We are excited and **the work of th** **NEW rom**

Several thousand man~~~~ come in to our editors every year and here are three extraordinary ladies who really impressed us.

We are sure you'll love them as much as we did!

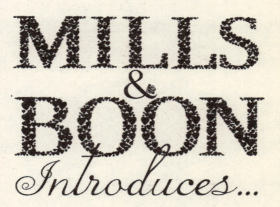

MILLS & BOON

Introduces...

ANDREA LAURENCE
SORAYA LANE
NATALIE CHARLES

Three brilliant new romances by super new authors: a passionate Desire™, an emotional Cherish™ and a thrilling, pacy Intrigue

MILLS & BOON

Introduces...

ANDREA LAURENCE

SORAYA LANE

NATALIE CHARLES

Published in Great Britain 2012
Mills & Boon, an imprint of Harlequin (UK) Limited,
Eton House, 18-24 Paradise Road, Richmond, Surrey TW9 1SR

MILLS & BOON INTRODUCES
© Harlequin Enterprises II B.V./S.à.r.l. 2012

The publisher acknowleges the individual copyright holders as follows:

What Lies Beneath ©Andrea Laurence 2012
Soldier, Father, Husband? © Soraya Lane 2012
The Seven-Day Target © Allison McKeen 2012

ISBN: 978 0 263 90223 5

009-1012

Harlequin (UK) policy is to use papers that are natural, renewable and recyclable products and made from wood grown in sustainable forests. The logging and manufacturing processes conform to the legal environmental regulations of the country of origin.

Printed and bound
by CPI Group (UK) Ltd, Croydon, CR0 4YY

What Lies Beneath

ANDREA LAURENCE

Andrea Laurence has been a lover of reading and writing stories since she learned her ABCs. She always dreamed of seeing her work in print and is thrilled to finally be able to share her books with the world. A dedicated West Coast girl transplanted into the Deep South, she's working on her own 'happily ever after' with her boyfriend and their collection of animals that shed like nobody's business.

You can contact Andrea at her website, www.andrealaurence. com.

Dear Reader,

You have no idea how long I've waited to write this letter to you, because it means that you're reading my very first book! The past year has been a life-changing whirlwind culminating in the pages you're holding in your hand. Thanks for coming along for the ride.

You get only one first book, and I'm thrilled that mine is Adrienne and Will's story. Some books are easier to write than others, and from the first moment this story popped into my head—oddly enough at 5:30 in the morning while I worked out on an elliptical machine at the gym—it was a joy to work on. The characters immediately came to life, and the words just flowed. From the beginning, I knew this special story would be 'the one.'

I can't wait for you to read Adrienne and Will's story and all the books that follow it. If you enjoy it, tell me by visiting my website at www.andrealaurence.com, like my fan page on Facebook, or follow me on Twitter. I'd love to hear from my readers! (*Wow, I have readers.*)

Enjoy!

Andrea

I've spent weeks trying to decide who to dedicate my first book to. It's not as easy as you think, especially when you have so many wonderful, supportive people in your life. There will be more books and more dedications, but this book would simply not exist without—

My Mother, Meg
For telling me my whole life that
I could do anything I put my mind to, and believing it.

My Boyfriend, Jason
For watching motocross and football with his headset on so I can write, and thinking chili dogs and takeout are better than a gourmet, four-course meal cooked at home.

And the Playfriends—Kira Sinclair, Kimberly Lang, Dani Wade and Marilyn Puett

For reading countless manuscript drafts, correcting my grammatical shortcomings, plotting in hot tubs and believing in me all those times I didn't believe in myself.

Prologue

"I am never taking this airline again. Do you know how much I paid for this ticket? Absolutely ridiculous!"

The sharp shriek of a woman's voice attacked Adrienne's ears the moment she stepped onto the plane and rounded the corner to first class. The woman sounded like she felt—although Adrienne was furious with herself, not a helpless flight attendant. She was going home a failure, but she had no one else to blame.

Her aunt told her that taking her father's life-insurance money to start a fashion-design company in Manhattan was a stupid, reckless thing to do. She'd be back in Milwaukee and broke within a year, she insisted.

At least her aunt wasn't right on all accounts. It had been nearly *three* years since she left. Adrienne had some moderate success, a few dedicated customers, but in the end, the cost of keeping afloat in New York City was more than she could take without a big break, and it never came.

Adrienne looked down at her boarding pass and started

eyeing the seat numbers for 14B as the line finally began to move. As she moved closer, she came to the horrible realization that the screamer was going to be her seatmate for the flight. The woman had finally calmed down, but she didn't look happy. Adrienne grabbed her book, stowed her bag in the overhead compartment and quickly took her seat, avoiding eye contact.

"I can't believe I got bumped from first class by a group of Japanese businessmen and crammed into the window seat. I can barely move my arms."

This was going to be the longest two hours of Adrienne's life. "Would you like to trade seats?" she asked. It was the one thing she could offer to save herself. As much as she would love to shove the woman up to first class, there were no seats unless she was amenable to sitting in the pilot's lap.

The little concession made a huge difference. "That would be wonderful, thank you." The woman's expression instantly softened and Adrienne could finally appreciate how attractive she was. A bad temper did little for her appearance. She smiled wide, revealing perfect white teeth and full lips, and for a moment she reminded Adrienne of her mother. They looked a lot alike, with long, straight, shiny dark brown hair and bright green eyes. She could be Adrienne's attractive, put-together older sister, really. Her suit was expensive and impeccably tailored. Her shoes were this season's hottest Jimmy Choos.

Adrienne suppressed a sudden pang of jealousy. This woman was better suited to be the beautiful and fabulous Miriam Lockhart's only daughter. Adrienne inherited her mother's fondness for fashion and skill with a sewing machine, but physically, she had more of her father in her, with his untamable kink to her hair and crooked teeth she couldn't afford to fix.

Adrienne undid her seat belt and stepped into the aisle to trade seats. She didn't mind the window, and to be honest, she should have a good view of New York City as it slipped away with her dreams.

"My name is Cynthia Dempsey," the woman said as she sat down.

Adrienne was surprised, figuring the woman would dismiss her once she'd gotten her way. Slipping her book into the seat-back pocket, she returned the smile, hoping the woman didn't notice her crooked teeth the way she'd noticed her perfect ones. "Adrienne Lockhart."

"That is a great name. It would look fantastic on a billboard in Times Square."

Or on a fashion label. "I'm not meant for the spotlight, but thank you."

Cynthia settled in, fidgeting with a large diamond engagement ring on her finger as they started to pull away from the concourse. Her fingers were so thin, and the band too large, that the massive jewel seemed to overwhelm her.

"Are you getting married soon?"

"Yes," Cynthia said, sighing, but her face didn't light up the way it should. She leaned in more like she was sharing gossip, as though her wedding would be the talk of the town. "I'm marrying William Taylor the Third at the Plaza next May. His family owns the *Daily Observer*."

That said it all. It *would* be the talk of the town. Adrienne was sitting three inches from the woman, but it might as well have been miles. She would probably spend more on her wedding than Adrienne had inherited when her father died. "Who's doing your dress?" The only common ground they could share was fashion, so Adrienne steered the conversation that direction.

"Badgley Mischka."

"I love their work. I actually interned with them for a summer in college, but I prefer daily wear that appeals to the modern working woman. Sportswear. Separates."

"Are you in the fashion industry?"

Adrienne winced. "I was. I had a small boutique in SoHo for a few years, but I had to close it recently."

"Where would I have seen your work?"

Turning in her seat, she gestured to the gray-and-pink blouse she was wearing. It had an unusual angled collar and stitching details that made it distinctively hers. "Since I'm out of business, this is your last chance to see an Adrienne Lockhart design."

"That's a shame." Cynthia frowned. "I love that top, and my friends would, too. I guess we just don't make it downtown often enough."

Three years Adrienne had worked, struggling to get her pieces out there. Sending samples to stylists in the hopes that something would make it into a magazine. Wearing her clothes out at every opportunity to catch the eye of someone with influence. It was just her luck that she would meet that person on the plane home.

"Ladies and gentlemen, we are next for takeoff. Flight attendants, please prepare for departure and cross-check."

Adrienne sat back and closed her eyes as the plane taxied. She hated to fly. Hated turbulence. Hated the feeling in her stomach when she took off and landed. She went through a reassurance ritual each time, telling herself cabs were much more dangerous, but it didn't help.

The engines roared loudly as the plane started speeding down the runway. Adrienne opened her eyes for just a second and saw Cynthia nervously spinning her engagement ring again. She didn't seem to like flying either. That made Adrienne feel a little better about her own fears.

The wheels lifted off, the plane shuddering as the air current surged them upward. The slight shake was enough for Cynthia's elbow to slip from the armrest, sending her ring flying. It fell to the floor between their feet, disappearing several rows behind them as the plane tipped into the air.

"Oh, hell," Cynthia complained, looking around her.

This was the absolute worst time for it to happen. Adrienne was about to say something reassuring when a loud boom sent all thoughts of missing rings from her mind. The plane shook violently and pitched downward. Adrienne looked frantically out the window. They weren't that far off the ground yet.

She clutched the arms of her seat and closed her eyes, ignoring the groans of the equipment and the screams of the people around her. The pilot came on to announce an emergency landing, the edge of nerves in his voice. It made Adrienne wish she'd paid more attention to the safety briefing instead of talking to Cynthia. Networking with dead people was pointless.

Doing what she could remember, Adrienne leaned forward, rested her head between her knees and wrapped her arms around her legs. Her eyes squeezed tightly shut as another loud boom sounded, the lights went out in the cabin and the plane lurched.

There was nothing left to do but pray.

One

Four weeks later

"Cynthia?"

The voice cut through the fog, rousing her from the grips of the protective sleep her body insisted on. She wanted to tell the voice to go away, that she was happier asleep and oblivious to the pain, but it insisted she wake up.

"Cynthia, Will is here."

There was something nagging at her brain, a niggling sensation that made her frown with confusion every time someone said her name. It was like a butterfly that would sit on her shoulder for a moment, then flitter away before she could catch it.

"Maybe I should come by later. She needs her rest." The man's deep voice pulled her closer to consciousness, her body responding to him against its will. Since she'd first heard it, he'd had that power over her.

"No, she's just napping. They want her up and moving around, engaged in conversations."

"What's the point? She doesn't know who any of us are."

"They said her memory could come back at any time." The woman's voice sounded a touch distraught at his blunt observation. "Talking to her is the best thing we can do to help. I know it's difficult, but we all have to try. Cynthia, dear, please wake up."

Her eyes fluttered open as she reached the surface of consciousness. It took a moment for everything to come into focus. First there were the overhead hospital lights, then the face of the older woman that hovered above her. Who was she again? She dug through the murky recesses of her brain for the answer. They told her she was her mother, Pauline Dempsey. It was discouraging when even the woman that gave her life barely registered in her brain.

That said, she looked lovely today. Her dark hair was nicely styled. She must've been to the salon, because the strands of gray were gone and it swung lightly, as though it had been trimmed. She had a silk scarf tied around her neck with flowers that matched the blue in her pants suit and the green in her eyes. Wanting to reach up and adjust the scarf, she was thwarted by the sling protecting her broken arm. Just the slightest change would've made it much more flattering and modern, although she didn't know why she thought so. Amnesia was a strange companion.

"Will is here, dear."

The worry slipped from her mind as Pauline pressed the button to raise the head of the hospital bed. Self-consciously, she smoothed her hair and tucked it behind her ears, readjusting her sling to make her heavy, casted arm more comfortable.

Sitting up, she was able to see Will seated at the foot of her bed. They said he was her fiancé. Looking at the handsome, well-dressed man beside her, she found that very hard to believe. His light brown hair was short but long enough on the top for him to run his fingers through it. His features were aristocratic and angular, except for the full lips she found herself watching while he talked. His eyes were blue, but she didn't know exactly what shade because she avoided looking him in the eye for long. It was uncomfortable, and she wasn't sure why. Maybe it was the lack of emotion in them. Or the way he scrutinized her with his gaze.

She knew absolutely nothing at all, didn't even know what she didn't know, but she had managed in the past few weeks to realize that her fiancé didn't seem to like her at all. He always lingered in the background, watching her with a furrowed brow. When he didn't appear suspicious or confused by the things she said or did, he seemed indifferent to her and her condition. The thought was enough to make her want to cry, but she didn't dare. The moment she got agitated, nurses would run in and give her something to numb everything, including her heart.

Instead she focused on his clothes. She found she enjoyed looking at everyone's different outfits and how they put them together. He was in his usual suit. Today it was a dark, charcoal gray with a blue dress shirt and diamond-patterned tie. He ran a newspaper and could only visit during lunch break or right after work, unless he had meetings. And he had a lot of meetings.

That or he just didn't care to visit her and it was a convenient excuse.

"Hello, Will," she managed, although it didn't come out quite the way she wanted. The multiple surgeries they'd done on her face went well, but there was more healing still to go. The accident had knocked out all her front teeth. They'd implanted new ones, but they felt alien in her mouth. Even after all the stitches were removed and the swelling had gone down, she had a hard time talking with the large, white veneers. And when she did say anything, she sounded like she'd swallowed a frog from the smoke and heat that had seared her throat.

"I'll leave you two alone," Pauline said. "Would you like some coffee from the cafeteria, Will?"

"No, I'm fine, thank you."

Her mother slipped out the door, leaving them in the large, private hospital room reserved for VIP patients. Apparently she was a VIP, because her family had made a large donation to the hospital several years back. At least that's what she was told.

"How are you feeling today, Cynthia?"

Realizing she wasn't sure, she stopped to take a personal inventory. Her face still ached and her arm throbbed, but overall she didn't feel too bad. Not nearly in as much pain as when she'd first woken up. If they'd told her she'd been locked inside a giant dryer, tumbling around for three days, she'd have believed them. Every inch of her body, from the roots of her hair to her toenails, had ached. She could barely talk or see because her face was swollen so badly. She'd come a long way in the past few weeks. "Pretty good today, thank you. How are you?"

Will frowned slightly at her but quickly wiped the expression away. "I'm well. Busy, as usual."

"You look tired." And he did. She didn't know what he looked like normally, but she'd noticed that the dark smudges and lines around his eyes had deepened each time she saw him. "Are you sleeping well?"

He paused for a moment, then shrugged. "I guess not. It's been a stressful month."

"You need some of this," she said, tugging on the tube that led to her IV. "You'll sleep like a baby for sixteen hours, whether you want to or not."

Will smiled and it pleased her. She wasn't sure if she'd seen him smile since she came to, but it was enough of a tease that now she wanted to hear him laugh. She wondered if he had a deep, throaty laugh. The suited man looking at her oozed a confidence and sexuality that even a sterile hospital couldn't dampen. Certainly his laugh would be as sexy as he was.

"I bet." He glanced down, looking slightly uncomfortable.

She never knew what to say to him. She was constantly being visited by friends and family, all of whom she'd swear she'd never seen in her whole life, but none of those chats were as awkward as talking to Will. She'd hoped it would get easier, but it just didn't. The nicer she was to him, the more resistant he seemed, almost like he didn't expect her to be civil.

"I have something for you."

She perked up in her bed, his sudden announcement unexpected. "Really?"

Her room had been flooded with gifts early on. It seemed like every flower and balloon in Manhattan had found its way to Cynthia's hospital room. Since then, the occasional arrangement came in from family or even strangers who heard about her story on the news. Being one of three survivors of a plane crash was quite newsworthy.

Will reached into his pocket and pulled out a small velvet box. "The airline called earlier this week. They've been sifting through the wreckage, trying to identify what they can, and they found this. They traced the laser-etched serial number on the diamond back to me."

He opened up the box to reveal an enormous diamond ring. Part of her wanted to believe it was a well-made costume piece, but after what she'd seen of her family and their large, plentiful and authentic jewelry, she knew it was breathtakingly real.

"It's beautiful."

Will frowned. Apparently that was the wrong response. "It's your engagement ring."

She almost laughed, but then she noticed the serious look

on his face. Owning a ring like that seemed preposterous. "Mine?" She watched as Will gently slipped the ring onto her left ring finger. It was a little snug, but with that arm broken and surgically pinned, her fingers were swollen. She looked down to admire the ring and was pleased to find there was a vague familiarity about it. "I do feel like I've seen this ring before," she said. The doctors had encouraged her to speak up anytime something resonated with her.

"That's good. It's one of a kind, so if it feels familiar, you've seen it before. I took it to be cleaned, had the setting checked to make sure nothing was loose, but I wanted to bring it back to you today. I'm not surprised you lost it in the accident. All that dieting for the wedding had made it too loose."

"And now it's too small and I look like I'm the loser of a boxing match," she said with a pout that sent a dull pain across her cheek. It didn't hurt as much as her pride. She had no idea what her wedding dress looked like, but she was certain that if she'd thought she looked better in it thin, the swelling wouldn't help.

"Don't worry, there's still plenty of time. It's only October. May is a long way off, and you'll be fully recovered by then."

"May at the Plaza." She wasn't sure why, but she knew that much.

"It's slowly coming back," he said with a smile that didn't quite go to his eyes. Standing, he slipped the ring box back into his pocket. "I'm having dinner with Alex tonight, so I'd better get going."

She remembered Alex from his visit the week before. He was Will's friend from school and quite the flirt. Even looking like she did, he told her she was beautiful and how he'd steal her away if she wasn't Will's fiancée. It was crap, but she appreciated the effort. "You two have fun. I believe we're having rubber chicken and rice tonight."

At that, Will chuckled. "I'll see you tomorrow." He reached out to pat her hand reassuringly.

The moment he touched her, she felt a familiar shiver run down her spine. Every single overworked nerve ending in her body lit up with awareness instead of pain. Her chest tightened, her hand involuntarily gripping his to maintain the connection it craved.

His touches, however brief or fleeting, were better than any morphine drip. Just the brush of his fingers against her skin made her feel alive and tingly in a way totally inappropriate for someone in her present condition. It had been that way since the first time he'd pressed a soft kiss against the back of her hand. She might not know him by sight, but her body certainly recognized her lover. The pleasurable current cut through everything—the pain, the medication, the confusion.

If only she reacted that way to a man who liked her. The thought was like a pin that popped the momentary bubble that protected her from everything else in her life that was going wrong.

Will looked at his hand, then at her with a curiosity that made her wonder if he were feeling the same thing. She noticed then that his eyes were a light blue-gray. They were soft and welcoming for a moment, an inner heat thawing his indifference, and then a beep from the phone at his hip distracted him and he pulled away. With every inch that grew between them, the ache of emptiness in her gut grew stronger.

"Good night, Cynthia," he said, slipping through the door.

With him gone, the suite once again became as cold and sterile as any other hospital room and she felt more alone than ever.

Alex sat sipping his drink on the other side of the table. He'd been quiet through the first two courses. Will always appreciated his friend's ability to enjoy silence and not force a conversation to fill space. He understood that Will had a lot on his mind, and letting him get through a glass of Scotch would make the discussion easier.

He'd asked Alex to join him for dinner because he needed to talk to someone who would be honest. Most people just told him what he wanted to hear. Alex was one of the few people he knew with more money than he had and who wasn't inclined to blow smoke up his ass. He was a notorious playboy and typically not the first person Will went to for romantic advice, but he knew Alex wouldn't pull any punches when he asked for his opinion on what he should do about Cynthia.

What a mess their relationship had become. To think that a few short weeks ago, he didn't believe it could get any worse. It was like daring God to strike him…

"So, how's Cynthia faring?" Alex finally asked once their entrées arrived, forcing Will out of his own head.

"Better. She's healing up nicely but still doesn't remember anything."

"Including the fight?"

"Especially the fight." Will sighed.

Before Cynthia had left for Chicago, Will had confronted her with evidence of an affair and broke off the engagement. She'd insisted they could talk things through once she got back, but he wasn't interested. He was done with her. He'd been on the phone with his real estate agent when the call came in that Cynthia's plane had crashed. When she woke up with no memory, he wasn't sure what to do. Continuing with his plan to leave seemed cruel at that point. He needed to see her through her recovery, but he would leave as planned when she was back on her feet.

At least that was the original idea. Since then…the situation had gotten confusing. This was why Alex was here. He could help him sort things out before he made it worse.

"Have you told her yet? Or should I say *again?*"

"No, I haven't. I think once she's discharged, we'll talk.

We're rarely alone at the hospital, and I don't want her parents getting involved."

"I take it she isn't back to being the frigid shrew we all know and love?"

Will shook his head. Part of him wished she was. Then he could walk away without a pang of guilt after her recovery. But she was an entirely different woman since the accident. He'd had a hard time adjusting to the changes in her, always waiting for Cynthia to start barking orders or criticize the hospital staff. But she never did. He made a point of visiting her every day, but despite how hard he fought it, Will found he enjoyed the visits more and more. "It's like she's been abducted by aliens and replaced with a pod person."

"I have to admit she was quite pleasant when I came by the other day." Alex put a bit of filet mignon in his mouth.

"Yeah, I know. Every time I visit her, I just sit back and watch in disbelief as she asks people how they are and thanks everyone for visiting or bringing her things. She's sweet, thoughtful, funny…and absolutely nothing like the woman who left for Chicago."

Alex leaned in, his brow furrowed. "You're smiling when you talk about her. Things really have changed. You *like* her," he accused.

"What is this, prep school again? Yes, she is a more pleasant person and I enjoy being around her in a way I never have before. But the doctors say her amnesia is probably temporary. In the blink of an eye, she could be back to normal. I refuse to get reinvested only to end up where I started."

"*Probably temporary* can mean *possibly permanent*. Maybe she'll stay this way."

"Doesn't matter," Will said with a shake of his head. It was just like Alex to encourage him to make a risky move. "She may not remember what she did, but I do. I can never trust her again, and that means we're through."

"Or this could be your second chance. If she really is a different person, treat her like one. Don't hold a past she doesn't even remember against her. You could miss out on something great."

His friend turned his attention back to his steak, leaving Will alone with his thoughts. Alex said the words he'd been afraid to let himself even think. Being with Cynthia was like meeting a woman for the first time. He found himself rushing from the office to visit her or thinking about how she was while he needed to concentrate on the front page flash for the *Observer*. And today…he'd felt an undeniable sizzle of awareness when they'd touched. He'd never had that intense a reaction to her before. He didn't know if it was the fright of nearly losing her for good or her personality change, but there was a part of him that wanted to take Alex's advice.

Of course, Alex didn't keep a woman long enough for the relationship to sour. It might not seem like it now, but the old Cynthia was still lurking inside her. That woman was miserable and unfaithful and stomped on his feelings with her expensive stiletto heels. Will had broken it off with her, and he had no doubt she'd be back before long. He wasn't going to lose his heart, freedom or any more years of his life to this relationship.

The doctors said she could probably go home soon. He was certain Pauline and George would want her back at their estate, but Will was going to insist she return to their penthouse so he could care for her. Having her at home was the natural choice. It was closer to the doctor, and being around her own things would be good for her.

And if it jogged her memory and she went back to normal? It would save him the trouble of breaking up with her a second time.

"Would you like to trade seats?"
The words floated in her brain, her dreams mixing reality

and fantasy with a dash of pain medication to really confuse things.

"My name is Cynthia Dempsey."

The words made her frown even in her sleep. Cynthia
Dempsey. She wished they would stop calling her that. But
she also didn't know what she'd rather have people call her.
If she wasn't Cynthia Dempsey, shouldn't she know who she
really was?

And she did. The name was on the tip of her tongue.

The boom of an engine bursting into flames dashed the
name from her mind. Then there was only the horrible, sickening feeling of falling from the sky.

"No!"

She shot up in bed, hurting about a half dozen parts of her
body in the process. Her heart was racing, her breath quick
in her throat. The nearby bed monitor started beeping, and
before she could gather her composure, one of the night shift
nurses came in.

"How are we, Miss Dempsey?"

"Stop calling me that," she snapped, the confusion of sleep
removing the buffer that edited what she shouldn't say.

"Okay…*Cynthia*. Are you all right?"

She saw it was her favorite nurse, Gwen, when she reached
over and turned on the small light above her bed. Gwen was
a tiny Southern girl with naturally curly ash-blond hair and
a positive but no-nonsense attitude about life. She could also
draw blood without pain, so that instantly put her at the top
of Cynthia's list.

"Yes." She wiped her sleepy eyes with her good hand. "I
just had a bad dream. I'm sorry for snarling at you like that."

"Don't you worry your pretty li'l head about it," Gwen
said, her thick Tennessee accent curling her words. She
turned off the alarm and checked her IV fluids. "A lot of
trauma patients have nightmares. Do you want something to
help you sleep?"

"No, I'm tired of…not feeling like myself. Although I'm beginning to wonder if that has anything to do with the medication."

Gwen sat at the edge of the bed and patted her knee. "You had some pretty severe head trauma, honey. It's possible you might never feel exactly like you used to. Or that you won't know when you do. Just make the most of how and what you feel like, now."

Cynthia decided to take advantage of the only person she could really talk to about this. Will wouldn't understand. It would just upset Pauline. Her mother spent every afternoon with her at the hospital, showing her pictures, telling stories and trying to unlock her memory. Saying she didn't feel like herself would just be an insult to Pauline's hard work.

"It feels all wrong. The people. The way they treat me. I mean, look at this." She slipped her arm out of the sling and extended her pale pink cast to show off her engagement ring.

"That's lovely," Gwen said politely, although her dark brown eyes had grown twice their size upon seeing the massive diamond.

"Don't. We both know this could feed a third-world country for a year."

"Probably," she conceded.

"This doesn't feel like me. I don't feel like some snobby uptown girl that went to private school and got everything she ever wanted. I feel like a fish out of water, and I shouldn't. If this is my life, why do I feel so out of touch with it? How can I be who I am when I don't know who I was?"

"Honey, this is a little deep for a three o'clock in the morning conversation. But here's some unsolicited advice from a Tennessee fish in Manhattan waters. I'd stop worrying about who you were and just be yourself. You'll go crazy trying to figure out what you should do and how you should act."

"How do I do that?"

"For a start, stop fighting it. When you walk out of this

room to start your new life, embrace being Cynthia Dempsey. Then, just do what you feel. If the new Cynthia would rather go to a Knicks game than the symphony, that's okay. If you've lost your taste for caviar and expensive wine, eat a cheeseburger and drink a beer. Only you know who you want to be now. Don't let anyone change that."

"Thank you, Gwen." She leaned forward and embraced the nurse who felt like her only real friend in her new life. "I'm being discharged tomorrow. Will is taking me back to our apartment. I have no idea what's in store for me there, but when I'm in the mood for burgers and beer, can I call you?"

Gwen smiled wide. "Absolutely." She wrote her cell phone number in the small notebook Cynthia had been using to keep notes. "And don't worry," she added. "I can't imagine any future with Will Taylor in it being bad."

Cynthia nodded and returned her reassuring grin. She just hoped Gwen was right.

Two

Will watched Cynthia walk through their apartment as if she were taking a tour of the Met. He had to admit the place felt like a museum sometimes with all the glass, marble and leather. It wasn't what he would've chosen, but everything served its designated function, so he didn't really care.

She examined each room, admiring the artwork, running her fingers over the fabrics and seeming visibly pleased with what she saw. She should like it, he mused. She and her god-awful decorator picked it all out.

Cynthia moved slowly, the stiffness of her muscles slowing her down. The doctors had changed the cast on her arm to a brace so she could remove it to shower for the last few weeks until it was fully healed. All the bandages and stitches were gone now and only the faintest of discoloration was visible on her face and body. If not for the slight limp and the brace, you might never know what kind of trauma she'd undergone.

Pauline had a hairstylist come to the hospital to do her hair before she was discharged. The hospital staff had to trim a good bit of the length off as it was singed from the fire, but the stylist turned their chop work into a chic, straight style that fell right at her shoulders. It was an attractive change, and he found himself admiring it as the town car brought them home. Her face looked so much better, and the hairstyle accented it nicely. A new style for the new woman in his life.

There was a thought that would bring him nothing but trouble.

Will turned and found Cynthia staring at the large engagement portrait they had hanging in the living room. *Damn.* He'd gone through the apartment and put away all her pictures as Pauline had asked, but he had to miss the giant one on the wall. As far as he knew, she hadn't seen any pictures of herself from before the accident. But now that she had, he expected her to have Dr. Takashi on the phone in an instant, threatening him with malpractice. Personally, he thought the doctor had done a great job even if she didn't look exactly the same.

But nothing happened. She stood silently studying it for a moment, and then she continued to the back of the apartment. The chime of his phone distracted him with an email from work, and he heard her shout from down the hall as he read it.

"This bathroom is huge! Is this mine?"

"Does it have a sunken whirlpool tub?"

"No."

"Then no," he said with a chuckle. "That's just the guest bath. Ours is off the master bedroom." And not three weeks before the crash, she'd complained that their bathroom was too small. He'd asked if she was throwing a cocktail party in there, and she'd scowled.

Clipping his phone to his belt, Will followed her to see if she'd gotten lost somewhere. He found her standing in her closet, her eyes glazed over at the selection in front of her.

After a moment, she reached out and started flipping through the neatly hung outfits.

"Dior. Donna Karan. Kate Spade. Are these…mine?"

"Every bit. You moved my stuff out of the closet six months ago to make room for your ever-expanding shoe collection."

At that, she turned to face the wall of shoes behind her as though she hadn't noticed it before. She whipped open a box of Christian Louboutins and stepped out of the loafers she'd worn home. The black patent-leather pump with the red sole slipped on without hesitation. "They're a little too big," she said.

That was odd. "Well, if your feet shrunk in the accident somehow, I'm sure you'll have fun replacing all of these with your new size."

She shot him a look of pure disbelief as she slid on the other shoe. She was a little unsteady on the five-inch heels at first, reaching out with her good arm to brace herself, then a wide grin spread across her face. Maybe now the bedazzled leather contraptions would be appreciated.

"I'm sure an insert would do the trick. I wouldn't dare waste all these." She turned back to the clothes, flipping through a few dresses he remembered her wearing at one society event or another. "Why is it that I recognize all these designers and understand their importance, but my own mother is a stranger?"

That was a good question. He had no idea how amnesia worked. Will ran his fingers through his hair and shook his head. "Maybe your brain just remembers what was most important to you."

Cynthia stopped in that moment and turned to him. The look of wonder faded from her face. "Did I really prefer shoes over my own family?"

Will shrugged. "I don't know. I'm not the person you confided in."

She slipped out of the shoes, placed them gently into their box and returned them to the shelf. No longer seeming to enjoy her closet, Cynthia brushed past Will on her way into the bedroom and disappeared down the hall.

He followed her out and found her sitting on the couch, staring blankly at the hideous modern art piece hanging over the dining-room table. "Are you all right?"

She nodded stiffly, but he didn't believe her. "I feel like everyone is tiptoeing around me. That there's an elephant in the room that everyone can see but me. If I ask you some questions, would you answer them for me? Honestly?"

He frowned but agreed before sitting on the couch beside her. They needed to talk, and there was no sense in putting it off.

"Are you and I in love?"

She certainly didn't hold back, so he opted to do the same. "No." Candy-coating the truth wouldn't help. She needed to know.

"Then why are we engaged?" Her wide green eyes looked a touch disillusioned.

"We're not."

"But…" Cynthia started, looking down at her ring.

"We were in love a long time ago," Will explained. "Our families were old friends, and we dated through college. I proposed two years ago, and then you changed and we grew apart. Your family doesn't know yet, but I broke off our engagement right before you left for your trip."

"Why?"

"You were having an affair. The benefits of staying with you were outweighed by the betrayal."

"Benefits? That sounds like an awfully cold way to talk about it."

"It's the truth. We didn't have a relationship left, really. Your father and I were collaborating on a project that would've been extremely lucrative for both our companies.

Your father prefers to work with family, so I was trying to see it through, hoping we'd weather the rough patch. When I found out you'd been having an affair for quite some time, there was no choice left. Even if the project fell through, the wedding was off. I told you I'd be out of here by the end of October. Plans obviously changed after the accident."

"You're staying?" She looked up at him with hopeful eyes that gripped at his heart. Somehow it seemed wrong to punish her for what felt like someone else's sins.

"No. I'll be here until you're well. Then we will announce the breakup and I'll move out as planned."

Cynthia nodded in understanding, but he thought he saw the shimmer of tears in her eyes before she looked away. "I must've been a horrible person. Was I always that way? You couldn't have loved me if I was."

"I liked the woman you were when we met. I wasn't fond of the woman you became after college."

She swallowed hard and looked down at the hands she had folded in her lap. She said she wanted the truth and she was getting it, even if it was hard to hear. "Was I nice to anyone?"

"Your friends and family, for the most part. You spoiled your little sister. But you had a short fuse if someone upset you."

"Am I anything like that now?" she asked.

"No," he said. "You're quite different since the accident."

"But...?"

"But, I wonder how long it will last. The doctor says the memory loss is temporary and anything could trigger it all to come back. At any moment, the woman sitting in front of me could disappear."

"And you don't want that to happen, do you?"

The face of his fiancée, so familiar, yet so different, looked at him. Her green eyes were pleading with him, and he noticed golden flecks in them he'd never seen before. It was beautiful the way the colors swirled together, pulling him in.

It made him want to keep looking, to find details he'd missed before. How long had he been with Cynthia but never really knew her? It made him wonder if he ever actually loved her or just the idea of them together. The smartest, most beautiful girl at Yale and the captain of the polo team. Both from wealthy families that ran in the Manhattan society circles. It was a match made in heaven.

But this was completely different. He wanted to know the woman sitting beside him. He wanted to help her explore the world and learn who she was and who she wanted to be. And he shouldn't. He should tell her it didn't matter if she got her memory back. But that wasn't true, and she asked for honesty. "No, I don't want that."

"You know," she said thoughtfully, "there's a part of me missing, and that bothers me. But from what I've heard, I think maybe it's better this way. Better if I don't remember and just start fresh."

Her words resonated with him. Alex had said this could be a second chance for their relationship. But could he offer it? This woman had betrayed him, abused his trust and threw away what they had together. Did the fact that she didn't remember doing any of it make a difference? He wasn't sure. "You always have a choice."

Cynthia's brow furrowed, a line deepening between her eyebrows in concern. Her last dose of Botox must've worn off during her hospital stay. It was refreshing to see her express real emotions, even if it cost her a few wrinkles over time. "What do you mean?" she asked.

"At any moment your memory could come back. When that happens, you always have the choice of continuing to be the person you want to be instead of going back to your old ways. You can make a fresh start."

She nodded, continuing to watch her hands and seemingly building up the courage to ask more questions. "I know you didn't like me, but were you at least physically attracted to me before the accident?"

"You were a beautiful woman."

"You're dodging the question," she said, her gaze meeting his. Her irritation brought a red blush to her cheeks that chased away some of the yellow discoloration from her bruises. She was so full of emotion now. Her skin flushed with anger and embarrassment, her eyes teared up with confusion and sadness. It was such a welcome change from the ice princess he knew.

It made him wonder what she would be like to make love to. Will's groin tightened, and he pushed the thought out of his mind. He was leaving, and he'd never find out the answer to that question, so it was better he didn't think about it. "I'm not. You were beautiful. Every guy at Yale wanted you, including me."

"That picture in the hall…"

"Our engagement portrait?"

"Yes. I don't look much like that now. I doubt I ever will again." There was another new expression on her face, a vulnerability that Will wasn't certain he'd ever seen before. Cynthia was many things, but she rarely showed weakness. The woman sitting beside him had a fragility about her that made him want to comfort her. He'd never felt that urge before. And he certainly shouldn't feel that way about Cynthia, of all people.

Unable to fight the need, he reached out and ran a thumb over her cheek. The swelling was almost entirely gone now. "Before, you were like a statue in a museum. Perfect, but cold." The tips of his fingers tingled as they glided over her soft, ivory skin. "I think flaws give character, and you're much prettier now. On the inside, too."

Cynthia brought her hand up to cover his where it rested on her cheek. "Thank you for saying that, even if it isn't true." Wrapping her fingers around his hand, she pulled it down into her lap, where she held it tightly. "I don't know everything I did to you, but I can only imagine. I'm sorry. Do you think you could ever forgive me for the things I did in the past?"

Tears gathered in Cynthia's eyes, and it made his chest ache to see her upset. The way she clutched his hand was like a silent plea. The guilt of crimes she couldn't remember was eating her up. She wasn't asking him to love her again. Or to stay. Just to forgive her.

Seeing her like this, spending time with her the past few weeks, had roused new and different feelings for her. Feelings that if left unchecked could lead him to getting hurt again. He couldn't allow that, even if every part of his body urged him to take the chance. But maybe he could offer her absolution. And then, in time, perhaps more.

"Maybe what we both need is a clean slate. To put everything behind us and start over."

Cynthia's eyes widened in surprise. "Start over?"

"Yes. Both of us just need to let go of the past and move forward. You can stop worrying about what you've done and who you were and just focus on what you want for your future. And maybe I can stop punishing us both for things we can't change."

"What does that mean for you and me?"

That was a good question. One he wasn't really ready to answer, but he'd do the best he could. "It means we start over, too. We're strangers, really. We have no reason to trust each other, much less love one another. What, if anything, happens between us will take time to determine."

"And what about this?" Cynthia held up her hand, her large engagement ring on display.

"Keep wearing it for now. This is our business. We don't need anyone offering their two cents, especially our families. This is a decision we have to make ourselves."

Forgiving her was the right thing to do. Cynthia nodded,

a faint smile curving the corners of her full, pouty lips. Her eyes were devoid of tears now and lit with the optimistic excitement of new opportunities. After weeks of seeing her so battered and beaten down, she was almost glowing. She did truly look beautiful, regardless of what she thought. So beautiful that he was filled with the undeniable urge to kiss the smile from her lips.

He leaned in, pressing his mouth gently against hers. It was little more than a flutter or brush across her abused skin. A silent reassurance that things would be okay even if it didn't work out between them.

At least that was the idea. In an instant, his whole body responded to the touch of her, and he knew the reaction at the hospital had not been a fluke. He'd felt a surge there but had convinced himself he'd just gone too long without sex. Maybe that was still the case, but every nerve ending urged him to cup her face and drink her in. But he didn't dare. For one thing, he didn't want to risk hurting her, since she wasn't fully healed. And for another, it was the first step down a rabbit hole he'd be unable to crawl back out of.

"Think about what you want your life to be. And what you want us to be," he whispered against her mouth. Then he pulled away before he changed his mind and did something he'd regret.

Cynthia didn't feel beautiful. She didn't care what Will said. That kiss was likely just out of pity. To make her feel better for realizing she'd been a miserable, beautiful woman once and a sweet, broken woman now. She could tell he was uncomfortable about it. His cell phone rang, and he immediately took the opportunity to disappear into what she supposed was his home office. She was left to her own devices to make herself comfortable and get used to her new, old home.

The problem was that it didn't feel much like home. The whole space had an institutional quality about it. She appreciated the clean lines and indulgent fabrics, but it was too modern for her taste. There wasn't a single piece of furniture that called to her to come and snuggle into it. The couch was firm, cold leather. The chairs were wood or metal without much padding. After poking around, she settled into the bedroom to watch television. The large, luxurious bed was perfectly comfy and the ideal place to lose herself in some mindless entertainment.

When that lost its appeal, she decided to take advantage of her bathroom and take her first real shower since the accident. She undressed and gently removed her arm brace, making a face when she saw how skinny and pale her arm was underneath. Then she stood languishing under the multiple streams of boiling hot water for a good half hour. The shower made her feel more human, more normal, but once she sat down at her vanity, normal disappeared.

They'd kept mirrors from her the first few weeks. Pauline—er...*her mother*—had insisted on it. She didn't want Cynthia to get upset. Cynthia didn't know how she was supposed to look, but it didn't take a mirror to realize there had been a drastic change, and not for the better. The pained expressions on the faces of those who knew her were enough. So she hadn't asked for a mirror.

Then one day Dr. Takashi removed the last of the bandages and brought a hand mirror with him. Cynthia hadn't wanted to look at first. She had no idea what she would find. Her mother was an attractive older woman, and her younger sister, Emma, was cute in an awkward, teenaged way, but she had no assurance she didn't take after her father. George was a regal, commanding man, but she wouldn't say he was handsome. He had a nose like a hawk's beak and eyes that appeared cold and beady when he focused unhappily on hospital staff.

Looking in the mirror that first time had been hard, but it had gotten easier. Every time she saw her reflection she looked better. The expressions on her family's faces were encouraging. But the one thing no one had done was bring her a photo of how she looked before the accident. Her mother had brought in a shoebox of pictures, pointing out different people for her to try to remember, but not a single one had her in it.

Returning to the apartment, one of the first things she was greeted with was a large canvas photo of her and Will. She was almost startled when she rounded the corner to the living room and came face-to-face with her former self.

It looked like the kind of engagement portrait that would go in a newspaper announcement. Her long, dark hair was swept over her shoulder, revealing large sapphire earrings that complemented the royal blue dress she had on. Will was looking handsome, yet casual, in khakis and a light blue dress shirt. They were sitting together under a tree.

The woman in the portrait had elegant, delicate features. Her skin was flawless and creamy, her eyes a clear, bright green. Her makeup was applied so well it took a keen eye to notice she had any on at all. She looked every bit the daughter and fiancée of two powerful Manhattan families.

She'd expected to be upset when she finally saw a photo of herself, but she found the experience to be oddly vacant. It was like looking at a picture of a stranger. Disconnected.

Now, watching her reflection in the partially foggy mirror, it was hard not to draw the comparison and catalog the vast differences. The high cheekbones and delicate nose had taken the brunt of the accident. Time would tell if the plates and implants Dr. Takashi used would bring back the prominent features.

Only the eyes and the smile looked like the portrait to her. Smiling in the mirror, she admired her new teeth. They were much like the photo, though they, more than anything, still felt wrong when she tried to eat or talk. And the eyes…well, the expression behind them was different. Perhaps when the photo was taken she wasn't so confused.

Her hairstylist had blown her hair straight after cutting it that morning. It was twisted up in a towel at the moment, but she knew the unruly kink would be back once it dried. She wondered how she would blow it out again with one good arm, then decided she didn't care enough to bother. Wavy hair was the least of her worries.

With a sigh, Cynthia poured a bit of lotion from the hospital into her hand and gently rubbed it into her face and neck. It was supposed to help with the scars and overall healing. Somehow, she doubted it would do enough.

More than anything, even if she never looked like she did in that portrait again, Cynthia wanted to feel right in her own skin. And she just didn't. Lotion couldn't fix that.

"I bet that felt nice after all those sponge baths."

Cynthia snapped her head to the side and found Will leaning casually against the doorframe, his hands buried in his pockets. He'd been working for so long she'd forgotten he was home.

Self-consciously, she tugged her towel up higher over her breasts and held it tight to keep it from coming undone. She could admit to herself she was attracted to him—the blush spreading across her face was evidence of that—but being mostly naked in front of him was a distinct disadvantage. They may very well have seen each other naked a hundred times, but she had no recollection of it. He was a stranger, like he'd said earlier. Everyone was, including herself.

He noted her reaction, stiffening instantly and taking a step back. "I'm sorry. This probably makes you uncomfortable. I didn't think about that. I'll go."

"No, don't," she said, reaching out to him before she could stop herself. She didn't want to be alone any longer. She'd wandered, confused and sad, through the apartment all afternoon, hoping anything would jog her memory. Having him here, even with her half-naked, was a welcome change.

He paused, then held up a finger. "I'll be right back."

Will returned a moment later with a fluffy, ice-blue chenille bathrobe. "This was your favorite. You liked to wear it in the evenings to curl up on the couch and read a book with your favorite glass of wine."

Cynthia stood, still clutching her towel, and let him drape the robe over her shoulders. She slipped into the enveloping warmth, dropped the towel to her feet and tied the robe closed. It immediately quelled her concerns, covering her from neck to toe.

With the hot shower and the soft robe, she really couldn't imagine feeling any better. At least until her fingers brushed his as she adjusted the collar. The glide of his skin across hers sent a tingle down her spine that had nothing to do with the cool marble and tile bathroom. She gasped softly and his fingers pulled away. She turned to look at him, her heart beating erratically in her chest. How did he do that to her with a simple touch? "This is great," she muttered sheepishly. "Thanks."

He nodded, stepping back, but still watching her in a way that made her want to readjust her robe under his scrutiny. She wished she understood what was behind his gaze. He had an intensity about him that attracted her, but she couldn't decipher what it meant when he focused it on her. Was it desire? Subdued anger? Curiosity?

"Are you hungry?"

Apparently, she was confusing the look of lust with hunger. "Yes," she admitted. The last thing she remembered eating was some manifestation of Salisbury steak before she was discharged.

"What would you like?"

"Anything but hospital food," she said with a smile.

"Okay," he said, matching her grin. "I'll go pick up something and bring it back. There's a nice Thai place not too far from here. Would you like to try that?"

"Sure. Just don't get me anything too spicy," she offered. She had no idea if she would like it or not, but that should be safe enough.

With a nod, Will turned and left. Seconds later she heard the front door open and close behind him.

To prepare for dinner, she detangled her hair and went to the closet in search of something comfortable. Some of the clothes were too tight, but Will mentioned she'd been dieting for the wedding. She flipped farther into the racks, finding some older things in a larger size. She was eyeing a stretchy pair of yoga pants when the phone rang.

For a moment, she was startled, not quite sure what to do. It felt like answering someone else's phone, but it wasn't. The call might very well be for her. Telling herself that it could be Will, she went into the bedroom and picked the phone up off the receiver. "Hello?"

"Cynthia?" the man's voice asked, but it wasn't Will. This voice was deeper, quieter, as though he didn't want anyone to hear him but her.

"Yes, this is Cynthia. Who's calling?"

The man hesitated for a moment. "Baby, it's Nigel."

Nigel. The name didn't ring even the slightest bell, although he said it as if it explained everything. But he called her "baby." She didn't like that at all. "I'm sorry, I don't remember you. I've had an accident and the doctors diagnosed me with amnesia."

"Amnesia? My God, Cynthia. I've got to see you. These past few weeks I've been going mad with worry. Your cell phone is disconnected. I couldn't get into the hospital because I wasn't family. All I know is what I read in the papers about the crash, and it wasn't much. Please tell me I can see you soon. Maybe tomorrow while Will is at work?"

Cynthia's stomach sank. Will hadn't elaborated on the details of her affair, but it didn't take much to realize Nigel was her lover.

Will's voice crept into her mind. *You have a choice.*

And she did. The past was the past. Will had offered her a clean slate and with it, perhaps a future together. At first, she hadn't been quite certain what to make of it. She had obviously been unhappy with Will before and wasn't certain if a bump to the head could make everything better between them. But she at least wanted to try. For now, she wanted Will to stay. The man on the phone would ruin any chance they had.

"No, I'm sorry."

"Baby, wait. I'll take an early train from the Bronx and meet you for coffee."

"No. Please stop calling. Goodbye." She disconnected and set the phone back onto the cradle. A few seconds later it rang again, the same number lighting up the screen. She didn't answer it. The phone finally went silent and she waited nervously for a moment, but he didn't call back.

That done, she took a deep breath and returned to the closet to get ready for her first dinner with Will.

Three

Will sat at his desk, staring blankly at his laptop. After dinner, he'd returned to his office to work as he usually did. He spent most evenings working. Newspapers didn't run themselves, and given that most of his days were filled with unproductive but necessary meetings, it was the only time he could dig through his email and actually get something done. Some people might've been bothered by the long hours he put in to keep the *Observer* at the top of its game, but Will didn't mind. In fact, over the past few years, his office and unending stream of work had become a sanctuary from his failing relationship.

And yet tonight, with at least a hundred unread emails in his inbox, he couldn't focus on the work. His thoughts kept straying to Cynthia.

He watched her roam around the apartment through the glass French doors that separated his office from the living room. When he'd left to pick up dinner, he thought things were okay between them. Better than okay if he let himself think too long about her shower-damp skin and the skimpy bath towel she was wrapped in. He hadn't seen that much of Cynthia's body in quite some time, and his visceral reaction to her was immediate and powerful. Fortunately the brisk walk to the takeout place had served as a cold shower, and by the time he had returned, he had it under control.

But now she seemed nervous around him. They'd eaten their Thai food in the dining room, filling the space between bites with harmless small talk. But he noticed an edge that wasn't there earlier. When the phone rang, she nearly launched from her seat to beat him to answering it, and it was just Pauline checking to make sure she was settled in. The mother and daughter chatted while he cleaned up dinner and disappeared into his office.

Will couldn't help but think that maybe she'd picked up on his attraction and it made her uncomfortable. He'd mentioned the possibility of a future together—nothing was impossible—but he wasn't sold on the idea. He just wished his body and brain were on the same page.

He wasn't surprised when she disappeared into the bedroom fairly early. She was probably exhausted after her first day out of the hospital. On top of the physical challenges, their talk had stirred up a lot of information that could be stressful to process. Dumping their past on her today was probably a mistake with her fragile condition, but she wanted honesty.

Given her nerves around him, he should probably sleep in the guest room tonight. It would make everyone more comfortable, and he could use the space to keep objective about all this.

With the apartment silent and dark, Will was able to focus on his work again. He finally shut down for the night near midnight. He would be up the next day by six, but those were standard hours for him. He could sleep when he was dead. Or retired. Whichever came first.

The next morning, he was up, dressed and having coffee by the time Cynthia stumbled into the kitchen. She was wearing navy silk pajamas under her robe, her hair pulled into a ponytail. Her eyes were still blurry and her face lined from a night of heavy sleep. The woman he knew would never let anyone, not even him, see her like this. She always emerged from the bedroom with her hair and makeup done. Will had to swallow his surprise in a large swig of coffee. He really needed to come to terms with Cynthia as a new person, but it was hard to change his every expectation of her.

"Good morning," she said, gently rubbing her eyes.

"Morning," he replied, getting up to refill his mug. "Would you like some coffee?"

"No," she said, wrinkling her nose. "I tried some in the hospital and didn't like it."

Will returned to the table and slid a plate with a couple pieces of buttered whole-wheat toast toward her. He couldn't stomach much more than that this early, but if he didn't eat something, he'd never make it through the morning column reviews. "I made some toast. There's tea and cocoa in the cabinet if you're interested."

Cynthia settled into one of the kitchen chairs and took a piece of toast from the plate. She seemed a lot more relaxed than she had last night, and Will was relieved. Perhaps some time alone in the apartment would help her adjust.

"I hate to leave so soon after you got up, but I need to get to the office. I'm going to try not to stay too late."

"You work a lot," she commented.

Will shrugged, rising from the table and putting his mug in the sink. "I do what I have to. Now, the maid should be here today around noon, so you won't be alone. I asked her to make dinner so we don't have to go out. She's planning to go through all the classic recipes so you can try them. I think we're up for pot roast tonight."

"Okay." She nodded, although her brow was wrinkled in confusion again.

"What's wrong?" he asked.

"It feels weird to have someone cook and clean up after me. I guess it probably shouldn't, but it does."

"I'm sure you'll adjust to the luxury of it in no time, especially once you try Anita's eggplant parmesan. She's truly gifted in the kitchen. If you need anything," he said as he slipped into his suit coat, "call my cell phone. I've left you a list of numbers on the refrigerator, including your folks and some friends if you get lonely."

"Thank you," she said, standing up to see him out.

They walked to the front door, where he grabbed his laptop bag. "I'll see you tonight." On reflex, he started to lean in to give her a goodbye kiss. In that fraction of a second, he noticed her eyes widen and her body tense up. Given her reaction after yesterday's kiss, it was probably a horrible idea, even as a casual goodbye. He stopped short, pulling back awkwardly, and instead threw up a hand to wave and darted out into the hallway.

Traveling down the elevator, Will could only shake his head. What the hell was he doing? He certainly wasn't acting like a man on the verge of moving out. He was getting sucked in by her, like quicksand. The more he struggled, the more he was sure to sink.

It was better he get to the office as quickly as he could. At least there, he knew what he was doing.

Cynthia stared at the closed apartment door, more confused than ever. Her heart had fluttered in her chest when she thought he might kiss her. Their kiss the night before hadn't really counted and just left her anxious for more. Will had set his hostility aside after their talk yesterday, but things were hardly on track for serious romance. She knew it was too soon for any of that. Kisses would only complicate things.

But that didn't stop her from fantasizing about what his kisses would feel like or how his mouth would taste. When he leaned close to her, the scent of his spicy cologne was enough to send her pulse racing. It made her thankful she wasn't still hooked up to hospital monitors that might give away her attraction to him.

Shaking her head, she locked the door and went back to her room to get dressed for the day. She wasn't exactly sure why—she had no intention of leaving—but it seemed like the thing to do. Reaching into the back of the closet, she pulled out a pair of khaki pants and a long-sleeved blouse in a dusty shade of pink and then slipped them both on with a pair of loafers.

Returning to the kitchen, she boiled water for tea and slathered another piece of toast with raspberry jam she found in the refrigerator. When the tea was ready, she poured a cup, grabbed her toast and went to explore the room Will had said was her private office.

She'd glanced at it briefly the day before but hadn't ventured inside. After their talk—and Nigel's call—she was afraid of what she'd find. Today, she wanted to tackle her past head-on and set it aside for good. She settled at the glass-and-chrome desk and ate while taking it all in. A large space on the desk was cleared off for her laptop, which had been destroyed in the crash. Stacked around it were glossy magazines and file folders. It was all very neat and precise. It made her want to reach out and shuffle some of the pages around. There was simply too much perfection.

Across from her desk were a red leather love seat and a chrome-and-glass coffee table. Several large advertising posters and a few framed magazine ads were hung on the wall for products she recognized. Her best guess was that these were campaigns she designed. Her family told her she was a successful partner in a Madison Avenue advertising agency.

Looking at them, a feeling of unease washed over her.

Not only were they completely unfamiliar, but she had no thoughts about the marketing strategies that went into them. All she could come up with was that she liked the dress one of the models was wearing. That was it.

Without her memory, she was going to need a career backup plan, and fast. Especially if Will opted to leave as planned. He'd left the door open for a relationship, putting the ball in her court to decide what she wanted. If she'd really hurt him as badly as he'd said, he was right to leave and she wouldn't blame him. But last night's discussion with Nigel had shown her that she did want to try for more with Will. She wanted him to stay, and not just for the financial support.

And yet, knowing he always had one foot out the door made her hesitant to invest too much. She might be the one to get hurt this time. It was a sobering thought that sent her scrambling for a chore to occupy her mind.

Cynthia opted to start shuffling through paperwork, partially out of curiosity and partially out of the hope that it might jog something in her head. She opened files and thumbed through pages about different campaigns and clients. Mostly it was unfamiliar gobbledy-gook. The advertising lingo was completely lost on her.

Setting them aside, she opened a drawer in her desk and fished around. At the front of the drawer were neatly stacked and aligned office supplies. Further back was a pile of envelopes. Cynthia pulled them out and eyed the outside. They were all addressed to her. Some of the postmarks went back as much as a year.

Picking the oldest one, she removed the letter and started reading it. It was a love letter from Nigel. An actual, handwritten love letter. It was sort of an odd thing to do in this day and age, but he explained in the first one how he thought it was the only sincere way to express how he felt. Email was cold and impersonal. She'd probably kept the incriminating letters for their sentimental value.

With a sigh, Cynthia sat back into her chair. She knew she'd had an affair, but being confronted with evidence of it was disconcerting. It was quite the romance they'd shared. He was a struggling artist she met at a gallery show. Since that time, they'd been meeting secretly at lunch, going away for weekends together under the guise of business trips and taking advantage of Will's long hours by flaunting their relationship in the apartment she shared with him.

The letters were more romantic than she'd expected from a fling. She couldn't know what she wrote back to him, but they seemed to be in love. It boggled her mind, not jiving with what everyone told her about herself. How did an uptown society girl fall in love with a poor artist from the Bronx? She didn't understand. Was she just using Nigel, or was she too embarrassed to be with him publicly? Daddy and Mother certainly wouldn't approve. Did loving Nigel and marrying Will somehow give her the best of both worlds?

Cynthia felt sick and was thankful to only have toast in her stomach. She thought she wanted to regain insight into her old life, but now she never wanted to remember the truth. She wanted to erase it all.

Piling the letters into a heap on her desk, she dug around for anything else incriminating. Her laptop and cell phone were gone, so any digital evidence of her relationship with Nigel went down with the plane. If and when she got a new computer, she'd purge anything left behind in her accounts. Will had already mentioned replacing her cell phone. She'd make sure to ask for a new number that Nigel couldn't get his hands on. In her office file cabinet, she found a folder with various cards from Valentine's Day and her birthday inside. None were from Will. Those were added to the pile, as were some photos of Cynthia and a blond man she didn't recognize. They looked far too cozy and the location far too tropical. She could take no chances with this. It all had to go.

By the time the housekeeper, Anita, arrived, Cynthia had

a fairly large stack of things to destroy. She went out to meet the woman in the living room. She was a pleasantly plump older woman with graying hair. Quite efficient, she'd already begun dusting the mantle over the fireplace when Cynthia found her there.

The fireplace. Perfect.

"Miss Dempsey." She smiled, although Cynthia didn't detect much sincere warmth behind it. "It's so good to see you back home. I'll do my best to stay out of your way."

Her housekeeper didn't seem to like her either. Did anyone? "Please, call me Cynthia. And you're no trouble. I'm happy to have someone here with me. Let me know if I can help you with anything. I feel bad just sitting around watching you work."

Anita looked as though she were struggling to hide the surprise on her face, simply nodding when she apparently failed. "Thank you, Miss Dempsey, but I can manage. Do you need anything before I get started?"

Since she asked… "Actually, I'm a little chilled this afternoon. I'd love to just curl up with a book in here. Any chance we could get the fireplace going?"

That Saturday was an unseasonably warm fall day. By this time in November, people were usually heavily bundled or shoveling out of the first snow, but it was in the high sixties. Will had started off that morning working in his office as usual, but seeing Cynthia wander aimlessly through the apartment tugged at him with guilt.

He'd made a habit of focusing on work to avoid dealing with her before the accident, but he didn't need to work this much. And for the first time in a long time, he didn't want to. He wanted to spend more time with Cynthia. Which is why he deliberately stayed in his office this long—the pull she had on him was too strong. But he couldn't stay in there forever.

Shutting his laptop down, he came out of the office and found her reading on the couch. She had a paperback romance in her hands. It hadn't come from any of the bookshelves in the house. "What are you reading?"

"A book I bought on the corner yesterday. I'm really enjoying it."

Will nodded, trying not to let his surprise show, because it just worried Cynthia when she realized she was doing something out of character. Honestly, the less she realized was different, the better. This Cynthia was all wrong, but all right by him.

"I noticed you had the fireplace going the other day, but it's fairly warm out today. Would you be interested in getting out of the apartment? Maybe take a walk around the park?"

The grin that met his question made him feel even guiltier for waiting this long. Her face lit up like a child in front of an ice cream sundae. She put her book down, carefully marking the page. "Should I change?"

Will hadn't really noticed what she had on before that. If he had, he might've had another surprise to hide from her. She wore a pair of tight, dark denim jeans, gray ankle boots and a soft gray sweater that went down past her hips. She'd put a hot-pink belt over it and some chunky pink bracelets to match on her good arm.

"Wow, pink," he commented.

She smiled and ran her hand over the belt. "I've decided pink is my favorite color. Do you like it?"

He knew the only reason Cynthia had that belt was for a retro eighties-style charity fundraiser they'd attended last year. She appeared quite taken with the splash of color now. Cynthia seemed to get a lot of enjoyment from putting an outfit together. It was a fun look for her. Her hair was down and slightly curly. Her face was fresh and free of makeup. She really looked lovely.

For a walk in the park, her outfit suited just as well as his khakis and polo shirt. "You look fine. Will you be okay to walk in those boots?"

She stood, feeling around in them for a moment. "I think so. They're pretty comfortable, and I think my daily strolls are paying off."

Will grabbed a light windbreaker from the closet and ushered Cynthia out ahead of him. They took the elevator to the ground floor of their building, waving to the doorman as he greeted them by name and held the large golden door open for them.

It didn't take them long to reach Central Park. They walked silently down the sidewalk, crossing over into the forest of reds, oranges and golds that autumn had ushered in. It had always been his favorite time of year. Fall in Manhattan was the best. The cooler temperatures, the changing leaves, the Thanksgiving parade...it just gave him a sense of inner peace no other time of year provided, like the world was slowing down in preparation for winter.

"I love the fall," Cynthia said, happily stomping on crisp leaves under her boots. "I think it might be my favorite time of year. Of course, I don't remember much about the other three seasons, so I'm withholding judgment for now."

Will smiled, reaching to his hip for the phone that had chirped several times since they left the apartment. He thumbed through the messages but didn't get very far before he felt Cynthia's insistent tug on his arm. He looked up to see her pointing at one of the city's million hot-dog carts.

"Let's find out if I like hot dogs."

Will slipped the phone back into its holster and followed her over to the cart. Something as simple as a hot-dog vendor had filled her with excitement. It was so contagious that he was eager to have one, too, and he hadn't bothered to in years.

They stopped at the cart and ordered two hot dogs and sodas—his piled on with sauerkraut and mustard, hers with ketchup, mustard and sweet relish. They found a bench and sat down with their lunch.

He'd polished off about half of his when he looked over and noticed Cynthia's hot dog was completely gone. She dabbed the corner of her mouth to remove some rogue mustard, still chewing the last bite. Apparently she did like hot dogs. "Would you like another one?"

"No," she said, shaking her head and sipping her soda. "That was just enough. There are a million things out there for me to try. I'll gain ten pounds if I overdo it. It's just one of many things I have to figure out."

Will watched her expression grow somber. She sipped her drink thoughtfully and watched a leaf blow by. He popped the last of his hot dog into his mouth, chewing and swallowing before he spoke again. "What are you thinking about?"

Cynthia sighed and sat back against the bench. "I'm thinking of what a mess I'm in. In a few weeks' time, you could be gone. I don't think I can go back to my old job if my memory doesn't return. I have no real skills I remember. I didn't even know if I liked hot dogs until a few minutes ago. What am I supposed to do?"

He'd considered this subject as he'd watched her lie in that hospital bed for weeks. She was fortunate that her income wasn't important. Anyone else might be crippled by it. "Well, you may not know it, but you do have a healthy trust fund and stock portfolio. You could live comfortably on that for quite some time."

"I'll go stir crazy in that apartment doing nothing. Especially if I'm there alone."

Will noted the way she looked at him when she said the last part. She didn't want him to leave. And sitting here with her in this moment, he didn't want to leave either. She needed to feel secure in her situation. At least then he would know she wanted him to stay for the right reasons. "I've also spoken to your boss, Ed. He understands the circumstances, and if and when you're ready to come back, okay. But if not…you could always try working for your dad."

"And do what? I don't understand any of that technical stuff. I don't want to get paid to sit at a desk at Dempsey Corp. playing solitaire just because I'm the boss's daughter."

He had to admire that. Working for her father or sitting around the house would've been the easy thing to do, but she wanted more. "You have the luxury of trying something new. You've got a world of opportunities ahead of you. What would you like to do? Anything interest you?"

She thought for a moment before she answered. "Clothes. Clothes are all that has really caught my attention. Not just buying and wearing them, but putting pieces together. Admiring the lines of a blazer or the texture of a fabric. I'm not quite sure what to do with it, though."

Will had noticed the last few weeks in the hospital how she had mentioned people's clothing, complimenting them, asking about fabrics and where they bought one piece or another. It seemed to be a natural interest for her. "Would you like to try designing clothes? Or maybe be a stylist for fashion shoots or something?"

Cynthia turned to him, her green eyes wide. "Is designing clothes really an option? I watched a lot of reruns of some fashion reality show in the hospital, and it looked interesting. I may not be any good at it, though."

"Doesn't mean it would hurt to try. We'll get you some sketch paper and colored pencils. See what you come up with. You don't have to be the next Versace, but you can play around and have some fun with it."

She broke into a wide smile and flung her arms around his neck. He was taken aback by her enthusiastic embrace, but he didn't pull away. He wanted to encourage this new side of her, even if he wouldn't be around to see it come to fruition.

Instead, he wrapped his arms around her and pulled her close. She buried her face in his neck and he breathed in the scent of her—a mix of a floral shampoo, a touch of perfume and the warmth of her skin. He recognized her favorite fragrance, yet it was different somehow. Something underlying it all was new and extremely appealing. His body noted the difference and responded to it despite his brain's reluctance. His pulse quickened and his groin stirred in an instant.

He had tried to wish away his attraction to her, and yet Alex's words taunted him. This could be their second chance. He'd offered them both a clean slate, and the only thing keeping him from taking this opportunity was his own stubborn sense of self-preservation. Yes, the woman he proposed to had abused everything he gave her. But this was an entirely different woman despite their resemblance. No matter how hard he fought it, she intrigued and aroused him like no woman had before.

What would it hurt to see where this could go, even if only to soothe his own curiosity? He could certainly keep his heart out of the situation to avoid disaster. If things went awry or she regained her memory, he could easily walk away, no harm done. And if he could keep their relationship going long enough to satisfy George Dempsey, it would boost his business. It seemed like a win-win situation if he could let himself give in to it.

Cynthia pulled away slightly, stopping to look up at him. She was clearly excited by her new design adventure, but her expression shifted as she gazed into his eyes. Something changed in that moment, and he could feel the difference, too. The attraction she felt for him was just as strong. He could tell by the way her breath caught, her lips parting slightly and tempting him closer.

She wanted him to kiss her. And he wanted to. He wanted to know how she would touch him. What sounds she would make. How she would feel in his arms. Letting his body and his curiosity win over, he leaned in and captured her lips with his own. There was an immediate connection when he touched her. This wasn't just a test. It was a real kiss, unlike what they'd shared before. A thrill raced through his body, a tingling in the base of his spine urging him to pull her closer. The need built quickly inside, pushing him to take more from her.

Cynthia leaned into him and placed one hand gently on his cheek. His tongue brushed hers, the taste and feel of her new and unexpected, like silk and honey. The hand resting on her hip slid upwards, caressing her side and tugging her to him. She whimpered quietly against his mouth, a soft, feminine sound that roused a primal reaction in him. He'd never been this turned on by a kiss in his life.

Everything about her, from the gentle caress of her hands to the flutter of her eyelashes against his cheek, started his blood boiling. There was an innocence, a sweetness. She had no agenda, no motives for offering herself to him. She just gave in to her desires and urged him to do the same. It took everything he had not to scoop her off the bench, carry her back to the apartment and claim her as his own.

Unfortunately, by the time he carried her four blocks to their apartment, he would realize it was a mistake. Pulling away, he stayed close, their breath warm on each other's skin. They sat still for a moment, his mind whirling with the implications of what he'd just done. He needed to keep his brain in charge instead of his crotch, or he'd make a mess of everything.

The loud melody of his phone broke the trance. The gap between them widened, Cynthia self-consciously straightening her clothes while he checked the caller ID. Apologizing, he took the call, ending the conversation as quickly as he could. "Let's go get you those art supplies," he suggested, when no other words seemed appropriate.

They gathered up their hot dog wrappers and soda cans, tossing them into a nearby garbage receptacle, and headed back out of the park and toward the nearest craft store.

This time, as they traveled, he felt Cynthia's fingers tentatively seek out his own. He couldn't remember holding hands with a girl since high school, and it was charming and unexpected. Hesitating for only a moment, he captured her small hand and they walked together out of the park.

With every step, he felt himself being pulled further in by the fascinating woman he refused to love.

Four

"I'm so glad you called me, Cynthia. I was wondering how you were adjusting to real life."

Cynthia smiled across the table at her former nurse, Gwen. She was glad to have someone to talk to. Anita the housekeeper seemed concerned every time she tried to strike up a conversation, and when she spoke to her family, they'd start on her again about coming to stay with them. Even her sister, Emma, had dropped hints, probably at their mother's urging. She enjoyed the time she'd spent with Pauline—they'd even had brunch on Sunday—but there were expectations there that she didn't know how to fill. Gwen was the only person Cynthia knew from after the accident, and she appreciated having someone around who didn't look at her as if she were possessed.

"It's been interesting. Fortunately, I've managed to avoid a lot of people. I guess since I was in such bad shape, they want to wait as long as possible to see me. I don't think it will last much longer. My mother is planning a big, fancy party

to celebrate my recovery. I tried to block most of it out yesterday when she mentioned mailing invitations and hiring an
orchestra to play. It sounds over the top and absolutely miserable."

Gwen smiled and squirted some ketchup on her cheeseburger. "The people in your life care about you, as weird as
all of this is for everyone involved. The sooner the new you
gets out there, the sooner everyone will adjust. Are you planning on returning to work?"

"I don't think so."

"Sometimes getting back in an old routine can help."

"Maybe, but I think it's an impossibility. I mean, if I were
a doctor, would you want me to jump back in the saddle and
operate on you, hoping my years of medical training would
magically come back to me?"

Gwen wrinkled her nose. "I guess not."

"I was in advertising, which I know isn't like brain surgery, but I remember nothing about it. I don't really have an
interest in it either."

"So what are you going to do? Become one of those society wives that organize fundraisers?"

"Uh, no," she groaned. "Right now I'm just trying something out."

"Do tell," Gwen urged, taking a large bite.

Cynthia thought about the pages and pages of clothing designs she'd sketched over the weekend. At first, it had been
a wreck. At least twenty sheets of paper had been crumpled into balls and tossed in the trash bin. But then they
started getting better. She let go of her inhibitions and the
ideas started flowing. The color combinations she put together worked even when she worried they wouldn't. The
pieces coordinated beautifully. She was itching to see some
of them leap off the page and onto a hanger. But that was a
whole other hurdle to climb over. She might be a good artist
and a horrible seamstress.

"I'm trying my hand at designing clothes. Just sketches right now, but I did what you told me and I'm following my instincts. Trying to do what my heart tells me feels right."

"Fashion design? Wow. Are you enjoying it?"

She couldn't hide her smile. "I am. I just sketch and sketch and when Will comes looking for me, I'm shocked to find I spent hours working on it."

"Sounds like you may be on to something."

"I think so. I mean, right now it's just sketches, but I'm thinking about getting a sewing machine and trying to actually make some of it."

"You should open a boutique and show at Fashion Week," Gwen encouraged.

Cynthia had to laugh at her friend's enthusiasm. "You are way ahead of me on this. First thing I have to do is figure out how to thread a bobbin. Then, if what I make doesn't suck, I'll go from there. I'm a long way from Bryant Park."

"But it's progress in the right direction. You're building your new life. I think that's great."

That made her feel good. She had Will's support, but a part of her wondered if he felt obligated to be her cheerleader. Her mother had feigned interest at brunch, but Cynthia could tell she'd been hoping her daughter would settle for being a society housewife like she was or at least go work for the family company. Knowing Gwen supported the choice made all the difference. "It is. I just wish everything else was working out, as well."

"Like what?" Gwen asked with a concerned frown.

"Like Will and me." Cynthia sighed, the weight of her situation heavy on her shoulders. He was sending conflicting signals. One minute he's discussing how she can support herself after he moves out and the next they're kissing on a park bench and holding hands. But even then, there was a part of him holding back. He was determined to keep one foot firmly out the door for a quick escape. That wasn't a good sign. "I don't know where I stand with him. With us. He seems distant sometimes."

Cynthia knew she couldn't tell anyone, not even Gwen, that they'd called off the engagement. Or about Nigel. He'd started calling again after Will left in the mornings. She'd considered telling Will, but it just seemed like dragging up the past after they had agreed to set it aside. Eventually he would stop calling. He had to.

"Maybe he's just not sure how to deal with the changes. You guys have been together a long time. It's like being with a new person. Whether the changes are good or bad, it's still an adjustment."

She looked down at her half-eaten burger and fries, which she was pleased to discover she adored, and nodded. Gwen was right. This had to be just as hard on Will as it was on her. Even as they kissed in the park, she could sense an internal battle raging inside him. The part that wanted her and the part that held back for whatever reason had fought hard. She wasn't certain which side won. They'd held hands in the park on the way home, but he holed up in his office after that.

"Has anything happened between the two of you since you went home?"

"Just a kiss," she said, the memory of it flushing her cheeks like a schoolgirl. Given her amnesia, it was like having her first kiss all over again.

"A kiss is something. If he didn't like you, I doubt he'd bother kissing you."

"But nothing has happened since then."

Gwen took a sip of her drink and shrugged. "I wouldn't worry about that. He might be concerned about your recovery. Or preoccupied with his company. But let me ask you a question. Do you *want* something to happen?"

Cynthia frowned. "What do you mean?"

"I mean, you've sort of inherited Will by default. Yes, you were technically with him for years, chose to be with him, but to the new you, he's a stranger. What if you just ran into Will on the street? Would you be attracted to him?"

Cynthia tried to imagine crossing paths with Will in an alternate universe where they'd never met. Perhaps she dropped something and he stopped to pick it up for her. The Will in her mind smiled and she found herself immediately drawn into the blue-gray eyes that watched her. The powerful aura that surrounded him was hard to resist, even in her fantasy. His strong build, his confident stride, the way he moved so gracefully yet with commanding purpose.

A pool of longing settled low in her belly and made her squirm uncomfortably in her seat. It was just like the memory of their kiss. Yes, she was attracted to Will. She couldn't remember their past, but her taste in men had certainly not changed since the accident, even if everything else had.

The question was whether she could allow herself to fall for him. He'd told her to think about it. And she had. She wanted to give them a second chance, but she didn't trust herself. She had no idea what she was capable of. She didn't want to hurt Will again. Letting this relationship and its baggage go might be better for everyone concerned. But it was difficult to ignore a man like Will.

"I think under any circumstances he'd be pretty hard to resist," she conceded.

"Then why are you fighting it? The hard work is done. You've already landed one of the most eligible men in Manhattan. Regardless of the past, I see no reason why you shouldn't allow yourself to indulge in this relationship."

Cynthia could think of a dozen reasons why she shouldn't be with Will and only one reason why she should. Unfortunately, that one reason had the tendency to trump all her good sense.

She wanted him. Badly.

And whether she should or not, she was going to try her damnedest to build a new relationship and keep him.

* * *

George Dempsey sat across from Will, the large mahogany conference-room table scattered with paperwork. The lawyers had prepared everything they needed for the product collaboration on the e-reader; the finer details just needed to get ironed out.

Unfortunately, Will could tell they wouldn't get very far today. His almost-father-in-law had more pressing issues on his mind.

"I'm worried about Cynthia," he said, staring blankly at a contract.

"The doctors say she's healing well."

"I'm not worried about her face," George grumbled, tossing down the page. "I'm worried about her head. Pauline tells me she's not going back to the ad agency, but she still refuses to work for me."

"I don't think she's passionate about electronics like you are. She never has been. Why would that change now?"

"Maybe because everything else has. She's doodling dresses all day. I feel like I don't even know my own daughter anymore."

"That's only fair. She doesn't know you, either."

George's brow furrowed in irritation. "Don't make light of this. I'm worried about her emotional health. And, frankly, I'm worried about this wedding."

Alarm bells suddenly sounded in Will's head. As far as he knew, no one but Cynthia and Alex knew about their breakup. They were toying with the idea of trying again, but nothing was set in stone. Their kiss in the park had been everything he imagined it would be and more, but it worried him. They had the potential of moving too quickly, crashing and burning before the ink on the e-reader deal had dried. He'd taken a step back and tried to distance himself the past few days. He ordered her a present to be delivered to the apartment and hoped to take her out to dinner tonight, but he couldn't predict the future. The paperwork on the table didn't mean a damn if George thought the relationship was in jeopardy. "She's been through a lot. A May wedding might be too soon. She could need more time to adjust."

George leaned across the table and speared Will with his steely gaze. "What about you? Are you getting cold feet?"

Will shouldn't have been surprised by the older man's blunt nature, but it always caught him off guard. "Why would you say that?"

"You two haven't been the lovebirds you once were. Back in school you couldn't keep your hands off each other. Even before the crash I sensed a distance. I don't want to believe you're a big enough bastard to leave her after her accident, but people shock me every day."

"I have no intention of leaving Cynthia in her condition. No one can guarantee what happens after that. Any relationship can fail at any time, even when you're trying."

George cocked a curious eyebrow up at Will. "You know I prefer doing business with family. They won't stab you in the back to please stockholders. If you have any reservations, you'd damn well better tell me before I sign off on this." George slid some papers across the table.

"Mr. Dempsey, this e-reader collaboration is smart business. It benefits both our companies. The *Observer* is a family company as well. We've got sixty years invested in its success. I understand your reservations, but know that with or without this marriage, we're fully behind the success of Dempsey Corp."

The old eagle eyed him, reading the sincerity Will hoped was etched into his face. He seemed satisfied for now. "You better be. But one other thing, Taylor."

Will hesitated to ask. "Yes?"

"I know a lot of people in this town. Business aside, if you hurt my little girl, I'll do everything in my power to crush you and this newspaper like a bug."

Will swallowed the lump in his throat and nodded. And to think, he'd only been worried that Cynthia might hurt him.

When Cynthia arrived back at the apartment from her lunch with Gwen, the doorman waved her over to the desk. "Miss Dempsey?"

Surprised, she went to the counter. "Afternoon, Calvin. How are you today?"

Calvin smiled and she noted the sincerity that hadn't been there the first time she'd met him. "Doing fine, Miss Dempsey. I have a delivery for you. It's fairly heavy. Would you like me to have it brought up?"

"That would be wonderful, thank you."

She continued on to the apartment, and within minutes there was a ring at the door. She opened it up to find one of the other building attendants, Ronald, carrying a large white box. "Oh, my goodness," she said, stepping out of the way. "Just set it over on the table."

Digging in her wallet past her newly reissued credit cards and ID, she took some money out for Ronald and thanked him as he quickly exited.

Alone, she returned to the box. The delivery slip was addressed to her. She couldn't imagine what it could be. She took a pair of scissors from the drawer near the entryway and sliced open the tape.

Inside was a big, beautiful, expensive, top-of-the-line sewing machine. She couldn't even lift it out of the box and had to settle for admiring it from the top. It was shiny white with chrome accents. Stuck down along the side of the foam packaging, she found the owner's manual. Since she had a while before Will would come home and help her unpack the sewing machine, she opted to study the instructions in preparation for its first use.

Around the time she finished reading, she heard Will at the door. Leaping from the couch, she rounded the corner to meet him just as he stepped inside. He looked at the expression on her face and then turned to the kitchen, where the large box was still sitting.

"I see it arrived."

"It did!" she exclaimed. "Did you buy it for me? It's wonderful."

"I ordered it this morning. They assured me it was the best you could buy and that they'd deliver it today."

Without hesitation, she put her arms around him, hugging him tightly and kissing him. Her intent had been to say thank-you, but once her lips met his, her plans unraveled. Will snaked his arms around her waist, pulling her tight against him. He had been distant since their last kiss and she'd thought maybe he wasn't interested, but there were no doubts once his tongue slid across hers and his fingers pressed hungrily into her flesh.

It felt so good in his arms. So...*right*...unlike everything else in her life. Most days, she felt like a body snatcher, wearing Cynthia Dempsey and her life like a skin. Nothing felt real or normal except sketching clothes and being with Will. Certainly taking another chance with Will was the right choice.

Pulling back at last, she said, "Thank you." She just knew her face was turning beet-red from being pressed so firmly against the full length of his body. It made her feel self-conscious.

Will didn't seem to notice. "You're welcome," he said with a devious smile. "If I'd known you'd react like this, I would've bought it two years ago. Or at least last week."

Cynthia smiled awkwardly at his statement, still wrapped tightly in his arms. She wasn't sure if she wanted him to let go or to pull her closer and kiss her again. "I...I've been reading up on how to use it," she stuttered.

He held on for a moment longer before releasing her to take a few steps back. "Already studying?"

The short distance was enough to clear her head and return her focus to the topic at hand. "Yes, I think I could have it up and running by tomorrow morning. Do you think we could take a little field trip tonight? I'd love to get some supplies to play with. Fabric, thread, maybe some buttons?"

Will let his computer bag drop to the floor and shuffled out of his jacket. "We can. I was actually thinking I would take you out for dinner tonight anyway. We can go by the fabric store on the way. Just let me change out of this suit."

Cynthia prepared quickly, knowing most fabric stores would be closing soon. He changed and they grabbed a taxi to whisk them to the Garment District. They took the old-fashioned elevator up to Mood, and she entered it like she would a sacred cathedral. Will loitered near the entrance doing business on his phone while she disappeared into the three stories of fabrics.

Triumphant, she greeted him a half hour later with a large black Mood bag filled with everything she might need. The dress form that wouldn't fit in the sack would be delivered tomorrow. One of the employees had helped her, making sure she had all the basics, and gave her a good idea of what to do with them.

It was all very exciting. She had this surge of energy she hadn't had since the accident. It was like the world had opened up to new possibilities. Fate had closed the door on her past, but as the operator slid open the metal grate of the elevator door, it was like he was opening a window to her exhilarating new future.

"Did you buy out the store?" Will asked, pushing open the downstairs door as she breezed past him.

"Not today. Maybe next week."

"It's good to have goals," he said with a laugh. "Are you ready for dinner?"

"Yes," she said. Lunch had worn off long ago, but she'd been too wrapped up in her new sewing machine to notice.

"There's a steakhouse a few blocks east of here that I've been wanting to try. Does that sound okay?"

"Sounds great."

Will took her bag and carried it for her as they made their way to the restaurant. As they stepped inside, Cynthia immediately felt underdressed and stopped dead in her tracks. The dark restaurant had paneled walls and deep burgundy tablecloths, delicately folded napkins and enough flatware to confuse an etiquette expert. Her slacks and sweater just didn't seem up to par. Will had to nudge her forward so the door could close behind them.

"This place is too nice," she whispered.

"You're fine," he assured, pushing her toward the maître d's desk. "Two, please."

Cynthia followed the two men through the restaurant to their table. They were seated at a secluded two-top in a corner where they wouldn't be disturbed by other diners. The waiter was obviously under the impression that they were on a date. It certainly didn't feel like one. At least not with Will eyeballing his cell phone again instead of his menu.

"Would you like to try one of our fine wine selections this evening?" the waiter asked when he arrived.

Will put his phone aside and looked expectantly to her, but she didn't know what to say. He'd mentioned before that she liked to drink wine, but she was really just craving a tall, cold glass of Diet Coke. So she said so.

Will nodded. "A Diet Coke for the lady and a merlot for me, please."

Once the server was gone, Cynthia tried to focus on the menu. There were so many things she hadn't tried yet, but there'd been almost nothing she hadn't liked. Except brussel sprouts. She had to remember to tell Anita that before she made them again. Tonight, however, she decided on a surf and turf to sample a few new items at once.

When the ordering was done and they were left alone with

their drinks, Cynthia noticed for the first time how romantic the restaurant was, especially their quiet little alcove. A large stone hearth contained a fire that roared on one wall, the warm lighting casting everything in a golden glow. She hoped it would do wonders for her skin tone, which still wasn't quite back to the perfect cream it once was. It certainly looked good on Will. The flickering of the fire sent shadows across the angular planes of his face and darkened his hair to a deep mahogany color. The flames reflected in his eyes as he watched her intently from across the table.

She drew in a ragged breath, her tongue darting across her lips to moisten them. His gaze dipped down to her lips for a moment and back to her eyes with a small smile. The heat of his stare made her intensely aware of her whole body. And his. The button-down shirt he'd changed into was dark green. It strained across his chest and shoulders, the hard muscles underneath fighting to be free of the restraint. Being pressed against him earlier had set her imagination wild. She wanted to know how those bare muscles would twitch under her hands. Or how the wall of his chest would feel when her breasts flattened hard against him.

"This place is very nice," she said, reaching for her soda and taking a large sip to moisten her suddenly dry throat.

"It is," he agreed, sitting back in his chair. "I'm glad we decided to try it."

"How was work?" Cynthia desperately sought out a topic of conversation that wouldn't make her think of touching Will and fisted her hands under the table to keep from reaching out to him.

"Busy, as usual. I saw your father today."

That would definitely cool her ardor. "Yes, Mother mentioned he was going to see you. How is he?"

"Good. We were going over the finer details of our product collaboration. It should be ready to launch in the spring."

"What are you two doing, exactly?"

"We're working on e-reader technology. His people have managed to create a touch screen so light, thin and cheap that before long, everyone will have one. We're hoping to even give them away with long-term e-subscriptions to the paper."

"Is your paper having trouble?"

"No, we're still performing well, but a lot of other papers aren't. It's all about the internet these days. I added online subscriptions a few years back, but I think e-readers are really the next big thing in the publishing industry. I want the *Observer* and Dempsey Corp. at the front of the surge. To take my company to the next level as a top-tier performer. It's what I've fought for years to do."

Cynthia nodded, although she had no real idea what it was all about. She loved the feel of a book in her hand, and it would take time before she would be willing to give that up to a gadget. But it sounded promising for the two companies. A big boost in the industry. Maybe if he climbed that peak, he'd be willing to sit back for a while and enjoy the view for once. She doubted it, though.

"Is that why we were getting married?"

Will paused, his glass in midair. "It's not why I proposed to you, no."

"But it's why you stuck around even though I was difficult."

"We both had our reasons for getting married, even if they were misguided."

"I would think that it was just good business, working together. Why do you have to marry me to seal the deal?"

"It's not like that," Will insisted. "My proposal had nothing to do with your father's company. That all came later. Just an incentive to stick things out when you became—to use your word—*difficult*. Your father prefers to work with family. When I broke off our engagement, I did it knowing that this project could be dead in the water the minute he found out."

"If this second try doesn't work out between us, will it hurt your company?"

"No, it won't hurt us. But it won't help either."

"I could talk to him. I mean, I'm the reason we broke up. He shouldn't penalize you and your employees because of something I did."

"That's a very sweet offer, but I don't think I'm in need of any of your heroics just yet."

Will reached across the table to take her hand into his own. The warmth of him enveloped her and radiated up her arm like sinking into a hot bath. His thumb stroked across her knuckles in slow circles, sending the tiny hairs on the back of her neck to attention. She wanted to close her eyes and lose herself in the sensation of his touch, but his gaze had her pinned in her seat.

"What makes you think this second try won't work?" he asked with a devilish smile that almost convinced her it would.

Almost.

Five

"You *kissed* her?"

Alex's disbelieving shout no doubt cut through the walls of Will's office and into the hallways of the *Observer* headquarters.

"Keep it down, will you? I deliberately employ some very nosy people around here, and not all of them are journalists. My admin is at the top of the gossip food chain."

Will got up from his desk and pushed his office door closed, flipping the lock to prevent interruptions.

"What's the gossip in you kissing your fiancée?"

"Well, for a start, she isn't my fiancée anymore."

Alex sat down in Will's guest chair. "Yes, but only I know about the breakup. Last time we talked you seemed pretty certain you were out of there once she was back on her feet. What changed?"

Will sat down at his desk and leaned back, weaving his fingers behind his head. "Nothing. And everything."

"I knew it. I knew when I saw that grin on your face at dinner that she'd gotten to you."

Will wasn't sure he liked the implication of that, but he had a hard time denying that she'd gotten under his skin. "I've never been this preoccupied with a woman before."

"So you're staying?"

"No. Yes. For the time being. Even if she woke up tomorrow with the temperament of a pit bull, I'm riding this out until she's recovered. We've agreed to start fresh and see what happens, but I still have reservations. This just spells long-term disaster."

"Then why did you kiss her?"

Will sighed. "Because I wanted to. And I haven't really wanted to kiss her in a long time. There is suddenly this chemistry between us. This electricity whenever I'm close to her. It's nothing like we ever had before. It's as though I'm with a completely different woman. A brand new relationship with someone who's soft and sweet and gentle. I mean, she giggles, Alex."

A blond brow shot up, curious. "Cynthia giggled?"

"More than once. At first, she was sort of lost, trying to feel her way around, but now that she's got her bearings, she's full of excitement and joy. It's like she's got a new lease on life. I like being around her. I'm happy when she's happy. I bought her a damn sewing machine."

"What? Why?"

"Because I thought she'd like it, and I was right. She's cleared out her office of advertising junk and has been merrily plugging away at making clothes."

"Is that what she's going to do now?"

"I guess. She can't exactly go back to the ad agency and fake it. I encouraged her to do what inspired her, and this is the direction she took. It makes her happy."

Alex nodded. "Which makes you happy. So what's the big deal, then?"

"It's all wrong!" Will shouted, slamming his fist into his desk. Hitting something let out some of the aggression he had pent up inside. His gut was a swirling mix of untapped sexual energy, confusion and frustration with no outlet. "She's sucking me back in when all I wanted was to get out. It almost makes me wonder if she's doing it on purpose. When I broke it off, she was insistent that we could work things out. Cynthia didn't want the embarrassment of calling off the engagement. She wouldn't even take off her ring because she said we'd talk when she got home. What if she's trying to trick me into staying by faking this whole thing?"

"You mean pretending she has amnesia?"

"I wouldn't put it past her. I couldn't trust her then, and I'm still not sure I can trust her now. All she did was lie to me for more than a year."

"She nearly died in a plane crash. Not even Cynthia could premeditate a plan like that."

Will frowned at Alex, his argument instantly deflating because he knew his friend was right. He was being paranoid. Letting his past distrust of Cynthia cloud his judgment. Of course she couldn't have set this up, but somehow it was easier to be suspicious of her than to let himself trust her. "Ah, hell. What a mess I've made of things."

Alex stood and went over to the small bar where Will kept his stash of water, soda and Scotch. "Want a drink?" he asked.

"No, help yourself," Will said.

Alex poured himself a few fingers of Scotch and walked over to the large picture window that overlooked the vast concrete sea of New York City. "I think you've gone about this all wrong."

"Enlighten me."

The real-estate developer returned to Will's desk and sat back down in his chair. "You offered her a clean slate, but you're still letting all that old junk mess with your head. Let's take a page from Cynthia's book, so to speak. Forget about your past with Cynthia. Forget about this collaboration with Dempsey Corp. Even forget you were ever engaged."

Will looked at his friend with distrust. Those were a lot of factors to just sweep off the table. "O-*kay*."

"Now," Alex continued, "with all that set aside, just ask yourself one simple question: Do you want her?"

Leave it to Alex to boil the situation down to base needs. But it made sense. Did he want her? Given that the blood pumped furiously through his body just from the sound of her laughter? Given that he'd locked himself in his office for hours with a miserable erection to keep himself from doing something stupid? "Yes."

"And with any other aspect of your life, what do you do when you want something?"

"I get it."

Alex shook his head. "You don't just get it, you tackle it. When you wanted to be student-body president, you campaigned like no one else. When you wanted to be the captain of the polo team in college, you worked harder than any other guy on the field. Cynthia could've had any man she wanted. But you set your sights high and you made her fall for you. You make things happen. It sounds like she's interested in you and you're interested in her. What's the problem?"

"It's not that simple. Yes, in your scenario it seems that way, but all those other issues still exist. I don't live in a vacuum."

"Yes, but what would it hurt if you guys gave this new relationship a solid try?"

Will knew the only thing that could get hurt was him, but that was only if he let it happen. Cynthia had the potential to really get into his head and into his heart, but he couldn't allow it to go that far. He didn't have a head injury to forget what Cynthia was capable of. But if he could keep his heart out of the equation, it would be better for business, and maybe he wouldn't mind coming home at night. "It wouldn't hurt anything," Will admitted.

Alex took another sip of his Scotch, a smug smile curling his lips. "Well, it's not my life, man, but if I were you, I'd go for it. March right out of this office and seduce the panties right off of her. Then enjoy it while it lasts. If she recovers and you hate each other again, so be it. You leave. You haven't lost anything that wasn't screwed before that plane went down."

"And if she doesn't recover?"

"They you'll live happily ever after. Simple as that."

It wasn't as simple as that, but it did give him something to think about. Will got up and poured his own small tumbler of Scotch.

Alex was right. He had told Cynthia he'd forgiven her, but deep down, he was still holding back. He hadn't committed himself the way he should've. And that wasn't fair to either of them. Will needed to let himself enjoy her, even if he couldn't let himself love her. Eventually something would ruin what they had, and he needed to take the chance while he still could.

Cynthia did the last bit of stitching and snipped the thread that ran from the cloth to the needle. She turned the dress right side out and shook it in front of her. It had taken her a few days, but her first piece was finished. She held it out to admire it and smiled. It wasn't bad.

She'd opted to start with the first design that called to her, regardless of whether it was too hard to tackle. It was a sleeveless shirtdress with a sort of fifties-era vibe. It buttoned down the front, with a sweet, rounded collar and a belt that tied at the waist. The skirt was full and fell just below the knee. She even considered constructing a crinoline underneath for fullness but opted to wait until it was finished to decide.

The silhouette was sophisticated, but it veered from the traditional with black-and-white zebra-printed fabric, splattered with hot pink and purple. The moment she saw the bolt of it sticking out of the racks, she knew it was the perfect choice for this project. She'd trimmed the edges and fashioned the collar and belt out of black satin that gave it a touch of shine and richness.

It was rockabilly meets the eighties. Funky, fun and unlike anything she'd seen people wearing. At least on the Upper East Side.

But now the real test. Slipping out of her clothes, she unbuttoned the dress and slipped it on. Turning and admiring it in the full-length mirror on the door, she was pleased and relieved to find she'd fitted it just right. After fastening the last button and tying the belt, the dress fit perfectly, flattering and forming to every curve.

It was just screaming for some black, patent-leather peep-toe sling-backs. Cynthia dashed down the hall to the bedroom and searched through shoeboxes until she found just the right pair. She slipped them on and then walked out into the living room to give the look a turn around the floor.

The sound of a loud cat-calling whistle made her spin on her heels.

Will was standing in the doorway, a look of open appreciation lighting his eyes. His heated gaze took in every inch of her, and she was fairly certain her skills at the sewing machine didn't have much to do with it. He smiled, shutting the door behind him. "Look at you," he said.

"Do you like it?" she asked, taking a twirl to make the full skirt swirl around her and torture him with the quick flash of bare thigh.

"I do," he said, swallowing hard. "I don't think I've ever seen anything like it."

"I just finished it a few minutes ago."

Will's eyebrows shot for the ceiling. "You mean you made that?"

"Yep. It's my first completed piece. I know the arm brace leaves something to be desired, but that will come off before too long."

"You went from a sewing-machine virgin to making a dress that is well constructed enough for the catwalk in three days? It took my little sister two weeks to figure out how to thread her machine when she took home ec. Her first dress looked like a purple potato sack."

Cynthia nodded. She'd had the same concerns when she first sat down. Fortunately, he'd bought her such a nice machine it practically ran itself. And sewing had simply come as second nature to her, which was frustrating considering how much of her previous life was a daily struggle. After reading over the manual once, the machine just made sense. Piecing together and pinning parts of the clothes on the dress form was easy. She might not know the name of every sewing doo-dad and gadget, but she would rummage through her things until she found what she thought would work. It was like she'd been doing it her whole life, which was impossible. And worrisome, honestly, if her joy of the new project hadn't taken precedence in her mind.

"I guess following my instincts has paid off. I'm really excited about making more. I was even thinking about making my dress for the party."

Will shrugged out of his coat and draped it over the arm of the sofa. "Ahh, yes. Your mother's soiree. It's the talk of the town. Choose your design carefully, as it might show up on the cover of every society paper and website in Manhattan."

Cynthia froze, mid-swish, her mouth falling slightly open. She hadn't thought about that. She kept forgetting that anyone gave a damn about what or who she was. There would be journalists there. Photographers. If she really wanted to be a designer, this would be the perfect launching board.

That, or they'd laugh her back to a figurehead VP job at her daddy's company. Who was she to just decide one day she wanted to do fashion? She had no training, no experience. Uncanny skill with a pencil and some scissors did not a career make.

"Maybe I should just stick with something in my closet, then," she conceded.

"Can't do that," Will said, closing the gap between them. "You can't be seen in something you've worn before. You've either got to buy a new dress or make one. And I think you should make one. Let everyone at that party know that Cynthia Dempsey has arrived, more fun and fashionable than ever."

Cynthia let her gaze drop from his, the compliment flushing her cheeks. "You're just being nice."

"No," Will said, standing directly in front of her and resting his hands on the small waist she accented with the cut of the dress. His fingers gently stroked her skin through the fabric, sending a warm awareness coursing through her veins. Her mouth went dry, her breasts tightening and aching to press against the hard wall of his chest.

Every time he got close to her, every time he touched her, she reacted this way. She just didn't understand. This couldn't be something new; this had to be chemistry and hormones at a base level. Something primitive. She couldn't squelch this reaction to Will even if she tried. And yet she had had an affair with someone else. She couldn't possibly feel this way and be with another man at the same time.

Will leaned in and pressed against her, and she was immediately pleased that she'd put on these high heels a moment before. The five-inch pumps put them on a level playing field. Mouth to mouth, chest to chest, hard length to soft belly.

"I believe I have my first fan," she said, her voice breathy and still slightly rough from the accident.

"Indeed." He leaned in and kissed her, capturing her mouth with unrestrained enthusiasm.

Cynthia met his advance with gusto. Their previous kisses, the way he touched her, had a hesitation like there was a war inside holding him back. Tonight there were no barriers. His tongue invaded her, his hands roaming across her body as though he were exploring new territory. She wrapped her arms around his neck, pressing her breasts against his chest and bringing his erection into direct contact with the sensitive juncture of her thighs.

Will moaned against her lips with the pleasure the pressure brought on. He slowly backed her against the living room wall and cupped one cheek of her ass, pulling her tighter to him. His lips traveled lightly across her jaw, still careful about the surgery she'd had, then moved down to feast on the sensitive curve of her neck. His hand drifted to encircle one of her breasts, his thumb stroking the hardened nipple that protruded through the fabric.

Cynthia gasped, the thrill of pleasure running down her back and exploding at the base of her spine into throbbing desire. She inched one thigh up the outside of his leg, hooking her knee around his hip. He pressed into her, the firm heat striking her sex. She couldn't contain her cry of pleasure. She'd never experienced a sensation like that before, and her body shuddered from the force of it.

Will continued sucking and biting at her neck, his fingers gently unfastening the chunky black buttons that held her dress on. Before she knew it, the top was undone to the waist and he was sliding his hands inside to caress her breasts through the thin lace of her bra.

Her breath caught in her throat as he left a trail of kisses down her neck to her collarbone and on to the valley between her breasts. He pushed aside the lace and took a hardened peak into his mouth, eliciting a strangled cry from her throat. Her fingers weaved into his hair tugging him closer. Now that she had him back in her arms, she didn't ever want to let him go.

Will's hand slid along her exposed thigh, pushing her dress higher as he moved. The tension in Cynthia's body increased with every inch, her body drawn tight as a drum. All her reservations about being with Will melted away. Nothing mattered but being in his arms right here, right now.

When his hand found the moist heat between her thighs, she thought she might explode with wanting him. His fingers stroked her gently through the silk of her panties, but it wasn't enough. Not nearly enough.

"Will, please," she whispered.

He pulled away from her breasts long enough to speak. "Please what? Tell me what you want, Cynthia."

A part of her flinched when he said her name. He'd said it a million times, but somehow saying it now, like this, brought the doubts back to her mind. She didn't want him calling her that. The concern was immediately wiped away by a tidal wave of pleasure as his finger made direct contact with her most sensitive spot.

"You," she managed, not quite sure she could form any other words.

Will's hand withdrew and she was about to revel in getting her way when she heard a soft ringing sound and realized he'd stopped because of the phone. She was about to chuck his stupid cell phone across the room when she realized it was the cordless phone on the table beside them. The caller ID was lit up with the last number in the world she wanted to see. He never called this late. There was no way she could hide the panic plastered over her face in that instant. No way she could pretend she didn't know who was calling.

Will pulled away, taking a full step back and leaving only her gelatinous legs precariously holding her up. When she looked in his eyes, the desire was gone, replaced only with the same cold indifference he'd had in the early days at the hospital. His jaw was tight, his face reddening slightly with an anger he refused to unleash even if she deserved it.

Instead, he turned and marched out of the room, slamming the apartment door behind him.

Completely deflated, Cynthia slid down the wall, her head cradled in her hands. With the phone still ringing, she picked it up from the cradle and threw it against the wall with a loud crack. The phone broke into several pieces, and that was enough to silence it, but the damage was already done.

Nigel had called again. And apparently Will recognized the number, too.

Six

By the time Will glanced down at his watch, it was after ten. He'd been pounding the pavement trying to figure out what to do. The cool night winds bit at his cheeks and forced his hands deeper into his pants pockets, but it barely registered in his brain as anything more than a nagging annoyance. He deserved the punishment for being that stupid.

He'd almost done it. Almost let himself go too far. Took Alex's ridiculous advice and set his inhibitions free. And what happened? Her lover called the apartment again.

Will could've let that go. Cynthia couldn't stop him from calling. But he'd hoped in that instant that she wouldn't recognize the number. That she would have the same blank look in her eye that she got when she met anyone else she should know and didn't.

But there was no denying the horror painted across her face. Cynthia knew exactly who it was. Knew exactly how poorly timed that bastard's call had been. His chest had grown so tight in that moment, he almost couldn't breathe.

He had to leave the apartment and get some fresh air before he suffocated.

She didn't remember her parents or her friends. Will, her fiancé of two years, was a total stranger. She didn't know if she liked hot dogs, for the love of God, but she remembered *him*. She'd even looked at Will, a glimmer of hope shining in her bright green eyes. Cynthia was hoping he didn't know who was on the phone. That he believed it when she said she wanted to put the past, and her lover, behind them. He was right not to trust her. The woman that betrayed him was still in there somewhere.

Spying an empty park bench, Will flopped down and decided to give his aching feet a break from their punishment. The shoes he wore to work weren't exactly designed for long strolls through the city. Hell, he was still wearing his suit minus the jacket he'd tossed aside. He'd accosted Cynthia the minute he walked in the door and then walked out without a second thought to how cold it was tonight. He hadn't eaten. Hadn't even checked his phone as it chimed and rang with repeated requests to contact him.

That plane crash was supposed to be their second chance. Her lover and all their other relationship baggage were supposed to be in the past. Just when he'd finally decided to take this chance seriously, she'd ruined it.

The blinking neon lights of the bar across the street from where he'd stopped beckoned Will to come in. He considered going inside and taking the edge off with some expensive whisky, but he knew drinking wouldn't help the situation. He was never one to just sit back and drown his sorrows. He always took action. And that was what he needed to do now.

Walking around Manhattan in the middle of the night wasn't going to fix anything. It helped him clear his head, kept him from doing something rash, but the only thing that could help him deal with this situation was probably asleep in their apartment.

Leaping back up after only a few moments rest, Will took the most direct route back to the apartment building. Cynthia had left on the entryway light, but the rest of the apartment was dark. He flipped on the living room lamp, illuminating the carnage that had once been their telephone. Based on the divot in the sheetrock, she'd slammed it against the wall.

Stepping around the plastic and metal bits, he continued down the hallway to their bedroom. He hadn't set foot into this space since the night she came home from the hospital. His clothes were in the closet of the guest room where he'd been sleeping, so there wasn't much point. He'd gathered his toiletries that night and had stayed out of her personal space while she adjusted.

Not tonight. Turning the doorknob, the light from the hall cast a beam across the king-size bed. He could barely make out the small bundle beneath the blankets. Will flipped on the lamp on his bed stand.

Cynthia was curled up tightly in the fetal position. She had tissue clutched in her hand and used tissues strewn over her nightstand. He could make out the dried tracks of tears across her cheeks. She'd taken it harder than he anticipated. She was so emotional lately.

"Cynthia," he said, shaking her arm softly so as to not startle her.

She muttered and shifted around, straightening out of her tight ball before her eyes fluttered open and her gaze fixed on him. They widened in an instant, and she shot up in bed even though he wasn't entirely certain she was fully awake. Her expression was panicked and confused, but as the fog of sleep faded away, her gaze hardened, protectively. She drew her legs up to her chest and scooted back against the headboard.

Will felt like a Goliath hovering over David, so he sat down on the edge of the bed and opted to face the wall so she wouldn't squirm under his gaze. "Why is Nigel calling again?" His voice was flat, unemotional. He didn't want her to shut down, and if he started yelling, she might.

"I don't know. He called the house the night I came home from the hospital while you were getting dinner. He kept talking to me like I knew who he was, but I didn't. It didn't take me long to figure it out, though." She shook her head and looked down at the tissue she was tearing to shreds in her hands. "He kept pushing to see me."

She looked back up at him, glassy tears sparkling in her green eyes. Seeing her cry was like an iron fist straight to his stomach. He wanted to reach out and soothe her, but he didn't react. For all he knew, this was a new tactic for manipulating him. He couldn't let her see that she was getting to him.

"Then I remembered what you said about choosing who I would be now. I couldn't do anything about what I'd already done, but I could put an end to it. So I told him I wouldn't see him and to stop calling."

Will's fists were curled tightly in his lap. He wanted to believe her, but a part of him had heard too many lies. "Why didn't you tell me? I thought we were starting over, being honest with each other?"

"I didn't want to drag it all back up. And he'd stopped calling at first. Then the calls started again. But I don't answer."

"I just don't know that I can trust you, Cynthia. I want to, but this doesn't help."

She flung back the covers and slid to the edge of the bed to sit beside him. She was wearing navy satin pajama pants with a matching tank top that left little to the imagination. The warmth of her hovered near, but not quite touching. His whole body hummed with the awareness of her, the scent of her skin making his brain lose focus. Will hated that even in this moment when he should despise her the most, he still wanted her. But he didn't pull away.

"You have no reason to trust me. And I have no reason to trust you. We're strangers. But I want more. I want this to work out. And I don't know of any other way to convince you of the truth."

Will looked down to see Cynthia slip off her engagement ring. She held it up and watched it sparkle in the light for a moment. "This isn't mine. You gave it to another woman. It's a symbol of our past and everything that has gone wrong between us."

Her fingers sought out one of his fists, uncurling it to place the ring in the palm of his hand.

"I know you're worried that one day I'll wake up and become *her* again. But you were right. I have a choice. Even if I recover my memory tomorrow, I'm promising you that I'm changing the person I was. I'd like to try making this work with you, with or without amnesia."

Since day one, Will knew her memory coming back would be the relationship killer. His interest and attraction to her would no doubt be erased by the return of her old personality. It was the thing he clung to, the last barrier he used to keep from letting himself get too close. And she'd just taken it away, leaving him exposed to her and their new possibilities together.

"Let's try to make a new relationship out of the wreckage of the one we destroyed. We can date, get to know each other as we are now. The world can continue to think we're engaged, including my father. And if and when," she said, her hand covering the one in which he held the ring, "you want to give that back to me…okay."

Cynthia watched Will's face for any sign that she wasn't about to be single and homeless, dragging two hundred pairs of shoes behind her down the street, but he was so hard to read. It wasn't until his other hand covered hers that she was able to take a breath.

"Okay," he agreed, although his face was still lined with concern. She understood that. She'd obviously hurt him.

Giving the ring back was evidence of her good-faith effort to make this work. In time, she hoped that they could make new memories to help mask the old ones. It would be a slow process, but she would take it one step at a time to be certain she did it right.

"I look forward to getting to know you," she said with a crooked smile and an awkwardly adolescent bump to his shoulder. "I like what I've learned so far."

His expression softened and he smiled, too. "It's been a long time since I've dated," he admitted. "I might be a little rusty."

"That's okay," she said with a shrug, "I don't remember ever going on a real date, so I'll be easy to impress."

At that, he laughed. It was the first real laugh she'd heard, and it was everything she hoped it would be. It was a deep, sexy rumble that vibrated in her chest and made her want to cling to him and bury her face in his neck.

"I'm glad your expectations are low," he said, turning to place a soft kiss on her lips. He pulled away immediately and stood up. "Good night."

She wanted him to stay, to pick up where they'd left off earlier, but she knew that wasn't the best idea. But the kiss held promise, just like their new relationship, and that was enough for her. "Good night," she said as he walked out of the room and then quietly pulled the door shut behind him.

Unfortunately, even as she switched off the lamp, she knew it was a lost cause. Sleep was no longer an option. She was as wired as if she'd chugged an entire pot of coffee. She'd gone to bed crying because she was certain she'd ruined everything. Now she had a world of new possibilities ahead of her. Her mind was spinning from their conversation, her thoughts bouncing around in her head. Cynthia lay there in the dark for nearly an hour, praying she would drift off to sleep, but it was no use.

She didn't have to get up early in the morning; she had nowhere to go, so she decided to put her energy to better use. Slipping quietly out of the bedroom and down the hallway to her workroom, she decided to do some sketching. She wouldn't run the sewing machine because the noise would wake up Will, but she could do everything else.

Her plan to make her own dress for her mother's party loomed heavy on her mind. It was an ambitious project to say the least, and she needed to start on it as soon as possible. Any design worthy of the event would be infinitely more complicated to construct than the dress she'd already made. It also needed to be well designed and perfectly suited to her style aesthetic. If it was going to be in newspapers, it needed to be the evening look she would use to close her collection on the runway. The wow piece that everyone could look at and say, "That's the latest Cynthia Dempsey design."

If that wasn't enough, she now had an added layer of pressure. She wanted to look good for Will, too. When she stepped out in this gown with her hair and makeup done, she wanted him to curse. She wanted him to threaten to rip it off her body and delay their arrival at the party—*if they arrived at all*—even though she was the guest of honor. To be honest, she wanted him to be as miserable with desire all night as she would undoubtedly be.

Will was a strikingly handsome man. Not pretty, like so many of the models in the magazines, but everything a man should be. Hard. Sophisticated. Confident. She'd seen him in everything from khakis to a suit, but she could only imagine how delicious he would look in his tuxedo. He had the broad shoulders and narrow waist that the jacket would cling to. His high, firm rear and solid thighs would be on display in his meticulously tailored suit pants. All he'd have to do is flash her one of his charming smiles and she'd be a puddle on the floor. Her best defense was a good offense, and she was going to make sure her new dress blew his mind.

Picking up her sketchbook, she flipped through pages to

see if any of the designs sparked her imagination. So far, she'd done a lot of casual wear and separates with a retro feel and modern styling. One of the sketches for a daytime dress caught her attention, and she knew that that was the piece she needed to use to transition the style into an elegant, formal look. The dress was fitted with a pencil-skirt silhouette and a sweetheart neckline that appeared to be like a corset atop a white dress shirt. It was a smart daytime look for the office.

Flipping to a blank page, she pulled out her colored pencils and started working on a new design. Like the daywear, this dress had a fitted silhouette, although instead of the skirt falling at the knee with a ruffled kick pleat, the gown would take it a step further by blooming into a full mermaid skirt. She echoed the neckline with a strapless sweetheart top that plunged deep in the center.

Losing herself in the sketch for an unknown amount of time, she added special details and penciled in the texture she hoped the fabric and beading she chose would provide.

Rubbing her eyes, she sat back from the picture and admired it with pride. Making this gown in time for her mother's party would be a challenge, but she could do it. The structure was actually easier to construct than sportswear. There was just one last decision to make—the color.

The theme of her collection had been a lot of black and white with pops of color. The dress would be stunning in black, but would it stand out enough? By the same token, she dismissed the bright pinks and teals other pieces had. That would be too much. Her gaze drifted over the pile of fabrics on the makeshift worktable that used to be a red sofa. It landed on a color she hadn't used yet, but that could easily be worked in. It was sure to be a stunner. She picked up the matching pencil off the table and started shading the dress, a smile curving her lips as she worked and brought the sketch to life. It was perfect.

Emerald green, just like her eyes.

* * *

Will found himself in the Flower District the next day after work. He hadn't been joking when he'd told Cynthia he was a little rusty where dating was concerned. He'd dated in high school and the first few years of college, but once he and Cynthia got together during their junior year, that was it. College girls hadn't required much wooing, and Cynthia had never been one for silly things like flowers and chocolates in the past. She wanted ice. He wouldn't have bought her an engagement ring guaranteed to get her mugged one day if she hadn't made it perfectly clear what she expected.

But now he had no idea what she expected. Well, actually he did. She expected very little, so any gesture would be welcome. That almost made it harder. He didn't want to slack off or not put in the effort she deserved because she was easy to please.

He picked up a bundle of roses. They were fresh and pink and reminded him of the color she blushed when he kissed her. Pink was her favorite color. Turning, he spied a few different types of lilies one stall down. Would she prefer something more exotic?

Will ran his fingers through his hair in exasperation and shook his head. He could only guess, so he opted to follow his instincts and go with his first choice. He walked to the counter, paid for the pink roses and hopped back in the cab that was waiting for him. Hopefully she would like them.

He rang the doorbell of their apartment when he got home instead of going inside. Her footsteps thumped across the floor as though she were running to the door.

"Did you forget your k—" she started as she flung it open, then she stopped when her gaze fell on the flowers in his hands. "Oh," she said, a smile lighting her face.

"I'm taking you on a dinner date this evening." He held out the flowers. "These are for you."

"Thank you," she said. "Let me put these in some water and I'll get ready."

Will nodded and followed her inside the apartment, shutting the door behind him. He watched as she searched the cabinets until she found a vase, unwrapped the flowers and arranged them in water before placing them on the kitchen table. "They're beautiful, Will, thank you."

"You're very welcome. I got us reservations for dinner at six-thirty. You'd better get a move on if we're going to make it on time."

Cynthia glanced at the clock and gasped, turning on her bare heels to disappear into the back of the apartment. Will waited patiently on the couch, wondering if she could manage to get ready that quickly.

Ten minutes later, he got his answer. She emerged from the back in a fitted black skirt and a ruffled white top with black details and stitching. She'd pulled her dark brown hair up into a bun and put on some lipstick that made her lips look pouty and plump like cherries. It was perfect.

"You look stunning," he said.

"Thank you. I tried to hurry."

"You did very well. We might even get there early."

They gathered their coats and caught a cab to the restaurant. It was an expensive Italian place, but not one of the society haunts where they might run into someone they knew. Not that she knew anyone. This being their first date, he wanted it to be private and without people gossiping about where they were and why her ring was suspiciously absent.

They were seated at a curved, burgundy leather booth for two, the table lit with the soft glow of candlelight. The sommelier brought him the wine list, and he was two seconds from ordering for her when he stopped. He didn't know what she liked anymore. "Do you want a diet soda, or would you like to try some wine tonight?" he asked.

She thought about it for a moment. "I'd like to try wine, but I want something light and sweet."

He nodded, taking the sommelier's suggestion for a brand of Riesling and a cabernet sauvignon for himself. Once they gave the waiter their order, they were finally left alone with a crusty loaf of bread and some herb-infused olive oil.

"Normally on a first date, I think I would ask a woman about herself, what she likes to do, where she grew up. Unfortunately, I don't think you know the answers."

Cynthia laughed and took a sip of her wine. "Mmm... this is lovely, thank you for choosing it. It might be hard, but maybe I can learn something about you *and me* while we're at it. Give it a try."

"Okay," he said, tearing a chunk of bread from the loaf and dipping it. "We'll go more esoteric, then. If you were trapped on a desert island, what three things would you take with you?"

"Well, if we're talking deserted with absolutely nothing, I say food, water and a toothbrush. If that kind of stuff is covered, then I say some books, a sketch pad with pencils and an mp3 player with a solar battery pack. How about you?"

"Given base needs are met, I would take..." he shook his head. "I almost can't even say. I wouldn't know what to do with a bunch of leisure time."

"What do you like to do for fun?"

"Fun? I just work. That's what I do. Occasionally Alex makes me play racquetball or you drag me to a party or a play. That's about it."

"Doesn't the paper own box seats at Yankee Stadium or something?"

"Courtside for the Knicks, actually, but I usually give the tickets out to clients and friends."

"Why? Don't you like basketball?"

"Yes. I just never make the time to go. You never wanted

to go with me, and Alex typically had a date or was traveling on business when I asked."

"When the season starts up again, I think I'd like to go. It sounds fun."

Will smiled as he tried to picture Cynthia at a Knicks game with a beer in one hand, nachos in the other, screaming at the players. "We can certainly do that. Anything else you'd like to try, assuming we go on a second date?" he said with a wink.

"Hmm..." She thought aloud. "Bowling, maybe. Or doing some of the touristy things around town. I don't remember any of that stuff, so it's like I'm a visitor."

"Do you mean like seeing the Statue of Liberty and Times Square?"

"Yeah. Maybe get one of those 'I ♥ NY' T-shirts."

Will had to laugh. The woman across the table from him surprised him every day. She really was an entirely different person. A sweet, caring woman with a zest for life and the simplest pleasures, like silly tourist fare. Maybe she really had changed for good. Enough that he could trust her with some of the feelings swirling in his gut but wasn't ready to say aloud.

"You know I work crazy hours, but I'll happily squeeze in some sightseeing with you if that makes you happy."

"It would. But tell me, why do you work so much?"

Will took a bite of bread to consider his answer. "When I took over for my father, Junior, after his retirement, it took a lot of hours to really get a feel for running the paper. Then things at home got strained and it was easier to bury myself in work. Then it just became a way of life."

"Isn't there someone else that can handle a lot of that stuff for you?"

He had a staff of hundreds of capable people, so he sincerely hoped so. "Probably, if I let them. But I like being involved. I don't want to be one of those disconnected CEOs in the ivory tower."

"There's got to be a happy medium. A line you can draw in the sand that says when you're working and when you're not. I mean, what would you say if I told you it was rude to constantly check your phone during our date?"

Will paused, his hand literally reaching out to compulsively check his phone when she spoke the words. His gaze narrowed at her and then he conceded with a nod. "I'd say you were probably right and offer to put it on silent." He held it up and flipped a switch, putting an end to the constant symphony of beeps, chirps and ringtone melodies. He wasn't comfortable turning it completely off in case there was a serious emergency.

"Well, that's a step in the right direction, I suppose. When was the last time you went on a vacation?"

"I took leave the Monday after your accident."

Cynthia frowned. "That's not a vacation. I'm talking sand between your toes and a frosty drink in your hand."

He thought back to his last trip and calculated how long it had been. "Sadly, it was after we graduated from Yale. Junior paid for both of us to spend a week in Antigua as a present."

"That was a long time ago. Do you have anything planned in the future?"

"Just our honeymoon. Two weeks in Bali," he said. "We reserved one of those little private huts over the water."

Will's mind instantly flashed to being on the beach with her. He knew she wasn't pleased with whatever weight she'd put on since the accident, but he didn't mind in the least. It gave a new fullness to her breasts and a roundness to her hips that would fill out a bikini quite nicely. He imagined rubbing thick, creamy sunscreen over every inch of her pale, delicate skin to protect it from burning. The undeniable desire to pull her into the water and taste the saltiness of her skin and the ocean mingling together washed over him. It was a fantasy worth indulging, even if not for a honeymoon. Two weeks in paradise, indeed.

"That sounds heavenly," she said, echoing his thoughts without realizing it. "Maybe we should plan something. Not necessarily two weeks in Bali, but something to get you away from work and me out of the apartment."

"Definitely," he said. Wherever it was, it had to have a beach, and he would buy her a pink bikini to wear. He'd already decided as much.

Just then, the waiter returned with their meals. "Wow," Cynthia remarked as she took in her large platter of pasta and immediately dug in. It provided him the luxury of watching her for a moment without her noticing.

Everything about Cynthia fascinated him. He supposed that having a brush with death could make you appreciate the smallest things, even fettuccine with clam sauce. It made him want to expose her to new things and shower her with gifts—not only because she deserved them but because she would genuinely appreciate them. He would take her on a tour of the city she would love, and as soon as the doctor cleared her to travel, they would be off to the nearest tropical locale. If she was too afraid to fly, he'd charter a yacht to take them there. But that would all come later.

First, he intended to expose her to another new experience. Once they got home, he was going to coax every type of pleasure he could from her body.

Seven

Cynthia could feel a change in the energy between them while they ate. At one point, she'd looked up from her food to find Will watching her intently. He'd barely touched his own meal, but the desire in his eyes made it obvious he was hungry for more than just pasta. She'd have to try tiramisu another night, because they were heading straight home after this course.

That was fine by her.

But as the elevator of their apartment building carried them up, Cynthia felt her nerves getting the best of her. She wasn't a virgin, but she felt as inexperienced as one. What was she supposed to do? She knew she was in capable hands with Will, but she wanted to please him, too. Hopefully he would understand and not think she was just bad in bed.

She also knew he probably couldn't help but draw comparisons from the past, and that worried her, too. Since none of her newer clothes fit, she knew she'd gained weight. Would he be disappointed to find that her body had changed? What if he wanted the lights on? Cynthia wasn't sure she was brave enough for that yet.

Will took her hand and led her from the elevator to their door. She let him guide her inside. He locked the door behind them, tossed his keys onto the table where the phone used to be and made his way into the living room.

When he reached up to turn on the light, Cynthia caught his hand. "How about just the fireplace?" she suggested. Even that light was too much, but she didn't want to sound immature. The fire would still cast shadows, and the dim glow would mask the imperfections she hoped to hide.

He nodded silently, going through the motions of starting a fire and gesturing for her to sit on the thick area rug in front of the fireplace. She kicked off her shoes and sat down to watch him. With the flames started, Will disappeared into the kitchen and returned a few minutes later with two flutes of champagne. "Have you tried champagne yet?"

"No," she said as she accepted the glass and watched him lower to the rug beside her.

"Then, to the first of several new experiences tonight I hope you'll enjoy." Will held up the flute and clinked it with hers.

Cynthia could feel herself starting to blush and hoped the fireplace didn't make it too obvious. She brought the glass to her lips and took in a sip of the sweet, bubbly drink. It was wonderful. She took another large sip. The fizz seemed to go straight into her veins, warming her whole body and relaxing the muscles that tensed as he lingered close.

"Do you like it?" Will asked, setting his half-empty flute on the nearby coffee table and then leaning closer to her.

"I do." She swallowed the last bit for a dose of liquid courage and set it aside.

"Good." He reached out to cradle the nape of her neck and leaned in to close the small gap between them. His lips met hers, and she instantly felt lightheaded in a way that had nothing to do with champagne. His mouth was warm and tasted sweet against hers. The feel of his fingertips massaging through her hair coaxed her eyes closed, and she gave in to the sensation of him.

She felt the heat of his hand on her thigh. It stroked gently through the fabric of her skirt, slowly inching it higher up her leg. The caress lit a fire deep in her belly that urged her to reach out to him. Cynthia pressed a hand against his chest, kneading at the hard muscles, but the starched fabric of his dress shirt didn't feel good against her palms. She wanted to touch bare skin. Starting at his collar, she worked at the buttons, pausing as she reached his waistband. There, the brush of her fingertips across his stomach elicited a deep groan of approval against her lips. It made her bolder, and she tugged his shirt out and undid the last button, slipping the shirt over his shoulders and exposing his chest.

This, she wanted to see. Pulling away from his kiss, she opened her eyes and took in the hard expanse of his chest, the ridges and planes of his body accented and shadowed by the flickering fire. It beckoned her to reach out, and she indulged. She reveled in the velvet glide of her fingertips across his skin. The muscles of his stomach jumped as her hand neared his navel, and Will shot a hand out to grasp her wrist. "Not yet," he whispered, moving her hand higher to rest on his shoulder.

Will kissed her again, and this time she could feel his hands move down her blouse, opening it as she had done to his shirt. For a moment her nerves returned, but her back was to the fire, so when he eased her blouse off, her chest was still cloaked in shadow. His hand slid like satin over her exposed back, grasping the catch of her bra and undoing it with a flick of his fingers. Without his mouth leaving hers, he slid the bra down her arms and tossed it aside, covering the aching globes of her breasts with his greedy hands.

Cynthia gasped against his lips as he pinched one hard-

ened peak between his fingertips and then soothed the ache
with his palms. The sharp sensation traveled straight to her
inner core, urging her body forward to press against him, but
it wasn't nearly enough to soothe the need building inside her.

Will unzipped her skirt at the hip and surged forward,
easing her back until she was lying flat on the rug. The movement exposed her body to the glow of the fire, but when she
caught him looking down at her with unbridled lust, her heart
leapt in her chest. For a moment, she was able to put aside all
her insecurities and bask in the glow of being truly desired.
It was a new and wonderful feeling, second only to the tingle
of his lips against her skin as he traveled down her exposed
chest. His mouth captured one tight nipple while his hands
moved lower to tug her skirt and panties down over her hips.
Only when he absolutely had to did his mouth leave her body,
and that was only to cast the last of her clothing, then his,
aside.

Cynthia sat up on her elbows and tried to admire what she
could of his body, but her plan to disguise her own insecurities had made it hard for her to see him, as well. She could
only see the shadow of his body moving, hear the crinkle of
a foil packet tearing open, then see the golden light on his
brown hair as his body slowly moved toward her. His hands
and mouth stroked and tasted every inch of her as he glided
up to cover her body with his own, shifting his weight to rest
on his hip and elbow alongside her.

His dark gaze fixed on her as his flat palm grazed over
her belly and then dipped between her thighs. He eased her
open to him and then let his fingers glide over her moist
flesh. Cynthia tried not to cry out, but the sensations overwhelmed her and she simply couldn't help it. She fought to
keep her eyes open and hold the connection, but the expert
movements of his hand sent her eyelids shut and her hips
rising up to meet his touch. The electric current of pleasure
running through her body was like nothing else she'd ever

experienced before. The pressure was building up inside of her, making her achy and hungry for more.

"Will," she whispered, her body no longer her own to control as he coaxed new feelings out of her. She couldn't imagine feeling anything more incredible than this moment, but she knew there was more. She wanted all of him and would feel incomplete until she did. "Please."

Nudging her thighs farther apart, Will settled in and hovered over her. His gaze never left hers as he rocked forward and found his home within her welcoming body. He filled her so completely that she gasped; the pleasure was almost more than she could bear. She'd waited so long for this, she wanted to lock her legs around him and keep him there forever.

But even she wasn't stupid enough to stop the delicious movement he'd begun. It was slow at first, inch by inch easing in and out of her body at an excruciating pace. His head dipped down to capture a nipple in his mouth and tug at it with his teeth.

"Oh, Will," Cynthia said, unable to do anything else but cling to the hard muscle of his arms. The climax was building inside her, but it was too soon. Far too soon. She wanted this feeling to last forever, and he wasn't going to allow it.

He released her breast and kissed her, the salty taste of her skin on his lips. She clung to him as he moved faster, thrusting inside her with increasing force. Every second brought another rush of pleasure, her nerve endings almost unable to take any more.

He seemed to enjoy watching the expressions on her face as her mouth fell open, her chest rising and falling with the rapid breaths of her oncoming orgasm. With perfect timing, he thrust home harder and harder, pushing her off the cliff until she had no choice but to dive into oblivion.

"Yes!" she cried out as the climax pulsed through her body. Her hips bucked against his driving pelvis, her back rising off the rug as her release exploded inside her. She got lost in the tide of ecstasy, her cries mingling with his as he found his own release.

Cynthia collapsed back into the carpet, Will throwing his leg to one side to put the bulk of his weight off her. They lay there together, a mix of heavy breathing and tingling bodies. That was the most incredible thing she'd ever experienced. Being in Will's arms, connecting with him like that, brought not only pleasure but a sense of peace she'd been lacking. She didn't delude herself into believing this was anything more than incredible sex to Will, but it was a start. If and when they finally made love, she imagined it would be even better. For tonight, she would let herself be happy with a successful first date.

Their first date. "So much for my reputation," she said, laughing as best she could manage between her harsh, ragged breaths.

Will tapped gently against the door to Cynthia's work-room and called her name. He heard the loud stitching of the sewing machine stop.

"Yes?" she said, her voice muffled by the heavy wood between them.

"We're going out tonight," he announced. She had been holed up in her workroom for days. They were going out whether she liked it or not. He didn't care if she went to the party in half a dress.

"I don't think I—" She began to argue, but he grabbed the doorknob and silenced her protest. "No, no, I'm coming!"

She flung open the door and quickly pulled it shut behind her. "No peeking," she reminded him with a frown.

"You've been working too much, and coming from me, that's pretty bad. I'm taking you out tonight."

"I really shouldn't," she said, backing into the room again, but his hand shot out to grab the door and keep her from retreating.

"If you go back in there, I will come in after you and carry you out. After I thoroughly examine your dress and ruin the surprise."

Cynthia glanced down at her raw and bloody fingertips and gave a resigned sigh. "I could probably use some time away. I'm making progress, though."

"That's great." Will slipped out of his sport coat and headed down the hallway to the guest room. "I'm going to change before we leave." He pulled off his shirt and tie, throwing them on the bed.

"I guess I should, too. Where are we going?"

"It's a surprise," he called out.

"Then how will I know what to wear?"

Will stepped back into the hallway and eyed her outfit. She had on low-ride jeans and a T-shirt, her hair down and loose around her shoulders. For what he had in mind, it was perfect. He was about to tell her as much when her mouth dropped open and a gasp of surprise escaped her throat. He looked down at his bare chest in confusion and then back to her red cheeks. They'd slept together only two nights ago, but apparently seeing him in full daylight was a whole new experience for her.

He was glad his abs met with her approval. His lips twisted in amusement for a moment before he spoke. "Stop that or we'll never leave the apartment. You look fine. Just put on a jacket and some comfortable shoes."

Cynthia's eyebrows shot up, but she didn't argue. She went into the master bedroom and reappeared a few minutes later wearing her jacket and with her running shoes laced up and ready to go.

He met her in the hallway wearing jeans, a gray polo shirt and his own pair of sneakers. It had been a long time since he'd worn jeans and sneakers. He forgot how comfortable they were.

She followed him to the door and he slipped into his leather jacket. "I take it we're not going to *Le Bernardin* tonight?"

"Nope." Will ushered her out of the apartment and down the hall.

"I have to admit, I'm a touch relieved. I'm too tired to worry about keeping my elbows off the table and which fork to use."

"I'm glad you approve."

"Any clues?" she asked in the elevator.

"Nope."

There was a touch of frustration in her eyes, but it was quickly erased with the light of excitement.

First, they hopped in a cab and he took her to a small underground pizza joint near the Theater District. He could tell by the look on her face that she was hesitant about it. The first time he'd walked in, he thought he might need a tetanus shot, but it was some of the best pizza in town. By the time she'd put away her second giant slice, he was pretty sure Cynthia would agree.

Then they walked a few blocks to 42nd Street. Every time they approached the entrance to a theater, she'd look around expectantly, but he would continue on past. No Broadway musicals tonight. Instead, he'd bought tickets to a Night Illuminations tour. When the giant double-decker bus rolled up, Will knew he'd made the right choice. Her face lit up immediately. The air was chilly on the top deck, but Will didn't mind. It gave him an excuse to wrap his arm around Cynthia so she could snuggle against his side. She asked him questions about sights they passed and he told her all he could. He'd always thought the lights of the city were beautiful, but sharing them with Cynthia made them even more special.

After about two hours, they'd seen all of Manhattan and

the tour dropped them back near Times Square. While she was mesmerized by a billboard, Will surprised her with an "I ♥ NY" T-shirt and a pretzel with mustard. They walked around for a while, and when she was nearly finished eating, she forced him into the four-story Toys "R" Us store to ride the indoor Ferris wheel.

It was an experience he would've skipped normally, but her excitement was contagious. "You had to pick the My Little Pony car, didn't you?" Will said as they stepped back out into the night. "We couldn't ride in the Monopoly car or even the Mr. Potato Head one."

"Is there something wrong with riding in a pink-and-green pony cart with rainbows and clouds?"

"Not if you're a five-year-old girl," he snorted.

"Where's your sense of adventure?"

Will stopped at a street corner and waited for the light to change before taking her by the hand and leading her to the other side. "I must've left it in my other pants."

"Speaking of which," Cynthia noted, "I like you in jeans. You look a lot more relaxed than you do in those power suits."

Will looked down at his outfit and shrugged. He was more relaxed, although he doubted his pants were the cause. He'd made the decision earlier in the night to turn his phone off. Before he left work, he informed his admin and his second in command, Dan, that he would be "unplugged" tonight. It was time Dan started earning his deputy title. It was hard to actually hit the power button, but within minutes, he could almost feel his blood pressure go down.

"I think it has more to do with the fact that I turned my cell phone off."

"Not just silent? Actually off?" Cynthia nearly choked on her last bite of pretzel.

"Yes, off." He was surprised she hadn't noticed, since it was constantly making noise, but with the honking cabs and tourist crowds, she might not have heard it, even with it on.

"What's that all about?" she asked, looking up to admire the sea of neon lights that surrounded them.

"You said I work too much. So I'm trying…something. It doesn't stop me from looking at the blank screen periodically out of habit, but it's a first step."

Cynthia broke into a wide smile. "Before long, I'll have you taking vacations and enjoying life outside the office." She turned to face him and reached up to wrap her arms around his neck. "I appreciate the effort. I know how important the *Observer* is to you."

He shrugged. "It is, but people are important, too. I'm trying to relax. Trying to enjoy my time with you." Will looked down at her, her eyes reflecting the neon. His hands had been resting on her hips, but now they snaked around her waist to pull her tight.

Cynthia eased up onto her toes and closed the distance between them for a kiss. The moment their lips met, the sounds of the city faded away. There was only the feel of his hard chest pressed against her soft one, the sweet taste of her mouth and the warmth of her skin.

Will felt exposed standing on the sidewalk. He slowly eased Cynthia backward into an alcove in the façade between stores and pressed her back into the wall.

Now they had the freedom to let their hands roam. Her palms flattened against his chest, feeling and exploring. Her fingernails scratched at his skin through the cotton of his shirt, eliciting a growl from deep in his throat.

Will leaned against her until her soft body molded to every hard inch of him. She gasped when he pressed his arousal into her belly and he closed his eyes to block out everything but the sensation of it. His tongue glided across hers, his hand daring to slide up her side under her jacket to stealthily cup her breast through the thin cotton of her T-shirt.

"Excuse me."

His eyes flew open as he took a step away from Cynthia.

They both turned and found one of the city's mounted police officers standing nearby. He looked down at them and shook his head as though he were expecting teenagers, not full-grown adults that could afford to do this at home.

"Times Square is a family place these days," he said. "Why don't you find a room somewhere?"

"Yes, Officer," Will said as he attempted to mask the grin on his face.

The policeman tipped his hat and signaled to the horse to continue its path down the sidewalk.

Will turned to her, pressing her back against the wall, but not daring to kiss her again. If he started, he doubted he'd be able to stop a second time. "We'd better go home before you tempt me to do something to get us both arrested." He spied a cab dropping someone off on the curb and waved it down.

Cynthia smiled and silently arched her back to grind against him one last time.

Will gritted his teeth together to keep a grip on his rapidly eroding control. "Get in the taxi, you minx."

Eight

The past few days, while passing in a blur, had been an exercise in restraint that Will could've done without. With the party looming close, Cynthia had become like an art exhibit in the Met. All he could do was admire her from a distance. He'd had a taste of her and he wanted more. With every day that passed by, the need within him built. Abstinence made the heart grow fonder, he mused.

They'd made a ritual of eating breakfast together in the morning before he left for work and she disappeared into her workroom. When he got home, he'd lure her away from the sewing machine for dinner. Once the dishes were cleared, she was back in her office working on her dress, despite his halfhearted attempts to lure her away. He was certain that if he'd been determined he could've succeeded, but he understood her drive. This dress was important to her like his paper was important to him. She wanted to do her best, and he didn't want to distract her.

That didn't mean he didn't lie in bed each night listening to the sewing machine whirr and ache to hold her. Fortunately, his celibate streak was coming to an end. Tonight was the party, and Cynthia's masterpiece would be revealed.

He slipped the last onyx stud through the buttonhole, adjusted his tie and shrugged on his black tuxedo jacket. Will glanced at his reflection in the mirror one last time, but things were as good as they were going to get.

Cynthia, however, had been in her bathroom for over an hour. He'd heard the water run, the blow-dryer and then a long silence where she was doing God knows what. He was glad he didn't have to worry about makeup and fussy hairstyles. He'd stopped in for a haircut earlier in the week and shaved after his shower, and that was about it.

He glanced at his watch and was pleased that they seemed to be on time so far. A limo would be picking them up downstairs in just a few minutes. Gathering his things, he sat on the couch to wait for her.

It didn't take long. The clicking of her heels on the hardwood in the hall caught his attention a moment later. Will looked up as she entered the room and nearly choked.

There were really no words for how amazing she looked. He rose to his feet, his mouth open but at a loss for what to say. Apparently that was good enough for Cynthia, who smiled and gave a turn in her gown. The dark green dress shimmered as the light hit the beads. It hugged every curve of her body, the neckline dipping down just enough to give him a luscious view of the swell of her breasts.

Across her bare neck, she wore an emerald necklace he'd bought for her when she'd made partner at her agency. The intricate gold design had nearly twenty emeralds inset into it, with the largest a teardrop that hung tantalizingly into her cleavage.

But none of it sparkled like she did. Her dark hair was twisted up off her neck with gold combs. Wearing her hair back let the pale beauty of her face shine. The matching emerald earrings dangled from each ear and brought out the brilliant green and gold in her eyes. She'd done her makeup perfectly with smoky colors that made her look sexy and mysterious.

She was simply stunning. He knew she worried about not looking precisely like she had before the accident, but her brilliant smile and personality made her glow more radiantly than she ever had before. The doctor had cleared her to remove the brace, so the chunky gold bracelets on her left arm hid the scar. Anyone who met Cynthia for the first time tonight would never know she was anything less than perfection.

"Gorgeous," he managed with a smile. "And the dress ain't bad either."

"Thank you," she said, her cheeks blushing with the compliment. For the first time he noticed her blush ran down her neck to her chest as well, turning the tops of her breasts an attractive pink color beneath the gold necklace. He wanted to run his tongue along the swell of her rosy flesh and bury his face into the deep valley between them.

Shifting uncomfortably as the fly of his tuxedo pants pressed into his arousal, he decided that focusing on her breasts was probably the wrong tactic if they were going to get through the next few hours. "Are you ready?"

"I am." Cynthia scooped up a small black purse and her wrap off the table.

Will offered her his arm as they walked out of the apartment and down to the lobby. Alone in the dark, private recesses of the limousine, he said, "You really do look dazzling. It's going to take everything in my power not to peel this dress off of you before we get to the party."

She smiled and turned to him. "Do I need to slide over and give you some space?"

"Don't you dare." His voice was a low growl as he slipped one arm around her back, the other gliding over her hip to actually press her closer. He wanted to pull her into his lap. To see her lipstick smeared across his stomach. How on earth would he be able to wait four or five hours to have her? He'd quickly become addicted to the woman in his arms.

"Could I offer you a little something to tide you over?"

Will arched an eyebrow at her. "What do you have in mind?"

She smiled and placed a hand on his cheek. "For now, just a kiss. Something to keep in your mind tonight when you're bored to tears and ready to leave."

Cynthia lifted her mouth to him. Her lips were soft against his, her mouth opening slightly. She tasted like peaches, he thought, realizing she must have some kind of flavored lip gloss on. It was intoxicating to drink her in as she deepened the kiss and let her silken tongue glide along his own.

He let her take the lead, knowing in his present state of mind, he'd take it too far and ruin Pauline's plans. He kept his hands firmly around her without roaming. But it was very, very difficult.

All too soon, she pulled away. "You're going to need more of that peachy stuff," he said with a strained smile.

"Thanks," she said, turning to her purse for her compact.

By the time the limo came to a stop outside the hotel, her lips were perfect and shiny and he had quelled the raging erection that wouldn't allow him to get out of the limo. She'd given him something to think about tonight, all right, but it was too dangerous a thought around all those other people.

Once they reached the party, it was absolute chaos. Dignified, well-dressed chaos, but a ruckus nonetheless. Cynthia's parents were greeting everyone as they came through the door of the ballroom, and her arrival was the official kickoff of crazy.

Will got the feeling that Cynthia had hoped to slip in unnoticed and get acclimated first, but the chances of that dissolved in an instant when Pauline announced her arrival to the entire room. He could feel her stiffen beside him as she was approached by person after person. They were all very sweet, fully aware of her condition and introducing themselves, but it was still an overwhelming sea of strangers for her. She held a tight grip to his arm, so he knew not to disappear and talk shop with any of the other publishing types he saw milling around the bar. He wasn't in the mood to do business anyway.

"Oh, Cynthia," one woman nearly shrieked as she came forward to embrace the reluctant amnesiac. "You look absolutely beautiful, darling. Oh," she continued on in a chatter when Cynthia stared blankly at her, "I'm sorry, I forgot. I'm Darlene Winters. I work for *Trend Now* magazine as the senior fashion editor. We've worked together for years on ad campaigns for the magazine."

Cynthia nodded, but he could tell she had a new type of nerves getting to her. A woman like Darlene Winters could kick-start her dreams of designing clothes, and she knew it.

"Let me look at you, darling," Darlene said, taking a step back. "That dress is absolutely stunning on you. Who are you wearing?"

Cynthia's mouth came open to speak, but nothing came out. Panic started creeping into her green eyes, so Will stepped in to intervene.

"You are looking at a Cynthia Dempsey original, Darlene. She designed and made this dress herself."

Darlene didn't have the kind of face that moved much after years of Botox and facelifts, but even then you could detect the expression of surprise. "Are you designing now? That's fabulous."

Will nudged Cynthia to respond. "Yes," she said, her voice quiet at first but growing more sure as she spoke. "I'm working on my first collection. This gown is the centerpiece. I'm very proud of it."

"You should be, honey. Listen, I don't want to take up all

your time, this is your party, but give me a call. I'd love to get together with you next week and take a look at what you're working on. This dress has me salivating for more."

Cynthia nodded and waved her hand casually as Darlene disappeared into the crowd. "Did that just happen?" she whispered to Will.

"Yep," he said with a smile. He turned to her and leaned down to plant a soft kiss on her peach lips. "Don't be afraid to tell people about your work. It's brilliant, and they should all know it."

She smiled up at him, her eyes glistening with tears of excitement and overwhelming emotion. This dream had quickly become very important to her. So it was important to him. He would support her in whatever way she needed.

The orchestra started playing a popular tune, and several of the people around them disappeared to pair off on the dance floor. He needed at least one good drink before he was loose enough to attempt that, so he decided to take advantage of the suddenly shorter line for the bartender.

"Let's go get a drink," he said. "It will make this easier for us both."

When they approached the bar, Will recognized the shaggy blond hair of the man in front of them. "Alex?" he said as he slipped his arm around Cynthia's narrow waist and snugly tugged her against his side for safekeeping.

Alex turned with a brand new drink in hand. "Hey, Will," he said, shaking his hand and then turning to look at Cynthia. His hazel gaze raked over her for a moment, lingering a second longer than Will liked on the plunge of her dress. He knew his friend had a hard time mentally switching out of playboy mode.

"Cynthia," he said with a smile, and just like that, he squelched the stalking panther and turned on the boyish charm that made him the favorite of older ladies everywhere. "You are looking mahh-velouss," Alex overexaggerated, leaning in to give her a kiss on the cheek. "You are a goddess at the sewing machine," he added.

Cynthia blushed and Will fought the need to pull her closer to him. His friend was harmless. He knew Alex had a strict code, and infidelity and seducing a friend's woman, even an ex, was a violation. Cynthia was safe. Every other woman in the room, however...

"Cyndi?"

Will's thoughts were interrupted by the arrival of Cynthia's sister, Emma. The teen was grinning with excitement, apparently having reached the age where Pauline would not only let her attend a party but wear a fancy dress and makeup, too. She was a pretty little thing who looked a lot like her sister, with flawless pale skin, high cheekbones and shiny, dark hair. The braces were probably a godsend, letting everyone know, including guys like Alex, that despite her tiny dress and attempt at being a grown-up, she was still jailbait.

A few more years and Emma would be out on the town giving George and Pauline heart palpitations.

Cynthia smiled and hugged her sister, letting the teen pull her away for a few minutes to talk about girly things, he supposed.

"I see you've charmed those panties off," Alex said, leaning in with a sly grin.

Will shook his head with a sigh. "You're awful. But if you don't mind me asking, how did you know?"

Alex took a sip of his drink and eyed Will with a mix of amusement and concern. "You're in serious trouble, man."

He frowned and turned to his friend, grateful Cynthia was distracted by her sister for a moment. "Trouble?"

"Yep. She's got you. I can see it when you look at her. I'd say you're one step away from being completely lost."

Will took a sip of his own drink, hoping the alcohol would muffle the alarm bells his friend's words had set off. He was giving this a second chance, but he thought he was being especially cautious to not rush into something he would regret. "Don't be ridiculous."

Alex slapped him on the back, a wide smile lighting his face. "I didn't say you should fight it, man. There's nothing quite like being completely lost to a beautiful woman. You look really happy with her. I just hope you let yourself enjoy it for once."

Before Will could answer, Alex gave him a wink, waved to Cynthia and disappeared into the crowd, back on the prowl.

After an hour or so, Cynthia finally got brave enough to leave Will's side and explore on her own. She'd had a few drinks and hors d'oeuvres, allowed her parents to take her around and introduce her to a million people and then sat through a miserable round of speeches in her honor.

But now she was alone, standing unnoticed near the edge of the crowd and sipping a glass of wine to help her unwind. It was all very overwhelming.

A man's hand reached for Cynthia's elbow, tugging her gently behind a decorative fabric panel in the ballroom. Perhaps Will's determination to resist ravishing her was wearing thin. She allowed herself to be lured away, setting down her glass, but she stopped short when she realized the man touching her was not Will.

She recognized Nigel from the photos in her office, although he didn't look nearly as happy as he had on the beach. His large, brown eyes reflected the same anger that was etched into every inch of his unshaven jaw. He had messy, dark blond hair and an ill-fitting tuxedo that was obviously rented at the last minute. In the photos, he'd had a bit of rugged, boyish charm, but at that moment, she wasn't entirely sure what she ever saw in him.

"Aren't you looking fancy tonight?" he said with a mocking tone. "That necklace alone could pay for three years of rent on my studio in the Bronx."

"Take your hand off me," she said, her voice as cold as she could manage.

"No way in hell, sweetheart. If I do, you'll run back to your rich fiancé."

"I told you on the phone that I had no idea who you were and had nothing else to say to you." She tugged, but his fingers pressed more cruelly into her upper arm. "How did you even get in here?"

"I used my last hundred dollars to rent this tux and bribe the doorman." Nigel smiled, apparently pleased with his ingenuity.

"Why? What do you want?"

His dark eyes pinned her and made her squirm uncomfortably. "I want the woman I love back."

"The woman you loved died in that plane crash. I may have physically lived through it, but I'm a different person now."

"So, you think you can just cast me aside because I'm not William Reese Taylor the Third?" he said with a sarcastic sneer that curled his upper lip. "You said you loved me."

Cynthia watched a touch of sadness creep into the man's dark eyes. They'd had something together, something that was still important to him. And for that she had some sympathy. But Will was important to her and she wasn't going to screw up her second chance.

"I don't know what kind of relationship you and I had, but believe me when I say it's over. Regardless of what I've said or promised you in the past, we're done. I'm working things out with Will."

She could feel rage coursing through his veins, the iron grip on her arm not lessening for even a moment. She was going to have a miserable bruise if he wasn't careful.

"You're going to regret using me, Cynthia." At that, he let go of her and stomped to the exit.

There was something about his tone that made her glad her building had a twenty-four-hour doorman. Once the door slammed shut, Cynthia flopped back against the wall with a rush of relief. She brought her hands up to cover her face so no one could see the horrified mix of fear, sadness and gratitude that he was gone. Taking a deep breath and running her hand over her upper arm to soothe where he'd gripped her, she painted on her best smile and melted back into the crowd. She moved immediately to her abandoned drink, swallowing a large sip of it and setting down the glass before someone saw how badly her hand was shaking.

"Pumpkin?"

Cynthia didn't get her wish. She turned toward the voice and found her father coming toward her with a look of concern on his face. "Yes, Daddy?"

"What was that all about? Do I need to call security?"

That was the last thing she wanted. The less attention drawn to this the better. "No, not at all. It was nothing."

Her father's sharp gaze focused on the red splotch Nigel left on her upper arm. "That sure looks like something to me."

"It's just a misunderstanding. I'm fine. Where's Mother?"

He shrugged, allowing her to put an end to that conversation. "I left her talking to that obnoxious woman from the country club. That always ends up being expensive."

Cynthia nodded, her nerves over the argument with Nigel slowly starting to fade. "I'm going to find Will. I'm hoping I can convince him to take me home. I'm exhausted. You'd better rescue Mother before you end up owning a house on Martha's Vineyard."

"All right," he said, leaning in to give her a big hug. "If you need me to take care of that, all you have to do is call," he whispered into her ear.

"You sound like a mobster, Daddy." She pulled away and smiled. "Everything is fine, really."

"Okay. You look beautiful tonight, pumpkin. I hope you

had a good time." He kissed her on the cheek and reluctantly stumbled off in search of his wife.

Alone again, she went to the bar and got herself a new glass of white zinfandel, which she could hold without shaking uncontrollably. Taking another sip, she closed her eyes, swallowed and took a deep breath. She needed to get a grip.

"There you are." Will's voice whispered close to her ear, his breath warm on her neck.

She spun in his arms to face him. "Hello," she said, pasting a smile on her face. "Are you having fun?"

He shrugged. "I've never really cared for these kinds of things. This party is for you, so naturally it's the best party ever thrown, but I'd just as soon rush you out of here and find out what's under that dress."

There was a heat in his cool blue eyes that promised he would make good on every word. The warmth of his hands on her sunk deep into her body, and the worries of a moment ago seemed to disappear. He had such a powerful effect on her. Having him so close, his cologne and warm male scent tickling her nose, was enough to make her want to rub against him and purr like a cat. She was about to suggest he take her home when he looked down at this watch.

"I guess we can't avoid it any longer."

Cynthia frowned in confusion. "Avoid what?"

"The dance floor. Come on," he said, taking a step back and holding out his hand to her. "We've got to take at least one lap around the floor before we leave. Pauline paid way too much for the orchestra for us not to."

"I don't think I know how to dance," she confided as he led her through the crowd. It was part of the reason she hadn't brought it up earlier. She'd rather look lovely in the crowd then stand out for looking foolish.

"Don't worry, I'm no Fred Astaire."

They made their way to the center of the floor where a large group of couples had already gathered. Will took Cynthia's hand in his, wrapped his arm around her waist and pulled her tightly against him. "We'll keep it simple," he said with a smile.

It was a good thing he meant what he said, because she could hardly think this close to him. The whole length of her body was pressed into his as they glided around. The song was slow and the steps were easy, but she hardly noticed anything but her handsome dancing partner.

"I'm going to have to keep a better eye on you tonight," Will whispered into her ear after a few minutes.

Cynthia felt her chest tighten but tried not to let the panic show in her eyes. Instead she turned to place her head on his shoulder so he couldn't see her face. "Why is that?" she asked. Had he seen Nigel?

"Because every eye in this room is on you, and every man here is drooling over how your dress looks like you were poured into it." His hand slid lower on her back to rest just above the flare of her hips. The heat sank into the base of her spine, a warm tingle starting there and working its way through her body.

Perhaps Nigel hadn't ruined tonight after all. "Mmm-hmm…" she murmured, her heart not slowing as the worry subsided but increasing with his caress. Her whole body was on high alert and aching for more of him. The few days she'd gone without his touch was far too long. "I *am* an excellent seamstress."

"Indeed."

"But how do you know they aren't looking at you? You're quite handsome tonight as well."

"Nope, but thank you for the compliment. If you've seen one monkey suit, you've seen them all. Tonight is all about you. And you deserve it."

Cynthia was a little startled by his statement. She'd been lucky. She doubted she'd been spared because she deserved it more than anyone else on that plane. To be honest, she should've been one of the last ones spared. "For what? Not dying?"

"You're a fighter. I'm so amazed at how you've handled everything that has been thrown at you the past few months. I didn't realize you had it in you. I guess I never really gave you enough credit. I was always too busy to really see who you were, only what you wanted me and everyone else to see."

Will stopped turning and they both became still in each other's arms. He reached down and gently tipped her chin up to him so she couldn't avoid his gaze. "I see you now, Cynthia. And I really like what I see."

Cynthia was trapped in the blue eyes gazing down on her with adoration and unmasked attraction. It was the nicest thing he'd ever said to her. It wasn't a declaration of love, but it was a step in the right direction. She'd held on to the dream of a real future together, but she figured it would take time. When she gave him back the engagement ring, it was a pledge to put in the necessary time and effort to fix their relationship. Perhaps it wasn't as broken as she'd thought. They could have a future together. One filled with love and laughter.

As she stood there, surrounded by the gentle glow of crystal chandeliers and drifting orchestra music, she felt her heart slipping from her grasp. She barely knew Will, but she didn't care. She knew he was honest and kind. He supported her like no one else had. He'd protected her from a world that seemed to come at her from all sides. He was a good man. A man worthy of the love that suddenly swelled in her chest for him.

Cynthia really did love him. And she wanted to tell him how she felt in this perfect moment, but she knew it was too soon. The night had been an emotional roller coaster, but she knew how it needed to end. She needed to find the solace and comfort she knew would be in Will's arms. And in his bed.

Maybe there she could find the courage to voice the words that wanted to burst out of her with their intensity.

Instead she said, "Kiss me." And he did without hesitation.

She melted into him, neither of them worried about her makeup or the fact that a hundred people were watching them. It was just him and her, two lovers in a bubble that no one, not even Nigel, could burst.

When they finally came up for air, Cynthia knew she couldn't stay at this party a moment longer. She needed to make love to Will.

"Now, we've danced. So take me home," she demanded with a wicked smile.

Nine

Cynthia sat expectantly in the limousine, eyeing Will as though he would pounce on her at any moment, but he wasn't about to start anything he couldn't finish. She couldn't walk up to the apartment carrying her dress, and she'd kill him if he ripped it off her the way he wanted to, so there was nothing to do but wait.

A little anticipation never hurt anyone. The past few days had taught him that.

But Cynthia wasn't having it. She moved over to the opposite seat, facing him. Having her out of his reach was helpful, but now he couldn't keep from looking at her. Which is exactly what she wanted.

Grasping at the fabric, she slowly inched her dress up her legs until they were exposed to the knee. He could see the bare flash of her inner thigh as she slipped out of her heels and stretched one pale, delicate foot across the distance between them. Starting at his ankle, it slowly snaked up his leg, gently caressing him as it went.

He tensed as her foot moved higher, slinking across his inner thigh. Will was firm, ready and aching for her touch. Her green eyes shone with a naughty glint as they locked on his. The corners of her mouth curved up in a knowing smile as her toes met with the base of his shaft and agonizingly slid up the hard length.

Will groaned aloud, his hands curving into tight fists at his sides. Thank God the privacy partition was up in the limousine. He didn't want their driver to hear him, and he couldn't keep the growl in his throat from escaping as her foot moved up and down in a rhythm set to make him absolutely crazy.

He would not reach for her, he told himself. They were almost home. Getting out of the car and upstairs might be an issue for him with her tiny pink-painted toes driving him to distraction, but he could do it.

"Aww," Cynthia pouted as the limo pulled up outside their building. "I was just starting to have some fun."

Will sighed in relief as she pulled her dress down and slipped back into her shoes. Cynthia gathered her things and slipped out of the door, which was now open and waiting for them. They made it upstairs in record time, the door slamming shut behind Will just as he thought he might explode if he didn't touch her soon.

But she moved out of his reach.

Taking a few steps back until she was highlighted in the dark apartment by the glow of the overhead entryway light, she held out a hand to urge him to stay where he was. He flopped back against the door, untying his tie to keep from choking on it as he realized what she had in mind.

Reaching up to her neck, she unfastened her necklace, exposing the wide, creamy expanse of her chest and throat. She set it on the nearby table and followed it one by one with her earrings and bracelets.

With a sly grin, she turned until her back was to him, looking over her shoulder with a wink. Her fingers moved up to her hair, finding the combs and pins that held it in place and removing them, letting her dark brown tresses fall in silky curls around her shoulders.

Then her arms twisted behind her and found the fastener at the top of the zipper. Cynthia undid it and then grasped the metal tab and dragged it down. Inch by inch, she revealed skin, his heart racing in his chest with every second that ticked by.

The zipper stopped just at the base of her spine. His eager eyes took in everything, including the fact that he'd yet to see evidence of any undergarments beneath that dress. No bra definitely, and he was beginning to think she hadn't worn panties either.

"Holy hell," he whispered, his throat becoming dry as a desert. All night there had been nothing between them but the elegant green material.

Holding the dress to her chest, she turned back to face him, her arms pressed so tightly that her breasts threatened to burst out of the top of her gown. They were tinged a pink color with a blush like her neck and face. It made him smile knowing she was trying so hard for him even when it was slightly out of her comfort zone. He wanted to tell her not to be embarrassed, that she was doing a damn good job, but before he could, she met his gaze with her own and the gown slipped to the floor.

It pooled at her feet, proving he'd been correct earlier. She'd worn a dress and shoes tonight, nothing more. If she'd told him that earlier, they never would've made it to the party.

She stepped out of the puddle of fabric, her graceful, nude body on full display for the first time. The expression on her face was a mix of nerves and arousal. Cynthia was giving herself fully to him tonight. Before, darkness had cloaked her just as she'd held back, but now her rounded belly and hips beckoned to him. Her perky, full breasts reached out with tight peach nipples that reminded him of her lip gloss from earlier. He knew they would taste just as sweet.

His body urged him to quickly close the gap between them, but he held his ground. As much as he wanted her, he wasn't going to rush tonight. Pushing away from the door, he slipped out of his tuxedo jacket and tossed it onto the coat rack. Taking one slow step after the other toward her, he pulled his tie off and threw it on the floor and then started unbuttoning one onyx button after the other.

He stopped just short of her, his shirt undone to his waist. Cynthia boldly reached out to tug it out of his waistband, undoing the last button and reaching up to slip the shirt off his shoulders. Her hands followed the fabric down his arms, her palms caressing him down his biceps, elbows and forearms until the shirt fell to the floor.

Will let her hands continue to explore as they ran over the muscles of his chest, sliding across the ridges of his abdomen and returning to unfasten his belt.

Her fingers were about to slip inside his waistband when his hand caught her wrist. She gasped in surprise. "I want to touch you," she said, pouting until he leaned in and wiped the frown away with his mouth.

Cynthia pressed her naked body against him, and he released her wrist so she could wrap her arms around his neck. The firm peaks of her breasts dug into his chest, the globes flattening to him as she struggled to get closer.

Their tongues and lips and teeth danced frantically together as his hands moved over her body, unfettered by the inconvenience of her clothing.

She gasped against his lips as one hand cupped her breast, her hips surging forward to press her soft belly against his pulsating erection. He groaned, closing his eyes and riding the wave of sensation she brought on. Her mouth took advantage of his pause to slide down his jaw to his throat, pressing soft kisses against his fevered skin. To his surprise, she bit him at the juncture of his neck and shoulder, sending a shock of pleasure that pushed him near the edge as she soothed the wound with her silken tongue.

She'd certainly gained some confidence since their first night together after the accident, and it was undeniably sexy. In one swift movement, Will dipped down and scooped Cynthia into his arms. She cried out in surprise and then giggled and nuzzled at his neck as they moved down the hallway to the bedroom.

"How very Rhett Butler of you," she said as he kicked the door open, switched on the light and laid her down on the comforter.

Will took a step back to admire the sprawled-out beauty on his bed. She looked so free and open to him. He had been given such a gift, and it had taken him this long to truly appreciate it. This woman was everything that he wanted. Four months ago no one could've convinced him that he would be where he was right now—with Cynthia naked, willing and on display for him. That he would be bursting with arousal and emotions he'd never felt before.

She was so beautiful it made his heart swell with pride that she was his. So full of life and energy it made him want to share his life with her. To experience it as her partner. Her lover. Alex was right. Will was lost. Despite his best attempts, he'd allowed himself to fall in love. Hopelessly, desperately in love with a woman who made him happy to come home from work every day. Who made him want to live life, not just write about it in the newspaper.

In that very moment, he had to possess her, heart and soul, and couldn't wait another moment. Without delay, he slipped off the last of his clothes, his gaze never straying from the feast before him.

Cynthia watched him anxiously through hooded eyes as he undressed, but her expression changed when she caught sight of his erection jutting proudly toward her. Her moist lips parted softly, and then the look of pleasure washed over her flushed face. With a smile, she crooked her finger at him to join her at last on the bed.

He'd waited long enough, and he wasn't about to deny her request.

Cynthia held her breath in anticipation as Will crawled onto the bed and covered her with his muscled body. The warmth of his skin seared across her exposed flesh, and a chill ran down her spine from the pleasurable contrast. He hovered just over her, her aching nipples dragging across his chest, the firm length of his erection grazing her stomach.

So close and yet so far away. She reached out to touch him, but he pulled back, moving down her body to settle between her legs. His hands ran up her shins, his palms tickling her as they moved higher. He knelt down and followed his hands with his mouth, first planting a warm kiss on the inside of her ankles and then traveling up her calves to the insides of her knees.

Knees were hardly an erogenous zone, but Cynthia's whole body was tense and sensitive to his every caress. As he gently parted her thighs, he exposed her moist core and her legs started trembling. She couldn't stop it, her body so weak with wanting him as his kisses traveled over her inner thighs, his fingertips tracing lazy circles across her skin.

By the time she could feel his hot breath tickling her dark, feminine curls, she thought even his slightest touch might send her over the edge. Will explored her with his hand first, running along the edge with his finger before slowly slipping it inside of her. Her muscles clamped down around him, desperate to hold him there, but it wasn't what she wanted. She wanted him.

He leaned in and his tongue struck her sensitive center without fail, the intimate kiss sending waves of pleasure through her body. Cynthia squirmed under his touch, her hips rising up to meet him and then pulling away when the intensity became too much.

"I need you," she whispered.

"You'll have me," he said, his voice deep and gruff with arousal. "I want to have a little fun first."

This time she whimpered as his fingers and tongue pushed her closer to the edge. She didn't want to peak without him. She'd admitted to herself tonight that she loved him. She'd exposed herself to him in every way, made herself so vulnerable she almost couldn't believe it. She wanted her first cries of pleasure as a woman in love to be mingled with his own. "Not without you. Not tonight, Will."

Her pleas were finally heard, and he moved back up her body, nestling between her thighs and looking down at her. He reached to the nightstand for a condom, and Cynthia sighed in relief that he'd thought of it when she'd been too overwhelmed with desire to think straight.

A moment later, he hovered over her, the tip of him pressing gently at her entrance. Without hesitation, he drove into her, and then he lingered—buried deep inside her. It was a powerful feeling, to finally join with the man she loved. So much so she almost had to fight back tears that the connection brought on. The words she longed to say hung on the tip of her tongue, waiting to be uttered, but he started moving inside her, and the time for talking passed.

Will dropped his weight on to his elbows, pressing his chest against hers. He kissed her, his lips and tongue melding with her own as he gently rocked back and forth. Every inch of their bodies were touching and molding together. Cynthia could feel every flex of his muscles, every shudder of strain as he fought to hold back the tides. But she didn't want him to do that. She wanted all of him tonight, leaving nothing behind.

"Love me the way you want to. Don't hold back," she said against his jaw.

Will didn't answer but buried his face into her neck. His rapid breaths were hot again her skin, his body stiffening to surge forward harder and faster than before. The delicious movement accelerated every impulse running through her nervous system, the pleasurable sparks lighting up all over.

It wasn't long before the tight knot of tension in her belly threatened to explode. Cynthia wrapped her legs around his waist and clutched at his back. The change in angle allowed him to drive deeper, a low roar of pleasure echoing into her ear.

She couldn't hold back any longer. "Will!" she cried out, as one long, hard stroke sent her over the edge. Her body was racked with convulsions of pleasure, her muscles tightening and pulsating around his firm heat. Her fingertips dug into the muscles of his back, scrambling for purchase as he continued to pound deep inside. At last, his own release exploded, his groan of surrender vibrating against the damp skin of her neck.

For a few moments, they lay motionless, their bodies a moist tangle of limbs and sheets. Cynthia struggled to draw a full breath into her lungs, but she couldn't. Her muscles were too tired and her heart too swollen with unspoken emotions. By the time the last throbs of pleasure subsided, she opened her eyes to see Will looking down at her.

"You," he said, propping up on one elbow and brushing a damp strand of hair from her forehead, "were amazing tonight. You were so worried about fitting in with those people, but it was effortless. You were so elegant and graceful. Every woman in that ballroom wanted to wear your clothing and hoped they'd look half as good in them as you did.

"And all the men…" he continued. "Well, let's just say I got to live out their fantasies tonight."

"I got to live out my fantasy tonight, too."

Will smiled, leaning down to place a soft kiss on her lips.

Her body responded to his touch, but her brain chased the heat out of her veins. It was time to sleep, at least for now.

He reached down to pull the duvet up to cover them, and then tugged Cynthia up to curl her back against his chest. Wrapped in the warmth of the blanket with Will beside her, they fell asleep, the lights still on, their clothes still strewn around the apartment.

Sometime before dawn, Cynthia woke up, still tucked in Will's strong embrace. She squirmed slightly to free herself from his grasp and sat up on the edge of the bed.

"Are you all right?" he asked, his voice sleepy and rough.

"Yes," she said. "I'm just thirsty, and I never brushed my teeth. Do you want some water?"

"No, I'm okay."

Cynthia pushed up from the mattress and walked nude into the bathroom. At the doorway, she paused and looked back at Will. She expected to catch a glimpse of him as he fell back asleep, but he was propped up on his elbow. He was watching her walk away, but the expression on his face was not what she was expecting. His brow was furrowed, his gaze burrowing into her backside, of all places.

"Is something wrong?" she asked.

Will shifted his gaze to her, the intensity only increasing as he studied her face just as thoroughly. "No," he said pointedly, although his contemplative tone made her wonder if that were really true.

Cynthia was too sleepy to worry much about it. She went into the bathroom and shut the door behind her. She chugged a cup of water, finished removing her makeup and went about her nightly beauty regime. Her body was aching, but fulfilled, and she was eager to crawl back under the covers and sleep in Will's arms until noon.

Returning to the bed, she switched off the lights and slipped under the sheets. Will had rolled onto his back and his eyes were closed. She snuggled into him and laid her head on his chest. Listening to his heartbeat, she realized she'd never been so happy. Finding a passion in sewing and design was nothing compared to finding a passion and love for Will. Tonight had been everything she hoped and wished for when she gave him back her engagement ring—a chance for them to start over and be happy together.

"I love you," she whispered into the dark once the rise and fall of his breath became steady and even against her and she was certain he was sleeping. Then she turned onto her side and closed her eyes, immediately falling asleep.

Although he was lying in bed with his eyes closed, Will was far from asleep. Ten minutes ago, he would've told anyone he was exhausted and content with the woman he loved in his arms. His business was doing well and his love life was better than ever. Somehow, all of that was snatched from him so quickly that he couldn't feel the pain of it being ripped away at first. There was just a mix of confusion and denial swirling around the sleepy fog of his brain. What he'd just seen was impossible. Incomprehensible. And yet there was no way to deny the truth.

The rose tattoo was gone.

He'd hated that thing from the moment she'd gotten it. Cynthia had gone off on a spring break girls' trip to Cancun their senior year at Yale. Sometime amongst the sun and surf and tequila, she'd decided it would be a great idea to commemorate the trip with a tattoo on her ass.

It was pretty and well done, but in the end, it was a red rose inked into her left butt cheek. He'd done his best to ignore it over the years, and when their love life fizzled, he'd forgotten it was even there.

Until it wasn't.

When he watched her walk away, the realization hit him like an iron fist to the gut. There was no tattoo. And not even the faintest hint of where one might've been removed by a laser without his knowledge. There was nothing. He didn't know what to say when she asked if something was wrong.

Yes, by God, something was very wrong. She was not Cynthia Dempsey, and that was a problem.

In an instant, his entire world came crashing down around him. The best relationship he'd ever had was built on nothing but lies. He could feel it disintegrating around him. Everything she'd said and everything they'd done in the past few weeks meant absolutely nothing.

Who had he just made love to? This woman, this Cynthia imposter…who was she, and how had she ended up living another person's life? The doctors said she had amnesia. Did she even know she *wasn't* Cynthia? Was this all just one tragic mixup, or had this woman deliberately taken advantage of her circumstances? Was it possible that despite her outward appearance, she was as manipulative as Cynthia?

All this time he'd been afraid to let his guard down because he didn't think he could trust Cynthia not to hurt him again. But he took the leap and found there was a greater pain he hadn't felt yet. The woman he loved, the one who'd gotten under his skin and made him question the way he lived his life, wasn't Cynthia at all. Cynthia never had the power to hurt him this badly because he hadn't allowed it. This time he'd let down his protective walls and permitted his mystery lover to shatter his heart, whereas Cynthia had merely cracked it.

It took every ounce of strength he had to keep his jaw clamped shut and swallow the hurt, confused words in his throat when she snuggled into his chest, completely oblivious to his discovery. The woman in his arms was not Cynthia. It was nearly impossible to wrap his head around the idea. His mind bounced around frantically, reliving every discussion, every touch, trying to determine if it had been obvious but he'd been too blinded by her light to see it.

No wonder Cynthia had cheated on him. He'd been with

her since college but he barely knew her anymore. They'd become so disconnected from their relationship that he couldn't even tell her from someone else. He, of all people, should've been able to tell the difference regardless of what some plastic surgeon's knife had done. He was a fool.

Will wanted to shake her and start throwing angry accusations, but it was 3 a.m. and he knew the answers wouldn't come. In the morning he would uncover the truth and then see what she had to say for herself. For now, all he could do was try to fall back asleep and hope the heartburn-like pain in his chest didn't keep him up all night.

It was then, as he lay in the dark praying for sleep to dull the pain, that the woman lying in his bed quietly declared that she was in love with him. And to think, up until that point, he'd thought the situation couldn't get any worse.

Ten

When morning had finally come around, the arrival of the sun did not make Will's outlook any brighter. In fact, he'd lay there wide awake the entire time. With each second that ticked by, the pain and confusion had slowly morphed into anger and suspicion. He got out of bed around seven and told her there was a pressing problem with the Sunday edition. He couldn't very well tell her he didn't want to be around her, pretending to bask in their post lovemaking glow. He wasn't a very good actor, and he wasn't ready to confront her until he had all the information. He wanted to have the advantage, and that meant doing the necessary research to figure out who she was and what she was after.

She—*he couldn't think of her as Cynthia anymore*—pouted appropriately and gave him a kiss to help keep her on his mind all day.

Oh, yeah, she'd be on his mind, all right. But probably not the way she imagined.

When he got to the office, he asked his weekend admin

to pull any articles the local papers had done on the plane crash. He spent two hours at his desk poring over the pieces published in his paper and other papers around town. There wasn't much information aside from details of the accident itself, the short list of survivors and what the airline was doing to ensure the tragedy would never happen again.

None of that was helpful.

Going down the hallway into the bullpen, where a large group of journalists worked in cubicles, he sought out the guy who had written all the articles for the *Observer*.

"Mike? Do you have a second?"

The journalist spun in his chair, a look of surprise on his face when he realized the owner of the paper was in his cubicle and not the guy across from him looking to borrow a stapler. "Yes, Mr. Taylor?"

"I'm looking for some information on Cynthia's plane crash. Do you happen to have any research materials left over that I can see?"

"Sure thing." Mike spun back around to his file cabinet and pulled out a green file labeled "Chicago Flight 746." "Everything I have is here, including any official faxes the airline sent."

"Is there a list of passengers and seats included?"

"Yes, sir."

"Excellent. Thank you, Mike."

Will took the file back to his office and flipped through the pages. According to the information from the airline, Cynthia was in 14A, a window seat in coach. That was unusual. A look at the first-class passengers explained it. Looked like a large group of Japanese businessmen traveling together. She probably hadn't realized what seat she was assigned until it was too late to change it.

Turning back to Cynthia's row, he noted the person beside her in 14B was a woman named Adrienne Lockhart. She had not survived the accident. Few had.

Firing up his laptop, Will pulled up his internet browser and searched for this Adrienne Lockhart. The first link was adriennelockhartdesigns.com, a site for a SoHo-based fashion designer.

A fashion designer. Will's stomach started to churn with dread. He was certainly on the right track. He'd hoped for a moment he'd find she'd sat beside a middle-aged attorney named Harold.

He opened the website up and saw on the homepage an announcement that the store was closing and thanking her patrons for their support. The announcement was dated the day before the crash.

Will clicked on "About the Designer," and before the page had almost fully loaded, he knew he had come to the right site. There was a photo of a smiling, dark-haired woman posted there. They could've been sisters with like features arranged in a slightly different way. She looked to be a similar build to Cynthia, but facially, there were differences. Adrienne's face was a touch rounder, her nose slightly wider. She didn't have Cynthia's high, prominent cheekbones or expensive, perfect teeth. Her hair had a sort of wavy kink to it, although it was the same dark color.

Clicking on the picture, it enlarged and he was able to zoom in on the feature he was most interested in. The eyes. He'd convinced himself that the gold in Cynthia's eyes had always been there, but he'd avoided her gaze so long he'd forgotten. Now he realized it was because it hadn't been there before. But it was certainly in this photo. If he enlarged the picture enough to show nothing else but the pair of green-gold eyes, it was like looking at Cynthia.

The Cynthia he'd made the mistake of falling for.

Cynthia Dempsey was not in his apartment. That woman was most certainly Adrienne Lockhart.

But why? How had this happened?

There had obviously been some kind of mistake at the accident site. Either the bodies had been thrown from their seats or they'd switched seats for some reason. He knew Cynthia hated the window, so he had no doubt she would needle the person next to her into trading. As badly as they were hurt, the women looked similar enough to be confused by rescue crews.

If Adrienne had woken up in the hospital, her face reconstructed to look more like Cynthia…it was an easy mistake for everyone to make. She had looked horrible, nothing like Cynthia at first despite Dr. Takashi's best efforts. They believed she was Cynthia because the doctors told them she was. But it was also an easy mistake to correct. All she had to do was say, "I'm not Cynthia Dempsey" the minute she could talk. But she hadn't. She'd feigned confusion and was diagnosed with amnesia.

Well, of course it would seem like it. She wouldn't recognize any of the people that came to see her. They'd never met. She wouldn't recognize their house or know anything about their life or her past. It made perfect sense.

Except she hadn't remembered who she really was either.

He'd always believed amnesia was the stuff of soap operas before Cynthia's accident. And now, knowing the truth, he was inclined to believe it still was.

The woman on that website was at the end of her rope. She'd lost her store, was flying back home to Wisconsin. She had nothing when she got on that plane. Even if there had been some initial confusion when she woke up with all the surgeries and drugs, there had to be a point when she realized there was a mistake and didn't say anything.

But why? Did the fancy life Cynthia no longer needed seem more glamorous? Rich parents, a penthouse apartment on the Upper East Side, a five-carat platinum engagement ring…certainly better than returning home a failure.

Better to go along with it, see how long she could get away with her game. In a matter of weeks, she'd overtaken Cynthia's life and set it on the course of the life she wanted. Not only was she designing, and miraculously well for a supposed novice, but now she had all the industry connections to get a collection off the ground.

It was certainly a big risk to take. She couldn't have known about the tattoo, but there could've been a million different ways to give her game away. Seducing him was probably the stupidest thing she could've done. Did she think he would be blinded by love and never notice the differences?

It had worked pretty well, so far. He'd dismissed the shoes being too big and the eyes being too gold. Cast aside doubts when she was suddenly a world-class seamstress. Suppressed his amazement when the personalities were like night and day. He supposed he had been blind. He hadn't wanted to see that no bump to the head could've turned the cold, indifferent woman he knew into the vivacious, loving woman who had charmed him from the first day in the hospital.

But perhaps that was all an act. If she were shrewd enough to steal another person's identity, all of that could just be part of the game. Be sweet, be loving, be innocent and everyone would love her too much to ask questions.

Slamming his fist into his desk, Will let himself focus on the pain radiating up his arm. The unpleasant sensation was the only thing in his life he knew was real and true. Cynthia or Adrienne or whoever the hell she was had wrapped him in such a web of lies that he didn't know what to believe. But pain didn't lie. It didn't turn your whole world upside down and confess its love to you in a ploy to hijack someone's life.

Well, no more. He wasn't about to be used for a second longer. He shut down his laptop and grabbed his coat off the back of his chair, then he marched out of his office to hail a cab for home.

Sunday afternoon Cynthia was filled with nervous energy. She should've been floating around on cloud nine after the amazing night she shared with Will, but something about this morning hadn't sat right with her. He'd come so far in his attempt to work less and spend more time with her. But this morning, he had almost avoided her. He didn't make eye contact. His lips had been stiff against hers when she kissed him goodbye. Then he'd dashed out the door to go to the office for a problem that someone other than the CEO could have fixed.

It made her uneasy. She thought last night had gone so well. She didn't know what the problem could be. Unless he heard her when she'd said she loved him. Cynthia had been certain he was asleep, but what if he wasn't? What if it was way too soon? She was a fool. *Always wait for the guy to say it first.*

As time went by without word from Will, Cynthia opted to call Darlene Winters. She should've waited until Monday, but she needed the distraction. She was pleased to find the fashion editor was still just as excited to view her work. She was to bring three pieces and her sketches to her office in the *Trend Now* magazine headquarters on Tuesday.

The problem was she only had three completed pieces: the gown, the shirt-dress and a coordinating skirt and blouse. If she took those three pieces, she didn't have the option of wearing one of her own designs. She didn't think any of her sketches could be completed in time, because she was short on the fabrics and supplies she would need. She'd just have to settle for the small fortune of designer clothes she owned.

She stood in her closet, eyeing the endless racks of items to wear. Cynthia had already picked out a deep purple skirt. She liked the pop of color, and the lines were similar enough to her collection that the style didn't contrast too much with what she promoted. But she still needed a blouse.

She flipped through hanger after hanger, the dollar signs adding up exponentially, but nothing caught her eye. Then she saw a glimpse of fabric in her peripheral vision. The flash of purple and white drew her down several feet to a long-sleeved blouse. She pulled it off the rack and looked it over. It was perfect, really. The purple and white stripes would accent the skirt, and some of the details in the blouse were very similar to what she'd been thinking about using in her own collection. Curious, she glanced at the tag on the collar.

Adrienne Lockhart Designs.

She looked at the name, staring intently at it for several moments as her brain tried to process the sudden influx of information rushing forward at once. It was like a dam had broken. Every memory she'd ever had bombarded her.

She remembered designing and sewing this blouse. The woman who bought it at her boutique was looking for a unique birthday gift. Her friend was the kind of person who had everything and she'd been struggling to find something different. Adrienne had hoped the woman would bring in more business, but nothing had ever come of it.

She could now picture her funky little shop with walls lined with clothing she'd designed and sewn herself. The fortune in her father's life insurance money she'd used to get started. The heartache of packing everything up to ship home to Wisconsin when it didn't work out.

Adrienne Lockhart.

The hanger slipped from her fingers to the floor, but she didn't bother to bend over and pick it up.

"My name is Adrienne Lockhart." She said the words aloud to the empty closet, and for the first time in two months, the niggling sensation in the back of her mind wasn't there. The name Cynthia Dempsey had always triggered a feeling that things weren't right. And they weren't.

Because Cynthia Dempsey was dead and buried in Wisconsin with a tombstone that had Adrienne's name on it.

A rush of emotion and confusion washed over her. She'd been living a lie for months. Fell in love with a dead woman's fiancé. Made love to him several times, all the while he believed she was someone else. How could she tell him the truth? What would he do?

He'd said he liked her better now than before, but would the fact that she wasn't Cynthia Dempsey change how he felt?

Never once when she thought about when and how she would regain her memory did it ever occur to her that she would realize she was someone else. Everyone thought she was dead. Cynthia's family thought she was alive. All of Cynthia's friends, the people who'd come to her party last night, pleased to see she was doing so well…how could she tell them the truth? How could she explain any of this?

Nausea swept over her. Rushing from the closet, she raced into the bathroom and lost her lunch in the fancy porcelain toilet.

Why hadn't she gone with her instincts? Alarm bells had been sounding the entire time to warn her that this life wasn't hers. She never had money or expensive anything. She was convinced that her tiny apartment in New York was an old janitorial closet. Her house in Milwaukee was a small, three-bedroom cottage in the suburbs that she inherited when her father died. The nicest piece of jewelry she owned was the strand of pearls that belonged to her mother. They were irreplaceable, but even then, they couldn't touch the value of Cynthia's jewels.

Rolling back against the wall, she wiped her mouth and was relieved that the engagement ring wasn't on her hand. It belonged to a woman from an entirely different world. That woman had been a successful advertising executive. That woman had clothes and credit card limits that Adrienne could only dream of. She was also a horrible person who cheated on her fiancé and made a mess of her own life.

Her one moment of relief was knowing she'd never actually done those terrible things. Nigel was a complete stranger. Along with everyone else, including Will.

Oh, God, Will.

Adrienne buried her face in her hands. This was such a mess. "How am I going to tell him?" she said aloud.

"How are you going to tell me *what?*"

Adrienne's head snapped up and found Will standing in the doorway of the bathroom. Things had apparently gone well at the paper. Not so much back here.

She immediately noticed a change in him. There was no softness in his eyes. His cold gaze was focused on her like a laser. His hands were thrust angrily in his pockets, his entire body tense from the chiseled line of his jaw to the wide, solid stance in the doorway.

"I…" she began, but couldn't find the words. What would she say? *My memory has suddenly come back, and I realized I'm not your fiancée. Sorry I slept with you.* Something like that?

"Why don't you do us both a favor and just come clean, *Adrienne?*"

Her eyes widened, her mouth falling open at once. He knew. Somehow he'd managed to piece it all together before she did. "I just remembered—"

"No way. Don't you even try to feed me some half-ass cover story about how you've just suddenly regained your memory because I've caught you."

"Caught me?" Adrienne's heart sank in her chest. She'd been worried enough that he'd be disappointed to find out she wasn't Cynthia but had hoped he'd understand the mistake. That perhaps their feelings for one another would overcome the reality of who she really was. But her hopes had been quickly dashed by the heated tone of his accusations. Apparently he was angry. And he somehow believed she'd faked everything for nefarious reasons.

"What a sweet stroke of luck it must've been for you. A failed business, no friends, no family, no money. Get on a plane and wake up a millionaire heiress with a new face making you the center of attention."

Adrienne climbed to her feet, tears she didn't want gathering in her eyes. "No," she insisted. "It isn't like that. I had no idea—"

"And to think I believed you'd uncovered a hidden talent, like some prodigy of the fashion world. Was it your plan all along to show your work to Darlene? Were you just using Cynthia's connections to further your career?"

"Why would I do that?" she asked. "It wouldn't be my career. It would be Cynthia's. This whole life was Cynthia's, and I knew I never fit into it. But everyone kept telling me this was who I was and that eventually I would remember."

"It's hard to remember a life you never lived."

The angry edge of Will's voice sent the tears spilling down her cheeks. She couldn't fight them anymore. "How did you find out?"

"You never should've seduced me, Adrienne. Dr. Takashi didn't work on anything but your face. It was a big risk to take off all your clothes and hope you looked the same from head to toe."

Adrienne flinched as her ego took the hit. Of course she never would've done that if she'd known the truth. Cynthia was perfect and thin and elegant. She was none of those things, and naked, it would be even more obvious. But she had to ask. "What was it about me that convinced you I wasn't her?"

"Cynthia had a rose tattoo. You don't."

Tattoo? That explained the odd look on his face as she walked to the bathroom last night. The way he'd stared intently at her rear end like the secrets of the universe were etched there. He was looking for a tattoo she didn't have. Their prior encounter had been dark, but that night the lights had been on while they made love and when she'd gotten out of bed. He'd known in that moment and she'd been stupid enough to turn around and tell him she loved him not twenty minutes later.

"Of course I don't. I'm afraid of needles. I would never have the nerve to get a tattoo."

"But you have the nerve to take advantage of a family that should be grieving the loss of their daughter?"

How could he think she would do that? Hadn't he learned anything about her in the past few weeks? "I didn't know. I swear I didn't know. Not until just now. In the closet I found a shirt—"

"The closet!" Will sneered, refusing to let her finish a complete thought. He obviously didn't care to hear anything she had to say in her defense. "I should've known the very first day you came home. Didn't know your own mother, but you knew when you'd landed the couture clothing jackpot. I bet you couldn't wait to see if you and Cynthia wore the same size."

"No," she insisted. "It was all real. Everything I said or did. I gave my heart to you, Will. I never would've done that if this was all a lie. I would never deliberately hurt you like *she* did."

A mottled red spread across Will's face, his nostrils flaring to indicate she'd said the wrong thing. "Don't you dare turn this on Cynthia. She may not have been perfect, but she never pretended to be anything she wasn't."

"Except in love with you." Adrienne couldn't help but shoot the sharp barb back at him in anger. "She probably never cared half as much for you as I do. She was in love with a broke artist from the Bronx. She was only using you as a cover so all her society friends wouldn't know she'd stoop that low."

Will shook his head slowly, the anger seeming to finish running its course, leaving him disillusioned and sad. "I never thought the woman I'd come to know the past few weeks would stoop this low either."

Adrienne tried to think of the right words for the moment.

The thing to convince him she meant everything she said. There was only one thing left. "I love you, Will."

"Get out."

Panic seized Adrienne, her chest tightening so suddenly she almost couldn't breathe. That wasn't the reaction she was hoping for. *Get out?* He couldn't really mean it. He wasn't cruel enough to throw her out with nothing. She didn't have a dime to her name. No cell phone, not even a driver's license. Everything she owned was Cynthia's. Adrienne had lost all her possessions in the crash. Even if she somehow managed to have her aunt wire her money, could she buy a bus ticket without ID? How was she going to get home?

"Will, please," she begged. She had to persuade him to see reason.

"I said get out!" he yelled, his voice booming in the acoustic bathroom.

In that moment, Adrienne knew the battle was over. There was no way she could convince him of the truth. Nodding, she started for the exit to the bathroom, waiting for him to step aside so she could get through the doorway.

"You think you know what happened. You think I'm a horrible person. I can't change that. But I meant what I said. I did fall in love with you."

He stepped aside to let her by but turned his face away, unwilling to look at her for the sincerity or truth of her words. He obviously didn't want to hear anything she had to say. Will had made his decision, delivered his verdict and executed the sentence. As far as he was concerned, Adrienne was as dead as everyone thought she was.

Defeated, Adrienne walked down the hallway, through the living room and out of his life.

Eleven

Adrienne stood outside the storefront that had once been her boutique. Her funky little shop had a banner across the window announcing the grand opening of a new Baby GAP. She could see the overpriced clothes for baby yuppies hanging where her beautiful, artistic creations once were. She wanted to cry. To scream and throw a rock through the window.

It was bad enough when she'd lost her shop. Not everyone had the talent to make it, and she was mature enough to understand that. But now she knew she did have the talent. With the right connections, Cynthia's network could've launched her career. Even if it had been as Cynthia Dempsey, it would've been fulfilling her dreams. And once again, she'd lost her chance.

Just like she'd lost her chance with Will. And that was even worse than her latest discovery.

She'd give up designing clothes to have the chance to make things right with him. He'd probably never forgive her or trust her again, but she wished he'd give her the opportunity to try. She'd never get it, though. Just like when he discovered Cynthia was cheating, he cut Adrienne from his life with one clean swipe. He was through. And even if he had second thoughts, they would come too late. Adrienne would be back in Milwaukee before long, working retail or finding some part-time job as a seamstress altering wedding dresses.

Somehow things were better when she was dead.

She clutched her arms to her chest, the cool breeze raising goose bumps across her bare flesh. She'd dressed for a lazy Sunday at home—a pair of comfy jeans, a cotton T-shirt and sneakers. She should've grabbed a coat before she left the apartment, but she didn't want Will to accuse her of stealing Cynthia's clothes. As it was, she was surprised he didn't force her out of the apartment naked.

It didn't really matter, though. No amount of cold air could distract her from the pain of the gaping hole in her chest. She thought she'd lost everything when the plane crashed, but she was wrong. What she'd lost since then was much worse. The man she loved hated her. The people she thought of as her family would, too, once they knew the truth. Adrienne didn't know what to do.

She'd wandered aimlessly through the streets with no real destination in mind and found herself in her old stomping grounds in SoHo. She didn't really know where else she could go. Hours had gone by and the sun was about to set, making her situation more serious by the minute. Her best option would be to see if she could crash at Gwen's place until she could get the money to go home, but she didn't have her phone number on her. Adrienne's only other choices were to show up unannounced at one of her old friends' places and give them a huge shock, since they thought she was dead, or find a homeless shelter.

From the penthouse to a semiprivate cot in just a few hours' time. It was such a disaster. And to think she'd woken up believing the world was hers for the taking. She was in love, her career was taking off…there was only the nagging worry about her persistent amnesia and what it would mean for her.

Well, standing on the sidewalk outside her store wasn't helping anything. She headed west toward the hospital where she could find Gwen and prayed she was on shift tonight. Adrienne was about to turn the corner toward Greenwich Village when she felt an iron hand grip her shoulder.

Just great.

Homeless, penniless, hopeless and now someone was going to mug her. And take what? All she had left was her pride, and that wouldn't go for much at the local pawn shop. Spinning on her heel, ready to fend off her would-be mugger, she found herself face-to-face with Nigel.

"What are you doing?" she screeched. "You scared the hell out of me." Adrienne jerked from his grasp and stumbled backward.

Nigel looked like hell. He hadn't changed his clothes or shaved since she saw him at the party, and she was willing to believe he hadn't slept either. His oversized tuxedo was wrinkled, his eyes bloodshot and wild with emotion and sleep deprivation. He looked like a man on the edge.

"How did you find me here? Did you follow me?"

Nigel nodded. "I've been watching your building and saw you leave. I followed you to try and talk some sense into you."

"You've been following me around Manhattan for hours?" A deep sense of unease was pooling in her already unsteady stomach. The last words he'd spoken to her were a threat, and then he'd started stalking her. She took another slow step back. If he had a weapon, she didn't want to be within swiping range.

"I did what I had to do. I need to talk with you."

There was a growing edge of hysteria in his voice that

Adrienne didn't like. "There's nothing to talk about, because I'm not Cynthia Dempsey."

"Oh, is that your new story?" Nigel sneered at her, his upper lip curling with irritation. "And who are you now, Miss High and Mighty?"

Why did no one believe her when she tried to tell the truth? "There was a mixup at the hospital. My name is Adrienne. They thought I was Cynthia, but I've regained my memory and know now that I'm not."

Nigel frowned at her. "Do you really think I'm that stupid?"

How could she prove it to him? Maybe the same way she'd unknowingly convinced Will. "I have no rose tattoo, Nigel. I know you would've seen it at some point. I'm not going to drop my pants in the street, but you can believe me when I say it. Will threw me out of the apartment because the tattoo was missing. That's why I'm wandering around Manhattan without a coat, a purse or a dime to my name."

Nigel struggled to swallow a hard lump in his throat. "If you're Adrienne, then where the hell is Cynthia?"

Adrienne squeezed her eyes shut. Every time she thought her life couldn't get worse, fate slapped her down and proved her wrong. Did she really have to connect those dots for him? She couldn't have him stalking her around town when she had no place safe to go, so she supposed she had to. "I'm sorry to tell you this, but Cynthia was killed in the plane crash. They confused us and thought I was dead instead of her."

If Adrienne had thought he was angry before, she was wrong. Nigel's jaw locked, his face flushing crimson with anger. "Stop lying to me!" He lunged toward her, and his hand flew before she could react. His fist made contact with her chin, sending her flying backward.

The last thing she remembered was the cold sensation of

the concrete sidewalk against her back and the loud thunk of her head as it hit the ground and knocked her out.

"I don't understand. What was she doing in SoHo without any money or identification? Was she mugged?"

Adrienne recognized the voice of Pauline Dempsey, her tone growing more shrill with concern. For a minute, everything was jumbled in her mind. Where was she? The last thing she remembered was fighting with Nigel. How did she end up in a room with Cynthia's parents? She was curious but didn't want to open her eyes. Her head hurt too much, and she was sure the lights illuminating her eyelids wouldn't help.

"It's possible, but I doubt it. The cops seem to think she was assaulted by someone she knew. The 911 dispatcher said the male caller gave her name. Without ID, no one would've known who she was otherwise."

"I bet it was that man from last night. I knew I should've called security. How is my little girl going to get better at this rate?" This time the voice was her father's. Or rather, George Dempsey's.

Was she in the hospital again? Wait...Nigel hit her when she told him Cynthia was dead. She must've been knocked pretty hard to black out.

"She's going to be fine. Fortunately, the man who hit her struck her jaw and not her cheekbones or any of the other parts that are still healing from surgery. She has a concussion, so we'll need to keep an eye on her for a little bit, but I don't think it's very serious."

"Very serious?" George's voice grew louder with irritation. "My daughter can't remember who she is, and you think another blow to the head isn't serious?"

There was no way Adrienne was going to be able to stay floating around in the dark sea that comforted her. Someone had to put a stop to this circus. She forced her eyes open, her hand coming up quick to cup her jaw when a groan sent a bolt of pain through her face. "Ow."

"Cynthia?"

They still thought she was Cynthia. Will hadn't told them the truth. She had the opportunity to end things differently than she had with Will, and she wanted to. She didn't want the couple that had been so kind to her to hate her the way he did.

Adrienne pushed herself up and looked around. She was in a hospital bed again, one very similar to the one she'd woken up in a few weeks ago, if not the very same. Pauline and George were standing to her left, the doctor to her right. And in the back of the room, leaning against the wall, was Will.

He didn't say anything when she looked at him. He just watched her with cold indifference. He hated her; she could tell as much from the stiff crossing of his arms and hardened jaw. But he hadn't told Cynthia's parents the truth. Why? He'd seemed angry enough to want to expose her to everyone, and yet he hadn't.

"Cynthia, are you okay? What happened to you? Were you attacked?" Pauline was at her side in an instant, rubbing her arm protectively.

Adrienne shifted her gaze from Will and turned to the woman seated beside her.

"I'm not Cynthia," she said as she softly shook her head.

Pauline and George both frowned and looked at one another with concern. "What's that dear?" Pauline asked.

"My name isn't Cynthia. I remember now. I remember everything. My name's Adrienne. Adrienne Lockhart."

Her two former parents turned from her to the doctor, their eyes wide with confusion and concern.

"Doctor, what's going on?" George demanded.

The doctor frowned and approached the bed. He pulled out a pen light and shined it in her eyes while asking her questions about dates and political figures. She got all the answers right, but that didn't seem to make him any happier. "You say you're not Cynthia Dempsey?"

"Yes," she said, nodding her head and wincing with the movement. That bastard had hit her hard. "I'm certain my name is Adrienne. I'm from Milwaukee. My parents were Allen and Miriam Lockhart." She looked at Pauline and then George. "I don't understand how this could happen. How could I be confused with another person?"

Pauline pulled away, taking a few steps back to cradle herself against George's side. Adrienne hated to see the pained expressions on their faces. She didn't have to tell them the implications of her announcement like she had with Nigel. Only a small child and a teenage boy survived the crash with her. If she wasn't Cynthia, then their daughter was amongst the casualties.

"Your accident was very severe, and you were almost unrecognizable." The doctor was already covering his bases for the inevitable lawsuit. "Do you remember living as Cynthia?"

Adrienne nodded again. "I do. I don't recall the day of the accident, but I remember everything else, before and after the crash."

"It appears as though your memory loss has been reversed, perhaps by the second blow to the head. And that leads us to another unfortunate complication. Please excuse us," the doctor said to her. "I need to speak with the Dempseys in private." He held out his hand and ushered the couple into the hallway for more damage control.

Adrienne took a deep breath and flopped back against her pillows once the door shut. She closed her eyes as tears formed and blurred her vision of the angry man across from her bed. She refused to cry again with Will still there, watching her. He'd never believe the truth—that her heart was broken—and would probably accuse her of crocodile tears for sympathy.

"You didn't tell them," she said at last when he continued to stand there without speaking.

"I wanted to see if you did the right thing first."

She opened her eyes and looked at him. It was so hard to look at the man she loved and see the naked rage of a stranger instead. He was nothing like the relaxed, happy Will who had kissed her in Times Square and swept her across the dance floor at her party. All that was left was the cold, hard shell of a businessman poised to take down a competitor. There was no reading him. It made it impossible to know if she'd passed his test. "And?"

"And you're a better actress than I thought." At that, he turned and strode from the room without glancing back.

With the slam of the hospital room door, the last remaining fragments of love and hope left in Adrienne's heart shattered, and she could no longer hold back the tears.

"You can stay with me as long as you need to. Or can stand to. My apartment is a fifth-floor walkup and only four hundred square feet, so I expect you to be gone by Wednesday."

Gwen held out a key and a slip of paper with her address. "You just make yourself at home. Eat whatever you like. You can probably fit in some of my clothes, too, although the pants might run a little short on you since I come from a family of elves. I'll be home around six in the morning."

Adrienne leaned in and hugged Gwen fiercely. When it was all said and done, the only friend she'd made since her accident was the only one she had left. It had been less than twenty four hours since the news of Cynthia's death, and already the world had lost interest in Adrienne Lockhart.

"You don't know how much I appreciate this," Adrienne said, fighting the tears that were a constant threat of late.

"Not a problem, honey. Now, keep an eye on your jaw and that lump of yours. It's a good excuse to have a milkshake for dinner. I'll check on you in the morning to make sure you don't need to see the doctor again."

After being discharged Monday afternoon, Adrienne had gone to meet Gwen. Her plans were to go to her apartment, surprise her aunt with the news of her miraculous resurrection and ask her to wire some money to her. From there, she could buy a change of clothes and hopefully get a bus ticket. Trains were too expensive, and planes were out of the question.

She waved to Gwen and headed for the elevator. When she walked out of the hospital, she stopped short as a black town car pulled directly in front of her. The window rolled down in the back, and she was surprised to find Pauline Dempsey looking out at her.

"Mrs. Dempsey?"

"Pauline, dear, please. Do you have a ride to wherever you're going?"

The answer was no. Gwen had given her ten bucks for the subway and a strawberry milkshake. "I was going to take the subway."

The older woman looked appalled. "Absolutely not. You're a magnet for trouble, my dear. You'll get mugged again."

The door of the town car flew open and Adrienne had to leap back to keep from getting hit. "Are you sure?" She wasn't entirely comfortable around Cynthia's family now. Things had to be awkward for everyone.

"Get in the car, please."

Adrienne did as she was told, the authoritative and motherly tone leaving no question. She imagined it was hard for Pauline to look at her and not see her daughter. To not want to treat her the way she treated Cynthia.

Once inside, she shut the door and found Pauline was alone. "Do you have an address to give Henry?"

Adrienne passed the slip of paper over the seat to the driver and the car pulled away from the hospital.

"I called to find out what time you were being discharged. I wanted to talk to you before you went home to Wisconsin."

"Talk to me about what? I told the doctors I don't remember much." Adrienne had hoped her memory of the day of the accident and meeting Cynthia would return, but it continued to be a black hole. She figured it was probably better that way if she was ever going to get on a plane again.

"Dear, I'm not fishing for information. I'm concerned for you. Whether or not you are my daughter, I sat in that hospital every day for five weeks drinking bad coffee and praying for you to recover. I was so proud of you Saturday night at your party. You are a beautiful, talented young woman, and your parentage doesn't change that."

"Thank you." She was mildly uncomfortable with the woman's compliments. "I'm very sorry about Cynthia."

The older woman nodded and looked down at the hands folded in her lap. "I loved my oldest daughter very much, but she could be very difficult sometimes. There were days I thought Will was a saint to even tolerate her, much less marry her.

"But these past few weeks with you have been so nice. Even through the tears and anxiety of the accident, you were always such a sweet person. I should've known then you weren't my daughter, but I hoped she'd made a change for the better. I think maybe I'll keep those memories as my last memories of Cynthia. End our relationship on a more positive note."

Adrienne nodded but took a moment to figure out how to respond. "My mother died in a car accident when I was eight. She loved to sew, and I spent hours watching her make dresses and play clothes for me and my dolls. After her accident, I climbed up to her sewing machine and continued her work. That's where I got my passion for designing clothes.

"But I've always had a hole in my life where she was concerned. It's hard for a teenage girl to grow up with a single father. They don't understand anything. And when he died a few years ago, I had nothing left.

"If not for the mixup, I would've woken up in the hospital completely alone and spent the weeks of my recovery without anyone who cared. Even though you aren't really my parents, having you and George there for me these few short months has been priceless. I missed having family so much. I know speaking to me might be difficult for you both, but please feel free to keep in touch."

Adrienne could see the tears in Pauline's eyes even in the dark cabin of the car. "Thank you," she said, leaning forward and hugging Adrienne. "I would love to keep in touch and see how you are doing, how your career is going."

"I'm not sure I have much of a career left, but thanks for your vote of confidence. Actually, I don't have much of anything left. It feels sort of odd to think of it that way, but it's true. Everything I had was Cynthia's."

"I didn't think about that. You lost it all in the crash, didn't you? How terrible. How are you getting home?"

"I'm going to have my aunt wire me money for a bus ticket. Given I've been declared dead, she's the only one with access to my accounts."

Pauline's hand reached out to rest on Adrienne's knee. "I want to do something for you."

Surprised, Adrienne turned to the older woman and shook her head. "No, you've done enough for me. That party had to cost you a fortune."

"Nonsense. I want to help you get home, and I won't take no for an answer. If you insist on the bus, so be it, but the train runs from Penn Station to Chicago and up to Milwaukee. I figure you're probably not interested in flying, but if you'll let me, I'd like to buy a ticket for you."

"I can't accept that. I feel like I've already taken advantage of everyone in Cynthia's life. I wouldn't feel right taking anything else."

Pauline turned to her purse, reached inside and pulled out her cell phone. Before Adrienne could argue, she purchased a one-way ticket in a roomette for departure the following day. After she hung up, she looked at Adrienne with a smile. "The ticket will be waiting for you at the ticket counter tomorrow. The train departs at three forty-five in the afternoon."

"That's really not necessary."

"I do what I want to, dear."

She certainly couldn't argue with that and frankly didn't want to despite her protests. Three days of buses and sleeping in terminals was not her ideal trip. "Thank you. For everything."

"You brought light into all our lives. Even Will's. I know he's taken all this pretty hard. I'm sorry if he's been a little standoffish. But he was happier with you these past few weeks than I'd seen him in years. Watching you two dance at the party, I was certain he was in love with you. I'll be the first to admit you were a better match for him than my daughter. Maybe once the shock wears off, he'll realize he loves you the person, not the name."

Adrienne tried to look embarrassed by her words, but inside she was really fighting back tears. She didn't dare leave herself the hope of Will changing his mind. How could this woman understand the situation so completely when Will, the man she loved, adamantly refused? His stubborn, suspicious streak had cost them a chance at real happiness.

The car pulled up to the curb and Henry got out to open the door for Adrienne.

"Call us when you get home safely. I expect to hear from you at least once a month so I know you're not in some kind of trouble. That was my rule with Cynthia, and now it's my rule with you."

Adrienne hugged the woman again. "Yes, ma'am," she said before slipping out of the car. She stood on the curb and watched the town car merge back into traffic and disappear down the block.

She was a little sad watching Pauline drive away but was glad to know they'd keep in touch. If she couldn't have the man she loved, at least a relationship with Pauline and George was more than she had before the accident.

Slipping the key from her pocket, she unlocked the door and headed up the four flights of stairs to Gwen's apartment.

Twelve

Adrienne's homecoming to Wisconsin was not nearly as grand as her party in New York. Frankly, it was depressing, but it was a reflection of her life and the turn it had taken. Her aunt Margaret picked her up at the train station. They had never been very close; Aunt Margaret hadn't liked Adrienne's mother, so of course Miriam's daughter was tainted as well.

When Adrienne came out of the train station, Margaret was waiting in the snow with her station wagon, a frown drawing deep wrinkles into her face. Just as when she'd called on Monday, there were no tears of joy to see her alive again. Not even a hug. Only a complaint about the traffic and that Adrienne's train had arrived at rush hour.

All the way home, Margaret talked about the hassle and expense of arranging her funeral. Adrienne figured she was mostly irritated because she'd gone to all that trouble for a person whose death gained her nothing.

As they pulled up to her house, she saw Margaret look at the place with a touch of disgust in her eyes. Adrienne had seen the muddy, uprooted For Sale sign in the back of the wagon when she got in. Margaret's mood was probably tainted by the fact that she wouldn't get to move into Adrienne's house now that she was miraculously alive. She'd always eyed the place with envy when Adrienne's father was alive and had pressed Adrienne to sell it to her after he died. She'd probably put her own place up for sale and started planning her housewarming party before she'd begun the funeral arrangements.

Fortunately, Adrienne had never bowed to her aunt's pressure. She'd kept it and had a place to come back to. It was the only home she'd ever known. Her tiny apartment in New York hadn't qualified. The penthouse with Will had never felt right to her. Only this place, with her childhood memories of her parents, could put her at ease.

Once she stepped out of the wagon and into her own driveway, she was no longer in need of her aunt's assistance. After Margaret drove away, she went inside and immediately started getting her life back. First were the necessary calls to "reverse" her death, and with a little quibbling and a lot of paperwork, her checking accounts and credit cards were reactivated and her utilities were turned back on. Then she cleaned the house from top to bottom to rid it of three years' worth of dust.

After that was done, Adrienne was left with the daunting task of starting her new life back in Milwaukee.

She supposed she should look for a job, but her heart just wasn't in it. She'd gone to school and worked hard to be a fashion designer. She could easily pick up seasonal work with Thanksgiving days away and Christmas quick on its heels, but selling clothes at the mall for minimum wage seemed like a waste. Adrienne wasn't broke now that she could access her money. A month's worth of living expenses in Manhattan could keep her for three or four in Wisconsin, where her house was paid off and her car was almost too old to insure.

Looking at what she had, she decided to put off the inevitable for two months to let herself get acclimated and work through the crippling emotions that slowed most of her activities to a crawl. She would lose any job she got if she stopped folding clothes and started to randomly cry in the middle of the store. And there was still the risk of that. At first, she thought she'd shed every tear she could for Will Taylor in the private roomette headed for home. But every now and then her mind would stray and the pain in her chest would grow so acute that the only thing to relieve the pressure was more tears.

To combat it, she kept herself busy. If she couldn't think of Will, she couldn't wallow in the grief of everything she lost. The boxes she'd shipped from Manhattan before her flight were sitting in the living room, untouched. Inside were all the unsold clothes she'd designed for her boutique. She carried each piece upstairs to her mother's old sewing room and hung them on the large aluminum clothing rack.

This, she decided, would be her new workroom. It already had most of the supplies she needed from the days she'd spent working on things in high school and during breaks from college. Using her mother's old sewing machine had always seemed to bring her luck and motivation.

Really, just sitting in the room where her mother worked was inspirational to her. The collection she began at the apartment with Will came to an end as quickly as their relationship. She knew she needed to do something different. Adrienne needed an outlet for all her emotional energy, and the new pieces she envisioned in her mind would be it. Her work was often the best therapy. It had gotten her through her father's fatal heart attack several years back, and it could get her through this.

Gathering up her papers and pencils, she sat down at the worn dining room table and started designing a new collection. One that would remind her of the happy times she spent with Will before everything went wrong.

The color palate was easy to determine. There were a couple blouses and skirts in the warm fall colors of their walk through Central Park. A burgundy leather jacket with dark brown palazzo pants that reminded her of the décor of the Italian restaurant where they had their first date. To accent the collection, a short, sassy sweater-dress in the shade of the pale pink roses he brought her. Then, as a finale piece, a full-length gown in the same soft, blue-gray color as Will's eyes.

It took her days. She even worked through Thanksgiving without realizing it because her aunt never called to invite her over. When it was done, she had a stunning thirty-piece collection ready and waiting for her to bring it to life on the dress form. A mountain of fabric dominated the floor of her living room in anticipation of weeks of construction.

In time, Adrienne had fairly successfully buried her grief in her work. The pain of losing Will had faded to a dull ache she'd learned to ignore until she lay alone and cold in her bed each night.

When the phone rang one afternoon, she was busy at the sewing machine. She wasn't prone to get many calls, so she ran to the cordless and answered, breathless. "Hello?"

"Hello. Am I speaking with Adrienne Lockhart?"

"Yes," Adrienne sighed. The woman's voice sounded familiar, but the odds were that it was a reporter who'd been in touch calling back for more details to add to her feature. While most of her family and society had ignored her since she came home, she got the occasional phone call from reporters in New York who were writing about the mixup and the untimely demise of society darling Cynthia Dempsey. Adrienne usually had very little to say and told them she couldn't remember the weeks she'd lived as Cynthia. It was easier that way. She didn't want to say or do anything that might cause the Dempseys or Will any additional pain.

"Adrienne, this is Darlene Winters with *Trend Now* magazine. I don't know if you remember speaking to me at the party or not."

"I do, yes. It's so nice to speak with you again." *Nice* was an understatement. Her heart was pounding in her chest so loudly she almost couldn't hear the woman on the other end of the line. "I'm sorry I wasn't able to keep our appointment."

"Completely understandable, although it's the first time I've been stood up by someone who miraculously recovered from amnesia. I have to say it's a fascinating story. I've been following it in the papers."

Adrienne felt a touch of elation slip away. Was she just calling to use their acquaintance to get the inside scoop? "It isn't as interesting as it sounds."

"Honey, I saw you and Will Taylor dancing. You can tell the papers whatever you like, but I know a juicy story when I see one. But that's not why I'm calling."

Spying a nearby chair, Adrienne slumped down into it. If Darlene had good news for her, she wanted to be sitting down. Likewise if it was bad news.

"I know you probably think I was only interested in your work because of who I thought you were. I have a lot of young designers clamoring for my attention, so—true—it did make me take notice when I otherwise might not have. But I've found myself thinking about your designs since you've left. I never got to see the rest, and I'm quite disappointed."

Adrienne wasn't sure what to say. She'd FedEx Darlene whatever she wanted. All she had to do was ask. "I appreciate the interest. It's a huge compliment."

"You deserve it. Listen, are you aware of the charity work we do here at *Trend Now?*"

She was ashamed to admit she wasn't. "No, but I'd love to hear more about it."

"Well, every year around this time we put together a charity fashion show. All the proceeds go to support art and design education in our local public schools. It's called the Trend Next show to help us grow the next generation of fashion designers. In the show, we feature four up-and-coming designers. It's a smaller collection, ten looks from each one, but it's great exposure for them. After the show, we also select one designer to be featured in a five-page spread in *Trend Now*."

It was a good thing she was sitting down. The pounding of her heart had stopped along with her breathing. She was frozen stone-still, waiting for Darlene to say the magic words. She had to say them. There was no other reason for her to call, right? That would just be cruel.

"We usually make our selections months in advance to give the designers time to work. But this year, one of our designers has fallen seriously ill and had to drop out of the show. I know it's short notice, but I wanted to offer you the chance to take his place."

"Yes," she said without hesitation.

Darlene stumbled for a moment over her sudden response. "Are you sure? It's in two we—"

"Yes," she interrupted. "It could be tomorrow and I'd say yes."

"Well, all right, then. I'll have my office overnight you all the show's information and paperwork you need to sign. The show will be Saturday the fifteenth, so I'll see you there with your ten fiercest looks."

"Thank you for this opportunity, Darlene."

"Knock 'em dead. Bye, now."

The phone sat silent in Adrienne's hand, but she couldn't move her thumb to hang up. She was showing in New York at an event sponsored by one of the biggest fashion magazines in the world. The exposure potential was incredible. And if her collection were chosen for the magazine...

Perhaps her career wasn't over quite yet. Maybe the pain and suffering of surgeries, fractured bones, broken hearts and shattered dreams would be worth it if in the end she could make something of the mess.

Adrienne hurried downstairs to the dining room, where her sketches were scattered across the table. There were thirty designs and not a single one existed off the page yet. She could work in some of the pieces she'd already made, but it might not be cohesive enough. She started sorting though, axing the labor-intensive knitwear and pulling out the ten items she thought would make the most impact, the last being the blue satin gown. Even ten pieces would be a challenge. It would mean working nonstop for two solid weeks, but she would do it.

She had to.

"Mr. Taylor?" His assistant, Jeanine, popped her head into Will's office. "Mr. Dempsey is here to see you."

Frowning, Will took a big sip of his coffee. He figured eventually it would come around to this meeting. The one where the e-reader deal would finally fall through. He'd managed to avoid George for a few weeks, probably because George was avoiding him, too. They'd seen each other at Cynthia's funeral, but, unexpectedly, it had turned into a circus.

Cynthia's lover had shown up, wailing and throwing himself over her casket. It hadn't taken long for people to figure out who he was and turn to Will with mixed expressions of bewilderment and pity. George and Pauline were horrified by the scene, but her father, at least, didn't look surprised. Apparently the deteriorating state of their relationship was public knowledge, despite how hard he'd tried to hide it.

After that debacle, Will had buried himself in work and Thanksgiving festivities with his family. But now all that was behind them. There was nothing but frantic Christmas shopping over the next few weeks, of which he was sure George Dempsey did very little.

"Send him in."

George came through the door, his suit looking a little larger than normal on him. The man was in his sixties, but today was the first time Will had ever thought about his age. He looked every year and maybe a few more. He had bags under his eyes, his wrinkles were more prominent with the loss of some weight, probably due to stress. Losing Cynthia must've taken a larger toll on him than Will had imagined.

"George, please, sit down."

With a curt nod, George settled into a chair. "How are you faring, Will?"

Truth be told, he was miserable, but not because of Cynthia's death. His feelings for her had died long before she did. But he did feel horrible about her death. No one deserved to die like that.

"I'm hanging in there. I think it's going to be a struggle to get through the holidays."

George nodded. "Pauline doesn't quite know what to do with herself. She started to decorate for Christmas, then kept having to stop because she'd run across something that reminded her of Cynthia and she'd start crying. Cynthia was always so busy, it just seems like she's working late and will call any time now. Then you remember again."

Will understood the feeling. His apartment had been a ghost town. He kept walking into his place at night expecting Adrienne to be there. To hear the excited thumps of her bare feet as she ran to greet him at the door. To see her sitting at the kitchen table with toast and tea. He had very quickly gotten used to having her there with him.

"I've been doing a lot of thinking, Will." George eased back in his chair. "This e-reader project we've been working on has a lot of potential."

Which is why I've decided to sell to the highest bidder and you're out, Taylor.

"Which is why I've decided we should go forward with it."

Will's eyebrows shot up, his surprise plainly obvious to anyone who chose to look. "What about blood and family and all that?"

George shrugged. "Cynthia is dead, Will. Emma is sixteen, and I'm not about to marry her off to seal this deal. As much as I like working with family, there's no one I know that can make this as big a success as you can. This is the technology of now. It needs to go forward. We've got everything in place to do that."

Will wasn't quite sure what to say. George had been adamant about this from the beginning. The turn of events was surprising, to say the least. "Thank you, sir. I'm glad to hear you're still interested in working with us."

"I am because you're a good guy, Will. You stuck it out with Cynthia and took care of her even when you and I both know you were on the way out. Then you tried again to make it work, even if it was with the wrong woman. That's the kind of dedication and loyalty I look for in a business partner." He paused, his expression softening in a way Will had never seen before. "You were almost my son, Will. And that's good enough for me."

Flustered wasn't even the right word to describe Will's state of mind, but he held it together. They chatted for a while about trivial things. Then he thanked George, promised to have his office send over the final paperwork later in the week and walked him out.

The rush of success-fueled adrenaline shot through his veins as if he'd been pulled back from a precipice. He knew this project was going to launch the *Observer* into the same peer group as the *Times*. He could feel it in his bones.

Will wanted to celebrate but slumped back into his chair

instead. The victory was sadly hollow without Adrienne there to celebrate with him. Despite the suspicion and pain he couldn't put aside, when it came down to it, she was the one he wanted to kiss and take out for a night on the town with endless champagne. And she was gone.

Suddenly Will's tie felt too tight.

His office had been his retreat since Adrienne left. He'd worked more hours than ever, avoiding their empty home and the feelings he couldn't face. Now the walls of his spacious office were closing in on him. He didn't want to be here a second longer. Without even shutting down his laptop, he got up from his desk and walked out.

"Mr. Taylor?" Jeanine questioned when he started down the hallway.

"I'm going home. Reschedule anything on my calendar. Dan's in charge."

Will didn't wait for her response. He didn't want to be here right now. He hailed a cab on the curb and headed back to the apartment.

When he finally walked in the door, he had his mail clutched in one hand and his overcoat thrown over his arm. He stood in the entryway, hoping the restricting feeling in his chest would abate now that he was away from work, but it didn't. And he knew why.

Frustrated, he yanked off his tie and tossed everything onto the bed as he entered the bedroom. The bed was made and had been since the day Adrienne left. Being in it without her had felt odd, so he'd returned to sleeping in the guest room.

Something felt off. He'd been fighting the feeling for weeks, but he was too stubborn and hurt to seriously consider what was really bothering him. Their fight in the bathroom kept replaying in his head each night as he tried to sleep. The expression of fear and heartache on her face. How she'd tried to explain something he hadn't wanted to hear.

He stopped outside of the master bedroom closet. He'd slammed the door shut in a fit of rage after Adrienne left the apartment and hadn't gone in there since then. Will hadn't gone into her workroom either. There were too many memories locked inside.

Twisting the knob, Will pulled open the door and walked in. The neatly hung rows of clothing were the same, the boxes of priceless footwear lined up as always. The only thing out of place was a piece of clothing on the floor. He bent down and scooped up the discarded blouse. Stitched into the collar was a tag that read Adrienne Lockhart Designs. Just as she'd tried to tell him.

A million curse words came to mind, all of them directed back at himself. He was a jackass. She'd tried to tell him that day, but he hadn't wanted to listen. He'd leapt to his own conclusions and pushed her way.

Why?

Because it was easier than admitting he'd let himself fall for her. Easier than admitting he'd made love to a woman he knew in his heart wasn't his fiancée. He got himself out of a sticky situation by making it all her fault.

Why had he immediately turned everything she said into a lie? She was in a plane crash and nearly killed. She went through hours of reconstructive surgery, weeks in the hospital. The poor woman's face had been smashed in so badly they couldn't tell her from another passenger, but somehow a head trauma severe enough to scramble her memory had seemed outlandish.

Perhaps she would've recovered earlier if she'd been exposed to things she knew. Maybe if her family and friends had come to the hospital things would've clicked sooner. But the problem was compounded by strangers and doctors insisting she was someone she wasn't.

Will should've spoken up instead of quietly, privately questioning every time she acted out of character. They could've cleared the whole thing up weeks ago. Saved himself the heartache. But then he would've missed out on the joy and passion, too.

He hadn't wanted to clear things up. He hadn't wanted the considerate, loving woman in his arms to get away. Things were better than they had ever been, and for once in his life, he just wanted to enjoy life.

But what was the point, when he just turned around and drove her off?

Will walked out of the closet and flopped down onto the mattress. He'd made a mess he had no clue how to fix. If he booked the next flight to Milwaukee and showed up at her door, she'd probably slam it in his face. That was what he deserved. That's practically what he'd done to her.

A shift of his weight sent a piece of his mail sliding to the floor. He bent to pick it up. It looked like a party invitation for something he wouldn't attend. He had a social pass this holiday, given most people would consider him to be in mourning. Or in hiding.

Tearing open the envelope, he realized it was his invitation to the annual Trend Next fashion show. Usually, he sent Cynthia with a check and stayed home. This year, he'd just mail the check direct. As Will tossed the card onto the bed, he noticed a tiny slip of paper floating to the floor. Curious, he picked it up to read it.

"Due to unforeseen circumstances, Nick Matteo is unable to show at this event. Designer Adrienne Lockhart will be showing in his place."

Will's jaw dropped. He never expected her to be back in New York so soon. And to be showing at the Trend Next fashion show…that was an incredible opportunity for her. And for him. He wouldn't go to Wisconsin. With only days before the show, she needed to focus on her work, not deal with the emotional upheaval of his arrival.

But after the show...

Will called the number on the invitation to RSVP. This year's check would be delivered personally.

Thirteen

"That's the wrong belt! Who put that on her?"

Adrienne dashed through the throngs of people to the line of models queued up to show her designs to the world. Whipping off one belt and replacing it with the cincher made from the same burgundy leather she'd used for a bomber jacket on another model, she took a step back and sighed in relief. That was close.

It had been absolute chaos for over three hours. The girls had to get their hair styled, their makeup done and get into their assigned clothes. Adrienne had to make sure each model had the proper accessories to finish off the look of each outfit. She was the last to go, so she'd seen how the other designers had handled their shows, but none of it could prepare her for her turn.

"Is everyone ready?"

After two weeks of working on a solid diet of caffeine, sugar and almost no sleep, she wasn't sure that she was. But ready or not, her chance had come. If she could make it through the next hour or so, she could sleep for a week to make up for it.

"Miss Lockhart, you're up." The production manager smiled and handed her a microphone. "Good luck."

Adrienne took a deep breath, straightened her own brown leather skirt and moss-green blouse, which was actually the eleventh look of the collection, and strode confidently out onto the catwalk.

It was nearly impossible to see the crowd. The bright stage lighting made her squint for a few seconds as her eyes adjusted. If not for the applause, she could have convinced herself there were only five people out there, which made the next part easier. She had never been good with public speaking. She was better behind a sewing machine, but this was part of the job.

When the applause finally quieted, she raised the microphone to her lips. "Good evening, everyone. My name is Adrienne Lockhart, and I'm thrilled to be sharing my work with you tonight. My collection was inspired by the almost unbelievable last few months I spent in New York. You might recognize my name from the local papers, but if you don't know, I'll fill you in. I almost died, got a new face, lost my memory, fell in love, fell out of love and finally found myself and my passion for designing again. Manhattan is a crazy town to get caught up in, and every moment of it is captured here tonight. I hope you enjoy it."

With a wave, Adrienne turned and disappeared around the corner, the wall muffling the sound of applause. As she passed off the microphone to a stage hand, the music she had selected for the show began. It was a beautiful melody with a heavy bass tempo for the models to stomp their hearts out to.

Before she could catch her breath, the first model took off and the show was on its way.

Here goes nothing.

She watched from a monitor backstage as each woman showcased the look she designed and selected for them. It was a parade of deep, rich tones, textures, fabrics and blood, sweat and tears. It was the perfect fall collection and the perfect reflection of her time with Will.

At last the finale dress was up. The blue-gray fit-and-flare organza gown was her crowning glory, a piece even more fabulous than the green dress she wore to her party. It was one-shouldered and gathered and draped tightly around the torso, exploding into a full, sweeping skirt that started just below the swell of the model's hips. She'd deliberately selected a fuller-figured model for this dress because breasts and hips were an absolute must for it to fit correctly.

Adrienne held her breath as the dress disappeared around the corner and all the other models lined back up for the final walk.

"Clapping and smiling, ladies," the production manager said as they started back down the catwalk. "That goes for you, too," he reminded Adrienne.

Pasting on a bright smile, she followed behind the ball gown, waving as the roar of applause nearly knocked her backward. She could still barely see the crowd with the bright lights, flashing cameras and the dark seating areas, but the sound they made as she came out was stunning.

This was her moment. Tears formed in her eyes as she took it all in, stopping at the end of the runway to give a short bow and blow a kiss to the audience. As she turned to follow the models backstage, she thought she caught a glimpse of someone familiar sitting in the front row.

It was just wishful thinking—her mind adding his face to another man's body because she wanted so badly to share this moment with him. Or maybe just tears mixing with spotlights to obscure her vision. There was no way Will Taylor was sitting in the front row of her fashion show holding a bundle of pale pink roses in his lap like the petal-colored fabric in her collection.

With a shake of her head to put the thought aside, she headed backstage and tried to focus on the joy. She wasn't about to let a mistaken Will sighting cause her to start moping and ruin this beautiful moment.

Fortunately, the chaos backstage pushed any remaining thoughts from her head. Models and designers were running around, and journalists and spectators were coming backstage to talk to people about the show. It made Adrienne wish she had someone here with her. Gwen had to work, and she hadn't felt comfortable inviting the Dempseys so soon after Cynthia's funeral. Unsure of what else to do, she returned to her staging area and started helping her models out of their outfits, hanging them back up neatly.

She was interrupted a few times by journalists asking questions. A couple wanted pictures, so she posed alone or with one or two of the models still wearing her designs.

"What was your inspiration for that beautiful blue gown?" one of them asked.

"That was the color of my lover's eyes," she said with a rueful smile. She'd searched through five fabric stores trying to find the perfect shade. Milwaukee didn't have anything as comprehensive as the shops in the Garment District.

The journalist wrote feverishly, took a few pictures and then disappeared to talk to someone else.

Before long the noise quieted, the models and journalists left and the designers and production workers began breaking down. Adrienne zipped up the side of the rolling garment armoire and scooped the last of the accessories into a drawstring bag she tied to the rack.

It was done. She'd nearly killed herself doing it, but she'd created a collection and had shown it on the catwalks of a Manhattan fashion show. If nothing else ever came of this night, she would be happy for this chance.

"Adrienne?" a woman's voice called, and she turned to see who was still hanging around. It was Darlene.

Adrienne didn't hesitate to give the woman a hug as she approached. "Thank you so much for this opportunity."

"Honey, thank *you*. When our fourth designer cancelled, I didn't know what I was going to do. You saved me, and you certainly didn't disappoint. Everyone is buzzing about your work. I think it was the best of the four."

"Really?" Adrienne had wanted to do a great job but figured that against designers with months to prepare, she'd do well just to not embarrass herself in front of the industry types.

"I was talking with Milton, the owner of *Trend Now,* and we both agree that your collection is the one we want to feature in the March issue. I just loved the leather, and that ball gown was divine."

Adrienne's mouth dropped open, appropriate words escaping her. "Are you serious?" was all she could come up with.

"Absolutely. I don't know how you did it, but the work was just outstanding. If you can stay in Manhattan through the week, we'll get the fashion shoot set up in a couple of days."

"Of course." Adrienne was staying with Gwen and had planned to hang around New York for a few days. She wanted to visit a couple friends from her pre-accident SoHo days and do some Christmas shopping. She always enjoyed the window displays and decorations that took over this time of year.

Adrienne handed Darlene one of her newly minted business cards with her cell phone number on it. "This is where you can reach me while I'm here."

"I'll call you tomorrow," she said. "Go out on the town and party tonight. You earned it."

She watched Darlene walk away. Once the fashion editor had disappeared around a corner, Adrienne flopped into one of the chairs at the makeup station. She was emotionally and physically spent, but she didn't care. She *did* have the talent to make it. Sometimes she wasn't certain, but validation couldn't come from a better source than Darlene. She didn't strike her as the kind to say great things when they weren't true. She wanted to sell magazines.

This might really turn things around for her. There was no way she could afford to open another shop, but maybe she could vamp up her website and send pieces to stylists who might actually use them in photo shoots for a change. Then maybe, just maybe, she could consider moving back and opening a storefront. Perhaps Gwen would be interested in sharing a two-bedroom place somewhere. Splitting rent would make life more livable.

"Are you planning on opening up a shop in Manhattan any time soon?" a familiar man's voice called to her, the deep tones echoing off the large empty space and concrete floors.

Her mind was playing tricks on her again. First she saw Will in the audience and then she heard his voice. It was going to take longer to get over him than she'd hoped. With a shake of her head, she turned in her chair and opened her mouth to answer, then stopped.

She wasn't crazy. Will was standing about ten feet away. He was looking more devastatingly handsome than ever, wearing jeans and a button-down shirt with a leather jacket over it instead of his standard suit. The angry expression she'd last seen on his face was gone, a bouquet of pink roses clutched in his hands.

Adrienne wouldn't allow herself to speculate on what his arrival, with flowers no less, meant. She'd survived a plane crash and managed to fulfill a lifelong dream. Certainly her string of luck was running out, especially where love was concerned. "No," she finally answered, standing to face him head-on. "As nice as this exposure is, I won't earn a dime off it if it doesn't build demand. I can't afford a store."

"That's a shame," he said. "I know a guy who has the perfect space for rent. He'd probably give you a great deal on it if you were interested."

Had he really come all the way down here to give her a tip on a real-estate opportunity? Apparently the roses meant very little. Just a gesture for her debut, she supposed. One of the other designers got flowers, too.

No matter how good the deal, she couldn't afford it, but she had to ask. "How great?"

"Free."

Adrienne shook her head and looked down at the square toes of her brown leather boots. "Nothing is free."

"Absolutely free," he insisted. "No strings attached."

He was just toying with her now, and it brought a surge of irritation through her body. The anger she couldn't express when he'd cast her aside rose to the surface, her cheeks getting warm and flush. "Why would he do that?"

"He doesn't need the money. And I think the owner feels badly about how things worked out for you."

Adrienne scoffed, crossing her arms protectively across her chest. "Things worked out great for me. I just had my first fashion show. I'm going to be featured in *Trend Now* magazine. My career is doing great. And you can tell '*him*' I don't need his pity offering. I'll get a place when I can afford to do it on my own."

Will's eyes widened at her angry outburst, and his brow furrowed in thought. This conversation obviously wasn't going the way he'd hoped. If he thought he could just march in here, offer her real estate and some roses and everything would be better between them, he was wrong. He'd broken her heart. Sent her out the door like a pesky vacuum salesman without a dollar in her pocket. She couldn't allow herself to trust someone who could turn on her so quickly. And there was no hope for love without trust. So what did they have left?

Nothing, it pained her to admit.

"When you came out before the show, you said that over the past few months you'd fallen in love. And out of it," he added with a slightly pained expression.

Adrienne had made that statement without thinking for a minute that Will would be in the audience. In truth, she did still love him. She ached to reach out and brush a stray strand of his hair from his forehead. She wanted to bury her face in his neck and cling to him so tightly he could never leave her again. But she wasn't stupid. The last time she was honest with him, he stomped on her heart. Will was a strategist, a businessman. She couldn't let him have the upper hand this time.

"So?" she challenged.

"So," he said, taking a few steps closer, "I wanted to know if that was true. Have you fallen out of love with me?"

Adrienne looked up, the most defiant expression she could muster plastered on her face. She wasn't about to fly into his arms and confess her love just to get cast aside again. "It is true," she lied. "I don't love you anymore, Will Taylor."

Will tried not to smile. He'd lied when he walked out of the hospital room that day. Adrienne was the worst actress ever. She couldn't lie her way out of a paper bag, much less feign almost two months of amnesia. No way she could be the master of deception he'd accused her of being.

But more important, she was lying now. She still loved him. He was certain of it. She just wasn't going to admit it. Will understood. He had hurt her, betrayed her. He knew how that felt. He didn't deserve her love, but he wanted it anyway. He just had to get her to admit it.

"I'm sorry you feel that way," he said.

"You broke my heart, and I'm not about to trust you with it again." Adrienne's voice trembled slightly as she spoke. He knew how hard it had to be for her to say that, especially knowing she did care for him. She was still his fighter.

Will nodded. "I'd like to help fix what I've ruined, but I understand if you're not interested. It's a shame, though," he said, taking half a step backward.

"Why's that?" she asked, moving forward as he moved back.

He could tell she was putting up a brave face but wasn't ready for him to walk away just yet. "Well, you see, the man is friends with a real-estate developer and got talked into investing in some property, but he's very particular about who he rents to. He's head over heels in love with a woman, but if she doesn't want the shop and doesn't want him, he'll be forced to lease it out to some overpriced teenage outlet."

"No!" she said, reaching out with a look of panic on her face.

"No, what?" he pressed, seeing the crack in her stern façade. "No, you want the store? No, you want me? Or no, don't rent it to a chain store?"

Adrienne shook her head, the fight abandoning her. "No to all of it."

Will slowly closed the gap between them and held out the flowers. "I brought these for you."

She accepted them, taking a deep breath of their fragrance. "Thank you."

"I'm sorry for how I acted. I'm sorry for not believing you. I was having trouble dealing with all of this, with how I felt about you and Cynthia, and I took it out on you."

She looked up at him, her expression open but not entirely sold. The flowers had been a nice touch, but they hadn't quite worked the magic he was hoping for. He'd have to take it up a notch. "The other day George came by the office and agreed on the e-reader deal. It took years of long hours to pull that together, and it meant nothing because I couldn't share the moment with you. Not Cynthia. *You*. Adrienne. In that short period of time, you became more important to me than anything. Than anyone."

She still didn't speak, but her gaze dropped to the roses, her knuckles gripping the stems and turning white with strain.

He moved in closer, bringing his hands up to gently hold the backs of her upper arms. He wasn't about to let her get away. "I know that I was horrible to you. And I don't deserve your forgiveness. But I'm asking for it. Because I love you, Adrienne. I've never felt this way about anyone before, and frankly, it scared me. But those weeks without you were like living with a part of me missing. And even if I can't have you, if I've ruined it, I couldn't bear to know you hated me."

He tilted Adrienne's chin up to look at him, and he saw the tears swimming in her green-gold eyes.

"I don't hate you," she whispered, trying to look away, but he wouldn't let her.

"But do you still love me?" he pressed.

"Yes." She nodded, a tear escaping and rolling down her cheek. "I love you, Will."

He took the roses from her, threw them onto one of the dressing tables and pulled her into his embrace, nearly crushing her against his chest. Will buried his face into the naturally kinky waves of her chestnut hair and breathed in the scent he'd missed.

"I'm so glad I didn't ruin it," he said, pulling away. "I was hopeful, though, so I brought this with me just in case."

Will took a box out of his pocket and eased down onto one knee in front of her. He watched with amusement and a touch of concern as the blood drained from her face. He wasn't sure if that was good or bad.

He held up the box to her. "Open it," he urged.

Adrienne reached out, her hand shaking, and took the velvet box. She opened it, her mouth dropping open as it tended to do when she wasn't sure what to say.

"It's not the same ring," she said, her brow furrowed.

It wasn't. It felt wrong to give her a ring that was intended for someone else. So he'd gone to his favorite jeweler and asked him to create a new ring especially for Adrienne.

It was a two-carat oval-cut pink sapphire surrounded by a ring of perfect, round diamonds and set in platinum. The jeweler was inspired by Princess Diana's engagement ring, recently given by her son to the new English princess.

Judging by the look on Adrienne's face, he'd made the right choice.

"Cynthia's ring was large and gaudy because that's what she wanted. I wanted your ring to be untraditional, beautiful and priceless. Just like you."

Will pulled the ring from the box and slipped it onto her finger. It fit perfectly, unlike all of Cynthia's things. This was hers and only hers.

"Adrienne, you have changed my whole world. I had been living half a life before you were given to me. Just going through the motions. I'd lost hope of ever being happy. But I was wrong. You showed me there was more to life than how I was living. You made me want to do and experience more through your eyes. And I want to continue to do that. For the rest of our lives. Marry me, Adrienne."

She dropped to her knees on the ground in front on him. Her eyes moved repeatedly from the ring to his face and back. "It's so beautiful. I don't know what to say, Will."

Will smiled and took her hands in his. "All you have to say is yes."

"Yes!" she said, launching herself into his arms. His weight was thrown off by the sudden attack, sending him rolling backward onto the concrete floor with Adrienne on top of him.

She straddled him, leaning down to put her palms on each side of his face, and kissed him. Will wrapped his arms around her and held her tight against him. It felt so good to have her back in his embrace again. He'd missed holding her so badly the past few weeks. His arms were empty and useless without her.

When his lips finally parted from hers, he took a ragged breath to cool his ardor. This was hardly the time or place for him to do everything he wanted to do to his new fiancée.

He was distracted as Adrienne started giggling.

"What?" he asked. One moment she was mad, then crying, then laughing. She would definitely keep him on his toes for the next fifty years.

"We're getting married," Adrienne said, as though he hadn't been present to hear the news.

"I know." Will pushed himself up until he was seated on the floor with Adrienne in his lap, her legs wrapped around his waist. "Does that mean you'll move back to New York and live with me?"

Adrienne nodded. "I have to go home and take care of some things, but it won't take me long. But if I do move back here, I want us to start fresh with a line separating our new life together from the past. I think the best way to do it would be to get a new apartment. Can we?"

"Absolutely." Will smiled. He'd been looking at places on the Upper West Side already. It was closer to the office, and the pace had always suited him better.

"And can we get new furniture? Stuff that isn't so...I don't know..."

"I *do* know." He laughed. He hated almost everything in that place. "And we can most definitely start over with decorating. We'll have an estate sale and only take what we want."

"Like my sewing machine." Adrienne grinned, the excitement of their new life together visibly forming in her mind. "I guess there's just one thing left to discuss."

"Ahh...here we go. The wedding plans, right? Let the circus begin."

Will didn't know what Adrienne's take on the wedding might be like, but he was certain it would be different, just like their life together would be different. And wonderful. And exciting. He couldn't wait to find out what their future would hold.

"Whatever you want, we can make it happen. I'll track down every pink rose in South America if you want it. Anything for you."

Adrienne smiled sheepishly. "That's wonderful, thank you. But actually, that's not what I was talking about."

Will arched an eyebrow in curiosity. She surprised him all the time. He'd proposed not two minutes ago. He figured her head would at least be wrapped up in designing her own wedding gown and bridesmaids dresses if not envisioning the whole extravaganza. "So, what's more important than planning our wedding?"

"You said something earlier about a rent-free location for my new boutique?"

Epilogue

The Daily Observer, Society Column
By Annabelle Reed-Graham
Saturday, October Twentieth
Central Park

I'm certain that all of my readers have been following the real-life drama over the last year that has been the romance of *Daily Observer* mogul (and my boss) William Reese Taylor, III, and his fiancée, the beautiful and talented fashion designer Adrienne Lockhart. I've been personally cheering for the couple through the ups and downs and have never been as excited to type an engagement announcement as I was this past December when the groom proposed with a flawless pink-sapphire-and-diamond ring reminiscent of the jewels of royalty. I've waited months with bated breath, but this past weekend, I had the privilege of attending their intimate autumn wedding.

For those of you expecting one of those large, stuffy and

expensive extravaganzas at the Plaza, you're in for a big surprise. While the bride's funky fashion sense and free spirit
are well known, no one was quite certain how the event
would unfold. Guesses ranged from hot-pink wedding gowns
to a ceremony on a rooftop, but we were all wrong. What re-
sulted was a beautifully traditional event with customized
elements that made this wedding uniquely their own.

The wedding ceremony took place in Central Park's
Shakespeare Gardens, where a gathering of less than a hundred close friends and family members joined the bride and
groom in celebrating their vows. The guests were serenaded
by an elegant string quartet while they waited for the bride's
arrival.

To everyone's surprise, the bride was walked down the
aisle by George Dempsey, the owner of Dempsey Corp. and
father of the late Cynthia Dempsey. The bride looked stunning in an ivory satin-and-organza gown, which she designed
herself. The strapless dress had a corset top, studded with
hand-sewn pearls and gold and silver Swarovski crystals set
in a mystical swirling pattern across the bodice. The skirt was
full and voluminous, swishing around the blushing bride like
a bell. If you looked closely, you could catch a glimpse of the
cheeky ivory and crystal flip-flop sandals she wore underneath it.

The flowers were expertly handled by Chestnuts in the
Tuileries. The bride's bouquet was a tight bundle of ivory
roses with pink tips and stephanotis with pink crystal centers.
The petal-pink ribbon around the stems matched the gown of
the maid of honor, Miss Gwendolyn Wright, a friend of the
bride and nurse at the hospital where the bride stayed after
her tragic accident a year ago.

The groom and his best man, Mr. Alexander Stanton, both
looked fetching in their Armani tuxedos. There wasn't an
ounce of nervousness in the groom. In fact, his gaze was focused so intently on his new bride as she walked down the

petal-strewn aisle, the rest of us could've gone home and he wouldn't have noticed.

The bride and groom exchanged customized vows under an arch woven with white hydrangeas and pink and ivory roses. I've personally written about more than a hundred weddings over the years, and I have to say I've never seen a couple beaming with as much love and joy as they did pledging their devotion to one another.

After the ceremony, guests were treated to a horse-drawn-carriage ride around Central Park to the Loeb Boathouse, where the reception was held. Guests sipped the night's signature cocktail, "The Barefoot Bride," a concoction of vodka, pureed strawberries and lemon seltzer, and dined on fun, non-traditional treats like filet mignon sliders, fried macaroni-and-cheese spoons and miniature corn dogs served in shot glasses with spicy Chinese mustard.

The warm wood tones of the rustic but elegant Boathouse were the perfect backdrop to the cream, rose and gold decorations. The walls were lit up in a delicate pink light, and each surface was covered in staggered sizes of ivory pillar candles and pink rose petals. Each guest table was draped with custom, hand-stitched rose-colored linens, embroidered with tiny pearls and crystals in the same swirling pattern as the bride's gown. The glow of more ivory candles highlighted the four-foot-tall gold trumpet vases overflowing with more roses, lilies and hydrangeas and dripping with strands of crystals and pearls.

When the wedding party arrived, the bride and groom shared a lively first dance to the unexpected "Never Can Tell" by Chuck Berry. They were later joined on the dance floor by the maid of honor and best man. Once the tempo of the music dropped, I have to admit I sensed something romantic happening between those two. Something to keep an eye on, since the best man is a notorious playboy.

The event was a feast for all five senses. After the first few

ANDREA LAURENCE 185

dances, guests were treated to a gourmet meal that included a
strawberry spinach salad, cold melon soup and a tender filet
with shrimp, garlic whipped potatoes and roasted asparagus.

True to the bride's style, the wedding cake was a fun and
funky creation from local bakery Cake Alchemy. Forgoing
the traditional sugar flowers, the square-tiered fondant cake
was decorated with a cascade of pink, ivory and burgundy
blown sugar globes. The four-foot creation featured alternat-
ing tiers of black-forest cake with cherry and cream filling
and white-chocolate cake with fresh strawberry-buttercream
filling.

After dinner, the bride reappeared in a shimmering,
cocktail-length fuchsia gown of her own design, and a swing
band kept guests dancing late into the night. As the cocktail
foretold, the bride and many of the ladies attending cast aside
their shoes to dance barefoot on the seamless white dance
floor, illuminated with the bride and groom's initials.

Attendees who overheated had the option of relaxing on
the pier, taking a trip around the lake in specially reserved
gondolas or indulging in the late-night appearance of a make-
your-own-sundae bar. It was a much appreciated treat after a
long evening of wedding celebration. I personally opted for
caramel and candied pecans with a creamy French-vanilla
ice cream, but the choices were endless.

Upon departure, each lady was provided with a silk drawstring satchel and each gentleman an embroidered handker-
chief by Adrienne Lockhart Designs. Inside the purses, they
found a card telling them that a donation had been made in
their name to the Trend Next Foundation, the same organization that helped launch the bride's successful career last year.

Before leaving, I had the opportunity to speak with
the happy couple. I asked them, as I ask all my brides and
grooms, what their wishes for the future were.

"My wish," the bride said, "is that we can spend every day

of the next fifty years as happy and in love as we are at this exact moment."

"Make it sixty years," the groom replied, sweeping the bride into a toe-curling kiss that brought a blush to this old biddy's cheeks.

I have to admit, watching the couple depart the Boathouse for their own horse-drawn carriage amongst the twinkling of sparklers, I got a little teary eyed. I hope the new Mr. and Mrs. William Reese Taylor, III, remain this blissfully happy forever. I've never met a couple who deserves it more.

* * * * *

Soldier, Father, Husband?

SORAYA LANE

Writing romance for Mills & Boon is truly a dream come true for **Soraya Lane**. An avid book reader and writer since her childhood, Soraya describes becoming a published author as 'the best job in the world', and hopes to be writing heart-warming, emotional romances for many years to come.

Soraya lives with her own real-life hero on a small farm in New Zealand, surrounded by animals and with an office over-looking a field where their horses graze.

Visit Soraya at www.sorayalane.com

Dear Reader,

I honestly believe that I have the best job in the world. After years of writing and dreaming of becoming a published author, I am so lucky to be writing romance novels for Mills & Boon® Cherish™.

In my pre-published years, I often wondered whether I would ever sell a book, but my determination never wavered. I wrote manuscript after manuscript, and looking back I feel that it was an apprenticeship of sorts.

I'm often asked: why romance? To me, the answer is simple. I like reading all different types of books, but when it comes to writing I love nothing more than a happy ending. There is nothing more satisfying than creating two flawed and conflicted characters, and taking them on a journey to true love. Knowing that no matter how much they struggle, eventually they will get the happy-ever-after that they deserve. And it helps that I believe in true love too!

In this story, Toby and Sienna are very true to the types of characters I love to write about. Toby is a former Special Forces soldier and, with two young children to care for at a time when he's struggling to know how to deal with his own issues, he's deeply conflicted. Sienna is like a blast of sunshine on a miserable day, but she also has her own troubles locked away inside.

My books often feature animals, and once again this is true to this story. I am so fortunate to live on a beautiful property in picturesque New Zealand, surrounded by our horses and with two gorgeous dogs, and I love bringing four-legged characters to life too!

I hope you enjoy Toby and Sienna's story, and I also hope that you'll visit my website to find out about my previous and forthcoming books. You can find me at www.sorayalane.com.

Soraya

For Carly

I am so fortunate to have you as my editor!
Thank you for believing in my very first book, and for all
your support and guidance since then.

CHAPTER ONE

TOBY Freeman slung his bag over his arm as he slammed the door to the car behind him.

Second Chance Ranch.

He paused to look up at the sign swinging from above as he passed beneath it, before looking ahead to the house. It wasn't anything over the top: a nice country home, with a fresh paint job to make the boards look new, and pretty flowers planted out front.

Still, it was completely different from anything he'd seen for the past eighteen months.

Toby stopped as if his feet had turned to tree roots, burrowing deep into the earth below. It was a child's call, the sound of a boy squealing. Happy, but squealing.

He fought the dual urge to call back to the boy or to flee. The latter was more appealing but he could just as easily have run to the sound. Because it was a sound that still filled his heart near to bursting, even if he had spent the past two years trying to repress those feelings. Toby was still human, was still a father, and sure as hell felt like he should still be a husband.

Only he wasn't. Because Michelle was gone and there was no point in thinking about her any longer. It only hurt, and he was sick of feeling like his heart had been ripped from his chest.

"Toby?"

His head snapped up. A woman stood at the front door, one hand on her hip and the other on the door handle. She was blonde, petite, and had a smile on her face so vivid that it almost made him forget what he'd lived through.

Until the weight of his memories crashed down with thudding insistence, like a black cloud waiting over him, destined to cast a permanent shadow.

Toby nodded, hooking his thumb deeper around the bag slung over his shoulder.

His response didn't seem to make her smile falter, didn't stop the kindness of her gaze. Like she was trying to pull him in, snare him with her niceness, only he didn't even know if he was capable of taking the bait.

"Come on in. There's two very excited little people waiting out back for you."

Toby's mouth was dry. He could hardly suck back enough air to fill his lungs. *They were here?* There'd been a message waiting for him, telling him they were safe, but he hadn't expected them to be here. Not already. Not before him. With a neighbor back home, maybe, but not *here*.

"My children?" His words were croaked, hard even for him to comprehend, but she nodded like she understood. That meant the squeal he'd heard before…

The pretty woman walked slowly down to him, as if he was a wild animal that needed coaxing. As if she was afraid of approaching him too fast in case he took flight. But her steps were confident and assured, like she'd done this before.

Toby's body tensed but he stayed still, watched as her hand curled slowly, gently around his arm, her skin warm and soft against his.

"Toby, I'm Sienna. We spoke briefly on the phone a couple of weeks back."

Toby wanted to reply, to have a proper conversation with her, but he couldn't. Because he kept hearing the squeal of only moments before, the happy noise coming from a child, and he suddenly wanted to put as much distance between himself and the sound as possible. Because if it was his son, or his daughter, then how could they ever be that happy with him as company?

He was like a derailed freight train, one that had crashed and was in need of serious repair. He knew it, but he was powerless to do anything about it.

"Toby?"

He looked up again, into sparkling blue eyes that seemed somehow to be filled with more happiness than he could imagine. Toby stared back. It was all he could do. He'd never found it hard to talk, but right now he was finding it impossible to form so much as a word.

"Toby, I wouldn't normally push any of my guests on their first day, beyond saying hello and showing them their room, but these aren't…well, they're not usual circumstances." She was still giving him that big Southern smile, but there was a seriousness to her gaze now.

Toby took a deep breath before answering, forcing himself to reply. "Why are they here already? Did my mom end up coming here, too?"

Confusion crossed her face, creasing her features. "You didn't know they were meeting you here? That I'd taken them in?"

He shook his head, not wanting to deal with this yet. Not wanting to deal with anything in the real world just yet. Because he needed time to figure out what had happened, to understand the twists and turns his life was taking.

"Your mom has been hospitalized. Her surgery date was pushed forward and they couldn't wait for you to get back. She told me there was no one else to take them in. I offered to care for them in your absence, until you were able to look after them. Until you arrived home."

He couldn't do this. He couldn't deal with them right now.

Toby wasn't even convinced this was the right place for him, whether he should have come here, and he'd wanted the time to adjust to being back. Not plunge straight back into fatherhood like nothing had happened.

His wife still and with her eyes open, staring up at him. Their newborn baby crying. A stranger's hand pressed to his arm, trying to pull him away. The one person in the world he'd thought was safe, snatched away from him without warning.

"I'm sorry, I…" Toby was embarrassed. He had never stuttered before in his life, but being here, dealing with this, it was impossible to know what to do and how to react. When the memories wouldn't let up for even a moment.

"Would you like to come in and see them?" she asked. "They're so excited about having you home."

Toby watched her, looked at this kind woman's face and wished he could feel as happy and free as she seemed to be. "I can't do this. I'm sorry."

He spun on his heel and kicked up the dirt as he walked back the same way he'd arrived. *He needed to go.* To get as far away as he could instead of dealing with all this right now. It was too much and he wasn't ready. Didn't know when he'd *ever* be ready.

"Daddy?"

Toby's heart thumped so hard it almost stole his breath away. He tried to keep walking but he couldn't, fought the urge to turn back, to look over his shoulder at the tiny voice calling out to him. Wished he could run from it because he was scared. Because, *damn,* he was scared. More so than a child on their first day of school.

"Daddy!"

This time Toby had to turn. If he hadn't he would have fallen to his knees.

He locked eyes with a boy he would have recognized anywhere. No matter how many years passed, how many continents separated them from one another, he'd never forget his son's face so long as he lived.

"Lochie." The nickname was punched out of him, took all his energy to expel.

"Daddy! Where are you going?" Lachlan sprinted toward him and tackled him around the legs, holding on tight, squeezing him like he'd never, ever let go. There was no fear, no shyness, only pure excitement.

Toby bent down until he was crouching, filled his arms with his son. Breathed him in, felt his small body scooped up into his, and couldn't help the shaking. The way his entire being almost convulsed from the shock of seeing him again, from holding his boy in his arms.

It was too much. Too much and yet not enough all at the same time. Too much to deal with, too little time to process what had happened and why he was back here.

Too fast for him to deal with being a parent again without Michelle. Even after all this time, coming back home, being back on U.S. soil, it was like the grieving process had started all over again.

"Daddy?"

Toby slowly raised his head. Standing beside Sienna, the woman he'd just turned and walked away from, was a tiny blonde girl who looked like an angel. Her fluffy golden hair like a halo around her head. The biggest chocolate-brown eyes he'd even seen were open wide and staring at him like she didn't know whether to watch him or hide.

Toby did fall to his knees then, was crippled with the pain of it. Couldn't see through the blurred tears in his eyes, couldn't breathe past the contracting in his lungs. *Couldn't feel because he hurt so damn bad.*

Because he'd never heard his daughter speak before. Hadn't seen her since she was less than a year old, before he'd left to go back to war. But without a doubt she was his little girl, because she was already the spitting image of her mom.

Toby kept his grip on Lachlan and opened his other arm to his daughter, couldn't take his eyes off her if he tried. *And still he cried.* Cried like a baby, like he hadn't cried in his life before.

Shuddering, soul-shattering tears.

"Holly," he croaked, arm waiting, hanging in the air for her to fill it.

"Come on, Holly," Lachlan called, holding on tight, encouraging his little sister.

Holly toyed with the edge of Sienna's shirt, peeked out at him. Then she ran like her life depended on it, flew across the ground as she raced toward him, little arms pumping.

Holly didn't say anything, just tucked into him, arms around his neck, her grip tight.

Toby had no idea how long they stayed like that, wrapped in one another's arms, but what he did know was that it felt *right*. That he'd have regretted it for the rest of his life if he hadn't turned back when his son had called out to him. *Just because he was a coward inside right now it didn't mean he had an excuse to behave like one.*

A hand fell to his shoulder, squeezed there, comforted him. It was a stranger's hand, but for some reason she calmed him like a mother would her child.

"Come on, Freeman family. Let's get you all inside."

Toby let himself be guided, but he didn't let go of his children, kept Holly hitched up in one arm and held Lochie's hand. He didn't know what to say to them, how he could ever look at them and not feel guilty for the mom they'd lost or the fact he hadn't been there for them, but he knew how to hold them. It wasn't that he didn't want to be a dad, he just had no idea where to start.

But right now, after seeing them, nothing else seemed to matter.

He watched as Sienna hoisted his pack and carried it inside, leading the way. Toby wished he could say thank you, wished he was capable of telling her how grateful he was that she'd taken his children in, that she'd been so kind to a stranger.

But he couldn't.

He only hoped that one day he'd be capable of saying the words that were circling in his mind.

Sienna Gibson kept the smile plastered to her face. She was used to being in control of situations, and this was not the type of morning she'd had planned.

When she'd opened Second Chance Ranch she'd been under no illusions. The men and women in need of her assistance were all troubled in their own way, and she had her routine of welcoming them and slowly helping them to land on their feet again. To transition back into civilian life from their time in the U.S. Army.

But Toby? Now he was another case entirely.

From the moment she'd locked eyes on him she'd known there was more troubling him than all the other soldiers she'd met combined. But what she hadn't been expecting was for him to seriously consider walking away from his children.

Because they weren't *her* children and she didn't know what the heck she would have done with them if he'd walked back out her gate. When his mom had phoned her and begged for help she hadn't had a choice. They were two innocent little people who needed somewhere to stay and someone to care for them, and she'd been happy to be that person. *Temporarily.*

"Why don't you two go and find Bonnie? I bet she's out looking for you in the yard." Sienna watched as the children looked at their father first before running off at her suggestion to seek out her dog. Like two little calves not sure about leaving the safety of the herd.

Toby hadn't moved from where he stood in her kitchen, so Sienna did what she did best. She put the water on to boil and started to talk.

"They're lovely children, aren't they? Your mom has done a fantastic job while you've been away."

Toby's eyes met hers, but it was like there was no one at home behind his gaze. Like the soul behind the pupils had checked out, his thoughts a million miles away. She'd glimpsed the man earlier, with his children filling his arms, but he wasn't there now.

"They've been little angels since they arrived but, boy, have they been looking forward to their dad coming home!"

she told him, knowing she was babbling but needing to fill the silence.

As Sienna fussed over the cups and coffeepot she saw Toby shuffle sideways. Only a little, but it was enough for her to know that she had his attention. That at least he was listening.

"They've been telling me all the things they're going to do with you, so I think you'd better get your rest tonight before they set you to work in the morning." Sienna laughed to herself, watching the pair out the window.

"They said that?"

Toby's deep, powerful voice took her by surprise.

"Yeah, they said that," she said softly, not wanting to push him or say the wrong thing now he'd said something back. "Lachlan's got a baseball glove up there that he's dying to use with you."

Sienna watched as Toby swallowed, wished she knew more about what was troubling the handsome soldier standing in her kitchen. Seemed like she was holding her breath waiting for his response.

"Sienna, why did you take them in?"

If she'd been surprised by his voice before, his question took her even more by surprise. "Why? Because caring for people is what I do, and I was hardly going to let them be taken in by Child Services when I had a perfectly good home to offer them." She paused. "Besides, your mom had no choice but to leave them, and helping others is important to me."

"Thank you." He was looking past her, at his children outside, but she could feel the compassion in his voice, knew that he genuinely appreciated what she'd done.

"It's no problem, honestly," she said, pushing a cup of coffee along the counter toward him.

"I don't know many people who'd do something for nothing."

She wasn't offended and she didn't think he'd meant anything by it. And it was true. She knew firsthand that most people did things with an expectation for something in return, but that wasn't her and it never had been. Besides, it was nice filling her home with people. It made her feel less alone.

"I had my reasons for opening this place, but it's never been about *me*. It's been about doing something for others." *She had memories to honor, someone she wanted to make proud.*

Toby's mouth moved only the slightest bit, the edge of one side curving into the smallest of smiles, but he kept his focus on his children. It gave Sienna the opportunity to look at him, to really look at him, and she found herself mesmerized by the intensity now shining out from his gaze. He was handsome. No woman would dispute it. Even with his hair buzzed off so that only a thick shadow of growth was visible.

But it was the power in his eyes that really struck her.

When he turned back he held her gaze for what seemed like forever before taking a sip of his coffee, his hand shaking slightly as he held the mug.

"I want you to know I'm here for you, Toby," Sienna told him, leaning forward so she could cover his hand with her own. "I want you all to feel at home here, because you're welcome to be here for as long as you need. It's what this place is all about."

She watched Toby as he looked at her hand. Like he

wasn't sure why her palm covered his fingers, why she was touching him. Why they were even sitting in her kitchen.

"Why are you doing all this for us? Why do you even want us here? Want anyone here?"

Sienna grinned at him and took a step back. This was a question she was used to, one she knew how to answer. Most of the soldiers who passed through her home asked it at some stage. Before they realized how committed she was to their recovery, to their future as well-adjusted citizens.

"Because I care," she said, maintaining eye contact with him so he knew just how truthful her words were, that it wasn't just some speech she'd rehearsed. "You can count on me, and my home will be your home for as long as you need it to be."

Toby had tears in his eyes again, a dampness that betrayed the real man beneath his tough exterior.

Sienna hated to see anyone cry, but right now she wondered if tears were the least of this man's worries. She knew firsthand that sometimes it wasn't worth fighting emotion, that it had to be released.

And Toby Freeman looked like a man and father in trouble. For the first time since she'd opened her doors she wondered if this was a guest she'd actually be able to help. As much as she liked to see potential in every soldier, Toby might just be in need of more than a little rest and relaxation. More than she could offer.

Sienna looked back out the window to the little boy and girl playing with her dog. She hoped for their sake that she was wrong. Because this man sitting in her kitchen had the potential to be a wonderful human being, a father who could care for and love his children.

She only hoped he'd be ready to help himself before it was too late.

CHAPTER TWO

TOBY was having an identity crisis. He'd never wanted to shirk his responsibilities as a dad, but after being away for so long it was tough to come back. *To this*. A world where he was meant to do everything for these little children in his care, where he was meant to know what to do and what they wanted.

When in actual fact he had no idea.

"Have you heard how your mom's doing at all?"

Toby looked up. He'd hardly moved since they'd sat and had coffee an hour earlier, and now Sienna was back.

"I…ah…haven't phoned the hospital yet," he told her. The truth was he didn't want to know just yet. Because he had a sinking feeling that she wouldn't be able to help him out with the kids any longer. Which meant he'd have to figure everything out on his own.

It was selfish, because she'd done so much for him and been there for him when he'd pushed everyone else away, and he hated the way he was thinking. It wasn't that he didn't care, because he did, he just didn't know how to tell her how he felt.

"I'm sure she'll be fine," Sienna said, breezing past him as if she didn't have a care in the world. "She was doing well the other day when I met her, but I know she wasn't looking forward to being cooped up for days on end."

Toby took a moment to watch her, this woman who had taken them in. He didn't know what the deal was with her, why she was doing what she did, but he wasn't going to complain. Or ask too many questions. He was grateful to be here, even if he did wish he'd been able to spend some time figuring everything out on his own first.

"Do you have children?" He didn't know where the question had come from but it was too late to take it back.

Sienna smiled. "No, but I've sure loved having your little ones to stay."

He glanced at her hand, noticed she wasn't wearing a wedding band and had no tan lines from where one might have been. But he wasn't going to ask. It was none of his business whether she had a man in her life or not.

"We officially opened a year ago now, and it's just Maisy and I. My housekeeper. You'll meet her later," she said, taking something out of the fridge. "Oh, and there's also the four-legged brigade."

Toby raised an eyebrow, watching as his children circled the yard with Sienna's dog bounding after them again. At least that answered his question. He shouldn't have cared, had no reason to care, but it was oddly satisfying to know she was here on her own.

"Want to come outside?" Sienna asked.

What he wanted was a burning hot shower and at least twelve hours in bed, but he didn't say that. Instead he nodded and waited for her before he followed her out the open back door. Sienna was carrying a plate of cookies and some sort of slice. He hadn't seen anything like it for…way too long.

Sienna spun around and almost knocked straight into

him. He took a step back, not wanting to make contact. Even by accident.

"Oh, sorry." She laughed, her head tilted slightly. "I have homemade lemonade in the refrigerator. Would you mind getting it? There's some glasses in the cupboard beside it."

Toby watched the easy way she turned away, her smile not faltering for even a moment.

"Kids! Come on, you little rascals!" she called.

Toby waited, paused before heading in to get the lemonade. His children flocked around her, skipping over from where they'd been playing without a moment's hesitation. They looked so innocent, so unaware of the turmoil that was his life or the way their happiness was so fragile it could shatter in less time than it took for them to devour their snack.

It broke his heart that they were growing up without a mom, and that they'd had to fend for themselves without him. Their grandmother was great, she'd been doing a fantastic job with them, but it wasn't like having a mom and a dad to tuck them in at night.

And now they were here. *With another woman*. One who wasn't even close to being related to them, playing and responding to her like she'd been in their lives for far longer than two days. Like *she* was the blood relative.

"Hey, Dad!" his son called out to him.

Toby raised a hand in a wave before disappearing back inside again. He tried to keep the smile on his face, fought the urge to frown and lose himself in his thoughts again, in the darkness he found there.

Dad. It wasn't a title he was even sure he deserved yet.

Instead of finding the lemonade he sank into a chair in the kitchen. He needed to sit, to just *be* for a moment. And try to make sense of what the hell was happening here and what he was going to do about his future.

The Humvee flipped. Toby was thrown sideways, found himself flung upside down. He couldn't feel his left leg, something was crushing it, but he fought hard to get out. Pulled himself clear, saw his wife and his children in his mind as he pushed through the pain.

Until it exploded. And he wished for a second that he'd exploded, too.

Toby tapped his fingers against his thigh, pushing at the memories, trying to tap each one away so he'd never have to suffer through them again. But after what he'd been through… He knew it had the potential to haunt him for the rest of his life, and he had no idea what the hell he was going to do to survive it. What he could do so he could *live* again.

Sienna was used to dealing with soldiers, but Toby was pushing her completely out of her comfort zone. She didn't know where to start with him, or quite how to broach the subject of his children or what was going to happen.

Because, as happy as she was to hang out with them, they were his children. *Not hers.* She didn't want that line to get blurred, because it would only make it harder when they left and moved on with their real lives. It was one of the few rules she imposed upon herself. *Never get too involved.* She'd lost enough in her life never to want to experience it again.

Sienna could see through to the kitchen, knew that he'd sat at her table awhile before rummaging through the refrigerator for the lemonade, but she didn't mind. Because it gave her more time to figure out what the best tactic moving forward was going to be.

"Can we show Daddy the horses?"

Sienna turned to find Lachlan standing behind her, his sister only a few steps away. She had to hand it to the wee guy—he was the sweetest kid she'd ever met.

"I'll wait here for your dad. You two run ahead, but stay on this side of the fence, remember?" Sienna told them.

They ran off, racing each other, Holly's tiny legs going flat out to keep up with her adventurous older brother.

Sienna looked over her shoulder and saw Toby emerging from the house again. "You found it okay?"

He nodded and set it down on the table, placing the pitcher in the shade. "Am I too late?"

Sienna closed the distance between them and sat down. "Not at all. They're just desperate to get down there and see the horses again. The lemonade can be for later."

The movement of Toby's eyebrows told her he'd heard, but he didn't say anything else.

"You know, when my brother came back from serving overseas he found horses a really good way to relax. It was a way for him to reconnect with the land, and maybe his thoughts, too."

Toby's head shot up, eyes connecting with hers. *Bingo.* It always worked. She only had to bring up the fact that she had an actual connection to a soldier and all the returned veterans looked at her differently. Suddenly had a whole new respect for her, or at least got that she understood part of what they'd been through.

"Your brother served?"

"Yup, two terms," she told him. "When we were kids he used to tie me up and tell me I was a prisoner of war, or sometimes I was allowed to be a soldier, too, but it was all he ever wanted to do. What he always dreamed of being when he grew up."

Toby looked thoughtful. He wasn't looking directly at her, but he was thinking. Was finally connected to what she was saying.

Sienna leaned over the table and lifted the pitcher, pouring a small amount into their glasses. "I'm new at this whole domestic-goddess routine, so I think we should taste a little before filling an entire glass. Just in case I've overdone the sugar."

Toby turned his body to face her then, the softest of smiles playing across his lips. "I was the same. My mom used to find war movies for me to watch and books to read, and I was addicted. It was all I ever wanted to be. A United States marine and nothing less."

Sienna didn't ask him about the reality, because she didn't need to. When her brother had returned she'd seen the reality in his eyes firsthand, knew that what he'd faced over there was something she could never understand. She'd tried, and he'd done his best to let her in, but he'd been haunted by what he'd seen and what had happened.

She raised the glass and took a mouthful. *Hmm.* "Okay, could be a touch sweet," she admitted.

Toby followed her lead and tried some. She laughed at his expression.

"It's awful, isn't it?"

"No!" She watched as he swallowed another mouthful, draining a good quarter of the glass. "It's great. Best lemonade I've had."

Sienna grimaced and tentatively tried another sip herself, this time larger. "You're lying. I know it's dreadful."

That made Toby crack another smile and Sienna realized she'd do just about anything to make him grin again, to witness his change in mood. He was handsome enough as it was, even looking glum, but the way his face changed when he was happy made him look like an entirely different man. His skin was tanned, sun-kissed from his life in the outdoors overseas, and his eyes were kind. The type that smiled all on their own, with a softness in his dark irises that she knew would be so easy to become lost in.

Sienna forced herself to snap out of it. She had rules. She wasn't to become too close to any of the soldiers who stayed here.

She looked away and picked up her glass again. "The children will like it, though, right?"

Toby put down his glass and leaned back in his chair, the most relaxed she'd seen him since he'd arrived. "Okay, well, if I'm completely honest it's perhaps a *little* too sweet for me. But I'm sure the kids will love it."

Sienna laughed—the kind of giggling, silly laughter that she wasn't used to hearing come from her own mouth. "I don't think I'm meant to be good at this sort of thing."

Toby raised an eyebrow. "It's not that it's bad…"

"But it's probably the reason why I still employ a housekeeper here, right?"

Toby stood abruptly, his face changing as quickly as his movement. It was like he'd realized they were laughing, chatting like normal people, and he didn't like it. Or maybe it had simply taken him by surprise.

"Time to find the kids?" she asked, her voice soft.

Toby's eyes met hers and she hardly recognized them. Gone was the soft, happy shine, to be replaced with the same dullness that had been there when he'd first walked in her door. Or attempted to run from her, she corrected.

This Toby didn't scare her, or make her want to put distance between them. This Toby made her want to help, because she knew how a man could change when he returned home. It wasn't the sort of transformation that required a leopard to change his spots, but it was about time and love and support. *And it worked.*

"Where are they?" His voice was gruff again.

"Down in the home field. Come on, let's go."

She touched a hand to Toby's shoulder as she passed, brushing her fingers lightly against him. To show him that she was there.

He didn't push her away, but he didn't acknowledge her either. They walked side by side, in silence, down through the gate at the end of the yard and toward the field. Sienna fought the urge to watch him, to drink her fill of the man moving to her left.

Because for the first time she wondered if she'd need to change her own rules. This time it might not be so much about not getting too involved as not getting involved at all.

She'd never thought about any of the men who'd stayed with her romantically before, wasn't even convinced that it was how she was thinking about Toby. *Not yet.* But there was something magnetic, something below the surface that was tugging her toward him.

He was a traumatized soldier with a family. He'd almost walked off and left her to care for his kids only hours before, and he'd struggled to make conversation with her in the kitchen earlier. She had valid reasons for not wanting to get involved with a man, for pushing away whatever yearnings she'd once had for a family of her own.

And yet here she was, trying to figure out what she could say or do to make him turn his attention her way. To make him smile and chat to her like they were just a man and a woman who *hadn't* met because of what he'd been through.

Sienna forced her eyes ahead and ignored the impulse to engage with him again. He was a quiet, reserved man, and she didn't need to push him. No matter how badly she wanted to draw him out of his shell, he needed time. She knew that more than anyone.

He was here to recover. Period.

Toby needed to make an effort. He knew he did. But putting his wants into action wasn't exactly coming easy. What he was thankful for right now was that his kids were busy playing and showing off their new skills, rather than expecting too much of him.

Sienna had been the same. Happy to do her thing without pushing him or asking questions, and he sure appreciated it.

"Do they get their love of horses from you?" she asked.

He watched Sienna as she put her arms back on the railings, eyes still on Holly and Lochie even though she was speaking to him.

"Maybe their love of dogs, but not horses," he replied. *They get that from their mom.*

Toby cleared his throat and forced himself to move closer. Holly was leaning into a little pony, trying her best to grapple with a brush like Sienna had shown her, and Lachlan was on the other side doing the same, only doing a more efficient job.

"You guys are doing great!" Sienna encouraged.

Toby liked that she hadn't probed any further.

"Do you think your dad will be up to going for a ride with us soon?" Sienna looked over her shoulder, a big smile on her face as she spoke to the children.

So much for liking her and thinking she wasn't going to push him too hard!

"Maybe not," he said in a quiet voice. Then he saw the two little faces, upturned and watching him, like all their hopes were pinned on him and only him. *Their father.* "Or maybe I could ride with you tomorrow?"

This time the kids smiled back at him, and it was Sienna's face that held all the concern.

"I'm sorry, I shouldn't have said anything in front of them," she apologized, voice low so they couldn't hear.

Toby shook his head. "No, it's fine. Not your fault."

Holly and Lochie were back playing, amusing themselves and talking to the pony as if she'd talk right back to them. It was seeing them behave like this, playing, as if there was nothing wrong in their lives, that filled him with hope. Because if his kids could move on like this, deal with everything that wasn't right or normal in their lives, then surely he should be able to do the same?

"I know my place, Toby, or at least I usually do," she explained. "But having the kids here has kind of…well, it's changed things."

He wished he didn't have to talk, but she was right. His children changed *everything.*

"I don't expect you to care for them," he said, wishing his voice didn't sound so flat. "I mean, I have no idea how I'm going to look after them, to be honest, but I will."

Sienna smiled at him so sweetly he could have sworn her eyes were sparkling with the effort of it. "You'll do just fine. I know you will."

Toby looked away, then back at her, cleared his throat again. "But you don't even know me," he said. "How can you say that?"

Sienna nodded. The barest of movements but one he didn't miss. "I don't need to know anything else about you except what I've already learned today," she said, her voice low. "Your children love you and you clearly love them, and as far as I'm concerned that tells me all I need to know. Anything that stands in your way is just a crinkle that can be ironed out in time."

Toby couldn't look at her, because he couldn't deal with what he saw in her eyes, in the expression on her face. Because she cared, and the last thing he needed was for either him or his kids to get too close to someone who cared too much about them. It wasn't like they would be hanging around for long.

He'd lost enough in his life to know that was one thing he wasn't prepared to negotiate on. He wasn't going to let anyone else close to him, into his heart, like he'd let Michelle.

"I tried to walk away from you today." He couldn't disguise the raw emotion in his voice or ignore the stab of pain inside. "I could so easily have kept going and not have stopped."

The smile on Sienna's face stayed firmly in place. "Yeah, but even if you'd walked away you would have come back. I might not know you, but I can see the love you feel for those kids and I know you wouldn't have been able to *stay* away."

Toby didn't look back at her because he didn't want to see the honesty in her gaze. Truth was, he probably *would* have come straight back, couldn't have left his children here in a stranger's care. But then again he wasn't the Toby who'd left almost two years ago. He was no longer the husband who'd put all his faith and love into his wife, the person who'd dreamed of getting old with one woman and no other. He wasn't the father who'd never wanted to leave the side of his son, or the man who'd scooped his baby daughter up into his arms and held her as his wife died on a hospital bed.

"Toby?"

He looked up as a hand closed over his, warm fingers threading through his own.

"Toby, why don't you head back to the house? Settle in?" Sienna suggested. "I'll hang out with the kids for a while and meet you back there for dinner."

He wanted to disagree, but she was right. The best thing for him to do right now was walk back to the house, be on his own for a bit. He wasn't any good around the children right now, and he needed to straighten everything out in his mind.

"Toby?"

He'd ignored her again without realizing. "Yeah, you're right. Are you sure?"

There went the megawatt smile again. "Sure as I'll ever be. You need to focus on *you* while you're here, too. That's what this place is all about, okay?"

Toby headed back for the house and tried to ignore the mental picture flashing on repeat through his mind. He didn't want to be attracted to her. *To any woman.* But the more he tried to forget what she looked like, the way she watched his children, the way she spoke to him…it made it impossible not to think about her.

Sienna was off-limits. *All women were off-limits.*

And the faster he accepted that the better. Michelle had always told him that if something happened to her she'd rather him be happy than miserable. *But then she'd always been the one person he'd counted on never losing, the one person he'd thought was out of harm's reach.* He might not be going back to a war zone again, and even if he'd been at home there would have been nothing he could do to save his wife, but he was never, *ever* going to fall into a situation he couldn't remain in control of, where he couldn't protect those closest to him.

Toby was here to figure out what the hell he was going to do now he was living back in the real world, and how the heck he was going to parent two kids on his own when he had no idea what he was doing.

Toby clamped his jaw shut and walked faster. It wasn't that he couldn't cope without his wife. He'd loved her more than life itself, but he'd come to terms with the fact he was never going to see her again, even if it did rip his heart in two sometimes.

But parenting on his own? That was another story altogether.

He wished he'd never had to come home.

CHAPTER THREE

TOBY lay back on his bed, the phone cradled in his hand. He'd been lying like that for a while now, trying to muster up the energy to phone his mom and finding an excuse each time he thought about dialling the number.

It was all too hard.

Being back here was supposed to be the easy part. He'd survived his tour when one of his buddies hadn't, and he was home for good. But *home* wasn't a term he could comprehend because *he had no home.* And now here he was staring at a phone, not brave enough to call the one person in his life who'd made sure that his kids had a place to *call* home. That they felt loved and cherished and secure.

Toby sat up and took a deep breath. No more excuses.

He waited, listened to the music played down his ear while he was put on hold after asking for his mom's room.

"Hello?"

His mom's calm, low voice made him forget everything. All the worries, the stress, *everything* fled his mind.

"Mom, it's Toby."

"Darling! Oh, it's so nice to hear your voice. Are the children okay? I'm so sorry for—"

"Thank you." He choked out the words, needing to say them now before it was too hard. Before he couldn't say anything. "Thanks, Mom."

There was silence, followed by a sniffle. Toby swallowed away his own emotion. His mom was the strongest woman he'd ever met, and she would never usually let anyone see or hear her cry. *Never*.

"Tell me about the children? Sienna seemed lovely, but I was so worried about leaving them."

Toby found himself nodding. "Yeah, they love her, and I think the feeling's mutual. You did the right thing, Mom."

Silence again, followed by a loud sigh. "I haven't been entirely truthful with you, Toby, because I didn't want to alarm you. Not with everything you were going through."

What? "Mom?"

"I have cancer, darling. The prognosis is good, but after my operation I have to have a course of treatment. I've put it off as long as I could. The doctor's warned me that it could be a while before I'm up to looking after the children again. Before I'm back home."

Toby shut his eyes. He couldn't say anything. Could barely process what she'd just told him. *His mom couldn't die*. She couldn't be going through this. Because he couldn't face losing another person he loved. Another person who was supposed to be safe, whom he was supposed to protect.

"Mom, you should have told me." His voice was a croak.

"No, I shouldn't have," she said firmly, her voice seeming to take on the strength his had once held. "I want you to enjoy those children, do whatever you have to do to move on, and promise you'll all be waiting for me when I'm well enough to come home. Do you hear me?"

Toby stayed silent. *She made it sound so easy.*

"Toby? Promise me. Promise me that you'll be able to look after those kids and enjoy being with them. She would have wanted you to be happy, to be the dad you were when she was alive."

Toby swallowed again, blinked away the dampness in his eyes. It was the second time today that he'd been on the verge of sobbing, of breaking down and not being able to fight his emotion any longer. It wasn't a feeling he was used to.

"I promise," he said, hoping he wasn't lying. *Wanting* to believe the words. "I'll do my best, Mom." It was all he could promise.

"Good. Now, stop worrying about me and go tuck those kids up into bed."

He ground his teeth together, trying to quash his anger at what was happening to his mom. "We'll leave in the morning to come and see you."

"Oh, no, you won't!"

Toby could tell when he wasn't going to win an argument with his mother, and from the tone of her voice he didn't have a chance with this battle.

"Mom, I'm not abandoning you when you need me. Okay?"

"Toby, I want you to respect my wishes," his mom told him firmly. "I don't want to scare the children by letting them see me like this, and I don't want you up and leaving them just to visit me either. So you stay put, and as soon as I'm ready to see you all I'll let you know."

Toby sighed, not wanting to upset her. "Okay, Mom. Just let me know if there's anything I can do."

He said goodbye and hung up the phone, then collapsed back onto his mattress. He was in no fit state to be tucking his children in or even parenting them, but he didn't have a choice.

Right now he was on his own and he was the best Lachlan and Holly had. And that terrified him. Made war seem like a distant memory that had been a far easier option than playing the role of solo dad.

"Toby, are you ready for dinner?"

He fought the urge to ignore Sienna's call and close himself off completely. Toby rose like a robot on automatic pilot and ran a hand over his spiky buzz cut. He looked at himself in the mirror—the darkness under his eyes, the emptiness of the gaze looking back at him—and then turned away. It wasn't the man he was used to seeing looking back at him. If his wife had still been here she probably would have walked straight past him in the street, not recognizing the soldier looking back at her.

"I'll be down in a minute," he replied, forcing his voice to comply.

Toby listened to Sienna's footfalls, heard her walk back down the hall. He straightened his shoulders, ignored his reflection in the mirror and turned on his game face.

He was a guest in someone else's home, he had children who depended on him, and he needed to act like the soldier he was. Just because he'd finished his last tour of duty it didn't mean he had an excuse to behave in any other way. Regardless of what had happened, no matter how he felt inside, it was time to pretend.

Like a soldier preparing to walk into enemy territory, he needed to channel the braveness that had seen him survive in the desert. Only once he was alone was he allowed to wallow, and not a moment before.

Toby was feeling uncomfortable. There was something wrong with the scene. With sitting in a kitchen, around a table, listening to his children talk about their day with a woman who wasn't their mom.

"Dad, did you love the horses?"

Toby snapped from the trance he'd slumped into and looked across at his son. Lochie had the darkest eyes, and a mop of hair that was just like his own when he let it grow out. He was unmistakably his boy. Not that he'd ever doubted it.

"I…ah…yeah," he replied. Truth was, he wasn't even sure he'd noticed any other horses besides the little pony they'd been grooming, and even then he couldn't recall its name.

"Will you ride with us tomorrow? Sienna says we're going to learn to ride properly while we're here." Lochie's voice was bright and clear, full of enthusiasm for life.

"Only if you say it's okay, of course," Sienna interrupted, worry lines creasing her face.

"Sure." He was hardly going to say no. "I'll be there to watch you."

"Daddy, read to us?" Holly asked.

This time he didn't find it so easy to reply. Because looking at the tiny girl across the table from him, perched on a cushion on the chair so she could comfortably sit at the table with them, stole his breath away. Left him unable to gasp even the shortest of breaths.

"I think she wants you to read them their bedtime story."

Sienna's gentle voice coaxed him from his panic attack. Toby found himself nodding. "Sure." He stared at the little girl with the massive eyes watching him back. She'd hardly eaten anything on her plate. His heart thudded. The last thing he wanted was to hurt them. No matter how bad he was at parenting, at dealing with everything that was going on, he had to be there for his kids. Without them he had no one. Was nothing. "I'd love to read to you." This time he forced out the *right* words, because he had no other choice.

"You will?" This time it was Lochie asking the question.

Even Sienna was watching him, giving him a look that he wasn't even sure how to interpret.

"Yeah, I'll read to you." Before Holly was born, before everything had happened, he'd always been the one to read to Lochie before bed. "Anything you want me to read, I'll read it."

He was telling the truth, speaking from his heart, and it felt good.

Better than good, it felt *right*.

"Do you want to bath the kids before bed?"

Toby placed the dishes into the sink and paused. Looked out the window even though it was dark outside. He turned around, pleased it was just the two of them. It gave him time to gather his thoughts.

"Sienna, I don't mean to be rude here, because you're doing so much for me, but…"

She took a step backward, placed her hands on the counter. Listening.

"I have no idea what I'm doing and I need you to tell me what to do."

"You're doing great, Toby. Honestly, you're doing great."

Her smile somehow managed to warm him. "You don't need to flatter me. I'm under no illusions here."

Sienna leaned forward and placed a hand on each of his shoulders. She looked him straight in the eyes, honesty shining from her face. "I'm serious, Toby. You're doing fine. You're a great dad and your children love you. Just believe in yourself, okay?"

They stared at one another, neither saying anything. Sienna broke the silence.

"To be honest, I don't know what to do with kids either, so I'm not exactly an expert here. I'm just doing what I can and that's all anyone *can* do, right?"

Toby relaxed. "You could have fooled me."

"Yeah? Well, you could have fooled me, too. You're going to be just fine with these two. I can tell."

Toby turned his back to Sienna and filled the sink with water, filling it up so he could do the dishes that wouldn't fit in the dishwasher. If he was going to talk he didn't want to be looking at her.

"It hasn't always been like this," he said, wishing it wasn't so hard to talk about. "I mean, once upon a time I seemed to know exactly what I was doing."

"You don't have to tell me anything, Toby. Don't feel obligated."

Sienna's kind words made him smile, but he continued. Because he needed to get this off his chest. "We'd been married four years, Michelle and I. Even though I was going to be away a lot, we both wanted children."

He shut his eyes as Sienna's hand touched his shoulder, squeezing, before she reached for the dish he'd just washed, starting to dry it. It was better this way, keeping busy while talking. Otherwise he'd probably never get it all off his chest. Sienna obviously knew he'd lost his wife, but...

Toby took a deep breath. "She went into hospital to have Holly, and it went from being one of the best days of our lives to being the worst day I've ever lived through." He gulped, tapped his foot hard in a constant rhythm, trying to keep his darkest thoughts at bay, staying focused on what he had to say. "I took Holly home on my own when she was only a few days old, and barely a year later I shipped out and had to leave my mom to care for them."

"Wow." Sienna was still drying, but she was looking at him. *Really looking at him.* "So how do you feel about Holly? Is it more difficult with her because of what happened?"

Toby had to answer honestly. He didn't know why, because he didn't know this woman, but he did owe her. In a way he owed it to her to brave up to the truth. Because she'd looked after his children when they'd had no one else, and she was giving him a lifeline in letting him stay here. *And she was the first person who'd ever asked him that question.*

Maybe after all this time he *needed* to talk.

"In the beginning, I would have done *anything* to have Michelle back. She was my wife and I loved her." There, he'd admitted it. "Does it make me a bad person for wishing our baby had died to save the life of my wife?"

Sienna had tears in her eyes. He could see them as clear as a mist settled over the sky. Toby looked back at his hands, submerged in soapy water in the sink. He didn't want her pity. Didn't want anyone's pity.

"I shouldn't have said that," he apologized.

"No." Sienna shook her head, blinking her tears away. "If there's one thing you can be with me, Toby, it's honest. If you're not honest here, if you can't be yourself, then how will you ever move on?"

He couldn't meet her gaze. Not yet. Because what he'd told her was what he'd been thinking for months. Years now. Only he'd never had the guts to say it out loud before.

"I think the way you felt is how anyone would have felt," she told him. "Anyone who'd give up the person they love more than anything in the world for a baby they haven't even spent a day with before would be lying. I'm sure of it."

Toby turned her way then, really looked at her, saw the honesty shining clear as day from Sienna's face. "Do you mean that?"

"Of course! I'm not the kind of person to say something just to please another. That's one thing you'll learn about me, Toby. I'm as honest as a…" She faltered.

"Priest?" he suggested, surprising himself that he was even capable of joking, given the subject matter.

Sienna laughed. "I'd like to think so."

They were silent again, standing side by side, but it wasn't uncomfortable. Not this time. "I still miss Michelle like crazy sometimes, especially now, but seeing Holly at the age she is…I don't know if choosing between them would be so easy. Those first few days, sure, but now…I wouldn't sacrifice her for anything or anyone."

Sienna put her fingers to her lips and Toby turned around, saw the children had returned.

"Thank you," he whispered, pleased they hadn't walked in at the wrong moment and heard some of their conversation. Not that they'd probably have understood, but still.

"I'm sure your wife would be proud of them," Sienna said. "And she would understand. Don't you ever feel guilty for your thoughts, or for being honest about them. It's far healthier to be honest with ourselves than pretend because we want to please someone else."

Toby pulled the plug out and watched the water gurgle down the drain. "She wanted children all her life. Even when we were in high school she was always harping on about having a family of her own one day."

Sienna stopped what she was doing and went to his children, put her arms around their shoulders and ushered them down the hall. "Then make her proud," she said back to him. "Be the dad she'd have wanted you to be and turn them into the people she'd want to see them become."

Toby paused before following, trailing after them.

She was right. She was absolutely right.

This woman he'd only known for a day, who'd looked after his children when she'd had no obligation to help, was speaking the most sense he'd heard in a long while. She wasn't trying to tell him what she thought he'd want to hear, or feeding him any lines about how easy it was going to be. She was just speaking the truth, plain and simple.

And he liked it.

So long as he didn't forget that he was sworn off women in a romantic kind of way, staying here wasn't going to be half bad.

CHAPTER FOUR

SIENNA was trying hard not to listen but it was even harder not to. She was folding towels and cleaning up the water that seemed to have splashed through her entire bathroom, attempting to stay away. Toby had started out a little shaky, not finding the rhythm of the story, but she could tell that he'd relaxed into the role of storyteller. And the kids seemed to be lapping it up.

She moved down the hall, leaned against the wall outside the children's bedroom. His mom had brought a truckload of books and toys when she'd dropped them off, and Sienna suspected they would have their dad reading all night if he agreed. She let her shoulders slump against the coolness of the wall at her back and listened.

Sienna shut her eyes as he read the story, listening to his deep voice, remembering what it was like to be read to as a child. He was a nice dad. She had no doubts that he'd eventually find his way with his children at his side, despite her reservations earlier in the day. But the look in his eyes, the almost pained way he answered when she asked him about *anything*...

It reminded her of Alec. When her brother had returned from his last tour of duty he'd struggled with everything. Catching up with friends, even simple things like doing the grocery shopping, had been a struggle. Sometimes she wondered if he'd ever have transitioned back into civilian life when he'd come home for good, but she'd never know. It was one of those questions that drove her round and round in circles and made her crazy. Because one part of her guessed that he'd never have reverted to the man he'd once been and another part, a more optimistic part of her, thought that he might have met a woman who'd have brought him back from the pain. Who could have helped to heal him, to bring back the fun-loving, always smiling brother that she remembered from their younger years.

And that was why she wanted to help other soldiers so badly. There wasn't a person who'd passed through her home that she hadn't wanted to reach out to, to help as best she could, but there was something different about Toby. Something about him that made her want to hold him close and not let him go until she'd figured out how to heal him.

Sienna wiped away a tear that had escaped her eye and pushed off with one foot from the wall. She passed the open door slowly, looked in at the little family she'd been listening to. Toby had his legs crossed at the ankle, sitting back on the bed. Lochie was tucked up on one side and Holly on the other.

A family. She sucked in the emotion she felt at seeing them all together, knew how stupid it was and forced herself to keep walking.

She was a grown woman and she'd had a beautiful childhood. It hadn't been perfect, but she'd been loved, and she'd had the best dad and brother in the world. There wasn't a day that passed when she didn't wish they were both still by her side, but she was doing her best and she knew they'd be proud. Years ago she'd sat curled up in the same room the children were in now, her dad reading to her until late into the night sometimes.

Years ago she'd thought a city career was more important than family, but she'd learned her lesson the hard way. If she was to do it all over again she'd do anything to enjoy those extra years in the community she'd fallen back in love with, spending time with her dad before he'd fallen ill.

"Sienna?"

A tiny voice called out to her and she was forced from the shadows. As she stepped through the door Holly scooted off the bed and came flying across the room to her.

"He doesn't read like you," Holly whispered in her ear.

Oh, boy. Sienna hoped Toby hadn't heard that.

"Sienna, come listen to the story," Lochie said.

She looked at Toby, tried to read his face. He was smiling, just a small half smile, but he wasn't saying no.

Umm. "Sure."

Holly grasped her hand tight and dragged her over to the other single bed.

"Don't you want to sit with your dad?" Sienna asked her.

Holly shook her head and snuggled in tighter to Sienna's side. She met Toby's gaze again and he just shrugged. He had his son beside him, but she'd sure bet it hurt that his daughter had picked a virtual stranger over her own father.

"Okay, let's listen to the story for a while, huh? Then it might be time for lights out."

Sienna folded the little girl into her and tucked them both down into bed. She'd looked after them on her own for a couple of nights before Toby had arrived and she'd coped fine, but there was something uncomfortable about being part of this particular scene.

She loved to fill her house with people, to make it feel

like a home. To make it feel like she still had a family. But this? She looked down at the child in her arms, couldn't bring herself to watch Toby—just hearing his deep voice read the story aloud was hard enough. They weren't her family and she needed to remember it. Because when they left she needed to wave them goodbye and move on. Just like she did when any of her guests left.

Sienna hoped the story was over soon.

Toby hesitated before entering. The aroma of coffee had woken him from his half-asleep state, and the smell of food was making his stomach growl. Loudly.

"Morning!"

Sienna's bright and bubbly voice tugged him into the kitchen. Even if he'd wanted to resist he couldn't, because there was something nice about being in a warm, welcoming home instead of the desert.

"Morning," he replied, trying to sound at least half as bright as she did.

"You sleep okay?"

Toby followed his nose and sat at the table, watching Sienna as she bounced around the kitchen. It was tiring just watching her. *Perky* would be an understatement for the permanent smile on her face and the way she danced about.

"I slept like I haven't in months," he told her honestly. In fact he probably hadn't slept that well in almost two years.

"The kids don't seem to wake until about half-seven, but I like to get things done early."

Toby could see that. She wasn't exactly slopping around in pajamas. Sienna was dressed for the day, her hair pulled up into a high ponytail, face made up and looking...

He looked away. *Beautiful.* That was what he'd been

thinking. She reminded him of the head cheerleader when he was a senior at high school, the one every guy had wanted to date. Only there was nothing superficial about Sienna. Or at least not that he could see. Beautiful, but with a humbleness that made her look more girl-next-door.

Something nudged his leg. Something long-haired and friendly.

"Bonnie!" Sienna exclaimed.

He reached down to give the dog a scratch. "She's fine. Don't worry about her." She had her tongue lolling out, a smile on her face like she was loving the attention.

"You don't mind? I've tried to get her to stay out of the kitchen, but I'm not so good at the whole strict-parenting routine."

That made Toby laugh. Her dog lay at his feet, letting out a low whine. "I've wanted a dog for years so she doesn't bother me. We'd always planned on getting one once I was back for good."

"Well, all I can say is that she's the best friend I've ever had," Sienna told him, pouring two fresh cups of coffee and sliding one carefully along the counter for him. He stood to reach it. "I tell her everything and she listens, plus I can lend her out to everyone who stays here, too, and she keeps every single secret she hears."

Toby wrapped one hand around the coffee mug, wincing at the scalding heat but not pulling away completely. At least the sting against his skin reminded him that he was alive.

"So you reckon I can confide in her, huh?"

"She can be your best friend while you're here and I promise she'll do the job well." Sienna held a carton of eggs up in the air, eyebrows raised.

Toby nodded in reply.

"Scrambled or easy over?"

Toby's tastebuds sprang to life. "Easy over. Definitely easy over."

Sienna's laugh didn't take him by surprise so much this time. He hadn't been in her company long, but her mood was kind of infectious.

Or not. He held on to the coffee mug tighter, enjoying the way the burning sensation made him stop thinking. About everything including his pretty host, even if it was only a temporary relief.

"I'm guessing you're hankering for all kinds of home-cooked meals, huh?" Sienna asked, pulling out utensils and starting breakfast.

"Like you wouldn't believe," he told her, and it was true. He'd been salivating about all the food he'd missed out on the entire journey back. "Only I was thinking I'd have to learn how to cook. That something you can help me with?"

"Ha!" Sienna laughed, cracking the eggs. "I've fooled you with my whole domestic-goddess routine. I'm a hopeless cook."

Toby cocked his head, watching her, trying to figure out if she was joking.

"Remember I mentioned that I have a housekeeper?"

He nodded.

"Yeah, well, I don't just have her because I need help cleaning and with the guests. It's the food I struggle with."

Toby couldn't help laughing back at her. "You sure look like you know your way around the kitchen."

Sienna turned from the pan to make a bow, laughing all the while. "I'll take your compliment, but I promise that my skills don't go any further than breakfast, and that's out of necessity. I can do a mean bacon and eggs, and waffles, too, thanks to my super machine, but that's it. Maisy arrives in a couple of hours and she'll handle everything else for the day."

Toby took a sip of his coffee. This woman really was something else. "So you're trying to tell me that you never cook dinner?"

"Nope. Never. Can't cook a proper meal to save myself unless it's frozen and just needs heating up," she confessed.

Toby slapped his hand on the table. "How about I make you a deal?"

Sienna spun back around, making eye contact before moving fast to grab a plate. "What kind of a deal?"

"While I'm here we both learn to cook. If I'm gonna be let loose as a single dad, the one thing I'll have to get good at is cooking."

"And what's my reason?"

"That it's laughable a capable woman like you can't rustle up a meal to save herself." Toby tried to keep his face straight but it wasn't easy. She looked beyond indignant.

"What do you call this?" she asked, one hand on her hip, the other holding his plate outstretched.

"I call that a pretty awesome breakfast, that's what."

Toby had no idea why he'd asked her to cook with him, why he was suddenly capable of chatting to her when he'd been finding it so hard to talk at all of late, but it was nice. A relief to feel normal if only for a moment in time.

Sienna tried not to watch Toby, but it wasn't exactly easy. He was pretty darn gorgeous, and she'd gone from wondering at one moment if she'd ever be able to help him to finding him magnetic and charming the next.

Off-limits, she reminded herself. She only had a few rules here, and being attracted to one of the soldiers was definitely breaking one of them. Aside from the fact that she didn't want to get too attached to anyone, she didn't need any complications either. Needed to be completely focused on what she was doing here at Second Chance Ranch.

But cooking? Wanting to learn with her? That was one huge step in the right direction for Toby. It sometimes took weeks to pull a soldier from his shell. She knew that better than anyone. And she hadn't exactly been feeling over-confident about Toby.

Sienna glanced down when she felt the sleeve of her shirt being tugged

"Morning, poppet," she said to Holly. The little girl had her hair all mussed up from bed and was standing shyly beside her. "You must have crept down those stairs as silent as a mouse."

Holly smiled, the corners of her mouth only just curving. She was the sweetest child. Sienna's heart had melted from the moment she'd opened her door and seen her standing beside her grandma. And after the way Holly had behaved last night she was guessing the feeling was mutual.

"You going to say hello to your dad?"

Sienna looked over at Toby and realized he hadn't moved. He'd stopped chewing, was completely immobile. When his mouth did move again it was like his food was so dry he could hardly gulp it down. Maybe she'd been a bit too quick to think he was coming completely out of his shell already. But dealing with the kids must be hard on him.

She raised an eyebrow at Toby, willing him to communicate with his daughter.

"Morning, Holly," Toby managed.

Holly twirled the bottom of her pajama top between both

hands, fingers playing with the fabric. Instead of answering him she slipped up beside him and stood there, her body angled slightly toward him like she wanted to be close but wasn't sure what to do.

Toby hadn't reacted straight away, but watching him Sienna saw it was like he suddenly remembered where he was and what he was supposed to do. "You want some toast?"

Holly nodded. She was the sweetest kid, but when she didn't know her dad, had last seen him as a one-year-old, it was a lot to expect her to accept him completely from the moment he stepped back into her life.

"One slice of toast coming right up!" Sienna saluted her little houseguest and gave her a pat on the head as she passed.

"Two!" Holly said back, scrambling up onto her dad's knee.

Sienna paused, then stopped herself, fussing with the toaster and finding jam in the cupboard. From the corner of her eye she could see Toby wrap one hand around his daughter's waist, his face less serious than it had been when Holly had first appeared.

He would be a good dad, she knew, but only if he received the help he needed. Because once he was back home with his kids and there was no one there to remind him what to do, to be the bridge between him and his children, that was when things would get tough.

Sienna twirled back toward Holly and then slowed, walking the toast over. Toby had seen her, had looked up, but he hadn't moved until their eyes had met. She'd seen him lean forward, touch his nose to Holly's hair and just breathe her in. Like he needed to soak her all up so he'd never forget her.

A noise from behind made Sienna turn back around. Lochie was standing with one hand buried in his sticking up hair, the other rubbing at his half-closed eyes. He looked hilarious—like he'd leaped from bed the moment he'd stirred without waking up properly.

"I'm starving," he announced.

"Hello, Starving. I'm Sienna," she replied, passing a grinning Holly her toast.

Toby started to laugh then, a deep-in-the-belly kind of laugh that made Sienna join in. It took her by surprise but she liked it. It was the first time she'd heard more than a light chuckle pass his lips. It even made Holly relax.

"I don't get it." Lochie was laughing, too, but only because they were.

"I'm being silly," Sienna told him, watching as he went to sit at the table with his dad and sister. "So just what is it that a starving boy like you needs for breakfast, huh?"

Lochie puffed out his chest at her, like he knew she was joking with him but he still wasn't completely sure whether he was being teased or not.

"A huge bowl of Fruit Loops. Then three pieces of toast."

Sienna shook her head, a smile on her face, and exchanged glances with Toby. Either the kid had woken up seriously hungry or he was trying to impress his dad with his appetite. Make out like he was a big tough marine, too.

She tucked her finger beneath Lochie's chin and tilted his head slightly, leaning down and forward so she could touch noses with him. "You're one of my favorite houseguests, you know that? Even if you two *do* keep forgetting your manners by asking me for things without saying please."

Sienna pulled away, stopping herself from giving him an impromptu hug. She was falling in love with these kids *way* too fast, and she knew how dangerous that was. She'd love children of her own one day, but right now that wasn't on the cards and she had no intention of spending time worrying about it. She needed to come to terms with who and what she'd lost before she even thought about her future. And even then she wasn't sure she would be brave enough to risk losing someone she loved ever again.

No matter how much Holly and Lochie reminded her of her own childhood, of kicking around with her kid brother, racing out to see the horses and hanging out with their dad in the kitchen, soaking up his every word each night at dinner, she wasn't going to get attached.

What will be, will be.

Toby knew he'd been quiet. Hell, he'd hardly been able to muster up a word when Holly had appeared. But Sienna was helping. Hell, was she helping! It was as if they'd known each other months, not less than twenty-four hours. She had a quietness about her that made him want to talk, and the way she was with his children, the way she seemed to know what to say and how to coax the people around her, was remarkable. Even if it *did* hurt that his daughter was more comfortable with Sienna than she was with him.

"You…ah…have many others staying here?" Toby had been wondering what the setup was, who else was here.

"Only two others right now," Sienna called back over her shoulder. "One of the guys has only been back in the country a couple of weeks, and the other one staying is almost ready to move on. He's been here nearly two months."

Wow. "That usual?"

Sienna placed a bowl of Fruit Loops in front of Lochie and sat down across from them. "You mean only having a couple of other returned soldiers here or them staying that long?"

"Both," he replied.

Sienna sipped at her coffee, probably less than lukewarm now, and looked at him over her cup. "I have three guest-rooms downstairs that I always have available. Sometimes they're all full, and sometimes they're all empty. Just depends."

Toby watched as she made a face at her coffee and scooped up both their cups. Clearly it was too cold for her liking.

"Another?" she asked.

He nodded and watched her rise. "And upstairs?" She hadn't mentioned the rooms they were staying in.

"I generally keep upstairs for myself. I have a sofa and television set up in one of the rooms, so I can be alone when I need to be, but there's the guestroom you're staying in and the one the kids are in. When they're needed I fill them."

He didn't like that they'd taken over her personal domain—not when she was being so kind. "We can all fit in down here in one room, if you want. I mean, you don't need to put us all upstairs." He wasn't sure if that had come out right, hated the way his voice sounded. No longer the calm, deep voice of authority he'd used when he'd led his men. Now he sounded like a regular guy not sure what to say to a pretty lady.

And that was definitely not the man he knew himself to be.

She leaned back against the counter, waiting for the water to boil. "Toby, please don't worry about where you're staying or what I'm doing for you, okay?" Her voice was soft, thoughtful. "What I'm doing here is something I've dreamed about for a long time."

He didn't know what to say back. It was easy for her to say, but not so easy for him to accept. He wasn't used to taking and not giving, to being the charity case.

Toby watched his kids as they ate, realized they were listening to the conversation, looking back and forward between him and Sienna like they were watching a tennis match.

"What I'm trying to say is that I don't want you to put yourself out," he said, more bluntly than perhaps he should have.

Sienna smiled, her personality vivid in that one expression. He couldn't see anything other than kindness shining from her face, except maybe a hint of sadness. But then perhaps he was reading that all wrong.

"I opened this place because I *wanted* to put myself out. Because I need to be there for others in need." She paused. "Does that even make sense? I'm not exactly the best at explaining what I mean sometimes."

Toby found himself nodding, wanting to understand. "Yeah, I think it does."

"Is it kind of like why you joined the army?"

He grimaced. Now the conversation was turning in a direction he wasn't necessarily comfortable with, but he'd started it. "Are you asking whether I joined the army because I wanted to help others?"

Sienna smiled at him over her coffee cup. "Was it?"

Toby wanted to shut his eyes and think, to go back in time and ask himself the question. "To be honest, I joined up because I wanted to prove that I was strong and tough, I think. Because I wanted to be one of the people who helped to protect our country, to be one of the good guys."

Sienna didn't say anything, just sat. He was starting to

realize that she always did that: asked a question, coaxed enough to keep him answering and let him talk. In a way he liked it, because she didn't seem to judge him. But then again he didn't know if he really wanted to talk in the first place.

"What about now?"

Sienna's question surprised him. *Now?* "I think it's about time we talked about something else."

If she was shocked by his response she didn't show it. Instead she clucked over his kids like a broody mother hen and made sure they were enjoying their food and ready for the day ahead.

"I think your dad needs to have some time on his own today, which means we need to come up with a plan," she told the children. "Any ideas?"

"Horse riding!" said Lochie. "You promised yesterday. *Please.*"

Toby watched as she expertly wiped jam from his fingers with a minimum of fuss.

"Sounds like a good plan. Toby?"

He made himself snap out of his mood. She'd asked a legitimate question about how he felt, about his career in the army, and he'd as good as bitten her head off. "I think horseback riding would be a great way to spend the day."

"You do?" Sienna had stopped what she was doing, was looking at him from where she stood.

"Yeah. Why not?" He tried to act like he was happy, like he didn't mind the thought of an entire day in her company, playing the happy and dutiful dad that he was supposed to be, riding an animal he'd have absolutely no control over.

He looked at his children and they watched him back,

slow smiles creeping across their faces. Holly looked excited about him joining them.

"Will you ride with us?" Lochie asked.

Sienna seemed to be holding her breath if the anxious look on her face was anything to go by.

"If I'm allowed to?" he responded.

"Of course you're allowed to. We might need to juggle a few other things, but let's plan to leave in an hour. Before it gets too hot."

"How about a picnic?" asked Lochie, his voice shy.

Sienna dropped an impromptu kiss to the top of Lochie's head and beamed at Holly, who looked so excited she was practically wriggling from her seat. "Now, *that* sounds like a brilliant idea."

Toby turned as he heard footsteps. A trigger of alertness fired through his body, diffusing when Sienna's hand fell to his shoulder.

"It's just Maisy here early," she whispered, somehow knowing that the noise of someone entering had sent him into protective overdrive.

"Hey, Maisy!" she called out, glancing at him as if telling him silently that it was okay.

"Morning, kids!" A booming voice rang out down the hallway, and Holly and Lochie sprang to their feet to greet the mystery woman.

Toby kept his hand wrapped around his coffee mug, taking the scene in. One day he was a soldier, flying through the air to land on home soil, the next he was part of a domestic scene that seemed more foreign to him than living in the desert.

He couldn't help but smile as the older woman bustled into the kitchen, his children trotting after her like eager puppies. Then his eye caught Sienna, and he wished he'd never looked up. Because he didn't need to be attracted to the way she smiled at Lochie and Holly, or be drawn to her tiny figure and bouncing blonde hair.

He was here to recover, not to fight his feelings.

Sienna caught him watching her and fixed her sunny smile in place, pulling him in even deeper. He cleared his throat, looked away, then back again. *Never again,* he reminded himself. He was *never* going to put himself in that position again, where he couldn't save a woman he'd committed to protect.

"Well, soldier, I think it's time for us to work on your weekly plan and then find some riding clothes for you."

Sorry, what? "Plan?" he asked.

"Maisy, do you mind if the kids help you with lunch? We're going on a picnic soon, but first I need to shuffle some paperwork with Toby."

Sienna's housekeeper gave him a wink and a grin before shuffling the children away. "Picnic lunch coming right up!" she sang out.

Toby stood when Sienna crooked her finger and pointed to the door, obeying like she was the one in charge. In a way she was. For the moment, anyway.

But walking behind her might not have been the best option. He looked away and started to whistle a tune, then almost smacked straight into her when she stopped without warning.

"What is that?"

He looked down at her, realizing how short she was now they were standing so close. "What's what?"

"That tune? My brother used to whistle it all the time."

Toby frowned. He had no idea what it was. "I used to

hear some of the other guys whistling it when we were out on patrol and I picked it up."

Sienna spun back around again and he followed. Only this time she was humming softly to herself as she led him into what he guessed was her office. It was oddly comforting.

Because since he'd been back he'd missed his crew like crazy. And with Sienna humming his tune it was like having one of his own nearby again.

"So, let's get down to business."

CHAPTER FIVE

SIENNA focused on the task at hand, and not on the man standing in front of her desk. She gestured for him to sit down as she did the same, but not looking at him was starting to become difficult. Plenty of the guys she'd met here had been handsome, and even more had been less troubled than Toby, but there was something about him that was drawing her like a mouse to cheese.

She wasn't fully in control of the situation and she didn't like it. Not one bit.

"So, we need to sort out a few things before we head off for the day," she told him, her voice businesslike. "I'm not sure how much you were told about staying here before you elected to come, but there are some formalities that we have to get out of the way so I can file all the right paperwork." She tried her best to reassure him with a smile. "All the boring stuff."

The look he gave her made her refocus on her paperwork. Fast.

"Some legal mumbo-jumbo or something?" he asked.

Sienna pushed a chart across her desk to him. "I've mocked up a schedule for you to look over, but of course it's open to change."

Toby's eyebrows arched, then bunched together as he looked at the sheet of paper.

She cleared her throat and pushed another few pages toward him. "There's also a disclaimer I need you to sign which formalizes your staying here, and some basic information about Second Chance Ranch and the options and activities while you're here."

"You make it sound like a summer camp." Toby's tone was humorous, but there was an underlying coolness to his tone that made a shiver trace the curve of her spine.

"You may not like the schedule now, but I can tell you that the way we operate here helps. I know it does because—"

"A *shrink?*"

Sienna's head snapped up. Toby was staring at the outline she'd given him as if it was going to attack him.

"If you want to call her that, sure," Sienna responded, trying to keep her voice bright and perky. "I think she'd prefer Dr. Aitken, but—" She stopped abruptly when Toby interrupted her. *Again*.

"I don't need to see a goddamn shrink."

Sienna wished he'd yelled. Would have preferred it to the cold, bone-chilling tone he'd just pulled on her.

"I know that you probably don't want to talk about certain things right now." She held up her hand, fixing her gaze on him, telling him that she wasn't okay with being interrupted. Two could play this game, and she knew exactly how to handle this kind of behaviour. "But part of my ranch being accepted by the army is the service that we provide, and that includes soldiers talking to someone. And that someone is a professional who I happen to call my best friend."

Toby still looked stormy, but he was sitting still and he hadn't said anything when she'd indicated for him to keep quiet.

"You don't have to tell anyone else what you talk about,

but you *do* have to go and see her. It's only mandatory once a week, and if you stay for a month then that's only four times. Unless you want to see her more. Okay?"

Toby's face seemed to crumple before her. He faded and lost that personality that she kept seeing bursts of from behind his eyes. Lost the intensity that he'd been projecting.

"I'm sorry." He said the words through almost clenched teeth, but she still appreciated the apology.

"Toby?"

He stared at his hands before responding, before turning the saddest eyes she'd ever looked into, in her direction. Sienna leaned forward and clasped the one hand he had resting on the desk, wrapped her fingers around it as best she could.

"You need to talk to someone in order to move on, and you need to try your hardest to rehabilitate yourself while you're here. Because this is where you can be yourself and start to heal."

"What if I'm not ready? What if I don't want to be helped?"

Sienna liked that he was being honest with her. Appreciated that he was trying to communicate his feelings.

"You *do* want to be helped, Toby. Because you have two little people out there in my kitchen who love you, who *depend on you,* and that's why you're ready. Okay?"

Toby kept staring at her, but he didn't nod. He didn't move so much as a muscle.

"I think what we need is a day out in the sun. You can look over all this tonight, once you've had a chance to think."

Sienna stood and pulled her chair out, ready to go. But Toby stayed still, motionless like a statue.

"There are days that I wish someone would understand, but most of the time I don't want to put anyone through what I've been through. I don't want to share it because then I'll know it wasn't just some nightmare that I can move on from. Forget about."

His voice was impossibly deep, and filled with so much raw emotion that it fixed Sienna in place, too. She wished she could tell him. Wished she knew how to convey what she held so tightly inside. But she didn't know him well enough to share. She needed to trust someone completely to let them into her private world, and she'd never admitted what had truly happened to any of the soldiers staying here. She'd managed to keep her past private.

"I've seen things, Sienna, things that you couldn't imagine but that I can't forget."

She held her brother's hand so tight that she worried she'd hurt him. But he didn't pull away and she didn't let go.

"I've seen a man I knew in pieces, his limbs blown clean off him, and so much blood that I kept thinking it must be like this inside of an abattoir."

"You can tell me, Alec. I'll listen to anything you need to talk about."

He shook his head, a wildness in his eyes that she hadn't seen before. "No. Because then you won't ever look at me the same again, and I need you."

Sienna dug her fingernails into the palm of her hand. "Sometimes the only way we can forget what we see, what we experience, is to talk. Because in passing those memories on we learn to lean on another human being, to share the load."

It was something her best friend had taught her—the doctor that she hoped could help Toby. Although she wasn't exactly one to practice what she preached. Not all the time, and especially not when it came to the tough stuff.

Toby didn't look convinced, but he stood and swept up the papers she'd prepared for him in one hand. "Tomorrow, then," he said. "Just let me try to get through today, and tomorrow I'll deal with all this stuff."

Sienna didn't mind. Not one bit. Anything to lighten the mood and she was keen. "I think it's time to test out your cowboy skills, then," she told him. "See what you're really made of."

Toby gave her a modest smile and she followed him out the door, pulling it shut behind her and flicking the lock. She'd left it open earlier, knowing the other two guests had already gone and because the Freeman clan were all asleep, but she wanted to make sure the room couldn't be disturbed while they were out. It was the one place in the house that she kept sacred, where she had her own stash of memories that she didn't want anyone else to know about.

"How about we find you some clothes to ride in?"

Toby paused and turned his big body her way. She resisted the urge to place her palm flat on his chest, to feel the strength there. It had been way too long since she'd been close to a man, since she'd felt hard muscle and flesh, and for some reason this soldier was making her think all kinds of thoughts she shouldn't.

Maybe it was a need to protect him, to nurture this strong war veteran until he was able to serve and protect those around him. Or maybe it was just that he was so darn handsome, even with his hair all but shorn off, and she was simply being a woman drawn to a good-looking guy.

"You have something in my size?"

Sienna nodded. "Yeah, right about perfect for you, I think." Toby took a step backward and she turned and led the way up the stairs. "I have a pair of jeans and a shirt of my brother's stored up here, and a great pair of worn-in boots you can ride in, too."

"You sure he won't mind?"

Sienna kept the bright smile fixed on her face, even though Toby couldn't see it, because that made it much easier to cope with. "No, he wouldn't mind at all," she replied.

Her brother would have loved what she was doing, and it was thoughts like that that kept her going some days. She might not have lost the love of her life, like Toby had, but she knew at least part of what he'd experienced. Which was precisely why she needed to keep him at arm's length. Because she knew what she could handle, and falling for Toby Freeman wasn't on her list.

Toby wasn't so much uncomfortable as feeling like he'd walked onto the set for a dude-ranch movie. Cowboy boots, a plaid shirt and faded-out narrow jeans weren't exactly his usual attire.

"Stop looking like a dog left out in the cold." Sienna seemed to enjoy making fun of him.

"Are you sure no one's going to laugh at me?" he asked, glaring at the grin on her face.

"You fit in perfectly now," she told him. "No one will even notice that you're not from around these parts."

Toby couldn't remember the last time he'd ridden a horse. His wife had made him go on a few trail rides over the years when they'd traveled around the country for a few months, but other than that he had little to no experience. Just because he lived in Texas it didn't mean he knew one end of a horse from the other.

"Where are the kids?" he asked.

"Waiting for us down by the horses already. I let them

walk on ahead, but they know not to go any farther than the fence until we get there, and there's no water or dangers between here and there." She stopped what she was doing and squinted into the sun. "If you look over there—" Sienna pointed "—you'll be able to see them. I never let them go anywhere I can't easily spot them."

Toby trusted Sienna's judgement, but he didn't want to take any chances where his kids were concerned. He couldn't risk anything happening to them. Not after what he'd already been through.

"Need me to carry something?" he asked, eager to get going.

Sienna finished filling one of the packs and passed it to him. "I'd love you to. One for each of us." She swung one of the packs up onto her back and called out to Maisy over her shoulder. "See you soon. We'll probably be half the day."

They walked in silence for a bit, but it felt nice. Comfortable. Toby hated talking for the hell of it, and he hated long drawn-out silences that grated past like nails on a chalkboard, too.

But he didn't mind being in Sienna's company one bit. Not so far, anyway, even if he had snapped her head off earlier in her office. And, unlike him, she looked perfect in cowgirl getup. Her blonde hair was plaited, falling over her far shoulder so he could only just see it, and a fitted shirt with the sleeves rolled up and tight jeans didn't do her figure any harm either.

Toby steeled his jaw and swung the pack to his other shoulder for something to do. *Stop looking.*

"You okay carrying that?"

Sienna's question almost made him laugh. "Yes ma'am," he replied, giving her a mock salute.

"Well, obviously I didn't mean was it too *heavy* for you," she said, rolling her eyes as if he'd made the stupidest joke in the world. "You could have a shoulder injury for all I know and meant to be resting up."

So did that mean she didn't know why he'd been discharged from the army? Why he'd been sent home? "I'm used to carrying a pack that can easily weigh seventy or eighty pounds, so I'll be just fine with this little featherweight."

Sienna kept walking but she was watching him now. "So, no ailments I should know about before you climb aboard one of the horses?"

He shook his head. "Nope, I'm good."

She seemed to think on that for a bit, but Toby was keen on changing the topic. He wasn't exactly comfortable talking about why he'd come home and why he wasn't going to be volunteering for another term offshore. His time with the army was up—for active service anyway.

"Have you lived here a long time?" Toby asked her.

Sienna gave him a thoughtful look, an expression he hadn't seen before crossing her face. Maybe sadness, but he couldn't be sure. "Here in Brackenridge?"

"No, here on this land," he clarified.

"This was my family home growing up, but things are different here now than they used to be, if that makes sense."

Maybe he'd been right. There was something there that he couldn't quite work out, something that was niggling her, worrying her. He could see from her eyes and the way she was flicking her fingers in and out, worrying her nails.

"So you bought this place from your parents?" He didn't want to pry, but talking about her kept the conversation away from him. When she wanted to stop, he'd stop asking questions.

"My dad passed away and left me the property, but I didn't want to farm the land. I've always loved being here, but I was never the one learning the ropes or preparing for a life of running the place. So I sold off most of the land— kept enough so I could have my horses and enough space so the property didn't lose that feeling I love so much."

Sienna broke away then. He could feel it. Like she was shutting off a part of herself, putting up a barrier to keep him out. The hesitant expression on her face turned into a happy smile, like it was a mask she wore to distract others from the sadness beneath the surface. Or maybe it distracted her from going too deep. Either way, he got it.

He remembered only too well smiling at neighbors when they came past with dinners for him, like they were all on a roster to make sure he had enough food to survive on after Michelle had passed. The way he'd be forced to smile back, stand tall, stoically thank them and wave them on their way. But when the door shut, when he was alone, he'd hunch over like he'd been sucker-punched, crying into his palms until the baby would wake and he'd have to pull himself together all over again.

"You were close to your dad?" he asked carefully.

Sienna's sunny smile seemed believable at the mention of her father, her eyes alive again. "Yeah, he was the best. I still miss him every day, but I know he'd be so proud of what I'm doing here."

"And your brother never wanted to run the farm when he got back?"

Sienna fixed him with her gaze, almost tricking him that

she was okay with the conversation until she patted him on the arm and pointed out the horses.

"See that big brown and white horse there?" she asked him.

He followed her point and squinted, knowing full well she'd swiftly changed the subject on him. "The massive one?"

"She's yours. I promise she'll be kind to you."

Toby raised his hand at the same time Sienna did, waving to his exuberant children as they jumped up and down and waved back. "So your brother's still away, then?" He had to ask, needed to know why he was wearing her brother's clothes, why she seemed so fond of him when she spoke of him, yet why there was no mention of him being here or coming back.

"Alec loved this place, and that gorgeous big mare you're going to be riding was his horse."

She walked away, stepped up her pace so there was a distance between them, but Toby wasn't going to push her any further. For whatever reason she didn't want to talk about him, and it was none of his business to find out. Maybe she just didn't like talking about her personal life, but he got the feeling there was a whole lot more to Sienna than met the eye. That her happiness wasn't as absolute as it seemed.

"Daddy, you look like a real cowboy!" Lochie looked beyond excited.

"You sure this is a good idea? I mean, we could always walk instead," he addressed his son.

Holly shook her head fiercely and Lochie looked offended. "Even Holly's fine on a horse, Dad. I thought you wouldn't be scared of anything."

Toby chuckled. "For the record, I'm not scared. It's just…"

"He's scared," announced Sienna, winking at him as she passed with a saddle slung under each arm. "Maybe you two should show him where the halters are and then take him out to catch the other horses. If he's not too chicken."

Toby watched as Holly whispered something to Lochie and they both burst into laughter. He owed Sienna a lot already, but putting a smile on those two little faces was something he'd never have a hope of repaying her for. Because when they smiled it seemed like his heart was slowly starting to defrost, piece by tiny piece. Once Holly started to accept him more he knew it'd all be worth it.

"Come on. Dad, you ready?"

Lochie reached out for his hand, his palm swallowed up when Toby closed his over the top of it. Holly was more shy, but he knew what he had to do. He bent slightly, holding out his arm, and Holly jumped into his hold with hardly any hesitation, letting him scoop her up off the ground. She looked a touch unsure, watching for Sienna like a hawk eyeing its prey, but she didn't once protest or pull away.

"Who will you ride, poppet?" he asked her, suddenly realizing that there were only three horses, and that his daughter was way too little to ride on her own anyway.

"Oh, she rides up front with Sienna," Lochie told him. "She has this massive big saddle and Sienna and her can both fit."

Right.

"And don't worry, Dad, she has helmets for both of us."

Lochie was full of information and Toby liked it. There was nothing nicer than hearing his boy talk, watching the way he looked out for his sister, the way he was trying to take charge like he was way older than his almost six years.

"Hey, Toby, wait up!" Sienna called out to him and he

turned. It was hard not to watch her, not to indulge in really drinking her in.

The smile that he'd thought could be hiding a multitude of feelings beneath its surface was so sunny and genuine now that he knew it to be exactly what he could see. And her eyes—they were so blue they were almost sparkling in the sunlight.

"You think I need some help?" he asked, still staring at her.

"I don't think. I *know.* These two can be devils to catch at the best of times when they know there's a long ride involved."

Toby waited until Sienna was beside him before he started to walk again, slowing his stride so she didn't have to rush.

"Thanks," she said.

"For what?"

"Slowing down so a short-ass like me doesn't have to run to keep up!"

"She said *ass,*" Lochie repeated with a giggle.

Holly laughed, too, although probably only because she wanted to copy her brother.

Sienna clamped a hand over her mouth, eyebrows pointed and eyes wide as she gasped. Toby just laughed.

"That's why I'd make a terrible mom," she said, shaking her head and mouthing *sorry* at Lochie.

Toby disagreed. The way she was with his children made him think she was perfect mom material. And he'd bet the kids thought so, too.

But it was stupid to think like that, to think of her in that role. Sienna was their host and nothing more, and even if he wanted something to happen between them he wouldn't let it.

Not now and not ever.

CHAPTER SIX

"So, now that I'm up here I might need an instruction manual."

Toby was staring at the horse's neck like he didn't trust her one bit and Sienna was finding it hard not to laugh. If she hadn't been so conscious of the little girl riding up in front of her, tucked back into her stomach, she probably would have given in to the humor of the whole situation. But she didn't want to make fun of their dad too much in front of them.

"You're going to be riding alongside me, and there's no narrow trails where I'm taking us, so she'll just follow my horse," Sienna told him.

He still looked unsure.

"Just keep your feet in the stirrups, heels down, and keep your reins nice and loose like I showed you. No yanking on her mouth."

"And she'll behave, just like that?"

"Yep, just like that. I told you, she's a sweetheart."

Sienna adjusted the rope in her hand and looked down at Lochie. "You okay?"

"Yeah, I'm great!" he told her.

Snow was a pro. She'd been the family pony since Sienna was a kid and she would trust her with the most precious of cargo up on her back. But Sienna kept a lead attached to her just in case. Even an old girl like Snow could take fright over something unexpected, and she didn't want Toby to worry any more than he already was.

"How do you make it look so easy?" Toby grumbled. "You've got Holly up front and you're somehow keeping control of the pony, too."

"I've been doing this for years," she said, nudging her horse into a walk. "Now, stop the moaning and enjoy the countryside."

He was all tense and rigid, and it took every ounce of her self control not to laugh.

"You know when you're out on patrol and you're alert to absolutely everything around you?" Sienna asked him.

"Yeah."

"Well, stop acting like that and relax!"

Toby scowled, but he couldn't keep it up for long. Not with them all laughing at him.

"I look that tense?" he asked.

"Yeah, Dad, you do," Lochie told him, peering around to look at his father.

Toby rolled his shoulders and wriggled his backside deeper into the saddle. "Better?"

"Heaps." Sienna clucked for all the horses to walk on. "Today is about fresh country air, hanging out with the kids and eating yummy food."

"Sounds a lot like what we all dreamed about when we were in the desert."

"Yeah? I'll bet you guys talked about all kinds of stuff you were looking forward to doing when you were back."

"Food was a big topic of conversation, but lots of the guys just wanted to get back home to see their families and never to see sand again."

They rode along. Sienna loved the familiar motion of her horse's gait. The children were quiet, looking around them, entertained by the passing countryside. "I know you didn't like the idea of the schedule, Toby, but it's not because I'm trying to organize you or because I want to control what you're doing," she told him in a quiet voice.

"I know." Toby let out a deep sigh. "I need to relax and stop trying to be in charge for once," he stated, as if it was the most natural thing in the world when she knew for sure that it wasn't.

"Which I know is impossibly hard when you're used to being the one leading."

He pushed his shoulders up into a shrug. "Yeah, but I've got no plans to go back, so I need to learn how to live this kind of life again. I need to get back to basics, and if that means talking to a professional then I guess I'll just have to swallow it. Lump it or leave, right?"

"Right." Sienna was surprised but she didn't let him see it. He was like a pendulum, swinging from one extreme to the other. She hadn't expected him to give in to talking to anyone that quickly. "One of the guys here, Matt, he arrived without saying a word and hardly spoke for a few weeks."

"What's he like now?" Toby asked her.

"He's part of a team of builders in town and he's like a different man. It's incredible how much he's changed while he's been here."

Toby seemed to have relaxed. His body was starting to move in time with the horse because he was no longer clinging on with his thighs as if his life depended upon it.

"So, what you're trying to tell me is that I could go from being damaged goods to a perfectly acceptable human being if I stay with you?"

She couldn't tell if he was joking or being a touch serious. Or both.

"All I'm saying is that I'm proud of what I've been able to achieve here," Sienna said. "If even one man out of five can come here and turn his life around, or just get back in touch with who he used to be and go on to be happy and content, then I know I'm making a difference. That it's worth it."

"And me?" Toby's voice was lower now, his tone deadly serious.

"If you want to be the man you used to be, whoever that was, then you'll find him. You've just got to want to."

She checked the rope tied to the pommel of her saddle with the tips of her fingers, so she didn't disturb Holly. The girl was tucked firmly against her stomach, the warmth from her back radiating into Sienna.

Toby was quiet, seemed satisfied, but then she couldn't hear what was going on in his head. She had the feeling that if she could hear his thoughts their ride wouldn't seem so quiet.

"Why did you start this place, Sienna? What *actually* made you do it?"

The quiet was suddenly disturbed and *her* head the one filled with a jumble of thoughts. But nothing was going to ruin her day out, with the sun beating down on her forearms, in the company of the two cutest kids in the world.

Not to mention a not-so-bad dad.

"I told you." She gave him her sunniest smile—the one she pulled out when she needed to make everyone around her feel good. She'd trained herself, knew how to push away memories and feelings when she had to. "When my dad passed away I sold the land and did something I'd always dreamed of."

Toby looked like he was deep in thought. "But what made you want to be so selfless? To give up what you were doing to help others? I mean, don't be offended here, but there's usually a catalyst for this sort of thing."

Sienna wasn't used to someone trying to help her, to delve deep into her past. She was so used to being the one providing the assistance. "Let's just say that one day I might tell you all about it." She gave him what she hoped was a firm look. A look that told him she didn't want to be questioned any further. "And until then you need to think about you and only you."

He didn't respond, but then she didn't mind. As long as he wasn't asking questions about her, then she was happy.

"Plus the kids," she added. "You need to think about you *and* the kids."

"And a way to repay you," Toby replied, his voice more raspy. Like he was shy. But she could tell from looking at him that he wasn't.

"A letter in the mail one day to tell me how great the kids are doing will be repayment enough." But as she said it she was already dreading the day they'd be leaving. *Because she was attached.* No matter how hard she wanted *not* to be, she was already wishing these kids would be in her life forever, in *some* sort of capacity. They reminded her too much of what it felt like to have a family again, of what she secretly coveted but was so afraid of at the same time.

And their dad wasn't half bad to have around either.

So much for the brooding, messed up soldier she'd met yesterday. She'd hardly seen that side of him today. Not really.

Although a stirring within her warned that he wasn't out of the woods yet. This stuff was *fun*. Today was *nice*. But the hard work would begin when he had to confront his problems, his past.

Doing that was never easy. She knew that from experience.

Toby didn't know why he was asking Sienna so many questions, or why he was even talking so much, but it was as if all the months he'd spent *not* talking had caught up on him. She was so easy to chat to, like his wife had been. The kind of happy, free spirit that could talk to an insect and turn it into a chirpy critter.

"So, is it usual to lose all feeling in your ankles with your heels pushed down this hard?" he asked her.

Sienna's body rocked softly with her laughter. "I think you're doing the whole rigid-soldier thing again."

"I think it's time for lunch." His backside was killing him and his thighs were already aching from trying to keep his balance.

"We haven't even ridden for half an hour yet! I can still see the house if I squint hard enough."

Toby disagreed. "You couldn't even pick out the house if you had my army-issue binoculars on, and as for the rigid-soldier thing…" He tried to wipe the grin off his face and for the first time since he'd been back didn't have a hope of doing it. "I think leaving that behind will take longer than a day, so give a guy a break."

Sienna tipped her head, hiding her eyes from him for a second.

It was a second he didn't enjoy.

"What do you say, kiddo?" He watched as she asked his son.

"'Bout what?" Lochie replied.

"Your dad wants lunch but I told him we haven't gone far enough yet."

Lochie tilted his head to the side, like he was thinking really hard, or maybe he just didn't want to say the wrong thing. Either way, Toby didn't want him trying to figure out what he *should* say. He wanted his kids saying what they really thought. What they *wanted* to say.

"Are you hungry yet, Lochie?" Toby asked him.

His son shook his head. "It feels like we only just had breakfast. But if you want to stop I don't mind..." His sentence trailed off.

"Then that answers it."

Sienna was laughing. He could see the gentle shake of her body. "Aye-aye, Captain," she said, bending her head down to whisper in Holly's ear.

Toby gave his horse a nudge like Sienna had showed him, to make her walk forward, and tried to make himself more comfortable in the saddle.

He wanted to know more about the woman hosting them. Wanted to know why she had the patience to help others, why she'd really started this place. And why she was alone here instead of married with a family of her own. But it wasn't his business, and he didn't have a valid reason for asking her anything more than he already had.

The sun was starting to beat down on his arms. Not with the ferocity that it had overseas, but enough to remind him that he was alive.

Alive when others weren't, so it was about time he stopped brooding and started to realize how fortunate he was. Enough of dwelling on the past, or wishing things had turned out differently, and more thinking about the future.

"So what are your plans now you're back, Toby?" Sienna asked.

Her voice drew him from his thoughts. She must have read his mind. "To be honest, I don't have much of an idea." He wasn't lying. He didn't have any plans and he hated floating. Hated not knowing what direction he was going in, especially when he was so used to his life being so structured. "I grew up in Houston and I still have a home there. It's where my mom's lived looking after the kids."

"I was an event planner before this, so I know all about facing new career challenges."

Toby felt his eyebrows shoot up. "Really? And you gave that up…?" He wasn't sure if that was the right wording.

"I guess I did give it up, but it was the right decision for me. I'd worked long hours for years, and leaving my job meant I could nurse my dad for a few months."

"Then you started this place?" It seemed every topic they started on turned back around to why she was doing what she was doing.

"Mmm-hmm." She looked out at the distance, like she was deep in thought. "I wanted to move to the city so bad as a teenager, and when I started work it seemed perfect. For a while." Sienna sighed. "But then things changed, and my dad was sick, and everything that had seemed so important in my old life suddenly seemed absurd and trivial. So here I am."

Toby didn't want it to seem like he was pushing Sienna into a corner again. He needed to dig himself out of this particular hole fast. "Plus it means you get to spend more time with your horses, right?"

That made Sienna smile. "Sure does. I ride whenever I can—long hacks around the farmland mostly. The new owner doesn't mind me pottering about so long as I close the gates behind me, and I've known our neighbor since I was tiny."

Toby hadn't ever really understood the whole horses obsession, although his wife had loved them, but being out here in the open was kind of nice. A different way to spend time in the outdoors, and less tiring than having to walk for hours on end, even if his backside *was* getting stiffer by the minute.

"See that tree up ahead? The one with the low-hanging branches?" Sienna asked them all.

"Is that where we're having lunch?" Lochie asked.

"Sure is." Sienna tilted her head slightly. "Wanna trot?"

Lochie almost leaped off his pony he was so excited. "Yeah!"

"Okay, remember what I told you. Sit deep and hold the pommel with your left hand. If you want to stop, just say *walk* and she'll respond."

Toby was smiling, listening to the exchange—until all the horses started moving faster.

Holy hell! "Sienna!"

She looked over her shoulder. "Oh, sorry, Toby! Hold on tight!"

He sure *was* going to hang on tight! Toby braced himself and tried not to bounce clear from the saddle, but it was a whole lot harder than Sienna or any of the riders he'd seen before made it look.

His teeth almost rattled from his head. Maybe walking for hours wouldn't have been such a bad option.

CHAPTER SEVEN

SIENNA sat with her back pressed up against a massive tree and her legs stretched out in front of her. Holly was lying flat out on her back beside her. Lochie was with his dad. She loved the time she was spending with the little girl, but she knew it would be better if Holly was spending more of it with her dad.

The little guy was acting like his dad had never left.

"Don't you love days like this?" Sienna had her eyes shut, and the feeling of relaxation was washing over her like the familiar touch of a lover. It was so different from the high-pressure life she'd led for so long, and she never for a moment regretted putting her career to bed for good.

When her dad had fallen ill, he'd been all that mattered, and it had sure put everything into perspective. She'd finished with the guy she'd been seeing when he couldn't understand why she wanted to care for her father, and she'd realized that her career and all the money in the world wouldn't make up for the years she'd lived in the city, not seeing enough of him.

"I haven't had a day like this in a long time."

Duh, what a stupid question she'd asked him. He'd been in a war zone for the last... "How long were you serving?"

"This time around? Around eighteen months all up." He made a face, squished one side of his mouth up in a pained kind of way. "It was too long, but then coming back any earlier might have been too soon, you know? I could have, but I just couldn't bring myself to."

Yeah, she knew.

"Did you ever want to do anything else? I mean, if you hadn't made it in the army?"

"Never." He said the word with absolute clarity. "I knew I'd make it and I did. There was never anything else."

Huh. Another similarity he shared with her brother.

Sienna watched lazily as Holly plucked at grass and Lochie rolled around, turning a leaf over in his hand and hunting for bugs or some other type of critter in the long grass.

"I think it's time to get back," she announced, not wanting to leave but knowing they'd already been gone too long. "Things to organize, animals to feed."

"Yeah, and I need to get back to call Mom. Check in on her," Toby said.

They didn't move, but Sienna at least made an attempt to stretch out her legs.

"Sienna, this friend of yours? The doctor?" Toby asked.

She waited, her face turned to him so she knew he was listening.

"Do you really think she'll be able to help me?"

His voice held so much uncertainty it made her want to wrap her arms around him and tell him everything would be okay. But she couldn't, because she hardly knew him and he'd hardly want her invading his private space.

What she could do was reassure him. "If I didn't have full confidence in her abilities, if I hadn't seen firsthand what she can do, then I wouldn't send even one soldier in her direction."

Toby nodded, like he wasn't sure he should have asked the question in the first place.

"You're brave and you're strong, Toby," she told him, willing the tears flooding her eyes not to fall. Because something about this handsome, brooding soldier and his little family was making her all troubled inside. "You have a family who loves you, and I think that's the most important start in the world."

"I want to help you," she told her brother, holding his hand so tight she was in danger of breaking his bones.

Alec gripped back tight, looked away like he couldn't bear to meet her gaze.

"No one can help me, Sienna. I can't get it out of my head."

He yanked at his hair, rubbed his forehead like it might help get rid of the demons.

"We'll get through this, okay?" she tried to reassure him.

Sad eyes, like a puppy on a pound's death row, haunted her with their troubles.

"No. No one can help me, not anymore."

When Sienna opened her eyes, fought against memories that she'd been able to keep at bay for so long now, Toby hovered above her. He held out his hand, offering her a help-up.

He was big. That was what struck her the most about him. At times he didn't seem so imposing because she knew he was troubled, but now... His broad shoulders blocked the sun from her eyes, his chest was like a wall in front of her. She started to imagine him with his hair grown out, without the stubble that grazed his chin and cheeks.

And then scolded herself.

She couldn't think about Toby like that. *Not ever.* Because she couldn't risk falling for a man like him. Losing her brother the way she had had been hard enough… She forced her brain to stop over analyzing.

She wasn't going to be so prissy as not to accept a hand.

"Thanks." She was supposed to sound confident but instead it came out more as a whoosh of air. Because all of a sudden she was too close to the handsome soldier.

Toby didn't say anything, but his eyes did. They spoke of confusion, uncertainty and something else she couldn't detect. Maybe didn't want to detect.

What she did know was that they stood there too long, too close, looking at one another, not saying anything. Not sure of what they should be saying.

"Home," Sienna managed, breaking the moment. "It's… ah…about time we went home."

Toby took a quick step back, then another. His hand went to his hair, sweeping back and forth across the buzz a few times.

"Kids, can you call Bonnie over?" Sienna asked.

Lochie jumped up and started calling out to the dog, who was off busy following her nose, and Holly trailed after him. Not saying anything, just happy to pad alongside her brother. Sienna didn't know what had just happened, why they'd both stood there like that, and she didn't want to speculate.

Toby was handsome and obviously kind. *But he was a father. He was a troubled soldier. Not to mention the fact that he'd just returned from the belly of hell in the desert and was supposed to be here to recover. Not to be ambushed by her.*

That thought brought a smile to her face. She'd never *ambushed* a guy in her life—was too old-fashioned or maybe just too shy to even consider asking a man out. So to think she was any kind of threat to this war-hardened marine would make her friends laugh.

"Come on, let's go," she ordered, bending to retrieve her pack and nudging Toby's in his direction.

He obeyed, nodding. "I'm thinking of walking. You know, to save my muscles?"

Toby made her laugh, softened the mood between them again. "Your butt and your thighs are going to kill you in the morning, but that's all part of staying in the country, right?"

He hauled his pack over his shoulder as if it weighed no more than a pound, scowling at her.

"Next time you could do some stretches first," she suggested, bending to drop a kiss to Bonnie's soft head as she reappeared.

"Who's saying there'll be a next time?" he grumbled.

She hooked a finger in the direction of his children. "They do. Because like it or not they love hanging out with my horses."

His expression suddenly turned serious, changed. "Do you think there's any truth to the concept of animals helping to heal humans? I mean, I've read about autistic kids coming a long way through riding horses—something about a beast sensing that they pose no danger."

Sienna closed the distance between them and reached out to him, let her hand fall over his shoulder. "I think that animals do more for us than we'll ever give them credit for." She paused, squeezed her fingers over the strong muscles above his shoulder, fighting the urge to lean against him, to connect with him. "If you're asking me if the horses are helping Lochie and Holly, then I'd say the answer is yes. But, to be honest, in this case I think Bonnie sitting guard beside their beds each night and curling up to them at every opportunity is a big part of their happiness here, too. Just like you being here has made them even brighter. And the more time you spend with Holly hanging out with the animals, the faster she'll be coming to you at every opportunity."

Toby turned to her. She wanted to step back but didn't. She stayed close to him, refused to let her focus falter, but the slow grin that spread across his mouth distracted her.

"So what you're saying is that we're going to need a dog?"

"Exactly. Every family needs one, if you ask me."

Toby pulled away from her—slowly, though, like he wasn't disliking their contact any more than she was.

"Come on, kidlets. Saddle up!" she ordered.

Toby sat back in the sofa. He'd managed to tune out the kids' show blaring from the television and was nursing a beer, eyes shut. Talking to his mom on the phone had made him worry all over again, but he was doing his best to block it out.

He didn't really want the beer, but it was nice to be kicking back with his feet up.

If he could only keep his memories at bay.

"Hey."

Toby's eyes shot open. The word was like a gun going off for the jolt it sent through him.

"Hi." It was easy to forget he wasn't in a private home as such, but he hadn't even thought about the other two guys arriving home at the end of the day. He stood, put his beer down and held out his hand. "Toby. Toby Freeman."

"Matt Richards," the other guy said, making firm contact with his hand as he introduced himself.

Toby sat back down and the other guy gestured over his shoulder.

"I'll grab a beer. Hold up a sec."

It gave Toby a minute to compose himself, to get his head in the right space. His brain almost hurt from trying so hard all day, from forcing himself to be a guy instead of a war-battered shell of a man. It hadn't been easy, and he'd thought he had a while before Sienna came back to compose himself. To remind himself how he had to behave, what was expected of him, why he needed to be thankful and all that.

Now he had another soldier to deal with—which should have been easier but was in a way harder.

"Holly and Lochie your kids?" Matt was back in the room, swigging on his beer like he'd been hanging out for it all day.

"You've met them already?" Toby was protective, suddenly didn't like the fact that this guy already knew his kids without him okaying it first.

"Yeah, they're great," Matt said, obviously not picking up on any hostility. Or if he was he was doing a good job of ignoring it. "I had dinner with them a couple of nights ago, with Sienna."

It was like an itch beneath Toby's skin, a prickle he couldn't dislodge. He had no claim over Sienna but he was going protective again. He needed to shut it off.

"You been here long?" Toby asked.

Matt grinned. "I thought I'd be in and out within a week, resented being here to start with, but I think I've clocked up almost two months and I hate the thought of leaving now."

"Sienna's a pretty good host." Was he interested in her? Had something happened between them? *Did he even want to know?*

"She's been fantastic. Been through a lot herself, I guess,

which makes her more understanding. From what she's said, anyway."

Toby nodded.

"Just arrived in?"

"Yep, two days ago. But I only got here yesterday morning," Toby replied.

"Active service?"

"You betcha." Toby guessed he should probably tell him where he'd been, who he'd been serving with, but he didn't want to go there. Didn't even want to think about what had happened on this tour—or the last part of it anyway.

"It's good to talk about it sometimes, you know? Get it off your chest and all that," Matt said, leaning forward slightly in the chair across from him. "But honestly? The best part about being here is forgetting what you've done and seen over there and just being a regular guy again."

Toby felt his eyebrows shoot up. Maybe he was going to like Matt a whole lot more than he'd expected to. Was he telling him that he wasn't going to ask about the war if he didn't volunteer to talk? That the last thing he wanted to do was remember either?

"Why does no one seem to get that some of the things we do and see over there need to be left there?" Toby asked him. "We all expect to be having a blast over there, but the reality is we're doing something great for our country, sure, but there ain't nothing glamorous about living in that hell-hole and doing what we're trained to do."

Matt gave him a mock salute and held his beer out, clinking it to Toby's. "We're gonna get on just fine. Didn't I tell you?"

Toby smiled back, even if he didn't feel like it, and took

another swig of his beer. "So, tell me, what's this doctor like?"

"Hot," Matt responded immediately, a grin lighting his face.

Toby laughed. "Seriously?"

"Seriously. And she's pretty easy to talk to, too. Once you stop ogling her."

Toby relaxed, sat back into the sofa and reminded himself that this was what he had to get used to now. Shooting the breeze, being a regular guy. Making friends. Even if he couldn't imagine the doctor could possibly be any easier on the eye than Sienna was.

"What's so funny?"

He almost dropped his beer. So much for being relaxed. He hadn't even managed it for more than a second.

Sienna was leaning in the doorway, arms crossed over her chest, beautiful big smile lighting her face. Waiting for one of them to answer her.

"Hey, Sienna. I was just introducing myself to the newbie."

She threw Matt a smile that made Toby's pulse race, made him clench his jaw harder than he should have. He didn't like that smile going in anyone else's direction, not one little bit. He hated his reaction even more, but he couldn't seem to do anything about it.

"I'm heating dinner up now. You want to wash up and meet me in the kitchen in say…" she checked her watch, her slim wrist rising in front of her "…twenty minutes?"

Toby nodded, never taking his eyes from her, watching until she'd disappeared.

"Toby?"

He looked at Matt. Toby had forgotten all about him when Sienna had been in the room.

"She's pretty awesome, huh?" Matt asked.

Toby stayed still, didn't nod or say anything. Didn't want to give anything away.

"You try and go there and you hurt her?" Matt was staring him down, tough as nails instead of the calm, easy-going guy of before, voice deep and threatening. "There are some guys who'd kill you or worse. *Me included*. Because she ain't just some girl, got me?"

Toby's pulse raced. He broke contact with Matt to look in the adjoining room, saw his kids there. It slowed his temper, made him forget about wanting to jump up and rip the guy's throat out for suggesting he'd hurt Sienna. He was a dad. That was his main role and he needed to remember it. No more reacting without thinking—not now he was back.

Instead he smiled, a slow movement of his mouth that held no warmth. "I hear you," he responded, his voice not even mildly hinting at the anger that was shooting through his insides.

"Good, then I was right. We'll get along just fine."

Matt stood and slapped him on the shoulder, a friendly enough gesture, but Toby still prickled.

He'd probably threaten someone, too, if he thought they were going to hurt Sienna, but was it because he liked her? *Like that?*

Toby had no intention of getting involved with anyone, of complicating his life any more than it already was and risking the pain—he'd suffered enough for a lifetime. But one thing was for sure: looking away from Sienna when she was around him was becoming nearly impossible. There was something about her that made his mouth go dry and his heart beat faster just being in her company.

Maybe it was the fact she'd taken his kids in. Maybe it was that she was being so kind, that he liked her values and what she was doing for others.

Or maybe he liked her in a way he hadn't even considered liking another woman since Michelle had died.

And that scared the hell out of him.

CHAPTER EIGHT

Sienna did her best to shoo Toby from the kitchen, but he wasn't budging.

"Come on, you're the guest. That means you get to sit back."

He shook his head. "Nope. Cook never has to clean up."

That made her laugh. She turned her back on him and started to fill the sink with water. "First of all, I'm not the cook. Heating up something in the oven does not equate to cooking." She squeezed some suds under the flow of the faucet. "And second…" Sienna didn't have a second. "Well, this is my house so I get to make the rules."

Toby didn't look like a man who took orders without making a fuss. "You're not going to wash all those, are you?"

She followed his eyes. "Oh, no, just the ones that won't fit in the dishwasher. The wine glasses and big plates."

He pulled open the dishwasher door and stood beside her, still not taking no for an answer. What was she going to say? *Out of the kitchen or you're in trouble?*

"You're not backing down, are you?" she asked with a sigh.

"Nope." He held out his hand.

"Fine, you can help. But I don't want you doing this every night, okay?"

Toby didn't answer her. She had a feeling he needed something to do. That he wasn't content just sitting around.

She needed to get the month planned out so he was focused, had things on his agenda. Men like him needed to be busy.

"Did Matt talk to you about what he's working on?"

Sienna could have sworn he stiffened at the mention of the other man, but maybe she was imagining it. She passed Toby a plate she'd washed and rinsed.

"He's a builder, right?" His question was simple enough, but she wondered if something had gone down between them when she'd walked in earlier. They'd seemed happy enough, had been laughing if she remembered correctly, but still, she hadn't exactly heard any of their conversation.

"I started talking to so many people when I started this place, and it made me realize that there were families who needed help when they lost their men," Sienna told him. Plus, she hadn't been able to imagine how it must feel to lose a husband for the widows left behind. She knew loss, but not the loss of a lover or soul mate. Those women had lost the fathers of their children. "There were so many widows struggling, with so little money, and I wanted to do something for them. Help them have a home for their families." She brushed the tears from her eyes with the back of her arm, her hands covered in the gloves she wore to do the dishes. "Matt's one of the guys working on the project."

"Hey…" Toby looked awkward, like he wanted to touch her but didn't know how to or what he'd do even if he was sure.

Sienna shook her head. "Sorry, I get all emotional just talking about what we're doing. It's our first house as part of the whole project, and it means so much to me."

He looked worried again, put off balance by seeing her tears. "Come here."

Toby surprised her by putting his arm around her. Waiting a beat before giving her a gentle hug, his big hand secured around her shoulder.

She couldn't resist it. Sienna let her head fall to the side of his shoulder. She was too short to rest it there, but able to take comfort from connecting with him regardless. It had been so long since she'd had someone to hug, had a man to comfort her.

Not a lover, or a boyfriend, but just a man. That feeling of protection and security you could get from any strong, dependable man. Her father and her brother had both always been there for her when she needed a hug, had held her like they'd deal with anyone who ever stepped in the way of her happiness. Of her safety.

"Thanks," she whispered, grateful for how brave he'd been in reaching out to her. Sometimes, even though she was surrounded by people each day, she felt more alone than she'd ever been.

"You're something special, Sienna, you know that?"

Toby's voice had changed, was huskier than before. So deep that it sent a chill down the back of her legs and back up again.

Sienna turned to face him before she pulled away, looked up and saw the man beneath those deep brown eyes flecked with gold. He didn't move, stayed immobile, and she felt as if she was fixed in place, unable to move even if she'd wanted to.

"Toby…" Her voice trailed off. She had nothing to say. Couldn't articulate what she wanted to say even if she tried.

They both hovered, neither doing anything.

He was gorgeous. Tough, handsome, troubled, *intriguing.*

She'd never worried about being attracted to a guest before, *but Toby?* Well, Toby was something different entirely.

Sienna wasn't going to do anything, but then she wasn't going to push him away either.

Toby moved in closer, somehow changed his weight so that his body was almost touching hers again, turned his chest almost to face her.

Sienna still had her gloves on, but she couldn't even think enough to pull them off. Her arms still rested on the edge of the sink, but she was so aware of Toby it was all she could focus on.

His head dipped, his lips moved closer to hers and she tilted her chin, waited for the moment where he'd kiss her. Sensed the quiver of anticipation thrum through her and was powerless to stop it.

Toby's breath was warm against her mouth…

"What are you doing to Sienna?"

Her hands fell into the water with a surprised splash. *Lochie!*

She met Toby's gaze and saw he looked as uncomfortable as she did, as embarrassed as the heat flaming her cheeks told her she was.

"Hey, bud," she managed, her voice bright and cheerful. Sienna turned to see both children standing in the kitchen behind them. "Your dad was helping me do the dishes and I…um…got something in my eye, so he was…ah…trying to see what it was for me."

"Oh." Lochie looked less than interested now, was shifting from foot to foot. Holly tugged at his arm and he gave her a nudge back. "We were just…we were wondering if there was any dessert?"

Sienna laughed, and listened to Toby do the same. Maybe they actually were young enough and innocent enough not to know what they'd almost witnessed. "Sure," she said.

Toby's fingers skimmed her waist as he moved past her. His touch was more powerful than if he'd made eye contact with her, made her suck in a breath and fight not to shut her eyes.

"There's ice cream in the freezer," she told Toby.

He looked over his shoulder, one hand on each of his children's heads, and stared at her. No smile, no frown, just a troubled stare. His eyes showed so much, said so much about who he was and what he was fighting, and at the same time gave nothing away. But one thing was for sure: he was rattled just like she was.

And Sienna was rattling so fast it was a wonder she didn't sound like a bunch of keys being danced around the room.

Sienna pulled off one glove and drew her hand up to her mouth, ran her fingers softly across her lips.

He'd almost kissed her. Toby had almost kissed her *and she'd wanted him to.* Like a lovesick teenager she'd puckered up and let him know she was okay with it, when she should never, *never* have let herself be put in that situation. She should have nipped it in the bud, should have known what would happen and foreseen how badly things could end if she even so much as entertained the idea of something happening between them.

Toby was fragile. He had just returned from active duty. He had children to learn to parent again. A sick mom to contend with. She couldn't go there. Couldn't survive falling for him and losing him. Having a family again and then facing being alone all over again.

Sienna put her glove back on and started to rinse the

dishes again, before pulling them both off. The kids hadn't had their ice cream! Toby had walked them out and probably had certain *other* things on his mind. The children hadn't had the dessert they'd asked for.

She pulled out four bowls and found some chocolate fudge sauce.

Her bowl was going to be loaded.

Sienna scooped up her last mouthful and slowly raised the spoon. She could eat another bowlful in the mood she was in, and couldn't care less about the calories.

"Yum," announced Lochie, holding up his bowl. It was as good as licked clean.

She should ask him to take it to the kitchen, but she didn't. He was snuggled up on the floor now, half on top of Bonnie, and Holly was tucked up at her dad's feet. It was the first time Holly had approached her dad like that without any prompting, so she didn't want to disturb the moment.

Sienna was on the other side of the room, siting in the deep leather chair that used to be reserved for her father. As a kid she'd often sat on his knee, but never in the chair, because her dad had worked so hard he'd loved flopping into his favorite spot at the end of the day to watch television.

She licked her spoon, not wanting to think about her dad right now. Thinking about Toby was taking up enough of her emotional energy, no matter how hard she tried to push him out of her mind.

When Sienna looked up again Toby was stroking Bonnie's rump with his foot.

"You know, this dog is lucky to be allowed inside," he said.

Sienna watched as Lochie wriggled even closer to her

beloved pooch, one arm around her neck, the other tucked under her as he tried to get comfortable, using her as a pillow.

"I've never understood why people get a dog, then leave it locked out in the cold," she mused. "I mean, you get a dog to be your best friend, or at the very least part of the family, and then you don't let them into your home? I don't get it."

Toby looked from her to the dog. "I've never really thought about it like that."

Sienna shrugged. "I think humans should only have a dog if they're prepared to love it like a child, but that's only my take on it."

"Seems fair," he agreed.

They both watched the television for a bit—some kids' movie—but Sienna guessed that Toby was about as interested in it as she was. Not that she wanted to consider what might be on Toby's mind.

"So, tell me how a girl like you is single." Toby said it as a statement more than a question.

Sienna took a deep breath, refusing to make eye contact. Where had that question come from?

"Tell me why you've suddenly gone from shy like a cat has your tongue to asking me questions that you've no business to ask." Sienna said it with a smile, but she regretted the last part. *Maybe he wanted to make it his business.*

She swallowed. Hard.

Toby didn't react, didn't take the bait. Just sat there waiting for her to answer.

"Maybe I'm not single." She kept her tone hushed, didn't want the children tuning in.

Toby seemed to follow her gaze, realized why she wasn't talking much louder than a whisper. "She's crashed."

Sienna watched Holly for a moment, saw the even rise and fall of her chest. She'd fallen asleep against her dad's legs, tucked in tight and safe. It made Sienna smile—until she saw the way Toby was staring at her. That made her swallow a few times too many.

"You know what I think, Sienna?"

She shook her head slowly.

"I think that you're not the kind of girl who'd almost kiss another man if you were involved with someone else."

Her cheeks burned. They stung with heat. Embarrassment was firing through her skin. Why did he have to bring that up?

"Toby, why is it you're suddenly so interested in whether or not I'm involved with anyone?" She forced herself to remain strong, not to lose her composure, no matter how rattled she was.

"I wish I knew the answer to that, Sienna." His words were honest, the simple truth. "I'm sitting here with my kids, thinking how nice it is. That it feels like we're part of a family."

Sienna resisted the urge to shut her eyes, to block her ears to what he was saying. Because she knew how hard it was for him to say, and it wasn't any easier for her to listen. "It's okay to enjoy being here, Toby. You don't have to feel guilty about that. And you *are* a family."

He looked down, hands turning to fists on his lap. "But you're not part of our family, Sienna. So why am I suddenly pretending like you are?"

His words hurt. Slammed into her like her body had been hurled into a concrete block wall.

"I'm well aware that I'm not part of your family, Toby,"

she whispered back at him, trying to block out the pain, not to let him see how much he'd hurt her with his words.

"I'm sorry. I didn't mean…" Toby's eyes filled with something she didn't understand, hadn't seen in them before. "Geez, Sienna, I didn't mean that like it sounded."

She tried to brush it off, outwardly anyway, but she needed to get up. To get out of here and make her way up to her own room so she could have some time alone.

"How about you put the kids to bed? Carry Holly up and tuck Lochie in. I'm sure he'll go straight off to sleep, too." He was looking pretty close to slumber already, all snuggled up to Bonnie. "I'll see you in the morning."

Toby reached out and grabbed her wrist as she passed, but only loosely, and she quickly slipped away from his touch.

"No," she whispered, her voice low but firm. She didn't know why he was reaching out to her, why he was touching her, and she wasn't going to wait to find out.

He couldn't reach out to her without tipping Holly over, so he stayed still, sat in place.

She should have known better. Better than even thinking about getting involved with a guest.

She'd never followed her heart over her brain before, and it wasn't time she started.

Sienna flicked the lights out in the kitchen, checked the back door on her way past and trudged up the stairs. Sleep always helped. Sleep and a long, hot soak in the bath.

Mmm. A bath was *exactly* what she needed.

Sienna lay back in the water and lifted her feet so her toes could curl along the edge of the bath. *This was exactly what she needed*. The warm water always seemed to help, took her mind off whatever was troubling her, and she loved being surrounded by sweet-smelling soap and light-as-air bubbles.

Delicious.

She stared at the ceiling and thought about what had happened. It had been a long time since she'd been with a man. A *really* long time. It was just that after breaking it off with her ex and moving back home she'd hardly had a minute to herself. She'd kept herself busy, refusing to think about being alone, about how lonely it was rattling around this big house without any family of her own. Without her dad or her brother, and without a man or any children.

Before, she'd thought her career was more important than a family. It hadn't been until she'd lost everyone she loved that she'd realized how wrong she'd been. Family meant *everything*.

But now that she knew how hard it was to lose someone, how much it hurt to be left alone, she didn't know if she could ever put herself in a position to be left vulnerable and miserable ever again.

When she'd turned thirty, lost her brother and then her dad, and realized she was alone, she'd vowed never to let herself be hurt again. But that was before.

So the fact that a gorgeous soldier staying in her home, with equally gorgeous children, was causing her heart to flutter wasn't *that* unlikely. It wasn't even necessarily wrong if she took out of the equation that she should be maintaining a professional distance. She was lonely, that was all, and she needed to get over it.

Besides, Toby wasn't ready for a relationship, was probably still pining for the wife he'd lost, and she wasn't interested in being someone's fling after too long in a war zone.

She'd never been that kind of girl and she wasn't about to start being that woman now.

Sienna sighed, sick of the conversation she was having inside her own head, and slowly lowered herself deeper into the water, wanting to submerge her entire body and hold her breath to forget everything for just a few seconds.

She stopped sinking when a knock sounded out, echoing through her bathroom.

"Sienna?"

It could have been any of the three men staying under her roof, but she knew it was Toby. Another soft knock echoed out and Sienna rose quickly, reaching for a towel and wrapping it around herself. The door to her bedroom wasn't locked and she was in the adjoining bathroom with the door open. If he turned the handle and looked in he'd see her.

"Sienna?"

She'd never thought of her safety or her privacy before, because she wasn't used to having anyone stay on the top floor with her.

"Just a minute," she called back.

Sienna rushed over to the vanity and checked herself in the mirror. Her hair was damp, so she ran her fingers through it and pushed it off her face. She dabbed at her cheeks, resisting the urge to apply some makeup. She still had a little bit on, and she could hardly keep him waiting in the hall while she made herself look pretty.

She squared her shoulders and opened the door.

It was Toby, all right. He was in his jeans, no top on, broad shoulders like candy to her eyes—tanned skin stretched over pure muscle. Like he'd been about to discard his lower layers and get into bed, then changed his mind.

So much for telling herself she didn't want to go there, that she was strong enough to resist him.

"Did I disturb you?" he asked.

She looked down at the towel around her body, tucked in tight between her breasts to keep it up. Heaven help her if it fell.

Sienna clutched it tighter.

"I was just getting out of the bath."

He nodded, looked down and then up again. "Do you… ah…want to go for a bit of a walk?"

A walk? Sienna had to focus on keeping her mouth shut and her eyes from popping. "Now?"

Toby looked embarrassed and she wished she'd just accepted.

"Sorry. If you're ready for bed and you don't want to…"

"Yes." Sienna reached out and touched his arm, felt the warmth of his skin, then withdrew her hand and reclaimed her grip on her towel. "Just give me a minute to get dressed and I'll meet you downstairs."

She gave Toby a quick smile before closing the door. She dropped her towel in the middle of the room and ran to throw open her underwear drawer.

Sienna eyed a pretty black lace set tucked away near the back but refused to let her hand reach that far. *He was not going to see her underwear or anything even close to her underwear.* She picked a plain black T-shirt bra and panties instead, and then wriggled into a pair of jeans and a sweater.

The man needed to talk, that was all. No reason for her to get carried away.

Toby tugged on a T-shirt and padded barefoot down the stairs. His shoes were at the back door, and he didn't want to wake the kids.

He felt more than heard Sienna behind him, but he waited

before turning. He needed a moment to compose himself, because what he was about to do didn't come naturally to him and he was starting to panic. A slow, steady panic, but panic nonetheless. One that had his pulse thumping a little harder than it should and the fingers of his right hand twitching.

They always did that. Like his trigger finger knew that he was focused on something and wanted the comfort of resting on a weapon. Only he wasn't in the desert now and he probably wouldn't hold another gun again. Unless he suddenly felt the need to protect himself and buy a handgun, which he doubted.

"Hey."

There was no backing out now.

"Do you want to just walk around here? I don't think we should go too far in case the kids wake up," she said.

Toby agreed. "I need some fresh air. We can sit here if you like?"

"No, let's walk. It'll do me good—even if we do just loop around the house a few times."

He didn't let himself look at her because he didn't want to. Didn't want to see the way she wrapped her too-big sweater around her tiny frame like she was cold and in need of warming up, or how young and fresh-faced she looked with hardly a lick of makeup on.

Toby shrugged away his thoughts and held open the door for her to pass through. "After you."

They walked slowly in silence, their footsteps magnified by the silence around them.

"I have this feeling like I'm alert to everything now," Toby confessed. "While I was away my entire focus was on being so aware of my surroundings. *Listening* for the enemy, *looking* for the enemy, *protecting* those around me."

Sienna was listening to him. He could tell from the slight tilt of her head, the way she was slowly swinging one foot in front of the other.

"You need to learn to shut it off, Toby, but it won't be easy."

Her words were kind, but they didn't help him. "Can you ever shut it off?"

He had no idea whether or not she could answer him, but he needed to ask someone. She'd met so many soldiers, seemed to have experience at dealing with things that he was going to have to trust her on.

Sienna stopped and reached out to him, took his hand and pulled him around.

"I think what you need to do is get a good night's sleep and go see my friend in the morning. You need to talk, and she's the one who can help you. She's dealt with what you're going through so often that I know she'll be able to talk you through it."

Toby searched her face with his eyes as much as he could in the half-light. He wanted to kiss her, to tug her in close to him and see what it felt like, what it would be like to have another woman against him, in his arms. To see if he was capable of letting someone close to him again, to open himself up and risk everything, put his heart on the line for a second time.

But he didn't.

Toby did reach out to her, though. He held up his hand, carefully so she could see it coming, and stroked the back of his fingers down her face, across her cheek.

"Thank you," he said in a low voice. "Thank you for

looking after my children, and for taking me in. Even if everything else falls through, at least I'll know that someone tried to help us."

Sienna looked angry, had a sudden wildness about her that made him drop his hand.

"Toby Freeman, don't you even *think* of talking like that! You *will* get through this and so will your children, and I do not want to hear about you *ever* thinking of giving up."

He stared at her. "How can you be so sure?"

Sienna laughed, but it was more of a nervous noise than a serious chuckle. "Because I get what soldiers have been through and I know how to help. I understand how you feel, Toby. Believe it or not, I know exactly what it's like, what you've been through."

Toby's back stiffened like a steel rod had been shoved up to keep it deadly straight. "Please don't say that, Sienna. I hate when people try to pretend they know what I've been through, because they don't. Just because you might be able to help me through a rough patch it doesn't mean you understand."

She didn't say anything back, but he could tell from the way she was watching him that she disagreed.

"Have you ever served, Sienna? Have you ever taken a life or seen a friend blown up in front of you? Have you ever lost the person you thought you'd be married to forever? Who you loved so much? Who you thought was safe and nothing could ever happen to her?"

Sienna shook her head. "No."

Toby had his hands clenched at his sides so tight that he doubted he'd be able to even walk without calming himself down. "Then don't *ever* tell a marine like me that you know what we've been through."

"Are you finished?" Her tone was businesslike, not warm or cold.

Toby glared at her. "Yes."

"Then it's time I said good-night. I've got a lot to do in the morning, so I think it's time for bed."

Toby stayed still, completely motionless, until she'd walked away. He'd been rude to her. To the woman who'd invited him into her home and taken care of his children for no personal gain.

Damn it! He'd asked her out here so he could open up and talk to her, so he could apologize for earlier, so he could figure out why he'd almost kissed her in the kitchen after dinner. Instead he'd insulted her and upset the one person who he could call his friend right now.

He hated that his life had become so complicated when two years ago he'd had it all worked out. Had known exactly what he wanted and where his life was heading.

"I love you," Michelle whispered into his ear. "But I'm going to miss you so much."

Toby hated saying goodbye. It was the only thing about his career that he despised.

"Do you know what I like about leaving you?" he asked her, kissing his wife on the cheek as she snuggled back into him.

"There's something you like?"

"I like that no matter what I'm going through, that you're always here. You're safe. So I know that I could lose so much when I'm serving, but not you."

She kissed him, palms to his cheeks. "You're a brave man, Toby." She kissed him again, on the lips this time. "And you're right. We'll always be here waiting for you when you get home."

Toby sank to the grass and pulled up his knees, dropped his head into his hands and pushed the emotion away so hard that it hurt. His eyes stung with the tears he refused to let out. His chest ached like he was physically in pain.

Michelle was gone. There was no changing that. He'd loved her with all his heart, but she was gone.

And now it was like *everything* had gone. There was nothing left inside him except when he saw his kids and held them in his arms. And then there was desperation inside of him, that voice inside his head that told him not to fall in love with them too much. To try to keep some sort of a distance from them, even though he doubted that was even possible.

Because he knew now that nothing was sacred. That there was nothing in life that couldn't be ripped away from you so carelessly that it was like that something or someone had never existed in the first place. And he couldn't voluntarily put himself in that position again.

Toby lay out on the grass, looking up at the stars. The ground was damp but he didn't care.

He'd pushed himself, made himself the guy he wanted to be since they'd gone out riding, but it wasn't easy, didn't come naturally anymore, and he was exhausted.

Maybe he did need to speak to someone. Maybe Sienna was right. But he also needed to come to peace with what had happened to him, and that meant jumping headfirst back into the past.

If he could do it—if he could find the strength to confront what had happened to him, who and what he'd lost—then maybe he would come out the other side a better man.

Toby put his hands over his eyes and spoke a silent prayer—one that he'd recounted over and over while he'd been away. Ever since Michelle had passed. This time he let his lips move silently, aware that he was alone and no one could see what he was doing. Not that he cared anymore.

Give me the strength to survive. Give me the strength to confront each day on my own, to be the father I want and need to be for my children. Give me the strength to live, and remember those I have lost.

Toby kept his eyes shut until he knew he was past the worst of the pain, until he knew the tears were gone again.

He was a member of the U.S. Marine Corps Special Forces Operations Command. He could survive in the worst conditions a man could be faced with—fight to the death, even.

So he *would not* cry.

CHAPTER NINE

SIENNA pushed papers around her office before sitting back and glaring at her computer screen as if it were responsible for all her problems. She knew what the problem was. She was just finding it hard to admit.

Toby. Toby was why she'd lain awake half the night and woken up with a crease on her forehead from all the worrying.

She looked down at the spreadsheet planner in front of her and picked up the phone. It didn't matter what he'd been through, or how much he was getting to her, she needed to stick to her game plan. It was why the army had been so accepting of what she was doing. Her approach worked. So she wasn't going to make any exceptions for Toby. Not a chance.

Sienna picked up the phone and dialled the number she knew by heart. Her friend picked up on the second ring.

"Sienna!"

"Hey, Charlotte." It was so good to hear her voice. "Are you on your way to work?"

"Just walking in the door now, and I've got fifteen minutes until my first patient for the day. Everything all right?"

Sienna sighed—sighs just seemed to be emitting from her constantly this morning—before leaning back in her chair. "Do you have any available appointments today?"

Her friend rotated around all the smaller towns and was usually booked well in advance.

"With that sigh, am I right in guessing the appointment is for you?" Her friend laughed. "Or have you finally met a soldier who's proving too difficult even for *you* to charm?"

Sienna loved this. Having someone to talk to—someone she'd known her entire life and could trust with anything. It was what she missed most about having her brother and dad around, although she hadn't realized quite how much she'd missed Charlotte until she'd moved back here for good.

"I have a new guest and I think he needs to see you sooner than later, if you get what I mean."

She could almost hear Charlotte nodding. "I'll take him in my lunch break."

"Are you sure? I'll drop a takeaway or something in to you late morning so you don't have to skip lunch."

"You don't have to, but it'd be nice, and I know you wouldn't ask unless it was important," Charlotte told her.

"Thanks, hon."

"No worries. Now I have to fly. I need to down a strong coffee and check my emails before today turns into a circus."

Sienna hung up the phone, a lightness that she hadn't felt before settling over her shoulders. Charlotte always made her feel better. Just hearing her voice seemed to relax her, and it always made her realize why Charlotte was such a great doctor.

"You organizing something for me?"

Sienna lost that lazy feeling and the uptight bunch was back in her shoulders. Toby was standing in the doorway to her office, leaning into it, big arms folded across his chest.

"How long were you standing there?" she asked, cheeks

on fire. She had no reason to be embarrassed, had said nothing that would offend him or anyone else, but she didn't like her private conversations being listened to.

"Long enough to hear you arranging an appointment."

Sienna stood and planted her hands on her desk, summoning up her most commanding voice. "Look, Toby, I know you don't think you need help, but there are a few rules here and in agreeing to stay here you are obliged to obey them."

The corner of his mouth had an upturn that made her furious, but he raised his hands before the smile spread.

"I came down here to tell you I'll do whatever I need to do. So if you want me to see the shrink today, just tell me what time."

Sienna stared at him before realizing she hadn't answered. "Twelve noon."

"All righty, then."

She didn't know whether to smile, laugh or scold him, but she decided to give herself time to think. To figure out what to say. Damn him!

"Are the children up?" It was all she could think of.

"They're in the kitchen. Maisy's fixing them something."

Sienna fingered a piece of paper to give herself something to do.

"Are you okay with looking after the kids while I see the shrink?" he asked, still leaning, casual as hell, like he belonged there, in her doorway.

"Her name's Dr. Charlotte Aitken," she told him with a polite smile, unable to look away, "and the children will be fine with me."

"Great," he replied, leaning forward like he was about to

spin around and leave. "If you could give me directions and a distance I'll work out how long it'll take to walk there."

Sienna burst into laughter, shaking her head as she watched him. Seriously, this guy was going to test every bit of patience and willpower she possessed. "I'll be giving you a lift, soldier, not making you walk all the way into town, so don't worry about that. I'll take the kids out for lunch while you're there."

Toby turned, then stopped, looked back at her. "Sienna?"

She waited, wondering what he was going to say.

"I'm not going back again, so I'm not a soldier anymore."

Sienna stood and crossed the room, stopping just in front of him. "You'll always be a soldier, Toby," she said, in a voice almost as low as a whisper as she placed a hand across his chest, covering his heart and tapping. "You're a soldier *in here,* and that means you'll still be a soldier in ten or even twenty years' time."

Toby's breathing sped up. So did Sienna's. But she pushed back with her palm before she could think too much about being that close to him, about being in his personal space.

"Why don't you have breakfast with the kids and hang out with them for a while? We'll aim to leave here about eleven-thirty, so I have time to grab Charlotte some lunch for you to take in for her."

Sienna walked back to her desk and sat down, readying herself at her computer again like she had a million things to do and didn't have time to chat. She *did* have plenty to do, but she doubted she'd get much done this morning.

Sienna stared at her computer until she knew he was gone, before looking back up at where he'd stood.

Toby was a good man, but that didn't mean she had any

right to look at him the way she wanted to. And after last night, after what he'd said to her outside, she should have known better anyway.

The morning had been hopeless, as Sienna had expected, but it didn't make it any easier to swallow. She'd spent years as an event planner, could operate under the most stressful of circumstances, yet she'd been unable to focus today. A complete and utter train wreck.

"You look hungry." Maisy was leaning on the kitchen counter like she was waiting for a yarn.

"I'm not hungry." Sienna started to pick at the muffin Maisy had pushed her way. "I'm only eating this because it looks so good."

"Taste good, too?" Maisy was smiling at her like she'd just been let in on a secret. She started to devour a muffin of her own.

"If I keep you on, I'll end up as fat as a house before Christmas," Sienna moaned, sitting down and gently touching her head to the cool granite.

"Am I right in guessing you're not flopped down like a dead flower because of my baking?"

Sienna could hear the amusement in Maisy's voice without even looking at her. "I'm just being overly dramatic," she mumbled. "Humor me for a while."

"Do you like playing these games to keep me guessing or do you want me to leave you alone?" Now Maisy sounded more serious, like she was tired of taking the bait and wanted the truth.

"I don't know what's wrong with me." Sienna pulled herself together, pushed her hair back off her face and finished eating her muffin. "I've met so many men since I started this place, but I've never... Oh, I don't know."

Maisy put down her food and moved toward her, tucking her arm tight around her and tugging her close. "Come here," she whispered, dropping a kiss into her hair.

Sienna couldn't resist, wanted to be pressed tight to the woman she regarded as an almost-mom to her these days.

"You've been through a lot, love. More than most could handle."

"What other choice did I have?" Sienna asked her.

It was a question she'd asked herself over and over so many times since she'd overhauled her life. Turned her back on what she'd once thought was important, moved back to her hometown for good. And Maisy knew everything—there was nothing about her brother and her dad that she hadn't shared with her.

"You lost everyone you loved and yet you're here, *fighting*," Maisy told her. "Sometimes you're a little hard on yourself."

Sienna knew what she was saying was true, but she still hated feeling like this. "You don't even know what the problem is."

Maisy kissed the top of her head again before taking up position again on the other side of the counter, preparing dinner and sorting out snacks. "Toby's the problem, Sienna. I know it and you know it. So let's not beat around the bush about what's troubling you."

Sienna's face flushed hot as she looked up. Guilty. Like a bear who'd been caught out with his paw in a beehive, stealing honey. "Is it that obvious?" Her question came out as more of a gasp.

"There's something about the man that's affecting you,

that's all." Maisy was matter-of-fact, no-nonsense. "You can't help chemistry, Sienna. It's one of those things that hits us when we least expect it."

"So what do I do?" She couldn't even believe she was having this conversation!

"You can do one of two things." Maisy rested one elbow down on the counter. "You can give in to it and see what happens, if you're brave enough."

"Or?" She wasn't even sure she wanted to know option number two.

Maisy put her hands on her hips, but it wasn't long before one hand was clutching her belly as she started to laugh. "Or leave town in a hurry."

Sienna scowled at her. "Thank you for your wonderful advice, Maisy." Just when she'd thought she was being taken seriously.

"Oh, you're welcome, missy. You're more than welcome."

She walked out to the sounds of her housekeeper laughing. "Keep this to yourself or you're fired!" Sienna called out as she walked down the hall.

Maisy's laughter only got louder. Sienna doubted she'd ever be worried about being fired.

Toby was staring at his kids like he was in danger of losing them right then and there. They were so innocent, so beautiful, that it almost hurt him to watch them. They were kicking around a ball, or more like Lochie was trying to teach his sister how to play whatever game it was, but she was sluggish, didn't have her heart in it. He hated seeing her flat like that, but she only seemed to really come to life with Sienna around.

"Holly!" Toby called. "Come over here."

He was sitting on the grass, plucking at strands while he watched them. Holly walked over, her bottom lip planted down into a pouty kind of frown. She stopped when she was in front of him without making eye contact.

"What's the matter, baby girl?" he asked, reaching out to grab hold of her arm, wiggling it until she came closer.

"Nothing," she whispered, wrapping her tiny arms around his neck and snuggling against his chest, her breath hot against his skin.

Toby could have held her like that all day without tiring of having her in his arms. The weight of her against him, the smell of Sienna's coconut-scented shampoo on her hair, the warmth of her cheek against his bare skin was like heaven. So was the fact that she hadn't resisted his affection. "Tell me what's wrong."

Holly pushed back against his chest and looked at him like the sky was falling in. "I miss Grandma." She flung her face back against him and started to sob.

Oh, hell. He was only just getting his head around talking to her and touching her. He wasn't equipped for dealing with tears and sadness.

"Sweetheart, we'll be with Grandma before you know it, okay?" Toby brushed the hair back from her forehead and planted a kiss there, not taking his lips from her skin. "She misses you, too, you know?" He'd only finished talking to her a few minutes before he'd stepped outside to play with the kids. "Grandma's very special, and you've stayed with her for a very long time, so of course you miss her."

Holly nodded against him, but she didn't loosen her hold.

"You guys ready?"

Toby looked up at Sienna's voice, but he wasn't any more ready to let go of Holly than she was to give up hold of him.

"Oh, I'm sorry, I didn't meant to interrupt." Sienna started to walk backward, back toward the house.

Toby smiled up at her. He didn't want her to feel she had to leave them. She'd been there for his kids when they needed someone, so he wasn't keeping anything secret from her. "It's fine."

"I just wanted to tell you that it's almost time to go. I'll be waiting outside in the truck."

Sienna disappeared as quickly as she'd arrived, and Toby pressed a final kiss to Holly's cheek before rising. "Come on, kids, let's go find Sienna."

Holly might be missing her grandma now, but he'd bet she'd be crying over leaving Sienna when the day came, too.

Truth was, it wasn't a day he was looking forward to either.

CHAPTER TEN

"How did it go?" Sienna wasn't optimistic. Toby's face was fixed in a mask of steel, angry, like someone had seriously nudged him in the wrong direction.

"Don't ask." He smiled at his children when he saw them, made an effort on their behalf, but Sienna could see it wasn't coming naturally.

"If you didn't like Dr. Aitken I'm sure I could find someone more suitable." Sienna was trying her best to be diplomatic, but in reality she had no idea who else she'd find for Toby to talk to—not at short notice. They'd have to drive to Austin, and even then who would be better than Charlotte?

Toby glared at her, then sighed, his shoulders dropping like a balloon with half its air released. "She was fine. Nice woman. I don't have anything against her."

Sienna bit her tongue, trying hard not to add the *but*. She waited instead, smiling and laughing at Lochie and Holly finishing off their little hot chocolates, glancing at Toby. He stood, walked over to order himself a coffee before pausing.

"Do you want another?"

She shook her head. "I'm fine, thanks. Any more caffeine and my hands will start shaking."

She tracked Toby as he approached the counter, ordered his coffee and strode back toward their table. When he was walking or standing he looked like he owned the world, could conquer the universe. But when he was trying to relax or talk, do regular stuff, he became awkward. Lost that alpha attitude and clammed up.

But right now, almost in front of her, he had the presence of a lion. Could take her breath away with the strength and power he exuded—as if he would take on anyone to protect someone he loved, would fight to the death if he had to.

And win.

Sienna refused to let herself appear rattled in front of him again and forced her hand to her coffee cup, swallowing the last of her coffee.

Toby dropped into the chair beside hers, leaning forward, elbows to his thighs. "It's not that I don't like your friend, Sienna. I'm sure she's a great doctor. But I just don't think I can talk like that. Talk about things that I don't want to relive, that I want to keep in my mind and not let out."

Sienna resisted the urge to take his hand, even though not reaching for him seemed unnatural. Made her fingers twitch with the need to comfort him with touch.

"You need to talk to someone, Toby," she told him, her voice low, "because if you don't you'll get to a point where your head is filled with what's happened. Where you can't move forward because of the memories you're reliving in your mind, over and over, and if you'd only let them out you'd be able to move forward with your life."

Toby looked crushed, but he straightened his shoulders anyway, like he was fighting with himself. He braced himself back against the chair and stared at her, his face not showing the faintest hint of expression.

"When I need to talk, I'll talk to you."

Her? Pain speared through her chest, like her heart was

being stabbed continuously with hot rods. She didn't want to be in that position again.

"I'm not the right person, Toby. I think you're best talking to a professional."

He stood. "No. If you want me to talk to someone then that someone will just have to be you." Toby reached for his coffee as the waitress brought it over in a take-out cup, smiling his thanks at her, his face not matching the stubbornness of his tone. "Come on, kids, let's go."

Sienna was the last to rise. She needed a moment to compose herself. The last time she'd been someone's confidante...*argh*. She was not even going to go there, compare when it was a different situation. They were different men. One had been her brother and one was a man who... She didn't know what Toby was to her.

"I can't talk to anyone else, Sienna. I'm sorry."

She held him close, shushed him like a mother would a restless child. "It's okay, Alec. I can listen. You just talk."

"It's like I have voices in my head sometimes. I can't..." Her brother tore his fingers through his hair. "I want to fit back in here so bad, but it's like I'm a different person. Hell, I don't even know what I'm going to do anymore."

Sienna kissed him as she pulled him near, let his head rest on her shoulder.

"You'll always be my brother, Alec. No matter what you've seen or done, you can tell me anything."

"Sienna?"

She looked up at Toby's call. He was already at the door with the kids and she was still loitering at the table.

"Coming."

Sienna walked fast in their direction, putting her memories where they should be—at the back of her mind. Not to be thought about anymore. Not if she wanted to move on from what had happened.

But if Toby wanted to talk to her how could she refuse him? Just because her brother had taken things into his own hands didn't mean Toby was going to. He needed to work through this stage, and hadn't she pledged to be there for him, to help no matter what? Wasn't that what Second Chance Ranch was all about?

Toby jumped into Sienna's truck and turned around to make sure Lochie had his seat belt on. He'd already put Holly into her car seat.

"Buckled up, bud?"

His son nodded. "Yup."

Toby had a chance to study Sienna as he turned around. He couldn't stop wondering about her. He had so many questions he wanted to put her way. But instead he sat and observed her, running his eyes over her face, her profile, her hair, her… Toby looked away.

There was no doubting she was beautiful. Smart. Courageous in her own way, in leaving a job behind to do something for others. He only wished he knew more, because from what she'd told him he doubted he'd even scratched the surface.

"Thanks for bringing me in today," he said, wanting to fill the silence with something. The kids were quiet, probably already nodding off to sleep in the back, and he hated that he'd been short with her a little too often. He didn't want to be rude, although for some reason he was doing it all the time. "I…ah…really appreciate all you're doing for us." He needed to stop telling her, but it was true. He still couldn't believe what she was doing for others.

Sienna took her eyes off the road for a split second. "I know."

Her sunny smile was back and he liked it.

Toby leaned deeper into the seat, enjoying being a passenger. Not having to worry about driving even if he did have plenty else on his mind.

Her sigh made him look up.

"You caught me by surprise earlier, but if there ever is anything you want to talk about I'm here for you. You were right about that."

"Thanks." He knew she wasn't finished yet, could see the worry of whatever was on her mind making her frown.

"It's just…" She paused, smiled, but in an awkward kind of way, not like usual. "I guess I understand more of what you've been through than you'd realize."

Toby prickled, imaginary spikes kicking up along his back, making the tiny hairs on his forearms rise. "Sienna, I don't think you realize what you're saying. I mean, I get that you might have been through some tough things, that you've lost someone you loved, but…" Did they *have* to have this conversation again?

Sienna kept her gaze fixed on the road, not breaking her concentration—or not visually anyway. "I know what happened to you, Toby. Well, enough of it, anyway." She glanced at him for a half second. "I know that you had an accident when your convoy came under attack in hostile territory, and I know that you lost your wife before your tour commenced."

Toby tried to contain his anger. He looked back, saw both of his kids were sound asleep.

"Just because you know a bit about what I've been through, it doesn't mean you can understand, Sienna. When

I said I might talk to you one day it wasn't because I thought you'd understand, it was because I knew you'd listen, would *empathize* on a certain level." His head was pounding, hard, like a grenade had fired nearby. "Please don't pretend that you can understand, because there is *nothing* in your world that could make you even comprehend what I've experienced."

Sienna stayed silent, looked like she was chewing on her lip.

"You'd be surprised what I'd understand, Toby, but if you want to pretend like you're all alone in your suffering, then that's your call to make."

Damn it! Now she was really getting under his skin.

"Okay, Sienna," he said, his voice cool. He didn't bother to try to make it warmer. "How about you tell me why you'd understand?" Hadn't they already had this discussion? Hadn't they already gone over this?

She moved her head slowly from side to side. "Another time, Toby," she told him. "I'm no longer in the mood to share, and there are some things I'd like to keep to myself."

Toby angled his body away from her and stared out the window. The world was passing by, disappearing as they drove farther toward her place. He liked it here, had no intention of leaving anytime soon, but he also had no intention of bringing up that particular subject again either.

Sienna was a good host. A *great* host. But that was all she was. She didn't mean anything more to him, and she sure as hell didn't understand what he'd been through or what had happened to him.

She couldn't and she never would.

No one would.

And that was just something he was going to have to live with.

Sienna was quietly fuming inside, but she wasn't going to let anger take her over. She'd made a decision a long time ago that she wasn't ever going to waste time feeling sorry for herself or getting riled up over things that had no place making her get all hot under the collar. And this was one of those situations.

Even if she did want to have a tantrum and scream and stomp her feet she wasn't going to. *No.* She was going to go for a ride on her horse, feel the wind against her face and smile up at the sky.

Sienna pulled on her jodhpurs, then a T-shirt over her head, and set off to find her boots.

"I'm leaving just as soon as I take the pie from the oven," Maisy called out to her but she wasn't even in a mood to chat with her housekeeper.

"I'm off for a ride. See you tomorrow."

Maisy knew better than to ask her what was wrong. Sienna held up a hand in a wave, glanced at Toby as he looked up from the paper he was reading, and walked out the door. She tugged on her riding boots and crossed the field.

By the time she was halfway to the horses she was smiling again.

No matter what the day brings, no matter how hard it is to smile and laugh, she had to be thankful for what she could do to help others.

It was her mantra, and she was sticking to it. Because if she didn't she knew how deep a person could fall into sadness and she didn't ever want to go there. Not again. Not personally and not on anyone else's behalf.

Because when her brother had taken his own life she'd had a choice to make: be a loner or a survivor. She'd chosen the latter.

Toby was starting to worry. What had begun as a slow niggle had become a persistent thud, and he wasn't liking it one bit. Not when he could be partially responsible for it.

He hated that they'd argued, but how else could the discussion have gone? She'd brought it up before, and he'd tried to explain then, but now he was starting to worry that he'd been too rude, that he should have just bitten his tongue. Because she was delicate and gentle, and the fact that he was responsible for wiping that never-fail smile from her face cut him up inside.

"Hey."

It was Matt. "Long day?" Toby asked.

"Yeah. You know, you should come to the site, see what you think."

"Do you need more hands on deck?" Toby had been thinking about the house project ever since he'd asked Sienna about it.

"You're kidding, right? We need all the help we can get!" Matt grinned as he flopped back into the chair. "It's hard work but it feels right, you know? Kind of like why I went into the army in the first place."

"I get it." And he did. Once Toby had grown up, joining the army had become less about glory and battle and more about wanting to do something positive. Fighting for his country and working hard to do something positive in another country, too. "Hey, Matt, can I ask you something?"

"Shoot."

"I don't know your story, or what you've been through, but has it helped talking about it to the shrink? I mean, I just don't think anyone can understand what's going on in our minds, what's happened to us."

Matt nodded like he understood. "I kept threatening to leave here when I arrived, refused to talk about things or even admit that I was having trouble adjusting," he confessed.

"So what happened?" Toby asked.

"Sienna happened."

Toby raised an eyebrow, tried to stay outwardly calm, but inside he was wild. He hated that another man was talking about Sienna like she meant something to him. Deep down he knew he had no claim on her. That nothing had even happened between them yet. At least nothing serious.

He didn't say anything back, waited Matt out.

"Sienna guided me, told me that she'd been through some pretty bad experiences and fallen into a dark place herself for a while, and I trusted her. Simple as that. *I trusted her,*" Matt said. "I don't know why, but it was like a switch had been flicked and I just talked to her and her friend the doctor until I had nothing left to say."

"Didn't you ever wonder how she could understand what you'd been through?" Toby had no idea if Matt had been through anything similar to him, but he knew that any soldier who was spending time here had been through a trauma of some sort.

"Honestly?" Matt shrugged. "Does it matter? She's been through something that she doesn't want to talk about, so who are we to question if her past is as bad as ours? If you don't let Sienna help you, then who the hell else will you open up to? If it wasn't for her, I don't know where I'd be right now."

Toby kept his body still, made himself think for a moment before doing something he might regret later.

A second passed and he still felt the same.

"Matt, I gotta go," Toby told him. "Thanks for the advice."

Matt grinned at him. "You're going looking for her, aren't you?"

Toby gave him a friendly slap on the shoulder as he passed. "I think I need to apologize now, before she gives up on me."

He didn't waste any time in rushing to the kitchen where his children were. Toby paused for only the briefest of seconds to look at Maisy playing with them. They were at the table making cards with glitter and bright colored pens. She'd been about to leave but the children had cajoled her into staying longer and he was glad. Otherwise he wouldn't have been able to go find Sienna. A tug inside of him told him he had to go fast, that she'd been gone too long, but he ignored it. He needed to find her, sure, but she didn't need protecting and she wasn't in trouble. Not every woman in his life was going to be stolen from him, needed his protection, but it wasn't a train of thought that came naturally to him anymore.

"Maisy, would you mind them while I go look for Sienna?"

The housekeeper glanced up, smiling like she was enjoying what they were doing as much as the kids were. "Sure. Everything okay?"

"Yeah, I just need to find Sienna. She's been out awhile."

"When she hacks out over the farm she's sometimes gone

for a few hours, so I wouldn't worry." Maisy paused, must have seen something on his face that made her want to help. "If you really want to find her, try the field that looks back down at the house."

Toby nodded at Maisy and strode out of the yard and toward the fields. He didn't care if he had to walk for miles, if it was dark by the time he found her. Sienna had tried to be there for him, and after everything else she'd done to make him feel welcome, to give him a chance, he needed to apologize to her right now. He'd been stupid and Matt was right. What did it matter if she hadn't been through exactly what he had? If she understood on at least some level then he needed to talk to her. Because he knew, deep down, that he'd never be given this opportunity to heal ever again.

Not to mention that he didn't need another black mark on his conscience.

He'd lost his wife and one of his soldier buddies, and it was eating him alive from the inside. *The memories, the failure of it all.* What he needed right now was to talk, no matter how much he'd been denying it, and the person he needed to talk to was Sienna.

Once he'd said sorry.

Toby covered the ground fast, not bothering to pace himself. He'd spent months staying fit, had stretched his muscles every day, and he'd started to feel cooped up lately. Even though his thighs had killed him after the ride yesterday.

Toby smiled, unable to stop it. The past few days might have been different than he was used to, but they'd been nice. Fun, even. Hanging out with his kids, being around Sienna… He had no idea why he'd been so hot and cold with her, but he needed to suck up his issues and say sorry before it was too late. And before she decided she didn't want to help him after all.

Toby was about to run through the gate that led up to the highest field when he spotted her. She was rubbing down her horse, her saddle resting on a railing. His heartbeat picked up slightly. Part of him had still been worried that something could have happened to her, so seeing her in one piece was enough to make him settle. Just a little.

As he neared he slowed, but he didn't take his eyes from her. She looked picture-perfect, with her hair in a braid so that it hung thick like a rope down her back. And she was talking.

He tried to tune out, didn't want to hear what she was saying to her horse. From what she'd said, Sienna liked to confess all her worries to her animals, which meant that whatever she was saying wasn't for his ears. And she'd been furious when he'd listened in on her on the phone the other day, so he wasn't taking any chances.

A loud bark rang out, startling him.

Bonnie. Toby bent into a crouch, waiting for the dog to trot over. She sniffed him then relaxed, obviously content that he posed no risk to her mistress. But now that Sienna knew he was there he had to figure out what to say. Fast.

"Nice ride?" he called out.

Sienna put down the brush that she'd been using. Her smile was more guarded than usual, but he liked that she didn't look angry. It told him he still had at least a chance at redemption after how rude he'd been to her in the car.

"There's something about being out here that helps clear the head. You should ride out with me and the kids tomorrow."

Before he could say yes, say anything else, he needed to

apologize. "Sienna, I'm sorry about before. I don't know why I was so hard on you and I should never have presumed that you wouldn't understand what I'm going through. What I've been through in the past."

She leaned on the railing, fixed him with a stare. Her expression was cool enough to make him want to step back. "How did you find out?"

What? He had no idea what she was talking about. "I just came to apologize, simple as that." What did she mean, *how did he find out?*

Sienna shook her head, not convinced. "Someone told you about Alec, didn't they?"

Toby wanted to stay still, to keep his feet fixed in place, but the compulsion to be close to her was stronger, the pull not one he wanted to resist. "Alec's your brother, right?"

Sienna turned away from him like she wasn't ready to face him, like there was something she had to keep hidden. She went back to brushing her horse, her hand moving in a constant and steady arc across the already gleaming horse-hair. "You really don't know?" Her voice was flat and she still wasn't looking at him.

"I never should have acted as if you haven't had your fair share of heartache, Sienna. It was immature of me to pretend like you'd had a perfect life. Whatever it is you want to keep secret about your brother is still secret. I have no idea what you're talking about and you don't have to tell me."

She stopped. Put her arms around the neck of her horse and hugged him like he was her best friend in the world. Sienna's cheek lay flat against the animal's neck; her eyes were half-shut.

"I've never told any of the soldiers staying here about Alec before. It's one of those things that I deal with better if I don't have to keep bringing it up. Guys like you? You've got enough on your mind without knowing about my past, too."

Toby bent toward her, arms crossed over the railing. Wanting to reach out to her. "What happened?" His voice was husky, sounded foreign to him. "He's away serving, right?"

Sienna shook her head, but she didn't manage to blink away the tears filling her eyes and sticking to her dark lashes.

"Sienna?" Toby didn't push away his feelings this time. He acted on what his heart told him was right. He closed the distance between them, jumping over the railing and putting his hands on Sienna's shoulders before pulling her away from her horse and drawing her in closer. She'd done so much for him already, and if he had to hold her while she cried then he was going to man up and do it. Stop over-thinking everything.

Sienna's body shuddered silently. Her fingers dug into his arms as she held on tight. And then almost as soon as they'd touched she was pulling away. She kept her eyes downcast, not looking at him, as she reached for her horse and unclipped him before opening the gate so he could join the other horses in the field.

"I found Alec on the farm," she told him, her eyes steady on a point in the distance. "He'd been gone awhile, and we always rode together when he was home. It was the first time we'd all been back here together, because I came home when Dad fell sick."

Toby stayed silent—except for the loud thudding of his heart as it seemed to echo in his ears.

"You lost both of them in a short time, didn't you?" he asked.

Sienna turned her beautiful big eyes up at him then, tears still glistening. "Alec had served nine months on his first deployment, and he hadn't coped well over there. I don't think it was anything like he'd expected it to be." She took a deep breath. "A week before he was due to ship out for his third term he took a gun and shot himself in the field. I found him lying there, and I felt guilty for a long time about not doing enough to help him."

Toby didn't know what to say.

"Less than a month later my dad lost his battle with cancer. So here I am, all on my own."

"Sienna, why did you feel guilty? What your brother did wasn't your fault." It wasn't fair for her to blame herself.

Sienna's mouth turned down, bottom lip wobbling. "Because I was the one person he truly confided in, and I didn't try hard enough to help him. If I'd made him talk to someone else, if I'd tried to do more... I don't know. Maybe it might have saved him."

"Oh, Sienna." Comforting Sienna suddenly seemed like the most natural thing in the world. Toby touched her back, ran his hand down to the base of her spine, then snaked his arm around her, drawing her in tight. He wanted to hold her so bad, to take away her pain, tell her over and over again how sorry he was for not listening when she'd been through easily as much as he had—just in a different way. "Some guys cope with what they have to do on tour, but some of us..." The words stuck in his throat, waiting there but so hard to release. "It's like you need to keep in it your head because you're scared that talking about it will make it seem real all over again."

Sienna burrowed her head into his shoulder, her body shaking. She was crying again and it hurt him. Pushed something within him that hadn't fired to life in as long as he could remember.

"He told me so much, Toby," she mumbled into his T-shirt. "He told me everything that had happened, every awful thing that haunted him, and he was so scared of going back. It makes me want to do everything I can to help other soldiers, so their wives or sisters or mothers don't have to go through what our little family did. It's why I want to help you."

Toby shut his eyes and held her even tighter. *So she did know exactly what it had been like for him over there. She might not know his story, how his tour had ended, but she knew what they went through when things went bad. Knew the brutal realities.*

"I love the army, Sienna, but I also know that every soldier is affected differently. For your brother..."

She rocked back in his arms, tear-filled eyes so big and innocent that she stole his breath away. "It's why I wanted you to talk to Charlotte so bad. I see Lochie and Holly and it breaks my heart to think that something could happen to you. Something that might seem different if you'd only talked to the right person."

Toby dropped a slow kiss to her forehead. His lips hovered. So hard to pull away when all he wanted was to tuck her up close to him again and keep her safe. But he needed to finish what he'd tried to say before.

"Just because your brother couldn't cope with his memories, with what he'd been through, doesn't mean you're going to lose anyone else or that I'm at risk of doing the same thing." He cupped her cheeks with his palms, forced eye contact. "I want to talk to you, Sienna, if you're okay with listening."

Sienna tilted her face slightly, away from his hands, but she was still looking up at him. Her skin was so soft beneath his hands, her breath warm as it touched his face.

"I can't help you, Toby. Not unless you want to be helped."

It was a whispered plea, like she was desperate for him to say that he was ready to be helped. And he was. It wasn't because he wanted to tell her what she needed to hear, it was because he *did* want her help, and he *did* want to move on with his life.

"I'll do anything you want me to do. Just please promise you won't cry again." He was hovering closer to her, drawn like a honeybee to the sweetest pollen-infused flower. He wanted to hold back, but he couldn't. He bent slightly, tucked one hand to her back to gently nudge her forward. "Sienna…" He exhaled her name, his pulse racing as his lips met hers.

She melted into him, mouth so soft, lips pillowy, and she kissed him back.

Then her hand shot between them so fast it took him by surprise, pushing him back enough so that their lips parted. He could have resisted, stood his ground, but her light touch told him she wanted to stop.

"Toby, I don't think this is a good idea." She didn't look up at him.

It might not be a good idea, but…

He swayed back on his feet, then changed his mind, pulling her against him, tugging her until she gave in, wrapping his arms around her and kissing the top of her head instead. Toby had no idea what he wanted from this, what their kiss meant, but he sure as hell knew that *not* kissing Sienna would have been a whole lot more unnatural than kissing her had been.

"You lost your wife." She said it as a statement, not a question, but she didn't push him away. Seemed content with her arms slung low around his hips, her head against his chest. For now, at least.

"Yes."

His wife was not something or someone he wanted to talk about. Not at this exact moment. Because when he thought about getting that close to another woman again, to someone like Sienna, the terror of it made his chest constrict. He couldn't lose another human being he loved again, and he sure couldn't stand to fail at protecting Sienna if he ever managed to let her in.

"I've lost too many people in my life, Toby, and I don't think I can go through that again."

He had no reply. He knew what that felt like on a different level, and in some ways he'd always thought the same thing. But Sienna…Sienna was doing something to him that he couldn't explain.

"I don't want to be your rebound girl, or someone you have fun with just because you're back from war. And I don't want to get close to you and then lose you, or have you walk away. I can't handle anything like that. Not now. It's too soon. I can't even imagine the pain of losing…" Her voice trailed off.

Toby sighed into her hair. He would tell her the truth if only he was sure what it was he wanted. His thoughts were a jumble. "I loved my wife, Sienna. I always will. I dealt with losing her as best I could, but I miss her like hell sometimes and wish she was here to parent my kids with me."

Sienna was starting to release him. He was losing her. What could he tell her that even started to make sense of what was happening between them when he didn't even know himself?

He needed to talk fast.

"You need to trust me when I say I'd never use you as some sort of *rebound,* but I'm not gonna lie to you, Sienna. I don't know where I'm heading, or what I want, but I do know that right now *I want you.*" He couldn't have laid his feelings on the line any better, been any more honest with her, but he could still sense she was about to flee. "I don't know what I have to offer you, because I can't deal with losing someone else either."

Sienna braved a look up at his face, like she was a shy schoolgirl, before standing on tiptoe and pressing a kiss to his cheek. "You're something special, Toby Freeman," she told him, squeezing his hand as she started to walk backward.

But...? Was there a *but* coming that he didn't want to hear?

She didn't say anything else. Left him standing there alone as she walked another few paces before opening a gate and letting herself back into the field with her horses.

He watched as she approached the pony first, bending down so she could scratch her, hitting just the right spot so that the pony nuzzled her hair in return for the attention.

Toby made himself look away, didn't let himself follow her—not when she obviously wanted to be left alone. He didn't know what had happened just now, or what it meant, but one thing was clear in his mind. He wanted to deal with what had happened to him, and he wanted to prove to her that she didn't have to fear losing anyone else in the same way.

Only he didn't know what that meant for him—what he

might have to offer her if it came to that. Just because he wanted to show her that he wasn't at risk of taking his own life, it didn't mean he could deal with the reality of opening himself up to losing her.

Toby turned to the house and took his time walking back. He had a lot of figuring out to do, and that started now.

CHAPTER ELEVEN

SIENNA trooped back to the house as the sun came down. She couldn't avoid going back any longer or else she was in danger of someone being sent out to find her. And she didn't want that someone to be Toby.

No way. Not a chance.

She slipped her boots off and went to wash her hands. Sienna could hear happy children's voices and it made her smile. They were the most delightful of kids, and she already knew she'd miss them once they left. No matter how hard she'd tried to keep a slight distance from them, to tell herself they were only here for a short time.

"Sienna, Sienna!" Lochie came racing in, skidding on the timber floor. "Daddy said you were out riding."

She bent to touch a kiss to his warm cheek. "I just needed to go for a ride on my own today, honey." Sienna had no idea if he'd understand that or not, but she didn't know what else to say to him.

"Daddy said it was so you could have some thinking time."

Hmm. "Then your daddy is very clever." Sienna ruffled his hair and followed him as he ran into the kitchen ahead of her.

"Sienna's home!" he announced.

She'd hoped there would be at least one of the other ex-soldiers present, that it wouldn't just be Toby, but she could feel his presence in the room as soon as she walked in.

Toby looked up, eyes flashing, and heat hit her the moment she saw him. All she wanted was *not* to think about the kiss, and right now it was all she could think about. Especially with him looking at her like that.

"Please don't tell me you've been waiting on me." The kids must be starving.

"No, we ate already, but Daddy said he was going to have dinner with you," Lochie announced.

Didn't kids just say the darnedest things?

"Oh." Sienna put her hands behind her back. They were trembling and she didn't want Toby to see. She had a gut feeling that he'd be the kind of guy to notice everything—he could probably tell that her heart was nearly jumping out of her chest.

"Early bedtime or a DVD?"

Sienna listened to both children groan at the start of Toby's question and then watched as they leaped up and down by the end.

"DVD—please a DVD!" squealed Lochie.

Holly raced off after him, giggling, like she wasn't entirely sure what the fuss was about but didn't want to miss out.

"Sugar overload while I was gone?" Sienna couldn't help but laugh as the children leaped onto the sofa in the other room, eager to do anything other than consent to an early bedtime.

Toby chuckled, but there was more burning in his gaze than just humor and she knew it.

She waited for him to follow the kids, to sort out what they were going to watch, before hotfooting it to the kitchen.

She pulled out a glass and spun around, before hovering back to the cupboard again and reaching for another. Sienna forced her hand to stop shaking and located a chilled bottle of Chardonnay in the fridge. She poured herself a half-glass, looked at it for a moment, then indulged in a long, slow sip.

Delicious. And exactly what she needed. To relax, for her confidence and to fight whatever the heck it was she was thinking and feeling about the man in her living room.

Sienna took another sip for luck, then one more. She hardly ever drank, just the odd glass with dinner or out with friends, but tonight it was the perfect remedy.

"Maisy left dinner for us." Toby's voice was like a billowy breeze touching her skin, making the tiny hairs on the back of her neck rise into prickles.

"She always leaves something good," Sienna mumbled, cradling her glass.

She didn't have the nerve to nudge Toby's glass closer, but she did nod to it before taking another sip from her own. Sienna was starting to get hot; the back of her neck was clammy. It had nothing to do with her ride or being outside all afternoon, either, no matter how much she wished it did.

"This for me?" Toby asked.

Sienna nodded again. She didn't seem capable of much else. What she wanted was to walk away and head upstairs, take something to eat with her and retire to her bedroom for the rest of the evening. *But she couldn't.* Toby was keeping her captive, making her stay put even though she wanted to run.

"You want to eat now?" She didn't know what else to say, or why she didn't just walk away.

"Suits me just fine," he replied.

Sienna fidgeted on the spot, unnerved by the way he was

looking at her, the way he was standing so tall and strong, so close to her in her own kitchen.

"I was going to go upstairs and change before dinner, but if you don't mind me in my riding clothes..."

The slight movement of Toby's head told her no. "I've been thinking about our cooking lessons."

She blinked twice, three times, and then met his gaze, her cheeks like an inferno was blasting within them. Damn him, bringing up something like that when she was all jittery.

"Cooking lessons?" she repeated.

Her plan had been to avoid him all night. To have dinner with all her houseguests or on her own and then retire for the evening early, so she didn't have to spend any time alone with Toby.

Not *this*. Not being so close to the man who was the reason she was jingling up and down faster than she could keep track of.

Toby crossed the distance between them, coming too close to her for comfort.

Sienna held her breath, squeezed the stem of her wine glass so hard that it was in danger of shattering in her hand. But Toby didn't touch her. He didn't kiss the breath from her like he'd done outside, didn't try to do anything except take his glass and raise it toward hers in a toast.

"To new beginnings," he said, voice low, like she was the only person in the world he wanted to hear his words. "I hope you can accept my apology for the way I treated you earlier today. I'm so sorry about your brother, Sienna, I truly am."

"Apology accepted," she replied, but her voice faltered as she touched her glass to his.

Toby watched her and suddenly she couldn't take her

eyes off his mouth, couldn't stop thinking about how good it was having his warm body close to hers, his hot breath against her...

No.

She jumped back, then sidestepped, tripping over her feet in her haste to escape.

"I'm sorry." Sienna apologized but she wasn't about to stop. She didn't want him talking her into staying because she needed time alone, away from his influence. Not that she even knew how he felt, but she didn't want to hang around and find out.

"What about dinner?" Toby's face crumpled, his wine glass forgotten as he forced it down onto the counter.

"I'm not hungry, Toby. I'm sorry."

Sienna was still carrying her glass but she didn't care. She didn't look in on the children as she passed them, didn't check to see the front door was locked, *nothing*. No matter how hard her tummy rumbled, or how bad she wanted to stay with him, she was staying upstairs. A long soak in the bath, some late-night television, and then sleep.

Toby was off-limits because he was a guest. Because he was a dad with beautiful children she didn't want to get too close to. Because he wasn't ready for a relationship or anything else right now.

And because if she let herself fall for him she could lose him, too. And losing a man she'd let herself fall in love with? That would be a pain far worse than she'd already experienced—on another level to what she'd been through. She couldn't put herself in a position of getting close to those little children, of being part of a family again, and then having them snatched away from her either.

"I'm here for you, Alec. Dad and I will always be here for you."

Her brother nodded. Sienna looked over his head and watched her father as he listened, not moving, not interrupting.

Sienna brushed away tears with the back of her hand, blinked furiously until she was in her bedroom. She hadn't known at the time it would be the last conversation she would ever have with her brother, and she couldn't stand to be in that position with Toby. Not ever.

She'd tried to be brave. She'd tried so damn hard. All these months she'd held it together, and one guest, *one man who'd suddenly entered her life,* had made it all come crashing back.

Tears flooded her eyes then, left her helpless as she pressed her back to the door and slowly sank to the floor, slumped. Sienna cried hard—cried like she hadn't since the last funeral she'd attended. Since she'd said goodbye to her dad.

The last time they'd all been together was when her brother had promised that everything was going to be okay. Then he'd killed himself, and her dad had died soon after.

Sienna had already lost everyone she'd truly, deeply loved, and she wasn't prepared to put herself through that again. Not for a long time and maybe not ever.

CHAPTER TWELVE

Toby woke with a fire in his belly that had been missing for longer than he could remember. His body was tingling, muscles desperate to be stretched, ready to do something. *For real.*

The house was silent, the only noise the low hum of snoring that he heard as he crept from his room and into the hall. He carried his running shoes, not wanting to be any louder than he had to until he was outside.

What he needed was a quick run to limber up, then breakfast before the kids woke and he had to help them with what they needed. Once Maisy arrived he would ask her nicely to look after them for a few hours, then he was going to make his way down to the building site. Even if he had to walk all the way there he was going to work on the project, help them do something for others. Make good his offer to Matt of giving the builders a hand.

Because one good turn deserved another, and after what Sienna had done for him and his own he wanted to do something for someone else, for no reason other than because *he could*. And he wanted to prove to Sienna how important her work was.

Toby laced up his shoes, stretched, then set a steady pace. He could feel it in his lungs, enjoyed the constant rhythm as he settled into a nice run. When he'd been deployed, exercising had been a huge part of what he did each and every day. Some days he'd been carrying a pack more than a third of his body weight, trudging for hour after hour on limited food and water. Here it was a luxury run, something he was doing just for him, and it was helping him to relax.

Sienna was the reason he was here, the reason he was able to parent his children while trying to figure out what the hell he was going to do with his life. Sienna had given him a chance. It was time he did something for her in return.

She'd been through hell herself, was like a frightened animal cowering from a heavy-handed master when he'd tried to get close to her. When he'd wanted so badly to kiss her again. But what Toby had here was an opportunity to prove to himself and to her that he was going to be okay. That she didn't have to be frightened of every troubled soldier doing something as traumatic as her brother had.

But what he couldn't help her with was her fear of loss. Because he felt it, too, as strongly as she did, so much so that it almost crippled him at times. He was terrified of experiencing what he'd been through again.

Right now, working on the housing project in town seemed like the right thing to do, and maybe, just maybe, it would help him to figure out what the heck he was going to do with the rest of his life. Besides being a dad.

Sienna crept down the stairs and prayed that Toby would be outside. She couldn't face seeing him, not after she'd bailed on him last night, but she also couldn't stay hidden any longer. Her stomach was growling like a wild beast from hunger, and she could smell something delicious wafting up from the kitchen.

Please let it just be Maisy.

Sienna peeked around the door, behaving like a stranger in her own home.

"Looking for someone in particular?"

Maisy made her jump. "Not fair!" she complained.

Her housekeeper was standing with her hands on her hips, clearly trying hard not to erupt into laughter. "It looks to me like you're hiding from someone, creeping around like that."

"Shh," Sienna hissed, nodding her head in the kids' direction. "I'm just... I don't know."

Maisy laughed and turned back to the stove. "I've just dished up a little something for the children. You've missed Toby and Matt, in case you were wondering." Maisy did a half turn, one eyebrow raised in question. "Owen went into town already. Said he was seeing Charlotte for his appointment today."

Sienna sighed and reached for a plate, holding it out for Maisy. She didn't usually eat a cooked breakfast, but this morning was going to have to be an exception. "Load it up, I'm starved." She had a heap of stuff to do today, and she needed to be recharged. Her other guests needed more time than she'd been giving them, too.

Maisy piled her plate high with mini-sausages, bacon, homemade hash browns and a couple of eggs. "Enough?"

"Mmm-hmm," Sienna murmured.

The children looked up as she approached them, full of smiles. They had colouring pencils and paper flooding the table, food long forgotten about.

"Your dad left you here today?" She had no idea where he would have gone with Matt. Not that it was any of her business.

"Yeah," said Lochie, tongue protruding slightly from between his lips as he concentrated on his drawing. "He said Maisy would look after us because he had to do some work."

Work, huh? She crunched a half piece of toast that Maisy had popped on her plate and thought about what he could be doing. What did she have on his spreadsheet that he might be up to?

Ah. "Did he go in to do work with Matt?"

She watched as Holly nodded.

Sienna ate most of her breakfast in silence, listening to Maisy bustle about the kitchen and hum under her breath as she cleaned things, watching the children as they kept themselves busy with their creations.

"You two want to spend some time with the horses today? Go riding again?" The words had hardly left her mouth before a wet nose pressed against her arm, nudging her insistently. Lochie was practically wriggling out of his seat, and Holly looked pretty excited, too. "Yes, you can come, too, Bonnie," Sienna told her dog, slipping her a piece of bacon under the table.

"Hey, Sienna."

She wiped her greasy fingers on a napkin and focused on Lochie.

"This is for you," he said, smile shy as he passed her the drawing.

Sienna could make out most of it: people, and what she guessed was a dog. Not a bad effort for an almost-six-year-old.

"Who is this?" she asked, pointing at the littlest figure.

"Oh, that's Holly." Lochie almost climbed on the table to lean over and point the people out to her. "And this is me, then you and Dad, and that's Bonnie."

Suddenly the toast in Sienna's mouth seemed overdry,

sticking to her throat as she tried to swallow it. "Um, it's great, Lochie. A really good drawing."

He shrugged like it was nothing special. "I wanted to draw our family, that's all."

Oh, wow. His family, but with her in it.

Sienna looked over her shoulder to see if Maisy was listening, but she was busy doing something else. Lochie was still watching her. Even Holly had looked up. Sienna didn't know what to say, but she needed to say *something*.

She wasn't part of their family and it wasn't a possibility. She was a friend, like a temporary aunty to them, but how the hell did you tell *that* to a kid his age? She sure couldn't explain to them the rapid beat of her heart and the way her entire body seemed to seize up at the thought. Having them here had been special, and she'd tried so hard not to get attached. Not to think too much about how nice it was to have a family back in her home.

"Who wants to go riding?" she asked instead, her voice full of a fake happiness that she hoped convinced them.

Lochie leaped up from the table and almost landed on Bonnie, which set her off in a series of excited barks, but Holly looked frightened, not moving from her chair.

Sienna went to her. "You okay, sweetheart?"

Holly nodded, but her eyes were big and round like saucers.

"Come here." Sienna scooped her up and popped her on her hip, even though she was way too tall to be carried like that for long.

Holly tucked her head in close, like she was tired, snuggling in.

"I love you, Sienna," she said, looping her arms around

her as far as they would go. "I love you to the moon and back."

Sienna's heart actually stuttered. It was hard to swallow again, or even to put one foot in front of the other. What was it with these kids this morning?

"I…ah…I love you, too," she told the little girl in her arms.

And it was true. She *was* falling in love with these delightful little children. But it wasn't healthy, wasn't realistic for her to feel this way about them.

She didn't want to get close to anyone, and she knew for a fact that once Toby was ready to move on he'd go back to his old life, away from here, *without her*. A holiday romance with him would only break her heart, and she wasn't ready for that.

Because her heart had only just started to repair. The stitches holding it together were only just starting to take. And she doubted she'd survive loss on any level again.

Especially not the loss of Toby if he came to mean any more to her than he already did.

Sienna hadn't spent time with Toby in days, besides the odd *hello* and polite chat over dinner with the others, and it was slowly starting to eat at her. She was irritable and she hated it. Especially when she was trying to focus on the new soldier who'd just arrived the day before.

It was different having children here, even if it was a nice kind of different. She had things to organize and plenty to do to keep her busy, so the last thing she needed to do was worry about Toby. Not his whereabouts or what he was doing.

A knock echoed out on the door to her office. Sienna

kept typing, needing to finish the letter she was writing before glancing up.

Oh.

She hadn't expected it to be Toby. Not when she'd thought he'd already left for the day.

"Busy?" His question hung in the air as she stared at him.

"I'm…ah…working on a proposal for additional funding." She couldn't think of anything else to say to him but the plain truth of what she was doing. Not with him suddenly in front of her like that.

Toby was dressed in jeans that needed a wash and a dark T-shirt, boots on his feet. He looked like he'd just finished a day of hard work, even though it was only… Her eyes flicked to the clock on the wall. Eleven o'clock in the morning.

"The guys say you're trying to get the go-ahead for another housing project." Toby walked in and sat himself down on the chair opposite her desk.

Sienna tried to smooth her hair down casually, wishing she'd taken more time with her appearance. If she'd known she'd be seeing Toby… *Enough!* He was a guest in her home and that was all. Talking to him was fine. She needed to catch up with him and what he was doing anyway—enter it into her logbook.

"Matt mentioned that you've been working on the house?" She wasn't coherent enough to talk about what she was doing. Asking him about what he'd been keeping himself busy doing seemed far more logical.

"Yeah, helping out as best I can." Toby shrugged. "Turns out I'm not that bad with a hammer or a paintbrush." His wry smile made her laugh.

"You've been down there working every day?" She

should have known what he'd been up to, but she hadn't wanted to hunt him down and ask.

His eyes were piercing as he locked them on her. "If you hadn't been avoiding me so much I would have told you."

Sienna fought the heat rising up her neck, didn't want him to see that he'd hit a sore point. "I've been busy, that's all, but I'm pleased to hear you've been there."

"I saw Dr. Aitken, too."

"Uh-huh." Sienna felt like she was treading water and only just keeping her head up.

"Sienna, look at me." His words were firm, commanding.

She pushed some papers around, stalling, but Toby didn't seem to be in a mood to be ignored. He wasn't the troubled soldier so much as the commanding officer right now.

He leaned forward. "Why did you want me here today?"

Sienna raised an eyebrow. "I have no idea what you're talking about. I never asked you to come here."

His fingers touched over her business card holder before he raised it to take a better look. "I had a message from one of the guys that you wanted me here. So here I am."

"I think someone's joking with you." Sienna wasn't sure what was going on—if he was teasing her, even—but it was weird.

Toby watched her like he was trying to figure out the situation as much as she was. Maybe he was doubting her, too.

"Oh, well. The carpet's going down today, and all the finishing touches, so there's nothing for me to do in town anyway." His eyes never left hers: dark brown, with the finest of gold flecks dancing in their depths.

Sienna stayed still for a moment longer, waiting for him to say something else, but when he didn't she rose and headed for the kitchen. "Maisy?" she called. Maybe *she'd* phoned for Toby?

"You don't think it was something to do with the kids, do you? Maisy could have…"

His voice trailed off as Sienna stopped and he almost crashed straight into her.

"Oh." Toby found his voice before Sienna did.

A basket sat beside the counter, clearly waiting to be discovered. Sienna plucked the note that was pinned to the top of it, holding it up so they could both read it.

I've taken the kids out for the day, so you two go off and enjoy yourselves.
M

Sienna nudged the lid open. Her heart was beating overtime, and she wasn't sure about turning around to see the expression on Toby's face. The food smelled delicious, whatever it was in there all wrapped up for them, but she dropped the lid back down quickly, her stomach suddenly churning.

"I think we've been had."

Toby's low voice made Sienna shut her eyes for a second, before turning to him with a smile. She didn't want him to know how rattled she was.

"I guess we're going on a picnic, then, huh?"

Toby grinned, shrugging at the same time. "Why not? I'd say we deserve a day off, wouldn't you?"

Sienna wasn't going to argue with that—but an entire day on her own with Toby? That was the part she wasn't so sure about. Not that she could do anything other than say yes.

"Okay. Just give me a few minutes first."

Toby nodded. "I need to take a shower and call Mom to see how she is today. I'll be back down soon."

Sienna stared and watched him go, tried to stop the quiver in her lips, the excitement building in her belly like birds playing in the breeze. She wanted to ask him how his mom was doing, but she couldn't find the words.

A day with Toby? She should have said no. But...

No buts.

Sienna went back to her office and saved what she'd been working on, shut her computer down and padded out into the hall. She still had bare feet, was only dressed in her jeans, with a sweater over her tank top to keep her warm. She needed to freshen up and get changed into something nicer.

Because if it felt like a date and sounded like a date she was betting it was one. Despite the fact they'd been set up.

She wanted to look good even if she was going to have to let Toby down gently if he had any ideas about something happening between them. Because it had been way too long since she'd been on a date, before she'd moved back into the house, and there was no way she was going to look anything other than pretty on a day like today. For a picnic out in the fresh air under the sun.

Sienna shut the door to her bathroom, rummaged through her makeup and set to work.

CHAPTER THIRTEEN

TOBY had to fight not to walk closer to her, but he knew his boundaries. Or what the boundaries should be. Sticking to them was the hard part, even if he did have a plan in mind.

Sienna wandered along beside him, looking as bright as the first flower to emerge after a harsh winter. *Pretty* would be an understatement, but it was a word that kept repeating in his mind. Her dress was summery, showing off bare, tanned shoulders and enough leg to make him smile. Maybe Maisy had been right. They would enjoy a day in one another's company.

"I've been talking to your friend Charlotte quite a bit," he admitted, needing her to know, not sure if she'd really absorbed it in her office earlier.

"Oh, okay."

He couldn't tell whether she looked alarmed or happy. "You were right. I needed to talk to someone and it turns out she was the right person after all."

Sienna paused, stopped walking for a second, then started again. Like she'd thought better of stopping for even a moment. "The other day, when we talked about Alec—"

Toby jumped in to interrupt, wanting to speak first. "You don't have to say anything," he said firmly. "When I told you that I only wanted to talk to you I was being selfish. It was unfair to want to burden you, especially after what you've been through." He smiled. "Another thing I have to apologize for."

Sienna smiled, but he missed the brightness that usually ignited her face. "I'm here because I want to listen, Toby, and I'll do my best. But something about you reminded me of my brother, and it terrified me."

He didn't know what to say in reply.

"And it still does." This time her voice was barely a whisper.

"I don't know what he went through, Sienna. Maybe one day you'll want to tell me, but right now all I know is what I went through, and it was…"

"Hell?" she suggested.

Toby moved closer to her and bumped his shoulder against hers, needing to be close to her no matter how much he knew he should be keeping his distance. "Hell and then some," he told her, fighting the urge to keep his thoughts to himself. Dr. Aitken had told him that he needed to open up to the people around him he could trust, and this was him doing his best. "I lost a friend and a fellow marine on the last mission I was assigned to. We were only a couple of weeks off coming home, and I don't know how I survived the blast when our Humvee was hit, but I did. And I'm so glad that I made it. At the time, maybe not. But now I feel like I've been given a second chance."

Sienna's face was hard to read, but he tried.

"That must have been hard," she said, "losing someone like that over there."

"Yeah, it was, but I don't need to tell you any more about it than that." He stopped, touched her shoulder, his hand resting there. "I'm not going to burden you, Sienna, and I'm not going anywhere, okay? You don't have to worry about losing me, and you also don't need to take on all my problems as your own. Whatever you're worried about, you don't need to be."

She looked skittish, like a foal on spindly new legs, but he didn't rush her. Stayed still, gave her the chance to push him away.

She didn't.

"Shall we have the picnic here?" Her voice was strained.

"Yeah, why not?"

Toby took a step back and set the basket down, stretching out a rug for her to sit on.

Sienna wiped at the sides of her mouth with a napkin. She was relaxed. Even though her heart started to race erratically every time Toby looked at her, she was starting to enjoy herself.

"It's nice doing nothing for a few hours," she mused out loud. "I seem to spend so much time in my office now, on the phone or organizing things, that I hardly even ride as much as I'd like to anymore."

Toby took her paper plate and paired it with his, before tucking them into a plastic bag and putting them away in the basket. He cleared the leftover food, too.

"It's nice just to sit and think, huh?"

She didn't know if she wanted to know what Toby was thinking about. Not when he looked at her like that—like she could possibly be on the dessert menu, eyes all hungry and...tempting. *Argh.* Her imagination had clearly been fuelled by an afternoon off, not focused on work.

But she kept going back in her mind to what he'd said before, about not needing to talk to her, and there was one thing—one event—he'd never mentioned since soon after he'd arrived, and she needed to know more. Because she had a feeling there was something or someone on his mind more than he'd probably like to admit.

"Do you want to talk about her?" She didn't have to say his wife's name for him to know what she meant.

Toby's response was raspy. "No." The air between them changed, tension firing.

"Because it's not something you need to talk about, or—"

He didn't let her finish. "Because I'm okay with not talking about it."

His voice was gentle this time, relaxed, and she believed him.

"I've…I don't know…come to terms with what happened as best I possibly ever will."

Sienna leaned into his touch when he reached for her like it was the most natural thing in the world, sighing in a way that sounded more like a cat purring. *So she'd asked*.

"What *do* you want to talk about, then?" Her voice was lazy, but she felt anything *but* lazy. Being this close to Toby was… There were no words to describe it. Even talking about his wife, or bringing the subject up, couldn't stop her from thinking about Toby as the strong, determined, handsome-as-hell man that he was. Couldn't stamp out the electricity surging between them.

Widower or not, she couldn't fight it any longer. If he made a move she'd be powerless to push him away. His hand against her was enough to make her melt, and the wall she'd so carefully built around herself was crumbling away.

"I don't want to talk about anything," Toby told her, cupping his hand beneath her chin, telling her with his hold that he wouldn't take no for an answer. That he wanted her to look up and into his eyes whether she wanted to or not. "I want…" He took a deep breath and blew it out slowly.

Sienna was captivated, like a bug caught in a web, unable to move, almost unable to breathe.

"You." The end of his sentence was a whisper, the smallest movement of his mouth producing a word more powerful than any other he'd ever spoken to her.

Sienna didn't have time to hesitate, to think about what was going to happen or where they were or what it would mean. His lips were brutal, rough, desperate. Not soft and gentle, as in their first hesitant kiss, but so insistent it was like he'd been waiting a lifetime to take ownership of her mouth.

She responded the only way she knew how. *Because she'd been dreaming of his hands on her for nights now.* Wishing that he'd make a move, that something would happen so she could get him out of her system. That she would have the guts to stop avoiding him.

But now that she'd had a taste of him the last thing she was going to do was let him go. Couldn't even imagine that they wouldn't be doing this again and again and again.

"Toby," she whispered, her lips skimming his ear before she carefully nipped at his earlobe, tugging ever so softly at his skin.

He growled low, like a big angry cat. "Do that again and you'll regret it."

Sienna giggled and bit down harder, not scared of what he might have planned for her. They hardly knew each other, and yet she felt closer to him right now than she had to any other person in as long as she could remember. *If ever.*

"That's it."

Toby tugged her deep into his body, yanked against his

hard chest. He kissed her with even more ferocity than before, dipping her before throwing her over his shoulder, hoisting her up so she was powerless to do anything other than comply.

"Toby, stop!" she squealed. "Let me down!"

"Quiet."

His growl was even lower this time. If she didn't trust him so much she might be scared. But him taking charge like this wasn't something she was going to protest to too much. *She didn't want him to stop.*

"Where are you taking me?" she demanded, thumping on his back as she wriggled and squirmed, loving every minute of being held by him even if she *was* bobbing up and down over his shoulder. "Your angry soldier routine doesn't scare me."

"Oh, but it should," he joked, giving her a slap on the backside before stopping abruptly and putting her on her feet. Playtime over. He swung her into his arms instead and Sienna slipped her arms around his neck, snuggling in close. He whispered, lips to her hair, his gaze suddenly serious, "Because I might never let you go."

Toby's words were tender now, holding so much meaning that she didn't know what to say back. How to respond. They'd somehow descended from awkward to playful and then relaxed. Something changed forever between them as they stood and stared back at one another.

"Are you sure you want to do this?" he asked, eyes staring straight ahead, like he was scared to look at her again in case she changed her mind.

She tugged at his hand and made him. Sienna had all of a sudden never been more sure of anything in her life, no matter what it was they might be about to do. "Thank you, Toby."

Toby's eyes locked on hers, full of so much *hope* that it hurt just watching him back. "For what?"

"For making me feel like everything's going to be okay. That I don't have to carry the weight of everyone else's problems on my shoulders. *For this.*"

"I thought you were the one supposed to be helping me while I'm here?"

Sienna snuggled closer as they crossed the distance to the barn. She played her fingers along the buttons of his shirt, teasing a few open, stroking her fingertips against the firm, taut skin of his chest. She'd refused her feelings for days, made herself believe that nothing could happen and that she wouldn't want it to anyway. But now... Toby was like a miracle cure that she was helpless to refuse. Powerless to pull away from.

"Watch it," he warned, his voice primal again, all tenderness gone.

Sienna walked her fingers higher, reaching up to plant featherlight kisses along the line of his jaw. "Or what?"

Toby's laugh vibrated against her, tickled through her entire body. "Believe me, this is one time you don't want me to be honest about what I'm thinking."

Sienna kept her mouth shut. The grass was wet and she'd much prefer to be carried like a princess to the barn. But so long as Toby had his arms wrapped around her she couldn't have cared less where they were.

Or how they'd gotten there.

CHAPTER FOURTEEN

TOBY swallowed what seemed to be a rock in his throat. His mouth was dry, his body somehow surging, like electricity was running through it.

He tipped Sienna back gently onto the hay. Bales were stacked all around them. She looked as unsure as he felt. Not unsure about wanting her, but about what they were doing, how it was going to change things. *Whether or not he was ready.* How he'd taken what felt like a massive step forward.

She'd asked him before about his wife, and suddenly the need to say something about it, about *her*, was a raw need begging to be released. It was like his thoughts were in order—like he knew what needed to be said and why he wanted to tell her things that he'd never wanted to share before.

He stroked her sun-kissed golden-blonde hair when she tipped her head closer to him, eyes shut, a smile playing contentedly across her face, like she was waiting for his touch, anticipating his next kiss.

Toby cleared his throat, hoped that talking to her wouldn't push her away. Because as much as he just wanted to be a regular guy, there were parts of him that made him anything but *regular*.

"She was the love of my life, Sienna."

He watched as her eyes opened and turned stormy-sad,

like a raincloud had taken over their usually bright hue. "I understand."

Toby moved his head slowly, side to side, not wanting her to think he'd changed his mind. "No, Sienna, I don't think you do."

She raised her eyebrows.

"She was the love of my life, Sienna. But you..." He was struggling with what he was trying to say. "I want this, too." He blinked away the tears in his eyes, not wanting to be distracted from anything other than Sienna and the feelings he wished he was better at expressing.

Toby didn't cry. He might have slipped once, but he had no intention of doing it again.

"But, Toby..." she protested.

"No buts." He reached for her hand, held it up to his lips and turned it, kissed the inside of her wrist while he watched her. "Let's just enjoy this. *Please.* No overthinking."

She looked like she was going to burst into tears, even as the corners of her mouth kicked into the beginnings of a smile. "You still love her, don't you?"

Sienna's words flooded his mind, made him hope she wasn't going to be upset when he told her what he had to say. *The truth.*

"I will always love her, Sienna. My children remind me of her every day and I'll never forget her. Not ever." Toby cradled her face in his hands. "But it doesn't mean that I can't love again. I..."

Sienna was hard to read. Her expression a mixture of so many emotions that he didn't know where to begin. But he needed to tell her now—wanted to tell her before their relationship changed forever.

"Sienna, I didn't mean for this to happen but I don't regret it, okay? I will *never* regret this or anything else that involves you."

"I'd never try to take your wife's place, Toby." She tilted her face up to his, her blue eyes twinkling as tears glistened in them. "*Never.* I need you to know that."

He pushed her sweater, nudged it off her shoulder. "I don't want to talk anymore, Sienna." His hand scooped around her bottom, pushing her hard against him.

Sienna didn't say anything back, but her body betrayed what she was thinking even if her words couldn't. She stood on tiptoe, tucking even deeper into him, kissing his neck, tracing her lips across his skin and closer to his mouth.

Toby moaned. "Sienna…"

"You don't like it?"

Her whispered question made his head start spinning, desire taking over his body. "If you don't stop that…"

"What?" She paused, lips hovering over his skin. "You'll do what to me, Toby?"

This time he wasn't prepared to play games. This time he didn't give her a second warning, or ask her if she was sure. This time Toby took command, eyes locked on hers as he walked her backward, against another hay bale. Because this was what they both needed—less talk and more action.

He lay her back, watched the way her long blonde hair fanned out around her, before nudging her knees apart and lowering himself carefully down over her.

Sienna laughed, the noise sending ripples through his body that only made him want her more.

"This is kind of prickly, Toby," she told him, still laughing.

"Tough," he said, lowering himself down even farther to press a possessive hot kiss to her mouth. "If you weren't so lippy I might have carried you to your bedroom—but then I do recall you liking the idea of the barn."

Toby pinned her when she started to wriggle, his kisses trickling farther down, lower, lips grazing her breasts.

If this wasn't love he had no idea what was.

If only he could admit it to Sienna.

Sienna toyed with the edge of Toby's shirt, nervous, not sure of herself. It wasn't like she had *no* experience, but it had been a long time since she'd been with a man intimately. *A very long time.*

"Are you scared?"

His whispered question made her hands shake. Sienna shook her head. *Not scared, terrified.*

She willed her fingers to obey, easing first one button then another through the buttonholes.

"Too slow," he told her, taking his hands from her body for a moment to raise the shirt above his head and discard it.

Sienna couldn't take her eyes from him. Toby was all muscle stretched under gloriously tanned skin. His arms were golden and chiseled, stomach taut. *Wow.* It almost made her want to cover herself, the upper half that he'd laid bare. *Oh.* At least she wanted to until his hands were back on her skin.

Toby's fingers moved lightly, so lightly, across her shoulders, tapering down to tease the skin around her breasts.

"Toby…" She couldn't remove his name from her lips.

He ignored her plea, covering her mouth with his instead of talking. His tongue was gentle yet probing, making her stomach flip and her toes curl as his hands skimmed lower, thumbs edging her dress farther down her hips.

"Let me love you, Sienna," Toby whispered, the tip of

his tongue wet against the curve of her ear. "I promise I'll be gentle."

Sienna let her eyelids flutter until they shut, lost in the delicious world of Toby and nothing else. She was too involved now to tell him no, beyond thinking of all the reasons why they shouldn't do this.

His hands and mouth left her body and Sienna's eyes flew open, alert. *No, please don't stop.* She'd never be confident enough to say it out loud to him, but…

Oh, my. He was taking off his jeans like he was a man on a mission. And as he grinned at her, like a panther about to devour its prey, she couldn't help but grin back, even though she was terrified, too.

Screw sensible.

Toby lowered himself over her again, his mouth taking possession of hers as she raised her arms to capture his shoulders.

CHAPTER FIFTEEN

SIENNA refused the urge to look over her shoulder at Toby wrestling his son to the ground. They'd wandered back to find the kids in the yard playing, and they'd all leaped around and played ball for a while.

She felt *naughty*. After what they'd done in the barn… Siena smiled to herself, fingers playing with a strand of hair as she walked inside. What she needed right now was a few minutes alone, to process what had happened. So much for planning on refusing Toby. For thinking she'd have any control over her feelings when it came to… She blushed at the thought of what they'd done. If her entire body could flush with embarrassment she'd be head-to-toe pink.

Toby was all man. Big, strong, caring, and well on his way to being healed.

Sienna sped up when she heard the phone ringing. She skidded on the timber floor and grabbed the cordless.

"Hello?" she gasped, out of breath from her quick sprint.

"Sienna?"

"Speaking," she replied, wondering who the older female voice belonged to.

"Hello, dear, it's Ally here—Toby's mom."

Oh, of course. "Hi, Ally. How are you doing?" Sienna smiled down the line at his mom. She'd warmed to her straight away when she'd met her. "We've all been thinking about you often."

"Well, it seems I'm doing okay. The operation was successful and the treatment didn't need to be as aggressive as they once thought. I'll be able to go home in about a week, so I thought I'd better give Toby an update since I missed his call this morning."

Was he planning on leaving as soon as his mom left hospital? A thick shiver ran through Sienna's body. Surely not… But then why not? His mom had looked after the children before, and he was doing well here. By all accounts he'd be ready to go soon.

Sienna gulped.

"Is…ah…Toby going to be joining you as soon as you're home?" Sienna asked the question as casually as she could, even though it tore at her inside.

Ally laughed. "Well, I don't know if I'll be up to looking after those children for a while yet, but if he's still desperate to get back home then I guess the answer is yes." She paused. "Tell me, dear, how's he been getting on? I never know if he just tells me what he thinks I want to hear."

Sienna didn't want to talk anymore. She wanted to run upstairs and be sick. Physically, gut-wrenchingly sick. "He's…ah…Toby's doing great, and I'm sure he can't wait to see you," she told her. "How about I go get him for you? Hold the line a sec, okay?"

She didn't wait to hear Toby's mom reply. Sienna put the phone against her stomach, squared her shoulders and called out through an open window to him.

"Toby!" Sienna watched as he looked up, tried to ignore the way his face lit up when he saw her standing there. "Your mom's on the phone."

He dropped the ball he was playing with and touched his son's head as he passed. She met him at the door, passing him the phone.

"Hey, beautiful," he whispered, brushing a kiss to her lips before placing the phone to his ear.

Sienna couldn't move. She stayed still, shutting out how she felt, wishing he hadn't kissed her again. Her fingers touched her mouth before she could stop them, before she had a chance to force Toby out of her head.

She'd wanted to protect herself, not to put herself in a position to lose someone she cared about. She hadn't wanted to get close to anyone.

Well, she hadn't. Toby hadn't made her any promises and she hadn't asked for any. Just because *she'd* presumed what they'd done this afternoon, how they felt about each other, meant something deeper, it didn't mean he did, too.

Him leaving soon, taking the children with him and out of her life, would be easier now than later down the track.

So why did she feel like her heart had been ripped out and she'd already lost someone she loved?

Sienna refused to watch Toby and the kids any longer. Didn't want to hear what he arranged or what he was talking about. Instead she headed upstairs for a shower and a change of clothes. She had work to do, things to organize, and the longer she let herself brood and think, the worse she'd feel.

"Sienna?" She noticed Holly standing in the kitchen, watching her wide-eyed.

"Are you okay? Your dad's on the phone to your grandma." Sienna mustered up a smile for the young girl.

Holly nodded, but she didn't move.

"I'm just going upstairs for a moment. Will you be all right here?"

Holly smiled at her before walking back outside.

Sienna needed to bury herself in her work, just like she always did. She had a press release to send out before the end of the day, for the opening of the charity house, and they were meeting the family ready to move in there tomorrow to walk them through the almost-finished home. They were expecting a media crew from Houston who'd shown an interest in the project from the beginning to meet them there, so it wasn't like she didn't have things to occupy her time.

Toby.

Toby was who she wanted to occupy her time with, was the reason her heart kept beating like an overactive windup toy. Toby and his perfect, beautiful, mesmerizing children.

But Toby was just a guest. No matter what they'd done, how she felt about him, or the kind words he'd said to her, he had a life, too. And that life didn't include her, so she was going to have to lump it.

End of story.

"Sienna!"

Toby's yell made her leap off her bed. So much for a quick catnap.

"Sienna!"

She jumped up and pushed her hair off her face. "Toby?" He sounded panicked.

The door to her room flew open. "Sienna, have you seen Holly? I've looked everywhere for her and…"

Sienna reached for Toby, trying to calm him with her touch. "Tell me when you last saw her. Where have you looked?"

"I haven't seen her since I was on the phone with my mom. I didn't realize she was missing and I've looked everywhere. Absolutely everywhere. I was keeping an eye on them but…"

Sienna couldn't stop seeing Holly's wide-eyed expression earlier in the kitchen. "Have you checked the stables?"

Toby's eyes locked on hers for less than a second before he spun and ran out of her bedroom, taking the stairs two at a time. She went after him but couldn't keep up. The man was on a mission, panicked about his little girl, and she didn't have a hope in hell of catching him.

"Toby! Toby, stop!" Sienna called loudly, trying to close the distance between them. "Toby!

The powerful run became a jog before he slowed and turned, running backward now. "I can't lose her, Sienna. I can't lose anyone else I love. Not ever again." His face was crumpled, his eyes full of unshed tears. "I can't lose my little girl."

Sienna started to run again as soon as he did. Holly could be anywhere. There were plenty of places she could hide. But the stables were the most likely.

"Let me go in, Toby. I think you need to catch your breath," she called.

Toby ducked through the railings and into the corral, and Sienna did the same.

He paused for a moment, but it was time enough for her to go through the door first.

"Holly? Honey, are you in here?"

Sienna waited, listening, and then she heard it. A gentle sob that almost made her gasp.

"Holly? Come out, sweetheart."

Holly crept out slowly from between two saddle racks, unfolding her body and squeezing out of her hiding place.

She was crying, tears streaming down her cheeks from swollen red eyes.

"Sweetheart, what are you doing down here? Your daddy was so worried about you." Sienna pulled Holly into her arms and cradled her.

"Holly?" Toby's deep voice boomed in the small space. "Holly!"

Sienna slowly let go of the little girl as Toby moved toward them, letting him scoop her up, holding her so tight it was a wonder she could breathe.

"Don't you ever do that again, you hear me?" Toby's tone was angry but he didn't let go of her. "I can't lose you, Holly, I can't deal with that. Not now and not ever."

Sienna reached out for him, put her hand on Toby's arm. "Don't scold her, Toby, she's scared."

"Scared? What the hell…?" He stopped when he realized that Holly was sobbing in his arms, crying so hard it sent goose pimples up and down Sienna's arms.

Sienna glared at him. "Holly, tell us what's wrong. Your dad's not angry. He's just been very worried." She shot him a look that told him not to disagree. "You can tell us, Holly."

"I don't—" she broke into sobbing hiccups "—want to go."

Sienna took a step backward, then forced herself to stop. Holly didn't need *her* flipping out, too.

"Miss Grandma," she sobbed, before burying her face into her dad's chest, "but don't want to leave Sienna."

So she'd overhead some of the conversation earlier when they were on the phone. *That made two of them heartbroken.*

"I'm going to head back, Toby. Let you talk to Holly."

The look he cast her pleaded with her to stay, but this wasn't something she wanted to hear. She didn't want to be a part of it.

Toby held his daughter with a ferocity that scared him. He forced himself to ease his grip on her small body and sank to the ground, holding her up until he could drop her into his lap. She sat between his legs, still hiccupping.

"I'm sorry," he told her, pulling her back so he could cradle her. "I was so worried something bad had happened to you."

Holly nodded. Her bottom lip was caught between her teeth when she looked back at him.

"I loved your mommy very much, Holly, and I'm scared of losing anyone else ever again. Do you understand? You're so special to me. Just like Mommy was."

Holly snuggled into him. "Why are we losing Sienna?"

Toby shut his eyes. If only he knew the answer to *that* question.

"We're not losing Sienna. I promise."

She seemed happy with his answer, or maybe she was just tired. But Toby wasn't happy. Not about being scared as hell earlier when he couldn't find his daughter, not about how upset Holly was at the idea of leaving, nor about how panicked he was feeling about walking away from Sienna.

He'd been so scared of opening himself up to loss again, to that kind of hurt, and he hadn't even realized that while he was pretending like he knew what he was doing he'd opened himself up to exactly that.

Toby kissed the back of Holly's head when she lay back against his chest.

What he needed to do was make a decision, and fast. He

either walked away now and nursed what was starting to feel like an almost broken heart, or risked staying here and the possibility of it shattering completely.

CHAPTER SIXTEEN

SIENNA willed her face to comply as she forced a cheery smile. This project was hugely important to her; it shouldn't have been hard to act happy and excited, but she couldn't wipe the feeling that a stormy rain cloud had been following her around all morning.

She'd avoided Toby and the kids for the rest of yesterday evening, busying herself outside and later in her office, but she couldn't stop thinking about them. About how she'd miss Holly easily as much as the little girl would miss her, and her dad…

She was missing him already. She wished she wasn't awash with double standards in her mind, but pushing him away and refusing to think about him wasn't proving to be as easy as she'd hoped it would be. It was the only option, but knowing that didn't make it any easier.

He was as scared of loss as she was, still loved his wife and was struggling with his past. Besides, it wasn't like he'd made a commitment to her. He hadn't asked her if he could stay, hadn't even had the decency to tell her that he would be leaving soon to move back home.

"Sienna?"

Someone was calling her.

She forced the bright smile again and walked out the door, emerging out onto the porch.

"You ready?"

Sienna nodded. The new family was still walking around inside, so excited they could barely contain themselves, but she hadn't wanted them to be pressured into too much press coverage. Just because they were thrilled with their new home it didn't mean they weren't struggling with the fact that there would be no man in the house. Aside from the massive portrait of the soldier they'd lost hanging in the hall, the man himself would never be stepping through that door to see his family.

"Do you want me right here?" Sienna asked, trying her hardest to focus.

"Yep. Just start talking, and if you mess up pause, then start over again," the cameraman told her. The reporter joined her on the porch and they both leaned against the railing like they'd practised earlier. "We'll edit it later."

"So, Sienna, tell us why this project is so special to you?" the reporter asked.

She didn't have to prepare—could speak straight from the heart on this subject—and she wanted to tell the truth. No hiding from her past any longer. "It's special to me because my brother was a United States marine and I lost him last year. I'm proud of the men and women who put their lives on the line to protect and serve our country, but I'm also very aware of the families left behind in some situations."

Phew, she'd done it. Hadn't faltered, had managed to speak nice and slow, just like she'd planned to.

"So this is a very personal charity for you?" the reported clarified, obviously wanting more information from her.

"It's…" Sienna stuttered, forgot what she'd been about to say. There had been a small crowd gathered before, and some of the guys working on the house had filtered out to listen and watch what was going on, but there was only one person who could make her falter. Make her struggle to breathe when before she'd been so composed.

Lochie was standing beside him, and Holly was in his arms.

Toby.

"Sienna?"

She couldn't take her eyes off Toby and his little family. Not even when the reporter said her name. *Damn him!* What she needed was not to see him, because she needed to push the silly fantasies she'd been indulging in from her mind, and to do that she needed him to disappear—for a little while at least.

"I'm sorry," she apologized, clearing her throat. "What I meant to say was that I have a personal reason to support a project such as this. I hope this will be the first of many homes we can provide within the wider community, for families in need who've lost a loved family member who hasn't made it home from war. Wives without husbands, husbands without wives, children without one of their parents."

Sienna excused herself as soon as she could and went back inside the house. She didn't want to face Toby—not right now, not *here*. She would wait for him to leave before she went outside again. She didn't know what they'd even say to one another—whether he'd pretend like nothing had changed between them.

"Sienna." His voice was unmistakable, and so was the warmth of his grip when his fingers closed around her forearm.

So much for hiding until he left. But, no matter how tumultuous she felt inside, she had no choice other than to face him.

"Hi, Toby." She braved up to him, turning and managing to dislodge his hand from her arm at the same time. "You here to see the house all finished?"

He stared at her like he was studying her face for an answer to a question. "Yeah, the house and you."

She turned her back, wishing he hadn't said that.

"What's wrong?" he asked, frown lines etched across his forehead.

"Me? Nothing." Sienna smiled at him. *He'd been expecting bubbly Sienna, and she was trying to distance herself as much as possible. Was powerless to pretend like everything was okay.*

"Don't give me that." Toby looked annoyed.

"Give you what?"

"Your fake smile. I've observed you long enough to know exactly when you turn on the fake charm." Toby crossed his arms across his chest like he meant business.

"I have no idea what you're talking about. I…"

Toby raised an eyebrow at her.

"Toby…" Sienna sighed. What could she even say to him without sounding all pathetic?

"I shouldn't have snapped at Holly yesterday. You were right."

Sienna stood still and Toby's eyes never left hers.

"Tell me what's wrong, Sienna."

She could hear voices, knew they wouldn't be alone for much longer. "We can't do this, Toby."

There went the creased forehead and the confused expression again. "By *this* you mean talk right now? Or are you referring to something else?" Toby asked her.

Sienna shut her eyes for a second and inhaled deeply. "There can be no *us,* Toby. That's what I'm trying to say.

I'm sorry. What we did yesterday was great, don't get me wrong, but we both know this can't go anywhere."

"I think you're wrong." Toby stroked her cheek with the back of one finger. "I've tried my hardest to fight this, Sienna, but when even my children love you it makes it hard to pretend like this doesn't mean something."

"I have to go." Sienna spun, his words echoing through her head. She couldn't deal with this. She wasn't going to let this turn into—

"Like hell you do." His voice was deep and dark, menacing.

Sienna took a step backward, not liking where this was going. "Toby, please. I—"

"No," he commanded. "I will not let you pretend like nothing happened between us yesterday when we both know that it was more than two people filling some sort of need. It meant something and I won't let you say that it didn't."

Toby's words were low, hushed, only for her ears, and it made them even harsher.

"Don't make out like I'm imagining something here, Sienna, because I'm not. I'm as scared as you are—but you know what? I'm gonna have to deal with it, and that means you have to, too."

Sienna didn't want to have this conversation. She went to stalk off again, to leave him standing on his own—because what could she say? How could she even start to explain herself?

How could she tell him how much she already loved him and his little family when it scared her so much just to admit it to herself?

"Don't you walk away from me," Toby ordered, before grabbing her arm again.

"Or what?" she demanded, glaring at him like she wanted him to burst into flames. "What the hell do you want from me, Toby?"

He shook his head, slowly, and her knees knocked, her legs like jelly.

"This," he hissed, before pushing her hard against the wall and possessing her mouth like a man who'd never take no for an answer, one arm pinning her and the other slammed into the wall above her head.

Sienna wanted to fight him, *tried* but failed miserably. Her lips parted for him and her body softened as his hands smoothed across her skin, skimmed her hips.

"Does *this* mean something, Sienna?" Toby whispered into her ear as he pressed decadent kisses there. "Can you feel *this?*"

Sienna refused to make a noise, furious that her body continued to defy her.

"Or this?" His mouth was hot against hers again.

Still she refused to answer. *What if someone walked in on them?*

"What is it you're scared of, Sienna?" he asked, his face so close, his nose touching hers as he stared into her eyes.

She gulped, swallowed over and over again. "Losing you," she murmured. "I'm scared of losing you, Toby. Okay?"

Toby pushed back and left a step of distance between them, one hand brushing back and forth over his cropped hair. "You don't think *I'm* scared of losing again?"

Sienna bit down on her lip, suddenly feeling tearful. "I can't go through losing someone again, Toby."

"What makes you think you're going to lose me? Why are you afraid of that?" he asked, his eyes flickering as he

stayed focused on her. "Don't you know how hard I'm struggling with that, too?"

"I know that you're leaving soon, that what we have is
just for now, and that's not something I'm interested in.
I'm sorry." Sienna brushed her cheek with the back of her
hand, quickly wiping away the tears that were gathering
and slipping down.

"I haven't decided what I'm doing, Sienna, but I came
down here today to—"

What? "I spoke to your mom, Toby. I know you'll be
back there soon, and I don't blame you." Sienna tried to
stop herself but she couldn't. The words were falling from
her mouth faster than she could think them. "I don't want
to get attached, Toby, because it'll only be harder in a week,
or a month, or whenever you go, so we need to pretend like
none of this ever happened."

"Are you finished?" he asked, a wry smile kicking up
the corners of his mouth.

Sienna stared back at him without answering. What was
so amusing?

Toby took her hand, holding it up and kissing her palm
before turning it back over. "I came here today to tell you
that…" He paused, pulling her in tighter to him. "That I
love you, and so do the kids."

"No." *He loved her?* She snatched her hand back and
held it up to stop him.

*Even if he did stay, even if she did let something happen
between them, would she ever stop worrying about losing
him? Would she ever be able to push away her fears? Because losing him, losing those children…that was something
she'd never recover from.*

"You don't think I'm scared, Sienna?" Toby was touching

her again, his torso less than an inch from hers. "You don't think it scares the hell out of me to even *think* about letting someone in again? To risk losing someone else that I care about." He paused, one finger tracing her cheek. *"Someone that I love."*

"Don't say that, Toby. Please don't." She wasn't strong enough to keep pushing him away. She wanted so badly to protect herself from hurt again, to keep herself from harm's reach, but she was starting to falter, to stumble.

Would it be so bad to let him in? To give herself a chance at the family of her own that she'd always dreamed of? To tell him that she loved him back?

Toby reached for both of her hands then, clasped them to his chest and tugged her closer. "I can say it because I mean it."

His voice was gruff, like he was as embarrassed about admitting his feelings as she was about accepting them.

"I love you, Sienna. Okay? I goddamn *love* you."

Sienna wanted to pull away, but her body wouldn't let her. Instead she let him draw her in, let her head fall to his chest and listened to the steady beat of his heart. It lulled her, calmed her, when before her own heart had been racing overtime.

"Do you love me back?" he asked, lips against her hair.

Sienna held him tighter, not yet ready to say the words but feeling them deep in her chest. She nodded, so he could feel it, and held on to his waist like she'd never let go.

She didn't move, let his words sink in, let the reality of what he'd told her sink in, too.

"I'm going to take the kids back to the ranch now, and I want you to think, okay?" he said. "Take all the time you need." Toby inched away, dropping a kiss to her forehead first, and then a slow, lingering one to her lips. "Just don't forget that I'm as scared as you. I'm scared, but I'm not prepared to walk away. Uness you tell me to."

Sienna stood and watched him go, missing the sound of his heart and the warmth of his embrace. She tracked his body as it moved away, his frame filling the hallway, his stride taking him away from her so fast.

"Sienna? Are you in here?"

She composed herself, smoothed her hair down in case it was out of place. It must be someone else wanting an interview or information.

"Just a minute!" she called back.

Toby had given her a choice, had opened himself up to her, and she needed to make a decision. Put her faith in the man she wanted so desperately to love, or hide away in her own little world instead of risking loss. Which would be cowardly, considering how brave he was being.

It sounded like a simple decision, she knew that, but the shaking of her hands told her it was anything *but* simple.

CHAPTER SEVENTEEN

SIENNA reached out to Holly and tucked her hair gently behind her ear, stroking her cheek as she pulled her hand away. She looked so sweet, so innocent sitting there, petting Bonnie like she was her most favorite thing in the world. She'd just arrived home and found Holly first, before seeing Toby, and she was pleased to have a moment just with the child.

"Holly, I need to ask you something."

Sienna waited for the little girl to look up. When she did she patted her knee, happy when Holly shuffled closer to sit on her. She started to loosely braid her hair for something to do.

"Holly, I really like your dad." She wasn't quite sure how to tackle this, what to say, but she needed to talk to her. Needed to tell her at least some of what was going on. "Do you mind if I spend time with you all? With your family?"

She needed to have a conversation with Lochie, too. He might be harder to impress, but right now it was just her and Holly, and the timing seemed right.

"Are you going to be my mommy?"

Sienna's heart thudded to her toes and somehow crawled its way back up to her chest. Holly could never understand how much she'd love to have a family, how much she'd like that to be true, but right now she didn't know *exactly* what was going to happen between her and Toby.

She loved him, she did, and it was stupid to keep pretending otherwise. If she hadn't been in love with him she never would have let this happen, and she knew he felt the same. But she wasn't going to walk away from what she'd built here either, what she'd worked so hard to achieve, and Toby had to prioritize his kids. They already had a home and he needed to take them back there. If not now, then sometime soon.

"Holly, your mom was a very special woman, and one day your dad will be able to tell you all about her." Sienna looked down and could see she'd said the wrong thing. Holly was too young to understand that kind of conversation. Kids this age expected straight up and down answers.

"So you won't be my mommy?"

"Holly—"

"Do you *want* Sienna to be your mommy?" Toby's deep, silky voice seemed to float straight through Sienna's body.

She turned, watched as he edged closer. His T-shirt showed off the brutal muscles that she knew he'd worked hard to get, but his eyes were softer now than they'd been when he first arrived. Lochie stood at his side, a little mini-me replica of his dad, just without the brawn.

"Toby, I don't think this is the right time to—"

He interrupted her again, stood in front of her with Lochie still at his side and dropped to his knees.

Sienna took the hands he held out to her, let them fall to her lap as he knelt in front of her. *Please don't tell me he's about to...*

"Sienna, I have two beautiful children who love you so much they almost burst with happiness every time you walk toward them." Toby was looking at her with such intensity that she couldn't look away, no matter how uncomfortable she was with the children listening. "You'd make the most amazing mom to them, if that's something you want."

She was forced to disconnect from him. She needed to look at Lochie and then at Holly, to see the smiles on their faces. *Toby was right.* She knew the children were fond of her, and she adored them straight back. She had loved her home being filled with their laughter and chatter, liked having them alongside her when she was out with her horses, loved tucking them into bed and feeling their warm breath against her skin when they kissed her good-night.

"I don't think we should be having this conversation here," she told him in a low voice.

Toby leaned back and pulled his two children against him, his arms around their tiny bodies making them seem even smaller beside his big frame.

"*Marry me, Sienna.* I want you to be my wife, and a mom to my children."

Sienna couldn't stop the tears as they ran down her cheeks. "But where will we live? What would we…?" All her fears poured from her mouth.

Toby laughed. He *laughed* at her! "We'll stay here, if you'll have us. Hell, I don't care. So long as we're with you we'll be happy—won't we, kids? We'll make it work. Even if I have to buy Grandma a house in town to keep her close by."

Lochie was nodding, his little face earnest, cheeks pink. Holly just looked confused.

"So you *will* be my mommy?" Holly asked, her voice so innocent it made tears spring into Sienna's eyes again.

She stared at Toby, saw the honesty within him as he held his children, waiting for her answer.

"We've only known each other a couple of weeks, Toby. Are you sure?"

"More sure than I've ever been." His smile met his eyes, showed her how honest his intentions were. "Let's take a chance, Sienna. This is one of those times that you just have to trust yourself, trust the way you feel. We both have to forget about what we've lost and give ourselves a chance."

She took a big breath, her body shuddering as she slowly released it. *It was now or never, and she didn't know how she'd live with herself if she said no.*

"Yes," she whispered, reaching out to Holly, even though it stole her hand away from Toby's. "Yes, Holly, I'll be your mommy—and Lochie's, too. If he'll have me."

She avoided Toby's gaze to see Lochie's reaction, loved that he was too shy to say anything when he was usually so full of chatter. He bumped shoulders with his dad, beside him on his knees, and wriggled like he didn't know how to react. But his smile gave away his happiness.

"So you'll marry me?" Toby asked, his eyes wide, hands shaking as he reached for hers.

"Yes!" She giggled the word, verging on hysterical. "Yes, Toby, I'll marry you."

EPILOGUE

SIENNA lay slightly on her side, her legs tucked up to make the position more comfortable. Toby was lying behind her, his body nestled into hers, resting on one arm so he could look over top of her. She tried hard not to shut her eyes. The sensation of his fingers gliding up and down her arm was close to making her fall into slumber.

"He's pretty kind to her, isn't he?" Toby said, kissing her earlobe.

Sienna looked at Lochie, watching him push his sister in the swing Toby had built for them, hanging from the massive tree in the yard. Lochie had just given up the swing to give Holly a turn.

"For a big brother, I'd say he's exceptional."

Toby's hand slid from her arm and moved to her belly, tracing circles in a tickling motion through the fabric of her T-shirt.

"That feels incredible." Her stomach was still neat, but it was sticking out enough to make her less than comfortable—except when Toby lavished attention on her like this. This was when she loved the extra weight she was carrying.

"What are we going to name her?" he asked.

"Isn't it bad luck to name a baby before she's born?" Sienna teased.

Toby laughed, the noise coming easily to him now. She

could hardly even remember the man he'd been that first day he'd arrived, because now he was so relaxed, so happy and easygoing, that she couldn't recall him ever not being like it. Come to think of it, she could hardly remember herself back then either.

"Michelle," Sienna blurted, finally brave enough to tell him what she'd been thinking ever since they'd found out she was pregnant with a little girl.

Toby's fingers stopped circling her belly, hovered for a moment before he let his open palm fall against it instead. "Michelle?" he asked.

"It doesn't have to be her first name. We could use it as her middle name, if you like. But I want to do something to remember her by."

Sienna tried to roll over and ended up half turned instead, but she was still able to look into her husband's eyes and see the smile on his face.

"I'd like that."

"Me, too," she said, tucking back into him and watching the kids again.

Toby had been so brave, even though she knew he was scared as hell of her having a child after the way he'd lost his first wife. She was so proud of him it hurt. But what they were going through felt so right—carrying a child that was so loved and wanted.

"Do you want to go riding after lunch?"

Toby tapped her on the stomach. *"No."*

Sienna laughed, resting her head on the grass as she sprawled out. "The doctor said I was fine to ride until twenty-eight weeks, Toby. Don't go getting all bossy on me, because I still have one week to go."

He growled, a low noise deep in his throat as he pinned her to the ground. "Are you *ever* going to obey me?"

Toby kissed her, didn't let her up until she gave in to him.

"I surrender," she squealed, halfheartedly trying to push him away. "But I'll never obey you."

"Hands off Mommy!"

Lochie burst onto the scene to rescue her, pushing his dad as hard as he could. Holly came flying in behind him, leaping on her dad to help her brother out.

Sienna rolled out of the way, laughing as she sat and watched them.

It was what she'd dreamed of her whole life and in the end had been so scared of giving in to. She let her hand flutter to her belly, as it always seemed to these days, like she needed to comfort the baby growing inside of her and tell her how loved she was.

She had a family again and she loved it.

"Mommy! Mommy! Come help!" Holly screamed.

Sienna crawled closer and grabbed Holly's hand, pretending to rescue her. Toby grinned and gave her a wink, making her heart thud to her toes at the unsaid words between them.

I love you, she mouthed, watching as he wrestled with Lochie.

His lips moved for her eyes only. *I love you, too.*

* * * * *

The Seven-Day Target

NATALIE CHARLES

Natalie Charles is a practising attorney whose day-job writing is more effective for insomnia than most sleeping pills. This may explain why her after-hours writing involves the incomparable combination of romance and suspense—the literary equivalent of chocolate and peanut butter. The happy sufferer of a life-long addiction to mystery novels, Natalie has, sadly, yet to out-sleuth a detective. She lives in New England with a husband who makes her believe in Happily Ever After and a daughter who makes her believe in miracles.

You can contact Natalie by visiting her blog at www.natalie charles.net.

Dear Reader,

I entered Mills & Boon's 2011 New Voices Competition armed with a first chapter and only the vaguest outline of a novel. I knew how the book would start, and I knew how it would end, but the middle? That was a little fuzzier. But as I uploaded that first chapter, reeling with a mixture of terror and optimism, I vowed that no matter the outcome of the competition, I would finish this book.

There was something about Nick and Libby's story that hooked me from the beginning. They are idealists navigating a dangerous and cynical world, trying to understand where they fit. Writing about them made me realise that I love romantic suspense because it reminds us that we can choose to be loving, selfless and brave in the face of our greatest fears. If we happen to fall in love—or back in love—with someone equally heroic along the way, well…I can't think of anything better than that. I hope you enjoy your time with Nick and Libby as much as I did.

This book was the winner of the 2011 New Voices Competition (yes, I still have to pinch myself when I say that!). Being named the winner and knowing that readers voted to see more of Nick and Libby humbles me to no end. This book is for all of you who supported me through this amazing journey, and for my fellow contestants, whose criticism and talent challenged me to be better.

With love and gratitude,

Natalie

For Ryan

You are my rock.

PROLOGUE

"I KNEW you would come."

The old man settled his shoulders against the arched back of his chair and folded his hands in his lap. Nick thought he detected a self-satisfied grin, but the room was dark except for the glow of the fireplace and the flames were fading. "You asked me to come, Judge Andrews," Nick said.

"And you listened." The logs shifted, sending a shower of sparking embers. "I like that about you."

Nick turned his eyes to the glass of whiskey in his hand, observing a frantic shimmer of light through the amber liquid. He'd noted the physical changes in the judge immediately. The bloodless gray pallor, the skin roped across the sharp angles of his skeleton. His once jet-black hair now lay thin and specter-white against the pink scalp. Yet those ice-blue eyes—the same ones his daughter had inherited—were still brimming with a sharp intelligence. She'd inherited that, as well. "Thank you, sir."

"Nick, you know me well enough to know that I have little patience for niceties," the judge said as he held a hand against the warmth of the flames. "That patience has all but disappeared in recent weeks, so I trust you'll forgive me if I cut right to the chase." He gazed steadily at the fire. "I have pancreatic cancer. I've been given weeks to live, months if I'm lucky."

"I'm very sorry to hear that, sir."

The judge avoided Nick's gaze. "Well, what can you do?"

The old man shrugged stoically, but Nick noticed a new pain behind the familiar gesture.

Nick took a sip of the whiskey, feeling the slight burn on his tongue. "How...how is Libby handling this news?"

"As well as can be expected, I suppose." The corner of his eye twitched. "These days she doesn't give herself time to handle much of anything—she's always working. Libby still thinks she can use the legal profession to save the world."

Nick's blood grew warmer at the thought of Libby. She was a prosecutor who took each of her cases to heart, tirelessly preparing for trial in the belief that if both sides performed to the best of their abilities the truth would prevail. As if she could bring order to chaos if only she worked hard enough. "If anyone can save the world, she can."

The judge pressed his lips into a slight frown. "Elizabeth is idealistic," he said. "It's an impractical quality that life will rid her of soon enough." He was quiet for a moment. "I need a favor from you."

"Sir?"

"Libby's in danger." He reached into his robe and removed a stack of letters bound by a rubber band. "These letters contain threats against her life. I have every reason to believe they are credible, and whoever wrote them promises to harm her after my death. I need to know that she will be safe."

Nick leaned forward to accept the letters and then opened the top envelope. He frowned. The prose was almost nonsensical, jumping from political ramblings about justice to a clear threat against the judge's daughter. "I can pull some strings within the Bureau, see if any of my colleagues can take a look at this."

The judge was perfectly still. "I don't want the FBI involved in this matter."

"The local police, then?"

"I don't trust the police. Besides, there are some parts of the past that are best left buried, and I don't want them digging around." He leaned forward. "I called you. I want you to resolve this alone."

Nick's stomach tightened and his mind began to race. He'd spent his time since their breakup trying to avoid thoughts of Libby. She'd played too large a role in his life for far too long, and he'd finally reached a point where he was able to break free from their shared history. To imagine his future without her. Nothing good could come out of seeing her again. "I don't think that's a good idea."

"Why? Because you and Libby were engaged?" The judge's gaze was level. Icy. "Come on, Nick. You know how to handle these things. You investigate violent crimes for the FBI."

"I'm on my way out of violent crime. I'll be training for public corruption."

The judge arched an eyebrow. "Running away, Nick?"

The words resounded like the slap of a glove.

Tension began to build in Nick's chest. "People change," he said. "My interest lies elsewhere. Besides, you want me to investigate a crime without the benefit of Bureau resources? How am I supposed to build a case?"

Judge Andrews's thin lips split into the suggestion of a smile. "I'd prefer that you take matters into your own hands and leave the justice system out of it. Call it self-defense, right place, right time." The judge shifted in his chair. "Since when have you cared about rules? The Nick Foster I remember always believed that the ends justified the means." His eyes grew dark. "You've always been a man after my own heart."

Nick returned his stony gaze. "I could get fired for this."

He shrugged. "Is that a problem?"

The judge's face was steely. Impenetrable. This was the Judge Andrews that emerged behind closed doors, out of view of the public eye. The cold, calculating politician who always got his way. The tyrant who'd made Nick's life hell when he was dating his daughter. "You're asking me to stick my neck out for a woman who hates my guts," Nick said in a low voice. "You want my services? It's going to cost you."

The judge didn't flinch. "I thought it might. What's your price?"

Nick ran a hand along the stubble on his cheek as he considered. "You would need to cover my expenses," he said slowly. "And let's just say that if I'm working on your dime I won't be looking to cut my costs. I would plan to hire some assistants."

The judge's gaze narrowed. "Of course," he murmured, his voice dangerously close to a growl. "I'm a fair man. You have three days to present me with a reasonable cost estimate for your...services."

"I didn't promise to make it reasonable."

The judge raised his chin slightly, as if the response had clipped him on the jaw. "Name your price, then."

Nick's shoulders knotted as he recalled the many times he'd felt those eyes sear into him, heard that mouth issue a cutting remark. To the judge, Nick had been just some kid from a working-class family—a harmless distraction that Libby would one day tire of. How many bitter nights since their breakup had that prediction festered in Nick's mind, coaxing him to the brink of rage? He'd never been good enough for the judge's precious daughter, and the judge had never missed an opportunity to remind him of that. But now...now the judge needed him. Now Nick had the upper hand.

He clenched his fist. "You want me to save your daughter's life?" he snarled. "Then I want this house. And I want your savings. I want your car, and your stocks and bonds." Nick squared his jaw and leaned forward. "I want everything you have, sir."

In the quiet dark of that March evening a harvest moon illuminated a field as expansive and frostbitten as the silence that settled between the two men. Nick glared at the judge, whose face was controlled except for a pulsing in his temple—an indication of barely suppressed rage. Nick's viscera trembled against the force of his own hatred.

"Fine," the judge finally whispered, the word escaping through a clenched jaw. "But only if you abide by my conditions."

CHAPTER ONE

Day One

THE envelope was addressed simply "To Libby Andrews," and the note inside was brief: *Are you still alive?* Libby stared at those words as she stood in her driveway, reading by moonlight. She would know the handwriting anywhere.

Nick.

Libby's mouth tensed into a line. So Nick was up to his old tricks again, was he? This was a game they'd played as children. He would leave her notes in improbable places—places she'd least expect to find them: her coat pocket, the inside cover of her algebra textbook, underneath her lunch tray. That had been the intrigue of it—that Libby had never known where the notes were going to appear, or what innocuous and often silly message they were going to relay.

Gianni's Pizza—best slice ever. You'll thank me. Or, *Did you see Mr. Diamond's moustache? He must be a nark.*

As the years had gone on, Nick had developed his own code for the notes. *Are you still alive?* meant that he wanted to come over. A light on her front porch meant he was welcome.

Libby balled the note in her fist. She hadn't seen Nick in over a year—not since the argument that had ended their engagement. Every now and then she saw his mother at the grocery store and she told Libby that Nick was doing well. She never offered more detail, but in a way that was all Libby wanted to know.

Libby walked back toward the house, her hands shaking as she debated whether she should turn on the light. If he thought they were getting back together…

Libby allowed the thought to trail as she unlocked the front door and closed it behind her. She looked at the switch to the light on the front porch. What was she afraid of? She was finally in a good place. So what if Nick came back, looking to rekindle their relationship? Libby could set him straight easily enough. After all, she thought with some satisfaction, she'd just helped to lock away a high-powered politician. Nick Foster, do your worst!

Libby flicked on the porch light and then turned to the pile of dirty dishes in the sink. Minutes later, there was a knock at the door.

"Nick Foster."

He heard his name before the front door swung open to reveal a very irritated Libby Andrews.

"You have got to be kidding me."

She had one hand firmly on the door, prepared to slam it shut in his face, and the other resting on her slender hip. It was nearly midnight, but she was still dressed in the same navy blue power suit she'd worn to court that morning.

The sight of Libby almost made Nick forget to breathe. She'd always reminded him of a Siberian forest, with silky black hair falling like bare branches against the new-fallen snow perfection of her skin. Both features paled against those now glacial blue eyes that were fixing him with a glare. She'd long ago mastered a look that made him suspect she viewed him as an entomologist would view a moth pinned to a piece of Styrofoam—as if he was the specimen and she the expert, and he'd better just cooperate.

For a moment Nick thought about pulling her close to him and tasting those beautiful bee-stung lips again. Show her who was the expert here. The thought made him smile just a little.

"Hi, Libby," he said.

"What are you doing here?" Libby demanded.

"Nice to see you, too."

They each paused, Libby glaring at Nick, and Nick returning her glare with a steady gaze.

Finally Nick broke the silence. "Can I come in?"

"No, you can't," Libby replied, folding her arms across her chest. "I only turned on the light so I could tell you to leave me alone. I've had a long day and I'm not in the mood for this."

"I know," said Nick in a self-assured tone, pulling himself to his full height of six feet one inch. If anyone knew Libby's many moods he did, and he wasn't intimidated. "I've been following the trial in the papers." He looked at her with admiration. "You actually convinced a jury to convict a state senator on corruption charges. That's a big deal."

"Yes, and it's a trial I've been working on for years, as you know," she replied. "And now that I'm officially on vacation for two weeks, I would like to go to bed." Nick lifted his eyebrows devilishly and Libby rolled her eyes. "Alone."

Nick shook his head and grinned. "There you go again, Libby, teasing me…" She started to shut the door, but Nick stopped it with one press of his strong hand. "Not so fast, Counselor. We need to talk."

"I have nothing to say to you."

"Well, I have plenty to say to you, and I need you to listen."

She reopened the door and Nick's hand dropped, but he remained close in case she tried to shut it again.

"Nick, we broke up over a year ago," Libby said, exasperated. "I'm happy with my life now, and I don't want to revisit anything. Oh, and this—" she shook her fist, brandishing the note he'd left earlier "—this is just creepy. I have email, you know."

Nick responded with a slight chuckle. "Believe me, Libby, I'm not here to reconcile. I'm here on business. You want me to flash my badge to make it official?" He reached into his pocket and removed his FBI badge, showing it to her. "FBI and all that."

Libby's eyes narrowed. "Seriously? It's official business?"

Nick started to affirm that, then bit back the lie. "We've both moved on, Libby. I'm not here to start anything, and I wouldn't be here at all if it wasn't imperative that we speak."

Libby hesitated, softening slightly. "I don't know," she said. "Can't this wait until morning?"

"I'm afraid not."

She inhaled and then released a deep breath. "Fine, come in. But make it quick." She opened the door to allow him inside.

Nick stepped into the little kitchen he knew so well. The smell of Libby's baking still lingered, and the scent of apples and cinnamon made him stop and say knowingly, "Baked apples and vanilla ice cream."

Her mouth opened, and then she shut it again. "I've been working late," she said.

"I know. It's what you snack on when you pull all-nighters. Apple pie, minus the best parts."

He noticed Libby twist her lips in an almost-smile, but then she turned to walk away, saying over her shoulder, "I'd offer you some, but we're making this quick."

Right.

He followed Libby to the little sitting room she'd set up in an alcove. "You must be visiting your mother," Libby said.

"She's staying with my aunt in Florida for a few more weeks. She won't set foot in New York until all the leaves are back on the trees." Libby turned on the lamp and Nick cleared his throat. "I was sorry about your father. Judge Andrews was a…good man."

Libby paused for a moment. "He was," she replied. "Thank you."

"Pancreatic cancer," Nick continued, watching Libby as she tidied up the sitting area. "I heard it was fast."

"You heard right. He died eight weeks after the diagnosis.

It was so sudden." She sighed, fluffing a small quilted pillow that had fallen on the floor. "It's been two weeks already, and I still pick up the phone to call him."

Nick's breath caught as she looked at him again. There she was: the sweet, vulnerable girl he'd fallen in love with the first time he saw her walking to school, her books pressed firmly against her chest as she giggled with her best friend. They'd both been twelve years old. Now her chin trembled, and she looked conflicted. "What is it?" he asked.

"Nothing," she said, placing the pillow in its proper place on the window seat. "It's just…" She sighed again and turned to face him. "I know Dad thought a lot of you, that's all."

That was a lie and she knew it. And yet she stood there, wide-eyed, watching for his response. Nick wondered what she was looking for. "He would have been proud of you today, Libby," he said.

Libby smiled faintly and seemed to relax. She gave a little shrug. "Yes, well…" She sat on a well-worn leather recliner and gestured with her hand to indicate that Nick should sit on the matching recliner across from her. Nick obliged, but not before admiring the curves of her lovely legs as she crossed them. He loved that Libby never wore pantyhose with her skirts.

His gaze darted to the exposed glass of the bay window. The woods behind Libby's house provided the perfect cover for someone to watch them undetected. Nick rose and pointed to the curtains. "Mind if I draw these?" He didn't wait for permission.

Libby watched him in puzzlement. "Do what you have to do, I guess." She studied him as he returned to the chair.

"So," said Nick, "I'll get right down to business."

Libby smoothed her raven hair absentmindedly. "Sorry, I should have offered you something to drink," she said.

Nick smiled. "I thought we were going to make this quick?"

Libby shrugged. "I didn't say it would be a large drink."

* * *

Frankly, Libby suddenly felt like she needed something to take the edge off. She eyed Nick. He was dressed in jeans and a black windbreaker jacket that was unzipped to reveal a dark gray T-shirt that hugged his lean torso nicely. His square jaw was shadowed with a slight stubble, but even if he'd been working all day his dark eyes still burned with a singular fiery energy. Yes, her ex-fiancé was seated across from her, looking better than ever. He was the same ex-fiancé who'd broken her heart, and yet here she was, practically biting her nails at the sight of him.

She didn't need this.

Nick's large hands rested easily on the arms of the recliner and Libby studied them, remembering the gentle pressure of those strong, certain fingers on her skin, the feel of his breath against the curve of her neck—

"I'll have a whiskey, if you have it," said Nick.

"Whiskey. Great." Libby started out of the room, then paused. "Oh, aren't you on duty?"

"It's no problem," Nick said with a wave of his hand. "This is the last stop on my to-do list tonight."

Libby shrugged and then darted into the kitchen. No, she didn't need this at all.

She was operating on sheer adrenaline after coming off a long and very public trial. After spending nearly two years on pretrial and investigatory work, and almost three weeks in the courtroom, a guilty verdict was no small victory. Libby was proud to say that it was hers.

After the jury had returned with its verdict earlier that afternoon she'd gone with some colleagues to Mickey's, a local bar a block from the prosecutors' office. Sitting in Mickey's, seeing her colleagues laugh and celebrate a hard-won verdict, watching the rich colors of their beverages catch the light… well, life had felt pretty good, and feeling good was a welcome change.

She ached from months of restless sleep, the physical and

mental exhaustion of being on trial, and the emotional demands of caring about what she was doing. The judge had graciously suspended the trial for two days so that Libby could arrange for her father's burial, but those had been her only days off in months. The constant working, racing, competing, all while carrying the weight of her grief…it had felt good to finally rest.

Then she'd come home to find that letter from Nick in her mailbox, and all the contentment she'd felt at Mickey's had evaporated in a hot little puff of smoke.

She couldn't explain his pull on her, or the way her entire body seemed to sit up and take notice when he entered the room. Still, every time she thought about Nick, which was less and less these days, Libby reminded herself that breaking up had been for the best. As lovers, their chemistry was undeniable, and Libby still reeled with the memory of their lovemaking. Nick aimed to please, and he did it spontaneously and with pleasure. But it was just physical chemistry. In every other way they were incompatible.

Libby shook her head, jolting herself back to reality. Compatibility with Nick no longer mattered. She'd recently started seeing someone new: a mergers and acquisitions attorney named David. They'd only been on a few dates, but David, although a little dull, was sweet and seemed fascinated by Libby. Sure, there hadn't been any sparks when he'd kissed her for the first time last Saturday, but sparks would come later, right? David called when he said he would. He was dependable.

Nick, on the other hand, was wrong on every level. Selfish. Arrogant. Impulsive. Still, Libby lamented as she poured their drinks, he looked good enough to eat, with that light brown hair cut to a no-nonsense length and that dimple in his left cheek that made her knees weak every time he smiled. He looked like he'd been spending a lot of time at the gym, too; his lean frame had filled out with muscle, and his broad shoulders appeared more imposing than she remembered. Fortunately he was still overly self-confident, proving that nothing about Nick had changed. She'd been right to break things off.

Presumptuous, she thought as she returned to the sitting room with a tumbler of whiskey for him and a glass of Merlot for herself. *God only knows what he thinks he's doing here.* Out loud she said, "Here you go."

"Thanks." Nick accepted the drink and nodded in Libby's direction. "Merlot?"

Libby couldn't help but fume as she returned to her recliner. "Are you going to do this all night?"

Nick blinked, wide-eyed. "Do what?"

"Pretend you know me," she replied. "The baked apples, the Merlot. What are you trying to prove?"

Nick held up one hand as if to shield himself from the blows of her accusations. "I didn't mean anything by it, Libby." He paused to watch her swirl her wine. "Pretend I know you? Libby, we've been friends for nearly twenty years."

She considered her wine and whispered, "Nick, there are lots of things you don't know about me."

"You're probably right." Nick took a breath. "But let's not revisit old arguments tonight." He raised his glass amiably, giving Libby a boyish smile.

"So," she said, curling her legs underneath her and ignoring his smile, "you said you had something you needed to tell me."

Nick eyed his whiskey, feeling a tug of guilt. He hadn't planned to tell Libby that he was on official business. That lie had caught even him off guard. He stole a quick glance at her. At least she'd seemed to buy his explanation. But he wasn't there on official FBI business at all. In fact he was just starting a brief vacation before being transferred to the Washington, D.C., office. No, this was not really an official anything. His reasons for being here were strictly personal.

Nick opened his jacket and pulled out a manila envelope. "I know you want me to cut to the chase, so here it is. This envelope was delivered to you today, and I wanted to be here when you opened it."

Libby's face darkened. "Wait a minute. You went through my mail—"

"Please," Nick said, holding up his hand, "let me explain. There are things going on that I'd hoped you wouldn't have to know about, but I think it's time you knew."

"What sorts of things?" she asked, her eyes narrowed in suspicion.

"I can explain, but first I need to know what's in that envelope." Nick watched her as she glared at him. "Look, at least I didn't open it, right? If my suspicions are wrong, I'll leave right away."

"And if they're right? What's going on here?"

"Please, Libby," said Nick, extending the envelope to her. "Trust me."

She hesitated, but then took the envelope and opened it, sliding her finger underneath the seal. Reaching inside, she extracted an eight-by-ten inch photograph. Her forehead wrinkled as she studied it. "I don't understand." She turned the photograph to show him. "It's a picture of me walking into the courthouse." She pursed her lips as she examined it. "I think this was taken on Monday."

Nick swallowed. The photo confirmed his fears. "Libby, do you remember that case your dad had? Will Henderson the serial killer? The trial was about thirty years ago."

She nodded slowly. "Sure. The Glen Falls Strangler. It was Dad's first big case. I was still in diapers, but I heard about it as I got older."

Nick leaned forward. "Do you remember how the killer stalked his victims? He sent them what he referred to as 'signs.'" Nick held up six fingers. "Six signs over six days, and on the seventh day he killed them. Do you remember hearing about that?"

Libby's face drained of all color as she watched him. "I do," she said softly. "Nick, what are you saying?"

"Sign number one," Nick said, holding up his index finger, "was a photograph of the victim in the ordinary course of their day. At trial, Henderson referred to it as—"

"Firing a warning shot." Libby dropped the photograph and clutched her fingers together in her lap to keep them from trembling. "Oh, God," she whispered.

"Libby," Nick started slowly, "Will Henderson is dead. He was killed in prison over two decades ago. But your father was receiving letters from someone threatening to harm you in the same way the Strangler harmed his victims. I met with your father before he died, and he asked me to protect you."

Her eyes grew wide. "He did?"

Nick nodded. "Libby, your life is in danger."

She was perfectly still as she stared at her hands. "Dad contacted the FBI?" Nick looked away, but didn't respond. "How do I know this is real? Why should I believe you?"

Nick reached back into his jacket and removed a small stack of letters secured with a rubber band. "Here," he said as he handed them to her. "These are the letters that your dad received. They make it clear that someone has been watching you very closely."

She thumbed through the letters carefully, examining the envelopes and squinting as she tried to decipher the frantic scribbles. They contained details about her daily routine: the roads she drove to work, the coffee shop she frequented, what she ordered for lunch. After several minutes she looked up, pale.

Nick gave her a pained look. "I'm sorry."

"Someone's been stalking me?" Her voice shook. "For how long?"

"It's hard to say," he replied. "The oldest postmark on those letters is from five weeks ago. I've only known about this for about three weeks."

Libby's jaw was slack. "Three weeks? And you allowed this to continue? You didn't tell me?"

Nick took a breath. He'd hired private investigators to watch Libby's house, to follow her undetected to and from work and to check her mail daily, keeping an eye out for the first sign. He'd been hoping that they'd catch the stalker without Libby ever having to know about it…and without him ever having to see Libby again.

"We've been trying to resolve this quietly. I didn't want to upset you. I've taken steps to ensure your safety, had someone nearby at all times just in case."

Libby rested her face against her palm. "This can't be happening." She glanced toward the floor at the spot where the photograph rested and tucked her hair behind her ears. "Seven days, huh?" she whispered. "And we're already through day one." She sniffed and her nose began to redden. "Why would someone want to…hurt me?" Her voice cracked.

"I don't know, Libby, but I'm going to find out. In the meantime, I'm going to be here, protecting you." He'd agonized about what he would do once the killer sent the first sign. Staying with Libby hadn't been his first choice, or even his tenth, but he'd reluctantly concluded that this was the best way to ensure her safety as the killer began to circle. No matter how painful their history, he simply couldn't trust anyone else to guard her once the signs began. "I want to stay here," he said firmly. "With you."

She shook her head. "I don't think that's a good idea."

Nick tried not to look startled. "Why not?"

Libby fidgeted with her hands. "I'm seeing someone," she said. "I don't want anything to be…confused."

He sat back. Libby was seeing someone? This was news. He had a hundred questions, but didn't want to appear too interested. "Look, someone's stalking you, and I don't think you should be in this house alone." He hesitated. "Where's your boyfriend?"

"Oh, he's not my boyfriend. I mean, we're seeing each other, things are good, and I don't want to screw it up." Libby swiped at her nose. "He's in Zurich for a few days."

Nick exhaled. "Then you're going to be alone if I don't stay here," he said. "Libby, I don't want you to be alone."

She eyed him and then looked at the floor, sniffing again. It took everything he had not to run over to her, wrap his arms around her and kiss those tears as they fell down her cheeks. Old habits.

"Fine," she sniffed. "But you're sleeping on the couch."

Nick rose. "I packed a bag before I left. It's in the car." He reached under his jacket and withdrew his gun from its holster. Libby's pupils grew large. "Lock the door behind me and don't open it unless I knock twice. Got it?"

She nodded silently. Nick walked out the door and waited on the step until he heard the click of the lock behind him. He took a deep breath to steady the pounding of his heart. Around him the world was sleeping, bathed in the milky light of a half-moon.

But Nick was wide awake. And somewhere a killer was watching.

CHAPTER TWO

Day Two

"'MORNING, sunshine."

Libby groaned, wiping a film of sleep from her eyes. Then she sat up and realized that at some point early that morning she'd fallen asleep, fully-clothed, on the recliner. Thick court transcripts were tucked around her, and more littered the floor. Her right hand rested on page 212 of day six of the Henderson trial. And a figure watched her from the doorway with obvious amusement.

"Rise and shine," Nick said, clutching a glass of water. After a furtive glance out the window, he parted the curtains slightly to admit a beam of sunlight.

Libby winced as he prattled on about something having to do with spring temperatures and daylight saving. "I hate morning people," she grumbled, running a hand across her mouth. God, was that drool on her cheek? And her skirt was practically riding up her thighs! She yanked it down. "What time is it?"

"Almost eight-thirty." His eyebrow arched rakishly as he visually scanned her. "I'm about to make some coffee, and you look like you could use some."

"I need a shower." Without another glance at the morning lark standing in her doorway, Libby skulked into the bathroom, closing the door firmly behind her.

She looked in the mirror—holy mess! Her mascara was

smudged and flaking underneath her eyes, and she had dark shadows all over her face where concealer from the day before had worn off. Her hair was parted oddly, rising up on the side of her head as if in rebellion. Libby's cheeks grew hot as she rubbed at the black gunk affixed beneath her eyes. No wonder Nick had seemed so amused.

She stepped into the shower and turned the water to its hottest setting. As the fog in her head cleared her stomach tensed. Someone was trying to kill her. A true Yankee, Libby thought in terms of utility, and she didn't know what to do with that information.

She stood beneath the spray of the shower, inhaling steam and the scent of jasmine soap. One thing seemed certain: Nick was lying to her. The FBI wouldn't take an interest in some creep sending her a photo of herself. No—not when there were terrorists and gangs and illicit drugs to worry about. Even the letters didn't seem to be enough to invoke federal jurisdiction. She couldn't imagine what federal crime had been committed, not even mail fraud. Then there was the way Nick had squirmed last night when she'd offered him a drink. He'd said that even though he was on duty her house was his last stop.

Last stop or not, Nick would never drink on duty.

"Official FBI business, my foot," she mumbled, turning off the water.

As Libby dressed and dried her hair she thought about those last weeks with her father, when he'd been uncharacteristically concerned about her welfare. He'd called several times a day to ask where she was, or to remind her not to walk alone to her car at night, then he'd bought a state-of-the-art alarm system for her home. Libby had assumed his concern had escalated because he was dying. Now she knew better.

Then her mind wandered to those last weeks with Nick, when everything between them had seemed so...*broken*. It hadn't been for lack of trying, because God knew Libby had tried to make things work.

They'd been engaged to be married for almost six months, and during that time Libby had planned a dream wedding, buying a simple, understated gown, selecting just the right flowers and invitations, and generally ensuring the day would be elegant and, above all, perfect. She'd done it all alone, as Nick had seemed to take little interest in the event. She would even invite him to taste cakes only to hear that he was working. He'd said he trusted *her* to select invitations and favors and music.

Libby had told herself that Nick's lack of interest in the wedding did not coincide with a lack of interest in his bride, but she hadn't been able to shake her suspicions. Worse, she hadn't been able to bring herself to finally tell him the truth about their future together, and how it would never be the future she knew he wanted. The resentment had built, until one day it erupted.

It had happened only a few months before their perfect June wedding. They had barely seen each other in weeks. If Nick was home early, Libby was working late, and weekends were nonexistent. Libby had gone home that night to find Nick in her kitchen, baking stuffed peppers.

"I thought I'd go ahead and make dinner," he said. Then he added nonchalantly, "Word came down today that I received that promotion. I'm being relocated to the field office in Pittsburgh."

Libby felt unsteady on her own feet. They'd discussed this promotion, and she'd made it abundantly clear that she was not leaving her father and a career she loved to move six hours away. Nick wasn't supposed to relocate. He was supposed to pack up his bachelor pad apartment so they could finally live together.

At that moment she felt a hundred angry words stick in her throat, but all that came out was, "I hate peppers."

Nick paused. "I thought you liked them."

"I hate them," repeated Libby, months of hurt suddenly

bubbling to the surface. "Hate is a strong word, and I hate peppers."

Nick stood, stunned, as Libby began to sob.

And the argument dissolved from there, with Libby accusing Nick of not caring about their wedding or about her, and Nick accusing Libby of burying herself in her work to avoid something. In the end she threw her engagement ring across the kitchen floor and Nick stormed out of her house. Libby brooded for an hour and then systematically gathered his possessions—his toothbrush, his BlackBerry, a college T-shirt—placed them into a box marked "Free" and left them at the curb. She never saw the ring again.

She waited for Nick to call, but he never did. Not to say goodbye, not to ask where his BlackBerry was. He was just gone.

Libby would never admit that she'd waited for Nick to return, but she had. For months each time her cell phone rang her heart had jumped in the hope that Nick was finally calling. She'd woken in the middle of the night, imagining she heard his car in the driveway, or the turn of his key in the door. His absence had become her most constant companion, filling the space in her life in unexpected ways, rending the future she'd so carefully planned.

Libby sniffed. Bacon. And coffee. Her stomach growled. Nick was in her house again, cooking the meals he used to cook. She squared her shoulders and headed toward the kitchen. Things between them had changed forever, and she was not about to let him forget it.

Nick was standing with his back to the doorway. He was barefoot, dressed in black mesh shorts and a gray T-shirt. He turned his head as she entered. "Coffee's ready, and I took out the cream and sugar."

Libby lurched gratefully toward the coffee, taking one of the mugs Nick had set out and filling it to the brim with the hot, black caffeinated goodness she needed to fully clear her head. She tasted it before adding cream and a little sugar. "This is really delicious," she murmured.

"That's because I bought it," Nick said matter-of-factly. "Enjoy a decent cup of coffee. My treat."

Libby's eyes narrowed slightly. "You don't like the coffee I buy?"

"You mean that stuff in the green bag?" Nick chuckled. "I don't know what that is, but it's not coffee." He turned his head and gave her a broad, easy smile, dimple and all.

Last night on her front porch Nick had been a tight coil of masculinity: hard, strong and poised to erupt like a spring gun if tripped. Now he seemed so boyish, with his bed-rumpled hair, bare feet and shorts, that Libby fought the urge to run up and bite him playfully on the neck.

It was only a fleeting thought.

"Hey, Nick?" Libby set her coffee cup on the counter. "What exactly are you doing here?"

His back was to her, but she saw his shoulders tense slightly. "I told you. FBI business. I'm protecting you." He scraped eggs and bacon onto two plates and turned to her. "Breakfast is ready."

Libby fixed him with the same steady gaze she used in court with uncooperative witnesses. "That's not true, is it, Nick? I've considered this from every angle, and I can't see why the FBI would take an interest in letters some lunatic sent to my dad."

Nick's dark eyes flashed. "What is this? A cross-examination?"

"Call it what you want." She folded her arms. "You've been lying to me, haven't you?"

His mouth tensed, accentuating the angular lines of his jaw. "I'm not supposed to talk about this, but a new order came down in our unit and we've started to—"

Libby held up a hand. "Save it. I want the truth."

They paused, staring each other down. Nick flinched. "Like I said last night, your dad asked me to be here, Libby. He was receiving those letters, and he was dying. He wanted to know you were safe. What was I supposed to say?"

"So the FBI isn't actually involved? It's just you?"

"It's just me."

"Why didn't Dad call the police?"

"I asked him the same thing. He said he couldn't call them."

Libby jutted her chin defiantly. "He believed my life was in danger, and he didn't want the police involved? No." She shook her head. "Dad would never put me at risk like that."

"Libby," Nick said in a steadfast voice, "it's the truth."

She started at the gravity of his tone, and when she spoke again her voice was softer. "Why would he do that?" She chewed on her lower lip as she thought. "It doesn't make sense. How are we supposed to build a case against this guy if the police aren't involved?"

Nick gestured to the two plates of steaming food he was still holding. "Can we sit down, at least? You look like you haven't had a decent meal in weeks."

He was right, and Libby had to admit the breakfast looked delicious, even if the bacon was burned. She nodded, and they sat at the little breakfast table.

As Libby dragged a forkful of eggs across her plate, Nick cleared his throat. "Your dad called me in March and left a voice mail. All he said was, 'Nick, we need to talk and I'm dying. So why don't you just come over?' That was it."

Libby smiled faintly. "Sounds like Dad."

Nick nodded. "He was a straight-shooter, all right. So a few days later I drove up and went to his house, and he told me that you were in danger but he couldn't go to the police."

"Why not?"

"He wouldn't answer my questions, except to say that that there were things in the past that should be left there." Nick looked down at his coffee. "He said that he didn't trust the police. He trusted me because...well, because of our history, I guess."

Libby ran her fingers along her place mat absentmindedly. "What did he mean about the past? And why wouldn't he trust the police?" She shook her head. "It doesn't make sense to me."

"Yeah, it didn't sit well with me, either." He took a sip of his coffee. "So I decided to honor the letter of his request, if not the spirit. I had to return to Pittsburgh, but I hired a couple of former FBI colleagues to keep an eye on you, to be your bodyguards. They've been checking your mail, by the way." Nick looked at Libby with a slight tilt of his head. "That's how I knew you'd received that photograph yesterday."

Libby clenched the place mat. "So you've been having me followed?"

"The way I see it, you already have a psychopath watching your every move. You may as well have a few good guys in the wings. Besides, they've also been doing some investigative work for me. They managed to track down those court transcripts I gave you last night."

The knot in Libby's gut loosened ever so slightly. If Nick had enlisted outside help from criminal investigation experts, he wasn't the only one protecting her, after all. She had her own mini police force. "These…investigators. Have they seen anyone suspicious?"

"The timing has been terrible, with you handling a public trial. You've been in court, surrounded by reporters and general busybodies…they haven't been able to identify a suspect." Nick shook his head as he continued. "I'm trying to honor your dad's request, but I hope you know I would never take risks with your life. Your dad didn't even want you to know about any of this until it became necessary, but I think we've reached that point."

Libby's brow furrowed as she processed this information. If her father hadn't trusted the police to protect her, then she wanted to know why. Still, she decided, that deathbed promise had been Nick's, not hers. *She* wouldn't hesitate to call the police in the upcoming days if it became necessary.

"Okay, Nick. Fine." She sighed. "You're the expert in violent crime investigation. What are we going to do?"

He sat back. "I've been looking over this file since your dad approached me, and I have a grasp of the basics, but I want to talk to someone who may have more insight." He finished his coffee and set the mug on the table. "We know it's not Will Henderson sending these letters, right? He's dead. So let's take that and work backward."

"Maybe Dad locked up the wrong guy? Maybe the real killer is still out there?"

"Could be."

"Or maybe it's a copycat?" she offered.

"Maybe," said Nick. "But whoever wrote those letters struck a nerve with your dad."

Libby went cold as she thought of the scrawled threats. "Nick," she said softly, "tell me what you know about this… guy. What are we looking for? What is he going to do?" She saw him turn his head slightly in hesitation. "Don't sugarcoat it. I prosecute these bastards. I can handle it."

"It's a little different when you're the target, Libby."

"Either we're partners or we're not," she said. "If you're here with me, sleeping on my couch and protecting me, then you have to make me your partner."

Nick hesitated. "Libby, it's better—"

"Nick," she interrupted, "listen to me." She waited until his gaze was on her. "I've come back from death before, remember? If I can beat cancer as a kid, I can handle this."

Libby's stomach still knotted when she thought about the time she'd gone to the doctor's office with a fever and left with a diagnosis of non-Hodgkin's lymphoma. After nearly a year of aggressive chemotherapy and radiation she'd been declared in remission, and ultimately cured. Being diagnosed with cancer at ten years old had been terrifying, and she'd fought like hell and beaten the odds. No one was going to tell her she couldn't handle something.

Nick's eyes moved across her face. "Okay." He reached for the carafe of coffee and poured another cup. "Let's assume we're dealing with the same guy your dad was dealing with in the seventies, okay?"

Libby nodded. "Okay."

"The guy's methodical. Precise. Sadistic." Nick took another sip of his coffee and set it aside. "He selects his victims carefully. He stalks them for months, learning their routine, becoming familiar with their territory. Then, when he's feeling comfortable, he begins with the signs."

Libby reached for the trial transcript. "I tried to find them here last night, in the transcripts you gave me, but couldn't."

"No need. I've memorized them." Nick held up one hand. "We've already received the first sign, of course."

"Yes." Libby shivered. She couldn't get that photograph out of her mind.

"Sign number two: he makes contact from afar. This could be any variety of things, but it seems that he would be present at some point in the victim's day. Hiding in the open, so to speak."

"So, is he going to say something to me today?"

"Hard to tell," Nick replied. "The contact with previous victims was subtle. It will probably be an uneventful day, but we should keep our eyes peeled." He continued counting on his fingers. "Sign number three: he sends a gift."

"A gift? What does that mean?"

"It's not something a normal person would recognize as a gift," said Nick. "It got pretty twisted, with him leaving pieces of his hair for the victim—things like that."

Libby shuddered. "Sick."

"Sign number four: he makes personal contact. He would call the victim and not say anything, or he would bump into the victim on the street—something like that. Sign number five: he lays a trap."

"A trap?" The skin on Libby's arms prickled.

"What the police learned during the investigation was that all of the victims escaped some kind of life-and-death situation before their actual death. One was mugged on the street, one was in a car accident." Nick's brow creased as he thought. "There were six victims total, and they were all a little different."

"Six victims?" repeated Libby, clutching her hands together to stop her fingers from trembling. "God."

"Yes, but Henderson was only prosecuted for three of them. The evidence on the other crimes wasn't strong enough."

"So sign five could be a lot of things, but in this sicko's head he thinks he's setting a trap of some kind?"

"It's about controlling the victim," said Nick. "Scaring her. Making her fear for her life. Hurting her."

"Like a cat toying with its prey." Libby's stomach turned. "And do I even want to know what sign six is?"

"That's the thing." Nick spread his hands wide. "We—they—never figured out what sign six was. Henderson was coy about it, and the victims never lived long enough to tell anyone about it. It must be very subtle."

Libby thought for a moment, biting her lower lip. "Tell me what happens on day seven, Nick."

His forehead creased as he looked at her. "He's not going to make it to day seven."

"Humor me."

Nick shifted in his seat. "All of his victims were found in their home, strangled. He…he would cut three fingers from the left hand. Seven days, seven fingers." He clenched his jaw. "He did it while they were alive."

The breath caught in her lungs and her hands flew to her mouth. Shaken to the core, Libby sat back and turned her head, looking out the window. "He tortured those poor girls," she said. Without thinking she glanced at her own trembling left hand, spreading her fingers out in front of her.

"Libby," said Nick, his voice firm, "it's not going to happen to you."

She balled her fist. "I wonder what made my dad think the letters were written by the same person who committed the crime?" she whispered, almost to herself.

"That's why I was thinking that we should find someone who was involved in the trial. A cop or a detective, maybe."

Libby tapped her fingertips on the table as she thought. "Jack MacGruder. He was just out of law school when Dad prosecuted the case, but he sat second chair at trial. Maybe he'll have some insight. Besides, he's been a mentor to me since the day I arrived at the District Attorney's Office. I trust him."

"It's as good a start as any," Nick agreed. He looked at the clock on the wall. "We should get going. I assume MacGruder is working today?"

"MacGruder is always working." Libby drained her coffee cup and stood up. "Thanks for breakfast. I'll clean up. Why don't you shower?"

Nick stood and stretched, raising his arms over his head. As he did so the T-shirt pulled just slightly above his shorts, revealing several inches of his taut midsection. Libby's eyes were drawn to the thin trail of golden-brown hair intersecting the bottom of his six-pack. An image flashed of the first time she'd touched him there, when she'd tucked her fingertips inside his waistband and felt his muscles quivering with the effort to restrain his desire. Her chest grew warm at the memory.

Libby looked away and busied herself with the dishes. "You know where to find the towels."

Nick began to walk out of the room and then paused. "Hey, Libby?"

She stopped her fidgeting and looked up. His upper body was turned back to her, his broad shoulders filling the doorway. He watched her with eyes that narrowed in concern, but his jaw was tense. "No one's going to hurt you. I mean it. Over my dead body."

Libby swallowed and nodded.

She gathered up the remaining dishes while listening to the familiar heavy fall of Nick's footsteps as he walked up the stairs. When he reached the top of the staircase she realized she'd been holding her breath and exhaled.

Reality was just starting to settle in. She was a sitting target for some lunatic who enjoyed psychologically tormenting his victims. Anxiety eroded her insides, leaving her so raw that it took all of her energy to pretend she wasn't hurting. Then there was Nick, so sure of himself, swearing to protect her. She liked to imagine he could. But, then again, she liked to imagine that things between them were different, and that he was there because he loved her. She liked fairy tales.

He's here because your dad asked him to be here, she reminded herself as she headed toward the sink. Nothing sexy about that.

Like most things in Libby's house, each towel in the bathroom had its particular place, and they were all folded identically and piled in the cabinet. Nick couldn't help but smile when he saw the familiar collection of nearly threadbare towels she'd bought in college and refused to throw out. She still had the offensively colored discount towels she'd fished out of a bargain bin in the middle of law school, and the souvenir beach towel she picked up in Myrtle Beach, with a shark in swimming trunks holding a surfboard, winking while giving a thumbs-up.

He selected the shark towel and unfolded it. He remembered the way she'd laughed the first time she saw that towel, and the tone of her voice when she'd declared it to be "all kinds of tacky." Mostly he remembered the kiss they'd shared in the middle of the parking lot after she'd bought the towel, his lips lingering on her taste of dried saltwater and coconut-oil lip balm.

The memory stung. Somewhere, at some point after that kiss, something had changed. The girl who had once giggled about tacky souvenir towels had become consumed with the grave task of constructing a tower in which to hide from the world. Libby's moods had grown dark and her life had become serious.

Nick thought it might have happened during those months he was at FBI training in Quantico but, looking back, he couldn't say for sure. All he knew was that for a while life had been better than he could have ever predicted. He'd been dating the girl he'd been in love with since they were children, and she'd seemed to love him in return. Then she'd disappeared without explanation, leaving in her place a distant, secretive woman who'd chosen to fill her free time with work.

Nick hung the shark towel on the hook next to the shower. The whimsical towel reminded him of the old Libby, the one who wore 'Saturday' socks on a Wednesday and spent all Sunday morning lounging in her Coke-bottle glasses and bathrobe, reading the *New York Times* and listening to jazz. That was the Libby who had curled up against him on the couch and wanted to talk about their day and their future for hours. That was the Libby who had embraced her world and its possibilities, who had accepted tackiness and imperfect boyfriends because she'd believed that life was better when slightly messy.

The memories caught in his throat. He missed the old Libby. He didn't know whether she still existed.

He turned on the shower and stood under the spray, letting it run over his face. He had no time to dwell on the past. Libby's life was in danger, and he had to focus on the mission at hand. He owed it to her father, and he owed it to her.

He showered quickly and debated shaving, but then decided against it, running his palm over the prickly stubble on his cheek. *It can wait,* he decided. *Everything else can wait.*

* * *

Jack MacGruder's eyes widened when he looked up from his desk and saw Libby standing there. "You're supposed to be on vacation."

"You just can't keep me away." Libby smiled and gestured with one hand to Nick. "Jack, you remember Nick Foster?"

"Of course." MacGruder stood to offer his hand. "Nice to see you, Nick."

"It's a pleasure."

In the late-morning light of MacGruder's small office he looked every minute of his fifty-seven years. His nearly translucent tissue-paper skin creased between his thick eyebrows from years of serious thinking, and around his eyes and mouth from years of equally serious laughing. "Please, make yourselves comfortable," he said, gesturing to two chairs in front of his desk. "You see, Nick, when you work for the State of New York for over thirty years you get a corner office with old wood paneling and an extra government-issued chair for visitors."

Nick smiled. "You also get windows that don't open, I see."

MacGruder waved a hand. "Oh, you can open them with a screwdriver if you get desperate. Don't ask me what qualifies as getting desperate."

Libby leaned forward. "Jack, we're not here on a social visit, actually. We have reason to believe that someone is trying to hurt me."

MacGruder sat back in his chair, his face stitched with concern, as Libby and Nick showed him the letters Judge Andrews had received before his death and the photograph of Libby walking into the courtroom.

"Someone is following the Glen Falls Strangler pattern," Libby said. "We thought we could talk to you, since you sat second chair on Will Henderson's trial. Maybe you have some insight into who would do something like this?"

MacGruder took a deep breath as he thought. "Will Henderson is dead, but you must know that already." He grabbed his bifocals from a corner of his desk and studied the letters, shaking his head. "It's uncanny," he mumbled.

Nick sat forward. "What's uncanny?"

"The handwriting. The phrases being used. 'I will lure your daughter to a fertile field and then slaughter her.'" Libby shifted uncomfortably and MacGruder quickly folded the letter. "Sorry, Libby. But that's the kind of language Will Henderson used in the letters he sent to his victims' families."

Libby's eyebrows shot upward. "He sent letters to his victims' families? I didn't know that."

"Oh, yes," said MacGruder. "The letters were loaded with similar images. Lambs to slaughter, pastoral scenes gone terribly wrong."

"Jack, I want you to be honest with me." Libby ran her fingers over her forehead, trying without success to release all of the tension that was pooling there. "Do you think Will Henderson was the Glen Falls Strangler?"

"I have no doubt."

Nick sat back in his seat, apparently startled by the speed with which MacGruder answered that question. "No doubt? None at all? Even when you look at these letters?"

"All the evidence pointed to him, and he practically confessed to the crimes. Now, you two never got to see Judge Andrews in action when he was practicing law, so let me tell you that to this day he was one of the finest trial attorneys I've seen. When he brought a case he felt every ounce of his responsibility. And with this one he knew Henderson was guilty. No," he said, shaking his head, "there's not a doubt in my mind that Henderson was the Glen Falls Strangler."

"You said that he practically confessed to the crimes, but there was still a trial," said Libby. "Why is that?"

MacGruder nodded as he thought about it. "That's right. He confessed to lesser crimes. Planting the signs, harassing the victims. We still had to try him for murder."

"Do we still have all of those files, or were they destroyed?" Libby asked.

"Your dad's files, you mean? We should."

Libby sat back. "Jack, we need to see everything you have on the Henderson trial, and we need to see it right away."

MacGruder shook his head. "That's all sitting in a storage warehouse, Libby. It will take a few days to get it here."

"You need to do better than that, Jack," Nick replied. "Libby's life may depend on it."

MacGruder looked out the window. "I'm not sure what storage facility we used. If it's the one in Stillborough, that's only an hour away, and I could make some calls for you."

"We'll wait outside," Nick said.

He rose and gently clasped Libby's hand, helping her to her feet. As she stood, she felt the warm pressure of his other hand against the small of her back. "Thanks," she whispered. She walked out of the office and Nick followed, closing the door behind them.

Libby paced the hallway before stopping to stare blankly at some photocopied newspaper articles taped to the wall. Nick approached her, edging closer until she smelled the spicy musk of his cologne. "I'm going to make a call over to the court records center. I want to see those letters."

Libby nodded. "Me, too."

Nick took his cell phone from his pocket and started to dial. Libby heard a click behind them as MacGruder opened his door. "I have good news and bad news," he said.

"Yes?" Libby walked over to him.

"The good news is we sent the case files to Stillborough. The bad news is they were stored in a unit that's had flooding problems, so I'm not sure what you'll find."

Libby and Nick exchanged a glance.

"We'll check it out," Nick said. "Thanks, Jack."

As they turned to walk away MacGruder grabbed Libby's arm. "Libby," he said. "I've worked around death and violence my entire career. I've paid for it with my marriage and most of my faith in humanity." His brow was knit as he looked at her. "That case, more than any other, still haunts me. I know I said I was confident Will Henderson was our guy, but…"

"But what, Jack?"

"Can I see those letters again?"

Nick handed him the pile of letters. MacGruder opened one and held a page to the light. After a few seconds, he gasped. "My God."

The words wrapped themselves around Libby's heart and squeezed. "Tell me, Jack."

MacGruder's large blue eyes were wide, his jaw slack. "The letters from the Strangler. They all had one thing in common."

Nick stepped forward. "What's that?"

MacGruder held the page to the light again, pointing at the top right margin with a trembling finger. "That mark," he said.

His finger indicated a faint watermark drawing. "A series of sevens," MacGruder whispered. "Henderson called it the seven-headed beast." He lowered the paper and turned to Libby, ashen-faced. "Libby, my dear. What have you gotten yourself into?"

CHAPTER THREE

LIBBY sat with her head on her desk, her arms folded to cover her face from the harsh fluorescent lights. Her head was spinning and she desperately needed a moment alone—except that Nick was right there, hovering beside her cubicle wall, offering her anything he could get his hands on.

"I told you, I don't want a glass of water. I want to sit here for a minute."

Her eyes were closed, but her senses were only heightened by the darkness. Libby heard the rustle of Nick's jeans as he walked to the visitor's chair she kept hidden behind the filing cabinet and sat down. She heard Nick pull the chair forward until he was almost next to her. Electricity coursed beneath her skin as she heard his breath and realized how close he was.

"How about a coffee? Or a tea?"

Libby groaned without bothering to lift her head. "How about five minutes alone?"

The chair creaked slightly as Nick leaned back. "I'll be quiet, then."

Libby took a deep breath. "Alone means alone."

"This is as alone as I'm leaving you."

She gritted her teeth. Her head felt too heavy to lift, and arguing with Nick over the definition of "alone" seemed too futile to be worth any actual effort. She sat like that for several minutes, trying to lose herself in the warm, dark cover of her own arms. But all she could see was that odd watermark and MacGruder's pale countenance as he pointed to it. All she could hear were the words in that terrifying letter. Her heart clenched and she sat up.

Nick was staring out the window at the parking lot, his brows knit. He turned his head. "You okay?"

Libby smoothed her hair back from her face and ran her hands along her cheeks. The dizziness had passed, but she'd certainly felt better. "Yeah, I guess so."

He was holding his BlackBerry, and he looked down as it started to vibrate. "That's Zack Troy. He's going to get copies of the letters the killer sent to the victims' families."

"Zack Troy?" Libby reached for a pencil and absentmindedly turned it in her hands. "Is that one of the goons you've had following me?"

Nick arched an eyebrow. "He's former FBI, a current private investigator. He's one of the good guys."

She laughed drily and began to doodle on a large paper desk calendar. The entire month was awash with various markings and appointments, decorated by hash marks, scribbles and doodles—except that two weeks were conspicuously marked "VACATION" in bold block letters. Libby tapped her eraser against that word.

"Not much of a vacation," Nick said.

She didn't respond, except to turn to him and say, "We're going to get this bastard, right?"

He sat forward until his elbows were resting on his knees. "Absolutely."

She placed the pencil back into its holder. "I'm going to hold you to that, Nick." She stood from her chair and grabbed her black jacket. "Let's get going. We've got some boxes to sort through."

The Stillborough storage center was little more than an enormous warehouse in the middle of a field, miles off the highway and accessible only by a narrow road riddled with potholes.

Nick was quite familiar with Stillborough. The prevalence of street drugs and violence had landed him and his colleagues in the old mill town more times than he could count. He hadn't even needed to consult a map during the drive from Glen Falls.

Nick pulled his car into a spot near the entrance. He turned off the engine and looked at Libby. "Ready?"

She'd barely uttered a word during the drive, which had been slightly over an hour. Every time he'd tried to begin a conversation Libby had murmured a terse response or remained completely silent, staring straight ahead as the road broadened beneath the vehicle. Now she looked at him with those wide blue eyes and an impenetrable expression. "I'm ready."

She stepped out of the car and proceeded toward the entrance without bothering to wait for Nick. He watched her for a moment, admiring the way her black wavy hair caught the sunlight, cresting midway down her back. His gaze then dipped lower, and he was momentarily hypnotized by the seductive sway of her hips as she marched away from him. Her focus was almost unbearably sexy.

They walked through a single glass door propped open to admit the cool springtime air into the dank warehouse. There was no reception area to speak of, just aisle upon aisle of gray industrial metal shelving, stacked floor to ceiling with cardboard boxes.

To the right was a small office with an open door and a man sitting behind a mound of paperwork. He looked up at them over the bifocals sliding halfway down his nose. "Can I help you?"

"I'm Libby Andrews, from the District Attorney's Office. I believe Jack MacGruder spoke with you a little while ago?"

"John Lankowsky. I manage the warehouse." John was bald, with small brown eyes that darted to Nick. "Are you a Fed?" he asked.

Nick's gaze shot to Libby as she tried to suppress a smirk. "Not today," he replied.

The man placed the paper in his hand on top of an already staggering pile on the desk and stood. "I had the boxes pulled a while ago. We have thirteen of them, but there may be a couple more."

"I'm sure MacGruder explained that we'd like to go through them," Nick said.

"You can do whatever you want for the next five hours," John replied. "But after that we're closing, and you'll need to leave them here."

Libby furrowed her brows. "Five hours?" She turned to Nick. "Thirteen boxes? We're going to need more time than that."

"We don't have more time than that, Libby." Nick nodded to John. "You have everything set up in a conference room, I assume?"

He snorted. "You could call it that."

He led them down a seemingly endless aisle to the very back of the warehouse, where a brown metal door opened to a small room with a Formica table. Cardboard boxes were stacked against the walls. Nick looked at the one closest to the door. The box was labeled "State v. Henderson #8."

"Here you go," John said flatly as he gestured to the room. "Make sure you keep this rubber doorstop in the door, because it locks automatically and you won't be able to get back in if you leave."

"Thanks," said Libby as she walked toward the boxes and began to read the labels.

Nick scanned the surrounding warehouse, looking for anyone or anything that seemed out of the ordinary. A few uniformed employees appeared to be taking some kind of inventory of the boxes a few aisles from the room, but the warehouse was otherwise eerily silent. He drew his hand toward his hip, unbuttoning his holster to have quick access to his gun in case the suspect decided to appear. Nick turned to Libby, keeping an eye on the door. "What do you think, Counselor? Any suggestions as to where we should begin?"

"Sure," she replied as she pulled a box from the top of a stack and set it on the wobbly table. "But maybe I should defer to the Fed in the room." She gave him a slight grin as she returned to the box and opened it.

Nick looked down at his clothes. "Jeans and a T-shirt. I hardly think it makes me look like a Fed."

"It's not your clothes, it's the way you carry yourself." She thumbed through the files in the box. "Let's just say that no one would think you taught kindergarten." She pulled a stack of papers from a file. "Here—I found the index."

Libby placed the papers on the table and ran a finger down the top sheet. Nick came closer, catching the sweet smell of her perfume. His eyes scanned the typewritten list. "What are we doing with this?"

"I don't know," Libby admitted. "I sort of feel like we're looking for a needle in a haystack, but I figure I'll know it when I see it."

The index was nearly thirty pages long, and listed the files in each of the boxes. Libby's eyes narrowed as she pored over the pages. "Dad was meticulous about his files. Everything in its proper place, labeled and cross-referenced."

"Sounds like someone else I know."

"Box five," she said, ignoring the remark. "It looks like that contains information about witnesses." She marched over to the stacks and began searching the box numbers. "You would think they would at least stack these things in some kind of reasonable order," she muttered.

"You would also think they would have better rodent control in a document storage facility," Nick said as he opened a box. "Here's box five, but it looks like someone made a nest out of a notebook."

"Yeah, well, half of these boxes are warped, and can you

smell the mold?" Libby groaned. "Why isn't anything ever easy?"

Nick was beginning to ask himself the same thing as she neared him and he was again encompassed by her smell. He didn't know what the fragrance was called, but he'd always found it intoxicating. He remembered nights in Libby's bed, when she was asleep, pressing his face against the side of her neck to inhale her scent: a heady mixture of woman and whatever this perfume was. Jasmine? Lilac? Like it mattered. Whatever the fragrance, it was making it impossible for him to focus on anything else.

He cleaned out the scraps of paper from the old mouse nest while Libby eagerly thrust her hands into the box. Nick watched with fascination as she removed a stack of files and took a seat at the table. The girl was unstoppable when she set her mind to something.

With every tick of the second hand on the large institutional clock on the wall, Libby felt her chest constrict. She wet her dry lips, fumbling through the documents before her with clumsy, cold fingers. *Contact from afar.* Would the suspect interrupt her to deliver his sign? She read the words on the page over and over, not making sense of the markings.

The clock continued its steady pulse. Each second brought her closer to day seven, and here she was with less than five hours to pore over thirteen boxes of court files in the hopes of finding anything to shed some light on who might be trying to hurt her.

Libby tucked her hair behind her ears. She had no idea what she was looking for.

The folders she'd grabbed contained pages of handwritten and sometimes typed notes, documenting her father's research in preparation for trial. Mostly, the notes concerned witness interviews. "Interesting," Libby said softly.

"What is?"

Nick was staring at her and she blushed, realizing that she'd been talking to herself. She pointed to the pages in front of her. "I'm reading notes from an interview Dad had with a detective. Apparently after Henderson was arrested for the Glen Falls killings a few mugging victims in a separate investigation identified him. Looks like he used to hang out near bus stops and rob old ladies." Libby shook her head. "Scumbag."

A man in an olive-green uniform appeared at the door with a cardboard box. "We found one more."

Libby jumped at the sound of the strange voice, but then relaxed when she saw the warehouse uniform. "Thank you. Why don't you just put it there?" She pointed to a space in the corner. The man obliged and then left the room.

Nick folded his arms across his chest and looked at the wall, apparently deep in thought.

"What is it?" she asked.

"Maybe nothing." He turned to face her. "But don't you think it's odd that a man would transition from mugging old ladies to playing this twisted psychological game?"

Libby blinked. "What do you mean?"

"In my experience criminals have their…modus operandi. They act in a way that works for them, and they don't tend to stray from that path."

"But there are plenty of criminals who evolve," she reasoned. "I've handled too many domestic violence cases to count, and I've seen abuse progress from verbal insults to murder. It happens."

Nick ran a hand through his thick golden-brown hair as he thought. "I guess I don't see it that way."

"Oh?" Libby lifted an eyebrow. "Then how do you see it?"

"In a domestic violence case the abuse doesn't change, it just becomes progressively worse. It's a matter of degree. Here you have a complete shift. If Will Henderson committed these crimes, we have to believe that he changed from a low-level creep who stole purses to a serial killer. And not just any serial killer, but a killer who tormented his victims and their families for days. He went from committing crimes of opportunity to becoming a calculated killer." Nick grew silent, his mouth forming a tight line. "I've dealt with serial killers before, and something isn't adding up."

She shrugged. "I suppose it's not fair of us to presume Henderson was guilty of those muggings when he was never brought to trial on those charges. Innocent until proven guilty."

"That's another problem," said Nick, leaning forward over the table. "If your dad knew Henderson was a suspect in this other investigation, why not bring charges?"

Libby's pulse began to escalate. She'd never understood the animosity that bubbled like lava between Nick and her father. He'd always told her that Nick was attracted to their family's money and prestige, and that she deserved better. In his mind, Nick lacked character. Libby had replayed those warnings in her head many times since Nick walked out, kicking herself for being so naive. Her father had remained loyal to her until the day he died, which was more than she could say for Nick.

"Eyewitness testimony is notoriously unreliable. Dad knew that."

"But here you have several victims identifying the same guy. That seems pretty reliable to me."

"Dad had prosecutorial discretion. Maybe he felt that there wasn't enough evidence to go to trial. Maybe he realized that Henderson was a serial killer, but not a mugger."

"Or," Nick said quietly, "maybe Henderson was a mugger but not a killer, and your dad locked up the wrong guy."

Libby's face grew hot. "Are you accusing my father of knowingly prosecuting the wrong person?" She tried without success to keep her voice from trembling.

Nick hesitated. "Libby, you know how much I…admired your father…"

"No, I don't." Her eyes began to well and she blinked back tears. Nick had despised her father, but she'd thought he knew better than to speak ill of him in front of her. He was dead and buried—why couldn't Nick just let it go? "Why would you even say something like that?"

Nick held up his hands. "I'm trying to explore all of the possibilities. Think about the pressure the police must have been under to find the Glen Falls Strangler. Mistakes could have been made. Maybe they reached a dead end with the investigation and let Henderson take the fall."

"Watch it, Nick." Libby's heart flailed in her chest and her hands shook. "My father was an honorable man," she hissed. "This is all speculation. You don't even have any evidence!"

"Well, that's true," said Nick. "But only if you don't consider the threats against your life evidence that the Glen Falls Strangler may still be out there."

The metal door slammed shut behind him. They both jumped.

"The doorstop must have been loose," Nick said, and he stood and walked to the door. He turned the doorknob but it wouldn't budge. "That's strange," he mumbled.

Libby's face was burning as she returned to the documents before her. She needed to calm down and remain level-headed if she was going to get through these boxes in time. "What's strange?"

"The door is stuck." Nick twisted and turned the doorknob, but it held resolutely still. He started knocking on the door. "There must be someone out there in the warehouse who can help us."

"Wait a minute." The blood drained from Libby's face as she rose from her chair. "Are you saying we're locked in here?" So much for remaining calm.

"I'm sure someone will hear us," Nick replied, but the tone of his voice did little to reassure her. He began pounding on the door, and the sound of his fist on the metal echoed through the room.

Libby's breath came in shallow gasps.

Nick turned to her, his eyes wide with concern. "Libby, have a seat. I'll take care of this."

She was frozen, her chest tightening as she felt how small the room was. She eased herself back into her chair and leaned forward until her head was between her knees. *Breathe,* she told herself. *There's plenty of air.*

But then her eyes were drawn to the corner of the room, where a thin white line was trailing from the box the warehouse employee had just brought in. *Smoke.* "Nick," she whispered, her throat clenched.

He was pounding on the door with both fists now and shouting for help. He didn't hear her. Libby was frozen. The smoke was coming out of some holes in the sides of the box, gathering thickly and bouncing off the ceiling to collect at the top of the room.

"Nick," she repeated, only slightly louder.

He continued to hammer at the door with his fists, and then turned to throw his shoulder against the door. He bounced off and winced, rubbing his arm. He stopped to stare at the same spot on which Libby's gaze was transfixed. His eyes widened. "Libby..." he said.

"Fire!" She jumped from her seat as a burst of energy coursed like a jolt of electricity through her marrow. Her muscles twitched, and she thought for a moment that she might be able to scratch through the cinder-block walls. "Oh, God." She joined Nick and started beating on the door. "Help us!" She grabbed the doorknob, twisting and pulling at it.

Nick raced to the smoking box and threw it to the floor. Flames leaped out the sides. "We have to smother it!" He stomped on the box, but that only succeeded in sending flaming pieces of paper flying. The fire began to spread.

"Why isn't the alarm going off?" Libby was nearly hyperventilating as the room filled with smoke. *Not this way,* she thought to herself. *I'm not dying this way.* She looked around and saw a red light on the ceiling. A smoke detector. "Nick, we have to set off the alarm!" she shouted.

He raced to Libby's side. "I'll lift you up. See if you can set it off manually."

Nick crouched down to wrap his muscular arms around Libby's thighs, squeezing her tightly before hoisting her toward the ceiling. The room was bathed in a thick haze of smoke and Libby fumbled blindly around the alarm, trying to find a button of some kind. "I don't feel anything," she said.

"Keep looking," said Nick, his voice hoarse. He coughed.

She pressed her fingers against the plastic. "Nick, there may not be anything. It was just a guess." She stopped as the smoke detector cover twisted off in her hand. A strangled scream escaped from the back of her throat.

Nick tensed. "What happened?"

"I broke it." Libby started to squirm. "Put me down. Now!" He obliged, and Libby tossed the cover of the smoke detector onto the table. Her eyes were stinging. "What are we going to do?"

Nick looked around the room and then pointed to the ceiling. "I think I see a sprinkler." He opened the nearest box and removed a thick stack of papers.

Libby coughed, trying to lift the weight settling in her lungs. "What are you doing?"

"I'm going to set off the sprinkler." He folded the papers lengthwise and held one end over the burning box. Once the paper caught fire, he sprinted to the sprinkler and held the flames against it. They waited.

"Nothing's happening!" She was on the floor where the air was less smoky, her breath sputtering.

The papers in his hand were burning furiously. Nick dropped them to the ground and doubled over in a coughing fit just as a bell began to ring. Seconds later a spray of dirty water began to stream from the sprinkler.

Nick lowered himself to the ground and crawled to Libby,

who was still seated by the door and coughing. "Are you okay?" He placed one hand on the back of her head and lifted her face with the other.

She gripped his forearms and nodded, still unable to talk. Several sprinklers were spraying now, and the floor was soon covered with cold water.

Nick pulled Libby against him and wrapped his arms around her. "It's working," he said, and the feel of his lips against her ear sent a shiver down her spine.

Nick's hard body was warm amidst the cold of the sprinklers, and the press of his arms around her shoulders felt so reassuring. Libby allowed herself to ease into the familiar comfort of his embrace as water poured around them and the suffocating smoke began to dissipate. She couldn't remember the last time she'd been touched that way.

They were still sitting in that position, shivering, when Libby felt a rush of air and saw a figure in the doorway. It was John, the warehouse manager.

"What's going on in here?" He coughed as the smoke billowed into his face.

Nick sprang to his feet, pulling Libby with him as he ran out of the room. Libby choked as clean air filled her lungs, and doubled over again in a fit of coughing. When she looked up, Nick had John's back pressed against the wall and was gripping his shirt in his fists. "Nick, stop!" She ran to his side.

"I want some answers!" Nick was inches from the man's face.

John had his hands up. "I don't know anything! Please!" His eyes were wide.

"Tell me who shut that door!"

"Nick." Libby placed her hand on his arm. "Please, stop."

He clutched the shirt tighter, but then let go. John scurried out of reach, smoothing his shirtfront with shaking hands. "I heard the alarm go off and came to see whether you two were all right. The fire department is on its way. And of course the police will follow."

"Someone shut the door and locked us in there," Libby said.

"I swear I don't know anything. I came to help."

Nick glared at him. "One of your employees delivered the box that contained the fire."

"One of my employees?" John's eyes narrowed. "Which one?"

"He was wearing a green uniform," said Libby.

The man snorted. "They're all wearing that. What did he look like?"

"Black curly hair," Nick replied. "Wiry build. About five foot ten or so. Late thirties, early forties."

Libby looked at Nick, impressed he'd observed such details.

John shook his head. "No one by that description works here."

Nick stepped forward, approaching him until their faces were inches apart. "You mean to tell us you have no idea who could've come by here and shut us in a room with a burning box?"

He met Nick's gaze. "I told you—I don't know anything." He paused before lowering his voice and saying gravely, "But I'm going to get to the bottom of this."

They heard sirens outside the warehouse, and moments later a group of firemen streamed into the building. Nick and Libby stepped aside to let them through, and John walked toward a group of employees. Libby realized for the first time that she and Nick were soaking wet, their clothes covered in the black filth that had come streaming from the sprinklers. She shivered.

"Libby," Nick said as he tried to place a hand on her shoulder. "Are you—?"

"I'm fine," she said, and then stepped out of his reach.

She didn't know what had happened in that room, when she'd suddenly felt content to sit in Nick's arms for the rest of eternity. Adrenaline, she reasoned. Nothing more. Life-and-death situations frequently brought people together. Whatever she'd felt, she couldn't indulge it. Nick was with her for a short time, and then he would be gone. She couldn't allow him to hurt her again. Thank goodness for fresh air and clarity of thought.

One of the firemen came out of the room, holding the smoke detector in his hand. "You two all right?"

"We will be," Nick replied. He nodded to the smoke detector. "You should take a look at that. It didn't even go off."

"Yeah, well—" the fireman lifted it up to show them and then continued "—it's a fake."

Libby's heart froze. "What do you mean, it's a fake?"

"It looks like someone has created a fake smoke detector. See? It's hollow." He handed it to Libby. "The real alarm was connected to the sprinklers."

She turned it in her hands. She hadn't noticed with all of the smoke, but sure enough the smoke detector was nothing more than a hollow piece of plastic, a battery and a red light.

Nick cursed under his breath.

The fireman scratched at his forehead. "A locked door, a fire and a fake smoke detector, huh? I don't want to scare you, but you should talk to the police. I'm trying to find a delicate way to say this…" He looked at Libby and Nick with concern. "Let's just say that it looks deliberate."

He returned to process the scene, leaving Nick and Libby alone.

Libby was still examining the smoke detector when she saw something white inside. "Wait a minute," she said, and ran her fingernail over the inside of the plastic. She caught the object and pulled it through the crack. A small piece of paper.

"What is that?" asked Nick.

His question was drowned out by the pounding of her heart in her ears as she clutched the paper with shaking fingers. Nick coaxed the paper from her hands and unfolded it. His face reddened in rage as he read the message.

"Nick, what's it say?"

She took the paper back from him, her stomach twisting. There were only three words on it—a message written in a childish scrawl: *Five more days.*

Libby's mouth went dry. "Contact from afar," she whispered. "The second sign."

CHAPTER FOUR

NICK wasn't sure what made him angrier: being a pawn in some psychopath's game, or seeing how that game had shaken Libby to the point where she was visibly struggling to maintain her composure. Her eyes grew wide when she saw the note that had been planted for her inside the false smoke detector, and for a moment her knees gave out beneath her. Nick and the firefighter both rushed to make sure she didn't fall to the cement floor.

"I'm fine, I'm fine," she told them, but Nick could feel her trembling as he helped her to right herself.

That was when the anger began to surge in his veins, until he saw white flashes in front of his eyes. He thought again about the man in the green uniform, delivering the box that had started smoking only minutes later. "Where is he?" he said in barely a whisper to no one in particular as he surveyed the surrounding warehouse.

A small crowd of uniformed warehouse employees had gathered near the commotion, and they were standing quietly by at a safe distance. Nick ran his gaze over each of them.

Libby folded her arms across her chest. "Where is who?" she asked shakily. "John? I saw him heading toward the front office a few minutes ago."

"Not John. The guy who delivered the box."

He caught a movement near the back of the warehouse out of the corner of his eye. The suspect was watching them from behind a shelf. Nick locked his gaze. "Stay here," he instructed Libby. The workers shuffled in confusion and alarm as he drew his weapon.

"Nick, don't—"

But Nick didn't wait for Libby to protest. He took off running, picking up speed when he saw that the suspect had turned to flee. "FBI—freeze!" Nick turned down an aisle at a sprint, trying to keep an eye on the suspect as he ducked around a corner. He came to the end of the aisle and stopped, looking around.

No, Nick thought. *He can't get away.*

He cursed himself for not paying closer attention when the man brought in the box. He was supposed to be protecting Libby, and he'd just allowed the suspect to wander into a room and nearly kill them. Who knew how many of those files had been lost as a result of the fire? Or how their own investigation would suffer as a result of the attempt.

The white flashes in front of Nick's eyes turned red.

A shadow brushed the wall of a side hallway and Nick gave chase in time to see the suspect open a door and run outside. Nick came to the door and then stopped. The doorknob had been removed. He saw a small wooden triangle on the floor and realized that the suspect must have propped open the door from the outside. Nick swore. He'd have to find another way out.

He continued running down the hall until he saw a door marked "Exit." Opening the door, he found himself in a parking lot and looked around, blinking as his eyes adjusted to the flood of bright afternoon sunlight. There were several cars in the lot, but as he turned, a white windowless van roared to life. Nick surveyed his surroundings. The gravel parking lot was surrounded by wire chain-link fencing. There was only one way around the building and to the street, and that was via the asphalt path on which Nick was standing. The van backed up and began to turn, sending a spray of gravel into the air.

Nick's eyes narrowed. *You want to leave?* he thought. *Then you'll have to get through me first.*

He raised his gun and stepped into the middle of the path, turning to square off with the van's driver. "FBI! Get out of the van!" Nick aimed the weapon at the driver.

The driver stopped a mere fifty yards away and they were both still, staring each other down. Nick trained his gun on the van and studied the man, taking in the square shape of his face and the close-set, almond-shaped eyes glaring at him. He noted the patch of black, curly hair peeking from beneath the cap of the uniform. "I said get out of the van—now!"

The suspect flinched, and for a moment Nick thought he was going to comply. But then a smile spread across the man's face, revealing a set of pointy white teeth. The van lunged forward—right at Nick.

Nick fired his gun at the windshield, ripping a web across the glass. The van veered to the right and Nick felt a brief surge of hope that he'd hit the driver. But the van righted itself and continued on its path.

Nick fired again, this time aiming for a front tire. He heard the bullet ricochet. The van continued, undeterred. Nick's heart beat wildly in his chest, his flesh burning with rage and adrenaline as the van careened toward him. He felt so powerful that he wondered if he could stop the van with his bare hands. All Nick could see through the shattered windshield were those teeth, peeking like fangs from behind the man's lips. The van came closer.

Closer.

The van wasn't going to stop, and the driver couldn't have seemed happier about it.

Nick jumped out of the way at the last moment and rolled to the side of the road, allowing the van to speed by. Then he rose to one knee and fired his gun after it, hearing the bullets ricochet off the back doors. Bile rose in his throat. The suspect had escaped.

His breath came in staccato bursts as he marched around the warehouse toward the front door. His heels dug into the ground with each step, the tension in his shoulders mounting with each crack of his foot against the pavement. The front door was propped open but the entry was vacant. The door to the office was closed. Nick walked inside and headed to the rear of the warehouse, back to the area where he'd left Libby and the firemen.

Libby was sitting on a chair, her shoulders wrapped in a gray blanket. She was talking to a fireman, a paramedic and a police officer, all of whom were staring at her with rapt attention. She was smiling at something the paramedic said. Nick clenched his fists.

"I thought you looked familiar." The cop beamed. "I have a copy of yesterday's paper—I should get your autograph."

Was she blushing? It sure looked that way as she lowered her eyes demurely and pulled the blanket tighter. "Oh, stop. My signature is worthless unless it's on a check."

"I'll bet you become a famous attorney some day." The paramedic smiled, giving Libby a little wink.

Nick saw those flashes of red again.

"Gentlemen," he said, his voice tense as he approached. "Special Agent Nick Foster." He flashed his credentials.

Libby stood, her eyes wide. "Oh, Nick, thank God you're okay. Someone thought they heard gunshots outside. A few officers went out to check."

"They did hear gunshots," he replied. "From my gun. The suspect was prepared to run me over."

Libby's hands, still clutching the blanket around her shoulders, flew to her mouth. "When is this going to end?"

Her voice sounded so childlike that Nick fought the urge to take her in his arms. Instead his eyes darted to the men surrounding Libby, delivering each of them an icy stare.

She stepped forward and placed a hand lightly on his forearm. "These gentlemen were trying to keep me calm while you were running around shooting at people."

"Ah. Then chivalry isn't dead, after all."

The police officer straightened his posture before offering Nick his hand. "Special Agent Foster, I'm Officer Donaldson. Ms. Andrews told me that you were both locked in that room when a fire suddenly started in one of the boxes. Is that right?"

"Correct," he said, his jaw tight. "And while you were here, talking to Ms. Andrews, the man who tried to kill us escaped. I need you to put out an all points bulletin on a windowless white van, New York license plate ending 'HGE.' The suspect should be considered armed and dangerous." Nick walked toward the room where the fire had been without waiting for a response, leaving the police officer, the paramedic and the fireman standing in stunned silence.

Libby followed him. "Hey, wait."

Nick stopped and turned toward her.

"What was that about?"

"What was what about?"

"They were being nice to me and you were rude to them."

Did she really not know? Nick wondered as he looked at her lovely face, her porcelain skin smeared with soot and the stagnant filth from the sprinkler water. Did she not know that those men had been flattering her because she happened to be a beautiful woman? Did she *really* not know that? He drank in her features. The soft, plump lips that formed her wide mouth, now slightly open as she questioned him. The strong chin on her heart-shaped face, those high, fine cheekbones. Her bottomless blue eyes seemed so confused. No, Nick realized, she truly had no idea why those men were talking to her. He sighed.

"Those men? They're useless," he said. "They're in here socializing while I'm risking my life trying to catch your stalker."

Libby pressed her lips together. Then she leaned toward

him and said in a low voice, "Nick, you lost the right to be jealous a long time ago."

She turned and walked toward the door to the document room, leaving Nick staring after her.

Libby's heart lurched when she saw the room. Chairs were overturned and water covered the floor. All of the cardboard boxes were soaked, and many of them were burned. The smell of smoke was so strong that her eyes watered.

A fireman and a police officer were examining the box that had contained the fire, and they looked up as they saw her. "Ma'am," said the fireman, "did you see who brought this box in here?"

Libby nodded, releasing one of her hands from beneath the blanket to tuck a strand of wet hair behind her ear. "Yes. It was a man in a green uniform. The one-piece kind of uniform. Coveralls. And workboots and a hat."

The officer looked interested. "So you saw him? You'd be able to identify him?"

Would she? In her experience as a prosecutor in the District Attorney's Office Libby was leery of eyewitness testimony. More often than one would think a rape victim would identify her attacker, exclaiming that she was certain of her choice, only to have that suspect exonerated by DNA evidence when the results of the rape kit were ready. If a victim's memory could fail after being face-to-face with her attacker, how could Libby expect that she'd be able to identify a man she'd barely paid any attention to?

"There must be security cameras," she said.

"There's one leading right to this room. Unfortunately someone blackened the lens with spray paint. We'll be lucky if we get anything decent from the others."

"Nick got a good look." She bit her lip. "I could do my best to identify him."

"That's all any of us can do," said the fireman, smiling

kindly. He gestured to the charred box in front of him. "Want to see what he did?"

Libby took a breath and held it. She nodded. The fireman waved her over to stand beside him. "It looks like this was some kind of a radio-controlled device," he explained, lifting a handful of melted plastic from the box. "It's a little hard to see anything, but this looks like a receiver of some sort." He gestured with a gloved finger.

Libby squinted at the plastic. "I'll take your word for it. You're saying that he dropped the box in here, armed with some kind of device, and then remotely created a spark?" A spark in a box filled with old paperwork would certainly be capable of starting a fire.

The officer shook his head. "Not just a spark. A flame." He lifted another piece from the box—this one metal. "This is a small blowtorch," he explained.

Libby's teeth began to chatter and she adjusted the blanket around her shoulders. "He wanted to do some damage."

"Do you have any idea why someone would want to hurt you?" The fireman's voice was soft as he watched for Libby's reaction.

That's exactly the question, isn't it? Libby thought wryly. She had no idea who would want to hurt her, or why. "I've been involved in some high-profile litigation recently. Maybe that set someone off."

"You know how people can get about local celebrities," Nick said from the doorway, trying to sound casual. Libby jumped—she hadn't heard him enter.

She pulled the blanket tighter. "These are my dad's old files. He died a couple of weeks ago." She gestured to the piles of boxes, burned or sagging with moisture. "He prosecuted the Glen Falls Strangler about thirty years ago."

"Oh?" The fireman lifted his eyebrows. "I remember that case. I was a teenager at the time. My older sister didn't feel safe in her own bed until that guy was locked up. This is a lot of material. Are you writing a book or something?"

"Uh…sort of." Both men looked at Libby now, and she shifted from one foot to the other before turning her head away from them. "I need to know whether these files can be salvaged. These are original documents, and duplicates don't exist."

"You don't mind if we go through them, do you?" Nick put a hand softly on Libby's back as she hunched under the weight of her circumstances.

The police officer shook his head. "Sorry, sir. And I'm real sorry to hear about your father, Ms. Andrews. But this is a crime scene, and you'll have to take it up with the police sergeant."

Libby felt the ball of anxiety in her stomach unfurl, spiraling to her throat and settling in a thick mass that she couldn't swallow. "Please," she said in a barely audible gasp. "We need these files."

Both men looked at her with soft eyes. The fireman said, "We're very sympathetic to your situation, Ms. Andrews, but—"

He was interrupted as Officer Donaldson barreled into the room. "Agent Foster, you may want to come with me."

Nick's face grew dark. "Why? What is it?"

"A body," said Donaldson, glancing at Libby. "We have a dead body."

Nick stood in the doorway to the office, wincing. He'd asked Libby to stay near the front door, telling her she had no business being so close to a homicide. She'd listened to him, but just barely, and she was craning her neck and standing on her toes to get a better look. "What happened?" she asked.

The warehouse manager was lying flat on his office floor in a puddle of blood. His throat had been cut. "John Lankowsky," Nick said to Officer Donaldson. "I gave him a description of the suspect, and he said the man didn't work here. He said he'd get to the bottom of this. He must have confronted him."

"Nick?" Libby called from her spot as she looked on.

"It's a dead body, Libby," he said impatiently over his shoulder. "That's all you need to know." He turned to Donaldson. "You need to clear everyone out of this area before your evidence is compromised."

"Yes, sir."

"What's going on in here? You're giving orders to my men?" a figure bellowed from behind Nick.

He turned to see a round face with two eyes, dark as flint, glaring at him. "Who are you?"

"Special Agent Nick Foster." He flashed his credentials. "And you?"

"Sergeant Katz," he barked.

The sergeant appeared to be in his early forties, with light brown hair beginning to gray at the temples and a rigid jaw. "Sergeant, I think Officer Donaldson can show you around. If you'll excuse me? I have to check up on someone." Nick left the room and approached Libby, who was hugging herself.

"What happened?" she asked, her lower lip trembling. "No, don't tell me. I don't want to know." She took a deep breath. "Yes, I do. What happened?"

Nick watched her. "It's the warehouse manager. His throat was cut."

Libby gasped and covered her mouth with her hands. Then a dark anger crossed her face. "There's no reason." Her blue eyes flashed as she spun to look at Nick. "What could be the possible reason for that poor man to die? To have his throat... cut?" She choked back her anger.

"Shh." Nick smoothed his hands down her arms. "I know."

"*Do* you know?" She yanked her arms away. "*Do* you know what it's like to wonder what you did to deserve this...torture? To know that someone is dead because of you?" Her anger was written on her face as she stepped away from him.

There was a time when Nick could have responded instinctively to her, known when she needed a hug or someone to talk to without being asked. But now the inches that physically separated them felt like miles, and Nick realized with a pang in his gut that he'd lost the ability he'd once had to comfort Libby.

"You're not responsible for any of this, Libby." His voice was soft, and without thinking he reached out to touch the tips of her fingers. Anything to bridge that gap.

For a moment Nick was certain she would yank her hand away. But to his surprise she allowed him to hold her hand, even relaxing her fingers to slide around his. Then she turned to him and her wide blue eyes met his, wrenching at his heart.

"Do you think we can go home soon?" she asked, and gestured to her wet clothes. "I want to change."

He swallowed. "Sure. I'm just waiting for someone."

She dropped her hand and folded her arms across her chest, tilting her head slightly. "Waiting for someone? Who are you waiting for?"

"Some friends who owe me a favor," he said. His attention was snagged by the movement of a dark SUV in the parking lot, and he watched as two men in black FBI jackets exited the vehicle. "As if on cue..."

The men walked confidently into the warehouse and looked around.

"Over here," said Nick with a slight wave of his hand. "Special Agents Morgenstern and Leonard, I'd like you to meet Elizabeth Andrews."

The men nodded. "Miss Andrews."

"Please, call me Libby."

Nick gestured to the back of the warehouse, where they could just make out a sliver of light from the conference room. "We're going to need all of the boxes from that room. Now, some of them are badly burned, but if you can see white on any of the documents inside, it goes. Got it?"

The men nodded. "Yes, sir."

Libby stared at Nick, her mouth slightly agape as he continued to give instructions to the agents.

"Load the boxes into your vehicle. I'm going to need copies of the contents delivered to Ms. Andrews' house as soon as possible. Then return the boxes to the Stillborough P.D. If anyone tries to stop you keep moving and tell them to come talk to me. Oh, and I need this to be done quietly. If your ASAC gives you crap about your whereabouts, I'll talk to him."

Morgenstern grinned. "Going rogue again, Foster?"

"Don't you worry about that," Nick replied stiffly.

"Better you than me." They turned and headed for the office.

Libby looked at Nick. "What's an A-sack?"

"Assistant Special Agent in Charge. Also known as a ripe pain in the ass." A slight smile spread on Nick's face as he caught the stunned amazement in Libby's expression. "You didn't think I was going to let you go home without those documents, did you?"

"I thought—" Libby stopped, and her face relaxed into a small smile of its own. "I don't know what I thought." She shook her head. "I have to hand it to you, Foster."

Foster. She'd used to call him that after he graduated from the Police Academy. She'd got a charge out of barking silly orders at him as if she was his superior. *Give me the remote, Foster,* or *Go make me some tea, Foster,* said with a laugh and a mischievous grin, as if she was trying to determine how much she could get away with. Sometimes, at unexpected moments, her usually mundane commands became deliciously sexy. *Touch me here, Foster.* Nick pulled himself back from the memory.

"So, are you making this a Bureau case, then?" Libby asked.

Judge Andrews' conditions were clear, Nick thought: no police—state or federal. He could jeopardize his payment by involving the Bureau, and he needed that money. He was still years away from making a decent salary, and in the meantime he had debts to consider. A car loan. Credit card payments. He also had to have a way to pay the private detectives he'd hired to guard Libby for three weeks. He looked at Libby and his stomach clenched. More importantly, Judge Andrews seemed to believe that they couldn't trust law enforcement. What if the stalker was a cop?

"No, it's not a Bureau case," he replied. "I just need some photocopies made."

The special agents had loaded a dolly with boxes and were streaming through the entrance area toward the front door.

Officer Donaldson observed them with wide eyes. "Hey, wait a minute!"

Nick saw him tug at the sergeant's sleeve.

"Sergeant, they're contaminating the arson scene!"

"What the...?" Sergeant Katz's face turned an alarming shade of purple. "Stop right there!"

"Keep going!" ordered Nick.

The sergeant's face grew even darker as he cursed. Loudly.

Sergeant Katz marched over to Nick and Libby. "Just what the hell is going on here?"

"I need those files, Sergeant."

"You Bureau guys are all the same," he snarled. "You think you're so superior. Are you telling me this is the FBI's case?" He studied Nick with those black glassy eyes. "Because if you think you can take those boxes from my crime scene—"

"We're on the same team here, Sergeant." Nick turned to face him. "In fact, I think I can help you."

The man scoffed. "With what? Your superior police skills?" The words were thick with derision.

"No, with information." Nick kept his voice level. "You want to impress the Stillborough Mayor? Be a regular hero to the Stillborough residents?"

Katz watched him warily, continuing to glower. "I'm listening."

Nick smiled slightly. "Stillborough likes its crystal, doesn't it?" Katz began to sputter, but Nick cut him off. "It's no secret, Sergeant. It's a little town with a big meth habit. I understand you had an incident on Christmas Day. A meth lab in a two-family house exploded, and two young children were killed in the fire. It made national news."

Katz reddened, looking slightly uncomfortable. "We're following up on leads."

"Of course you are," said Nick. "But what if I told you that the Bureau is watching the person who caused that explosion closely, and that I can give you some insight to his location?" He shrugged nonchalantly and stuck his hands in his pockets. "We have an informant. Your boy is a small player in a big drug ring we've had our eye on for a long time."

"Are you serious?" Katz leaned in closer. "Don't jerk me around—"

"I'm quite serious, Sergeant. You make that arrest and you'll be a local hero, tough on crime, tough on drugs." Nick touched his shoulder and whispered, "We can work with you and make that arrest part of a larger drug bust if you can hold out for a little while."

Katz did not move. "And what do you want in return?"

"I want to make copies of the documents that were stuck in that fire. My colleagues will be careful to not disturb any evidence, and they'll return the boxes tonight. I also want you to keep me apprised of any developments in this case." Nick straightened, pulling back his broad shoulders until he towered over Katz. "*Any* developments, Sergeant. That means I get to know which officers are handling the evidence and responding to any related calls, and every move they make. The FBI is prepared to bust the guy you're after in the Christmas Day case, and if you want to be the one to get the credit you'll treat me as a partner in this investigation."

Katz sucked his teeth, and his face twisted as he thought, but after a few moments had passed he turned to Nick and said gruffly, "Deal." He extended his hand.

Nick broke into a broad smile and accepted the sergeant's handshake. "I'll be in touch, then."

Libby grabbed Nick's arm as Katz walked away. "Nick," she whispered, "what does that mean?"

"It means the sergeant is going to help me watch his officers as they process this case. If your dad said that we can't trust the police, I want to know everything that they're doing." He placed his hand gently on her back. "And it means we need to get you home so that you can finish going through those documents."

"I never took you for a diplomat," Libby said over her shoulder as they walked toward the front door. "You're just full of surprises."

Nick quickened his pace to hold the door for her. "You know what they say about desperate times," he replied. But beneath his cool exterior his chest swelled at the smile she gave him.

CHAPTER FIVE

LIBBY wandered toward the stove as the teakettle began to hiss and whistle. Every inch of her body ached with fatigue, and they were only halfway through the files stacked in her dining room. "Would anyone like some tea?" she asked over her shoulder.

"No, thanks," came the chorus of replies from her living room.

She closed her eyes and took steadying breaths as she waited for her tea to steep. Special Agents Morgenstern and Leonard had dropped off the boxes and left, and almost immediately Nick's private investigator buddies, Zack Troy and Ben Sterling, had appeared to fill the vacancy.

"Troy and Sterling," she'd said as she looked them over. "Yes, that sounds like a detective agency, all right."

"It's actually Sterling and Troy," Ben had replied with a lopsided grin and a wink of one of his cobalt-blue eyes. "Pleasure to finally meet you, Libby."

She lifted the tea bag from the steamy water and squeezed the excess fluid into her cup. Between Ben's stunning blue eyes, Zack's almost-but-not-quite-too-long wavy chestnut hair, and the dimple in Nick's devilish grin, Libby was certain she had three months covered on a "Hot Guys of Law Enforcement" calendar. Under different circumstances she might have considered herself one of the luckiest women around. But then, there was the whole serial killer thing.

She wrapped her hands around her mug, holding it gingerly as the heat spread to her fingers. After they'd arrived at her house, Libby had excused herself and drawn a hot bath. She'd added bubbles and lain in the tub for nearly forty-five minutes as she tried to slow the thoughts racing through her mind. How long had it been since she'd been able to close her eyes without hearing a hundred frenetic thoughts vying for her attention? When had her neat, orderly life suddenly taken this wild turn?

After the bath water had chilled, she'd dressed in an unseasonably warm sweater and heavy socks, trying to suppress the numbing cold icing her veins. It hadn't helped, and so she'd made tea. She wasn't convinced that was helping, either.

Libby could hear the rustle of papers and the murmur of voices in the living room as they sorted through her father's files. She felt something in her stomach spark at the deep rumble of Nick's voice. *My own body is working against me.* She took another deep breath. Yes, Nick was attractive. He was take-charge. Sure, she'd found it almost unbearably sexy when he'd stood up to that Sergeant What's-his-face. Then she'd pinched her arm and told herself to snap out of it. She'd been in love with Nick before. Hopelessly, mindlessly in love. She'd been in the kind of love where she'd gotten butterflies in her stomach at the sound of his car in the driveway, or the ring of her cell phone when he called. She sighed. These butterflies felt unnervingly similar to the old ones.

Libby shook her head. They weren't in high school anymore. Nick was no longer the captain of the soccer team or the boy that the other girls crowded round each time he went to his locker. Libby remembered the way that Nick had taken all of that attention in stride. He was always so confident, so unflappable. Libby had never admitted to Nick that they would never have spoken if he hadn't approached her first. She'd always had a paralyzing crush on him.

She took a sip of her tea. No, she wasn't a schoolgirl, and

she wasn't going to allow Nick to have that kind of power over her heart and her mind. The minute she allowed him that control would be the minute she opened herself to being hurt. She would never allow anyone to hurt her the way Nick had hurt her when he'd walked out the door. *People who love you don't leave.* The thought was like a probing finger against a still-open wound.

Nick didn't love her. Nick loved himself, and she'd learned that the hard way.

He'd been at FBI training in Quantico when she'd mentioned that she had a medical problem that required further testing. "I don't want you to worry," she'd said. "But the doctors want to rule some things out."

"I'm sure it will all be fine," he'd replied.

But it hadn't been fine. A series of blood tests and ultrasounds had revealed that Libby had entered premature menopause as a result of the cancer treatment she'd received as a child. The diagnosis had left her numb. She'd told herself that she didn't want children, anyway. She had a career she loved. She had goals. That was enough. The lies had kept her going for a while, but eventually she hadn't been able to ignore the gut-wrenching pain of seeing a mother with a young child, or the sudden shame she had felt about her body. The diagnosis had permeated every aspect of her life. It had become who she was.

Libby hadn't been able to bring herself to tell Nick that she was infertile, and he'd never asked how the tests went—as if he'd forgotten entirely. As if, she'd had to admit, he didn't even care. Once he'd come back from Quantico, he'd been engulfed by his new job, and Libby had allowed herself to drift away, finding it easier to be alone than to face the prospect of his rejection. One day, when the time was right, she'd tell him that she couldn't bear his children. Sometimes the confession had reached the tip of her tongue before she'd bitten it back, afraid that if she was honest he would leave her. So she'd never told him—and he'd left her anyway.

And yet now that he was back in her life she realized the temptation to be with Nick was still there. She'd never been afraid to be alone, but now Libby felt an ache in her chest at the thought of him leaving in a few days, taking his voice, his footsteps and his cologne with him. He filled her home with something intangible, something she still missed.

She was unsettled by the realization.

"Hey, Libby?"

Speak of the devil. Nick was standing in the doorway, back-lit by the lights in the living room. He held out his hand. "Your phone has been vibrating."

"Oh." She walked over to take her cell phone and typed her password. "Just some text messages. From David."

She felt Nick watching her, and she tried to keep her face inscrutable. David was in Zurich, negotiating some corporate merger, and he'd sent several messages to say hello and to tell her how much he was looking forward to seeing her when he came home. Libby's heart cleaved with guilt. She needed to stop spending so much time dwelling on the past and start thinking about her future. David was a nice guy. Reliable. Stable. David was her future, not Nick.

He walked nonchalantly past her and opened a cabinet to retrieve a drinking glass. "We ordered pizza, if you'd like some," he said.

"Yes, I saw the boxes sprawled across my living room floor. Thanks, but I'm not hungry."

"Not even for Harry's Pizza?" Nick smiled. "I ordered pepperoni."

Damn, Libby thought, there was that dimple again. "No, thank you. I just…" She lifted her shoulders. "I guess I lose my appetite when people are trying to kill me."

The smile faded from Nick's face. He hesitated for a moment and then put the glass on the counter. "Libby," he said. He didn't continue.

"I know. I shouldn't joke like that. It's not funny." She started to take a sip of her tea, but the way he was looking at her sent her pulse racing, and her hands felt unsteady. She put the mug down.

"That's not what I was going to say."

She lifted her eyes to his. "What were you going to say, then?"

He walked over to her until they were inches apart, until Libby was nearly breathless from the pounding in her chest. Nick reached out his hand to cup Libby's chin in a familiarly possessive gesture—one that had never failed to make Libby's knees weak. He caressed her face with a slow gaze, his eyes devouring her hungrily. She wondered if he could feel the thrust of her pulse against the pads of his fingers. She wondered if he noticed the way he'd just stalled the breath in her lungs with his stare. She hoped not.

Nick leaned forward then, coming down toward her face, his lips slightly parted. Libby, so cold all day, felt heat spreading through her as she closed her eyes and opened her lips in anticipation of contact. But then she felt the soft touch of Nick's lips against her forehead. He pulled away and smoothed her hair from her face.

"I'll save some pizza for you, just in case."

She nodded feebly, trying to swallow her disappointment as he took his glass of water and walked back toward the living room. *Convinced now?* she thought angrily, trying to stop the sting of humiliation. Nick was the one who'd left. He'd gotten over her a long time ago, and the sooner she accepted that, the better.

She eyed her phone. She'd cloistered herself away since the breakup, and she had no one to blame but herself for the loneliness. Nick had moved on, and he wasn't coming back.

She grabbed the phone and sent David a reply: *Miss you, too. Can't wait until you come home. Maybe I'll pick you up at the airport.*

Nick wandered back into the living room and pointed at Zack. "Hey, feet off the couch. Better yet, you shouldn't be wearing shoes at all in here."

Zack looked at him with amusement. "Yes, sir." He gave Nick a mocking salute and turned to Ben. "Next thing you know he'll be telling us we have to eat our pizza with a fork and knife."

"My grandfather owned a pizzeria in the city. He'd turn over in his grave if I ever suggested that you eat pizza with a fork." Nick settled himself to the floor and leaned against the base of the love seat. "But I know how Libby is, and she'd take your head off if she saw shoes on her couch."

Ben turned to Nick and asked in a conspiratorial whisper, "Hey, what's the story with you and her? Did you used to hook up?"

Nick flinched at the crude term. He saw no need to rehash their long history with Zack and Ben. "Hooking up" implied one-night stands and sex without strings attached. Libby, to the contrary, had walked around for years while carrying his heart in the palm of her hand. "No, we never hooked up."

"Hmm," Ben nodded thoughtfully. "That's too bad. She's hot."

"She's hot in that smart teacher kind of way," Zack agreed. "She's probably out of your league, Foster."

"Enough," Nick warned.

"Well, if you're not going to make a move, maybe I will," murmured Zack as he rummaged through a folder.

"You do so much as look at her the wrong way…" Nick growled. He'd meant it as a good-natured threat, but his tone was more ominous.

"Hey!" Zack laughed warily and held up a hand. "Easy. I'm just joking."

Libby entered, clearly oblivious to the exchange the three men had just had. Nick watched her as she moved gracefully across the room and settled herself on a pillow on the floor. He felt helpless, watching her in her heavy sweater. A wool sweater in April. She was scared out of her mind and putting up a brave front. He felt ashamed, thinking of that moment in the kitchen when he'd been consumed with a need to kiss her, to fold her into his arms and cradle her against his chest. His response had been all wrong. Libby was vulnerable and he was supposed to be protecting her. Kissing her would only complicate matters, and God knew matters were already too complicated.

She noticed his gaze and gave him a wan smile. "So, are you finding anything?"

"Not too much." Ben shrugged. "I keep coming across all of these campaign flyers—'Jebediah Sinclair for mayor.'" He picked one of the flyers up and handed it to her.

"Of course." Libby nodded as she read the flyer. "Jeb Sinclair. He and my dad were good friends. David, my boyfriend, is his son."

Nick flinched. So he was her boyfriend now? He noticed her glance at him furtively from the corner of her eye before she continued.

"Gosh, I remember going door to door with Dad for Jeb Sinclair when I was a kid." She smiled. "I collected his campaign buttons. I think I had a few shoe boxes filled with them."

"Sinclair," Nick said thoughtfully. "I remember him. I never knew David, though."

"David went to private schools," Libby replied. "I knew him when I was much younger, but only recently met up with him again at a fund-raiser. I believe Jeb was the longest-serving mayor of Glen Falls. I think he was elected in 1976, and he was one of Dad's biggest supporters when he ran for judge."

She looked at Ben and Zack. "Judges in New York are elected, so politics were a way of life in my house."

"Michael Andrews was highly respected, first as a prosecutor and then as a judge," Nick said.

Libby turned and gave him a grateful smile. Nick looked away, feeling slightly guilty. She'd always adored her father—and why not? Judge Andrews had doted on his daughter and shown her only the best sides of himself. Nick had never told her about the many times the judge had pulled him aside and informed Nick that, in his mind, Libby deserved someone with more brains and less brawn.

"My daughter deserves an intellectual equal. A doctor or a lawyer, Nick," Judge Andrews had sneered. "Not a *cop*."

Nick still ground his teeth at the memory.

But then he thought of his last meeting with the judge, when he'd been forced to agree to give Nick his entire estate in return for his assistance. Everything he ever owned would belong to Nick, and all because Judge Andrews was hiding something in his past from the police. He couldn't help but feel some satisfaction. Truly, revenge was a dish best served cold.

"That reminds me," said Zack as he stood and walked to retrieve a pile of folders from the corner. "Your father was the one receiving the threatening letters, wasn't he?"

"Yes," Nick said.

Zack produced a pile of photocopied letters. "I went over to the court record center, like you asked, Nick. I copied quite a few letters for you."

"These are the letters that Will Henderson sent to the families of his victims, correct?" asked Libby.

"Correct."

Nick glanced over the documents. To his untrained eye the handwriting looked the same as the handwriting in the letters Libby's father had received. If it *was* the same, then perhaps the Glen Falls Strangler was still at large. But Nick was not prepared to draw that conclusion himself. "I want to have these compared to the letters that were sent to Judge Andrews. I'm going to scan these and send them over to a handwriting expert at the Bureau to see what she thinks." He looked at Libby. "I'll ask her to put a rush on it."

"Good." She nodded. "Anything else?"

Nick was happy to see her reach for a piece of pizza. She was looking too thin.

"I'm learning more about this Will Henderson," said Zack. "Seems he was a small-time crook for a good part of his life. Frequent brushes with law enforcement for shoplifting, purse-snatching, things like that. Nothing violent, from what I've seen. I have to say I'm a bit puzzled as to how Henderson became suspect in a string of homicides. Nothing I've seen suggests that he should have been considered."

Libby shot Nick a look, as if she was wondering if he'd planted that idea with Zack. He gave her a slight shrug—they'd never discussed the issue. He felt rather vindicated that Zack also found it odd that a petty career criminal like Will Henderson would become a serial killer.

"Lots of serial killers begin as petty criminals," said Libby.

"But the crimes serial killers begin with are more antisocial in nature," Zack explained. "They set fires and torture animals. Grabbing purses and stealing cigarettes doesn't seem to fit the profile."

"I think I can answer your question," said Ben as he flipped through the notepad on his lap. "I came across something earlier that made me think Henderson had signed a confession of some sort."

"Yes, that's right," Libby said eagerly. "Jack MacGruder mentioned that Henderson had practically confessed to the killings."

"Right." Ben rubbed the spot above the bridge of his nose as he searched his notes. He looked up. "Maybe we should review the timeline so that we're all on the same page."

"That would be helpful," said Nick. "You two have been researching the details of this case for weeks."

"And the devil's in the details," said Ben. "Okay, then. Let's start at the top. 1971: victim number one. Trish Cummings. Twenty-three years old, a waitress at a greasy spoon in the center of town."

"You make it sound like you're reading a police report," Nick said.

"Sorry. I've been assembling the details piecemeal."

Ben had had his legs stretched out on the floor in front of him, but he shifted and bent one knee up. He had a way of talking animatedly with his hands, and Nick watched him with bemused interest.

"Trish's parents received threatening letters at their home and threw them out without going to the police. Apparently Trish was a pretty girl who had no shortage of male admirers, so they just assumed that the letters had been sent by another one." He held up his hands. "Weird, I know. But that's what they said."

"They were probably in denial," said Libby as she absentmindedly twirled a lock of black hair around her finger. "Who wants to believe that someone would want to hurt their child? It must have been easier, emotionally, for them to convince themselves that whoever wrote the letters actually loved their daughter."

Her comment made Nick remember why Libby was such a great prosecutor. She put up a hard front, but she innately understood victims and their families and had a deep sympathy for their struggles. With Libby there were no crocodile tears or phony emotional pleas—she was unapologetically herself in the courtroom. Juries loved her for it.

"Whatever the reasons," Ben continued, "they didn't go to the police. Trish was found strangled in her apartment, and three of her fingers were cut off. A gruesome scene."

"To say the least." Nick eyed Libby, prepared to redirect the discussion if necessary. She was listening intently.

"Now, the police had no way of knowing at that point that a serial killer was on the loose," Zack said. "They became suspicious almost nine months later, when twenty-two-year-old Lea Patricelli was killed in the same manner. Again, there were letters to the family, but they didn't contact the police."

"Even if the police began to suspect a serial killer after Lea's death, they were reluctant to utter the *S* word for a long time," Ben said.

Libby tilted her head. "The *S* word? Oh, you mean *serial*."

"Exactly," Ben said. "Having two brutal murders occur in one town is one thing, but when you inject the words *serial killer* into the mix, you risk widespread panic."

"But eventually the police were open with the public about what was happening, right?" Libby asked. "And the murders still continued?"

"The police came forward after the fourth murder. That time the victim was thirty-six-year-old Mary Rogers. From what I can gather from the newspaper clippings I've read, that's the first time the media reported a serial killer was loose." Ben studied his notepad. "Yes, that's when the newspapers began to issue specific warnings about letters being sent to families. They didn't learn about the six signs until much later, when Henderson was arrested. He explained everything."

"So Henderson told the police about the signs, then?" Libby sat back. "That's compelling evidence of his guilt."

Nick turned to her. "What are you thinking?"

"Let's assume the police had a bunch of evidence from the crime scenes, including a lot of things they didn't understand or view as significant. Let's also assume that they never told Henderson about this evidence. Wouldn't it be strong evidence of Henderson's guilt if, as part of his confession, he was able to explain the significance of evidence the police never told him they had?"

Nick nodded slowly. "Yeah, I can see that."

Libby gave him a triumphant smile. "So you see? Henderson *must* have been the killer. Even if it doesn't make absolute sense for a petty thief to become a serial killer, this is great evidence that in this case it happened that way."

"Libby, I understand why you would be relieved about Henderson being the real killer," Nick began slowly. "After all, that means your dad prosecuted the right person and that the original killer isn't after you now. But Henderson is dead, so none of that tells us who is threatening you, or why."

"Did he have a wife?" Libby asked. "Kids? Maybe we should talk to them."

"No kids, and the wife died while Henderson was in jail," Ben replied. "She took her own life shortly after her husband was sentenced."

Libby winced.

"There's also one other problem with Henderson being the killer," Zack said. "I found a note about an eyewitness who was interviewed early on in the investigation of the case. She claimed to have seen someone lurking around the second victim's home. According to this witness, she saw this person leaving the scene of the crime, his clothes covered in blood."

"Eyewitness testimony?" Libby's eyebrows rose. "I'm confused. I thought there hadn't been any eyewitnesses to the crime."

"I thought the same thing, Libby," Zack said. "But then I saw this note. Clearly there was an eyewitness, but she was never called upon to testify at trial."

Libby frowned, her whole face a jumble of confusion. "Well, why on earth wouldn't Dad call an eyewitness to testify at Henderson's trial?"

"From what I can figure," Zack replied, "it's because the eyewitness would have sworn that Henderson wasn't the one she saw that day."

Nick saw Libby pale. "Wait a minute. Let me get this

straight," she said as she leaned forward. "Will Henderson signed a confession. Not only did he confess, but he gave the police reliable information about the evidence they had collected, further strengthening his confession. And now you're telling me that there was an eyewitness who would have testified that Henderson *wasn't* the person she saw leaving the second victim's house, covered in blood?"

"Here—you can see for yourself." Zack handed her a file.

Nick walked over to Libby and sat down to review the file with her. It contained several newspaper clippings in which Lea Patricelli's neighbor claimed to have seen the killer brazenly leaving her house in broad daylight.

"Harriet McGovern," Nick read aloud. "Oh, damn—she was seventy-three at the time."

"Seventy-three years old in 1972? I don't think we're going to get an interview." Libby continued to sort through the papers in the file, coming across some handwritten notes on sheets of yellowing paper. "Looks like Dad had the opportunity to sit down with Harriet." She squinted. "Is this even written in English?"

"Here, I've always had an easier time reading your dad's writing." Nick took the paper. "This says that Harriet was having tea on her porch at three o'clock in the afternoon when she saw a man leaving Lea Patricelli's house, covered in blood."

Ben, Zack and Libby sat in rapt attention. "Did she say what the man looked like?" Ben asked.

"It looks like she did, if I'm reading this correctly." Nick had his finger against the paper as he focused on the barely legible writing. "She said he was extremely tall, well over six feet. Light brown hair. Does that say 'red'?" He showed the paper to Libby.

"It looks like 'ruddy.' 'Ruddy face.'" She sat back. "That's an interesting description. So she saw an extremely tall man with light brown hair and a ruddy face. I don't even know what Will Henderson looked like."

"Is there an opposite of that description?" Zack asked. "Because Henderson was no taller than five foot eight, with fair skin and dark hair."

"Even if his complexion became ruddy every now and then," said Ben, "it doesn't seem likely that Henderson would be confused with an extremely tall man with light hair."

"I don't buy it." Libby sat back.

"Which part of it?" Nick asked.

She stuffed the papers back into the file and shrugged. "Any of it. This is an interesting footnote to the case, but I just don't see how one person's supposed eyewitness account should carry the day." She closed the file. "Look, I know I sound like I'm defending my dad, but you have to understand, he was building a case. Sure, it makes sense that he interviewed someone who claimed to be an eyewitness, but if he didn't think she was a reliable witness he wasn't going to put her on the stand." She handed the file back to Zack. "The defense didn't call her, either, and her testimony could have introduced reasonable doubt. Mark my words—there's more to this story."

There was passion in Libby's voice, and Nick couldn't help but stare at her. Her cheeks were slightly flushed and her bright eyes reflected that keen intelligence that he'd always found so irresistibly sexy. Her generous lips were slightly parted as she waited for Zack's response. Nick touched his own mouth, thoughtlessly imagining Libby's taste.

"I'll defer to your experience, Attorney Andrews," Zack said good-naturedly. "But you wanted to know all of the details, so I'm giving you all of the details."

Libby relaxed her posture slightly. "You're right. You're just the messenger, and I shouldn't be arguing with you over this." She ran her hands over her face before folding her arms tightly across her chest. "I think I should try to get some sleep. Zack and Ben, you're welcome to stay over, if you'd like. Actually, I think I'd sleep better if you did. Safety in numbers."

Ben and Zack smiled.

"Thanks, Libby," Ben said. "We'll probably stay up late looking through these boxes and then crash on the floor, if it's okay with you."

"That's fine. Nick can show you where the blankets are." Libby stood.

Nick felt Ben and Zack looking at him quizzically, and suppressed a sudden urge to knock the smug smile right off Zack's face. He rose and followed Libby to the foot of the stairs, out of sight of Ben and Zack.

"Hey," he said, touching her arm lightly. "Get a good night's sleep."

She paused, trailing her gaze across his face. "Is that really what you wanted to say?"

Nick's stomach tensed. That was one of the things he wanted to say, but he had a hundred more to add. He wanted to know what had happened between them. How they could have gone from best friends and lovers to virtual strangers. He wanted to know what had made her pull away from him to begin with, to distance herself until, terrified of her silence, he'd decided to leave her before she left him.

"I'm trying to make this better, Libby. I'm trying to fix this so you can go back to your normal life." He brushed his fingers through his hair. "I really do want you to sleep well tonight. You need to get some rest."

Her face softened slightly and she reached out to touch the tips of his fingers. The feel of her skin made his breath catch in his throat.

"Thanks, Nick. I want you to sleep well, too."

Nick watched as she turned and climbed the stairs, which creaked under the weight of her footsteps. He waited until her figure had entirely disappeared into the darkness of the second-story landing. Then he waited longer until he saw a sliver of light pierce the dark and he knew that she was safely in her bedroom.

CHAPTER SIX

Day Three

LIBBY pointed to a white Victorian house with a wraparound porch and a wooden sign in the front yard advertising "Everett Adams, Attorney-at-Law."

"There," she said. "Just pull in to that little driveway, and there's parking in the back."

Nick followed her instructions, parking the black Toyota Corolla in a space between two SUVs. "Your chariot has arrived."

Libby started to open the door and then looked back at him. He was wearing a light black V-neck sweater that clung just enough to the hard curves of his arms. *Focus, Libby!* "You can wait here."

"I don't think so." Nick opened the door and stepped onto the gravel.

"You know, you don't need to escort me everywhere." The tone of her voice was one of annoyance, but secretly Libby had breathed easier after Nick had insisted upon driving her to the center of town. She'd never considered herself to be helpless by any measure, but having Nick around made her feel that much stronger. It didn't hurt his case that he'd finally shaved that morning, and that she'd caught a glimpse of the gun in its holster, hidden beneath his jacket. He was looking exceptionally dangerous on a number of levels. Also, he smelled mouthwatering.

Focus!

"I'm meeting with the attorney for my dad's estate, Nick. Last time I checked, he's not the guy who tried to set us on fire yesterday."

He gave her a wry smile and closed the car door. "Nice try, Andrews. Come on, you're going to be late."

They followed the driveway to the back entrance, located at the top of four wide wooden stairs painted in a light blue. Libby always looked for an excuse to visit the period Victorian homes and converted businesses that lined Glen Falls' Main Street. The buildings were maintained in period-appropriate hues of mossy greens, sienna reds and earthy browns, and often contained ornate architectural details like stained-glass windows and patterned chimneys. In a few weeks' time this stretch of Main Street would become especially vibrant as the sweetly fragranced blossoms of pink dogwood, magnolia and weeping cherry trees brought it to life. Even on such an overcast day visiting Main Street was a welcome distraction.

Everett Adams had converted the Victorian home that now housed his thriving estate-planning practice and preserved many of the home's charming details. "Isn't that wallpaper incredible?" Libby whispered breathlessly as she studied the rich burgundy walls accented with gold scroll. She shrieked as Nick started to sit on a plush bench decorated with golden-hued fabric. "Nick, that's an antique!"

They were greeted by a middle-aged woman with wiry chestnut-colored hair and darkly framed glasses that she wore at the tip of her pointy nose. "Ah, Elizabeth Andrews," she said with a little smile. "My, if you aren't the spitting image of your father."

Libby smiled warmly. "I have an appointment to see Attorney Adams."

"Of course. I'll let him know you're here. My condolences, honey. Your father was a lovely man."

"Thank you."

Nick and Libby stood off to one side of the reception area while the woman picked up the phone and said, "Attorney Adams? Elizabeth Andrews is here to see you." After a moment she placed the phone on the receiver and turned to Libby. "He'll be right with you, honey."

"What are you two meeting about, anyway?" Nick asked.

"I'm the executrix of Dad's estate," Libby said. "With James living in California, I guess Dad thought it made more sense for me to handle this business." Libby sighed. "Honestly? I could never stand estate work. I took a course in property law because I had to, but I've always found it to be a unique form of intellectual torture."

Nick stiffened. "You're talking about settling the estate *today?*"

"Yes. I want this done with. I feel like the sooner Dad's estate is closed, the sooner I can get some closure myself."

Nick nodded. "I can understand that."

There was a creaking of the floorboards and an older man with fine snowy-white hair appeared, his arm extended toward Libby. "Good to see you again, Libby."

"Nice to see *you,* Everett." She gestured to Nick. "I'd like you to meet a friend of mine—Nick Foster."

"Oh, yes." Everett's smile tightened. "Nick Foster."

Libby's eyebrows shot up and she turned to Nick, who gave her an easy smile as he shook Everett's hand. "Attorney Adams has done some legal work for me."

"Well, Libby, why don't we get started? Nick, are you staying here or joining us?"

Nick looked at Libby. "You know…why don't you just go ahead? I'll be here when you get out."

Libby nodded, feeling a slight relief that Nick understood the need to keep certain things confidential. She would be safe with him waiting in the reception area, she had no doubt, and he didn't need to be involved in such mundane matters as paying her father's debts. She followed Everett into the office and closed the door behind her.

Everett walked behind a large oak desk and gestured with one hand to a red-cushioned armchair. "Please, have a seat. I appreciate you coming here this morning, Libby," he said as he settled into his chair. "I wanted to review certain details of your father's estate plan with you."

"What kinds of details, Everett?"

"For starters, you know that your father's will left his entire estate in a trust and named me as the trustee?"

Libby had been unpleasantly surprised, after her father's death, to learn that he'd elected to do some untraditional estate planning. Rather than leaving his possessions directly to his children, he'd placed them all in trust.

"Yes, I do know that. I was hoping that we could review the terms of the trust today." Her father had never discussed how he intended to divide his estate, and Libby was curious.

"Actually, we can't discuss that. Not yet, anyway." Everett sat forward and folded his hands on his desk.

Her eyes narrowed. "Why not?"

"There are certain conditions that must be met before the terms of the trust can be disclosed to you." He shrugged apologetically. "Those were your father's wishes, and I'm sure you understand that I am bound to follow them."

"Conditions?" Libby shook her head and tried to quell a gnawing in her stomach. "What conditions? And why would the trust document be secret? Isn't it a public document?"

"No. Wills are public," Everett said as he reached for a mug on his desk and took a small sip. "Trust documents are not."

She rubbed at her forehead as she tried to understand what was happening. "So basically what you're telling me, Everett, is that Dad has planned his estate in order to hide something from me and James?"

Everett arched an eyebrow. "I wouldn't say that your father was trying to hide something, *per se.*"

"But he was, wasn't he?" Libby felt a surge of adrenaline as she contemplated the possibility that Everett had assisted her father in doing something untoward with his estate. "He knew that a will would have to be made public, and so all it says is that his estate will be placed in trust. The trust document, which actually details how the estate will be divided, is being kept secret."

"Only for a little while—until the conditions are met." Everett lifted his hands helplessly. "You understand that I can't disclose what those conditions are just yet? But I don't anticipate this taking much longer."

Libby took a deep breath and held it for a count of ten. She had to calm herself. She exhaled and said quietly, "You said you had some other matters to discuss?"

"Yes." Everett opened a manila file on his desk and handed Libby some papers. "We need to focus on settling your father's debts. Since you're the executrix of the estate, I wanted to keep you informed." He gave Libby a smile, and she countered it with a stony glare. Everett cleared his throat. "I will be publishing a notice in the newspaper this week. Any debtors will have a certain period of time to come forward, and after that any claim will be extinguished."

There was a small tasseled pillow on the chair, and Libby teased the silky threads between her fingers, remaining silent.

Everett looked slightly uncomfortable as he shifted in his chair. "My office has prepared several checks to pay known debtors of your father's estate. I will need you to sign them as the executrix." He slid a small stack of checks across the surface of the desk. "There is a pen right in front of you."

Libby took the pen and began signing. The checks seemed innocuous, even boring. Her father's final electricity and telephone bills, a check to the oil company. She paused and stared at the next check. "'Independent Protection Company,'" she read. "What is this for?"

Everett was reading a letter on his desk. "They sent a bill. I don't have it on hand."

There was that gnawing again—this time accompanied by anger at Everett's nonchalant response. He was purposely making light of this payment. "I want to see that bill," she said.

Everett sighed, as if she was being tedious. "I'll have to look for it, but your father left specific instructions for that one."

"Everett," Libby said, "this is a check for fifty thousand dollars. If you want me to sign it, I want to see a bill."

He spun to face her and then sat back in his chair. "If you don't sign it they will still get paid, Libby. There are provisions in the trust document."

She rose from her chair and leaned over the desk, her heart thrusting and her face hot. "I want to see that trust document, Everett," she hissed.

"I told you, I can't show it to you yet."

"Are you stealing from my father's estate?"

"What?" His eyes widened, then he rolled them. "Libby, calm down."

"You're asking me to sign a check for fifty thousand dollars to some company I've never even heard of. You can't produce a bill, but you can tell me that they will get paid whether or not I sign this check. Everett, what the hell is going on here?"

He was quiet for a moment. Then he said, "Take a deep breath and sit down. I'll explain."

She reluctantly did as he asked.

Everett continued, "I'm going to talk to you attorney to attorney, all right?"

She crossed her arms. "All right."

He smoothed a hand over his white hair. "It may be that your father had some debts that he never discussed with you. I knew your father for decades, and he was an exceedingly private man."

"Yes, he *was* private." Libby studied him suspiciously.

"I am not stealing from your father's estate," Everett whispered. "I watched you and James grow up. I was your father's confidant and friend, and, although I didn't know her as well, I thought your mother was a lovely woman." He tilted his head. "What's happening to you, Libby?"

She felt her shoulders tense. "Why would you ask me that?" Her voice trembled.

"You seem angry. Scared. You know I'm in a difficult position. Professionally, I must maintain a certain level of confidentiality, and yet it upsets me personally to not be able to answer your questions."

A knot rose in her throat. His calmness in the face of her strong accusations left her cheeks hot with shame. Of course she knew deep down that Everett wasn't stealing from her father's estate. Whatever her father had elected to do with his money was his choice, and she'd unfairly lashed out in anger.

She swallowed. Then she signed the check and returned it to the pile. Stacking them neatly, she slid them across the desk and rose. "You'll call me soon, then?"

Everett eyed her. "I will."

She nodded silently, pressing her lips together. Then she turned and walked out of the office.

Libby looked like she was on the verge of tears as she left Everett's office. Her face was pale, her mouth pulled tight as she struggled to maintain her composure. Nick stood. "What happened in there?"

She stopped in front of him, and then he could see the tears pooling beneath her blue irises. She started to open her mouth and then stopped, wiped her eyes.

"Never mind," said Nick, feeling a growing alarm. "You sit here."

"No," she managed. "It's fine."

"No, it's not," he said. "Sit here and wait for me." Without bothering to knock, he opened Everett's door and closed it behind him.

The attorney spun around in surprise. "Nick," he said.

"What just happened with Libby? Why is she crying?" He balled his fists.

"I'm not sure," he said. "She seems to be having a difficult time with her father's death." He gestured to the armchair. "Please—sit."

Nick walked stiffly to the chair. "Libby loved her father. You know that?"

"Yes, I do. She always looked up to him."

"Looked up to him? She idolized him. He's the reason she became an attorney—and you know she wants to be a judge one day, too?"

"From my perspective, she is not struggling so much with her father's passing as she is with the terms of his estate." He gave Nick a pointed look. "The estate plan is…unusual, as you know."

Nick's stomach dropped, and he wondered what had transpired between Libby and Everett. "I don't know anything about the estate plan." Nick eyed him from beneath his dark brows. "I haven't seen the documents, Everett."

"Please call me Attorney Adams," he snarled. "And you know *exactly* what the documents say—that you essentially blackmailed the judge with his daughter's life in return for his entire estate."

Nick clenched his jaw. "We had an agreement, that's all. There was no blackmail involved. The judge didn't trust the police, and so he turned to me for help." Nick sat back. "I have my expenses, and I need to be paid for my services."

"Yes, you have certainly seen to that. You will be well provided for."

Nick hesitated. "Does Libby know?"

"About the terms of the trust?" Everett tightened his mouth. "No, she doesn't. She doesn't yet know that she and her brother have been disinherited because her ex-fiancé made some despicable…*agreement* with her father."

Nick glared at him. "I'm risking my life for her. I'm risking my job—"

"Oh, spare me." Everett rolled his eyes. "I hope that you are happy with your choices. Let me assure you that you have a very sizeable amount coming to you if you comply with the judge's conditions." Everett looked at him coolly. "You *are* in compliance, correct? The police have not been called?"

"An attempt was made on our lives yesterday," Nick said. "The Stillborough police were called to the scene of an arson and a murder. I'm watching them closely and receiving updates from the sergeant. No one knows what has been happening to Libby, and there is no reason anyone would look into the judge's past." He paused. "I assume that does comply with the terms of the reward, correct? The police can be involved as long as they don't have any reason to reopen the Glen Falls Strangler files?"

Everett nodded stiffly. "I believe that would comply." He cleared his throat. "Ms. Andrews just signed a check for fifty thousand dollars. That money will be placed into an account and used to pay your expenses while the estate is being settled. These things take some time, but I'm sure you understand that."

Nick didn't respond.

Everett picked at the corner of the desk as he thought. "Is she going to be all right?" He looked at Nick, his eyes creased around the edges in a display of concern.

Nick's throat tensed. "Yes. Of course she is." He stood. "You'll be hearing from me shortly."

"I'll be waiting with bated breath, Mr. Foster."

Nick left the office without another word, closing the door behind him.

The receptionist looked at him with a tight-lipped smile. "She's outside," she said. "Poor thing. These meetings are difficult for many clients."

Nick bolted out the back door, relieved to find Libby safe.

A generous spring rain filled the air with the scent of earth. She was standing on the porch, leaning over the rail. She didn't turn when he came outside. He stood next to her and mirrored her posture, resting his elbows against the wooden porch rail. He watched the rain gather in an indent in the gravel parking lot.

She held her hand out into the rain, then brought it back, rubbing her thumb and forefinger together. "Sometimes I feel like I didn't know him at all." She flicked droplets of rainwater. "I have so many questions, and there's no one to ask."

Nick turned his head to her. Libby's chin was trembling. "What would you ask your dad?"

She threw up her hands. "Where to start?" She counted on her fingers. "One: I want to know what he knows about whoever is trying to hurt me. Two: I want to know why we're not supposed to call the police. Three: I want to know why he went to such lengths to keep his estate planning a secret." She turned back to the rail. "I just feel like he was hiding so much."

Nick frowned. "Is that it? Just those three questions?"

She leaned over the rail again. "Yeah, I think so."

Nick considered the questions himself, thinking back to that last meeting with the judge. The judge had told him that he had reason to believe the threats against Libby were credible, and Nick had interpreted that statement as an admission that Will Henderson might not have been the Glen Falls Strangler. Nick would give anything to ask the judge what, exactly, he knew about that subject.

Libby picked at the small paint chips on the wooden railing. "It's day three," she said softly, darting her gaze around the parking lot. "He's going to leave a gift today."

Nick's face was still. "Ben and Zack are watching the house. My gun is loaded. We're prepared if he tries to make a move."

She straightened and turned to him. "Can we go somewhere?"

"Where do you want to go?"

"I don't know. Somewhere else. Somewhere safe."

"Okay. I'll surprise you."

The falls were swollen from the spring rain, and they heard them roar as they sat in the parking lot, waiting to see whether anyone had followed them to the park. Libby had spent the drive watching behind them, her gaze glued to the side-view mirror. They'd been driving for nearly fifteen minutes before she'd realized that Nick hadn't said a word, and that he was also watching. But no one had followed them to this spot, and no one had pulled into the parking lot behind them. Still, Libby clenched her fists as they got out of the car.

Nick and Libby walked to the base of the waterfall: a clearing with a small wooden bench where people could sit and watch the water tumble fifty feet.

Libby's pulse had skipped when Nick had drawn the car to a stop at this spot—did he remember that day when he'd left Libby a note in her locker, asking her to meet him here? Did he remember when she'd appeared, breathless and perspiring from the bicycle ride, her hair loosening from the braid she'd so carefully prepared that morning? Or the way he'd been waiting on that bench, and how he'd risen to meet her, walking over with a smile like he knew exactly what he was doing, like he'd planned the moment for years? And then he'd pulled her against him for the very first time and kissed her. He'd held her to him in an embrace and she'd pressed her ear against his chest to feel his heart fluttering like a bird. Did he remember? Because she remembered. She kept that moment etched on her heart.

Nick was holding a large black umbrella with one hand and her elbow with the other. "Careful, the path is muddy," he said as they approached the falls.

When they came to an area beneath a ledge where the ground was dry, Nick folded the umbrella and rested it against the rock. Neither of them spoke, and as they watched the falls

Libby imagined the trajectory of a single drop of water plunging from the top of the hill to the base.

She squinted, trying to isolate that droplet. "I feel like I can think here," she said.

"I know."

She felt a warmth beginning in her chest, spreading slowly to her extremities, as if her blood had disappeared and her heart had begun to pump tingling heat through her body. It was happening, wasn't it? Despite her best efforts, despite knowing better, she was falling for Nick again. Her life was in such disarray that she hardly recognized it, and yet here, alone with Nick, she felt safe.

"Do you remember that time we hiked up to Overlook Point?" Nick asked, pointing to the spot in the distance. "We could see the entire valley—the town, the falls—everything."

Libby smiled. "I remember. We only did it once, though. Why was that?"

He shrugged. "Life is too short to do things twice."

Her smile faded. Did he apply that same reasoning to relationships? The heat in her veins started to dissipate. Nick was gorgeous, and intelligent and strong. He was a gentleman who held the door. But he was here to help her through a difficult time. After that he would be back in Pittsburgh, living his life without her. She couldn't help feeling the way she did, but she'd be a fool to entertain any thoughts of a future with Nick.

Still, she couldn't help but ask, "Do you ever miss it here?" *Do you ever miss me the way I miss you?* Because she was realizing that she missed him, and that missing him hurt.

"Glen Falls?" He was quiet for a minute as he considered the question. "Sure. I grew up here. I love the downtown, and I have a lot of friends here."

Her heart beat harder against her sternum. "Why did you leave?" she whispered, the question rising from her throat of its own accord.

She was looking at the falls and he was looking at her. She

felt his stare coasting over her profile. No doubt he was wondering what kind of conversation she was looking for, what she meant by her question.

"I had the opportunity to work on violent crime in Pittsburgh. I was needed there." He frowned. "You know that."

It sounded so perfectly reasonable—as if he'd had no choice but to pick up and leave his fiancée right before the wedding. "You didn't have to go," she whispered. "Something would have opened up here."

"Maybe. But Glen Falls is a small town. I could have been waiting for a long time." She heard him sigh. "Anyway, none of that matters now," he said.

She felt something painful rising from deep in her chest cavity, making its way to her throat. He'd simply been looking for a way to escape from her, to finally break away from the familiarity of their relationship. God, but she was a fool. She held her breath and bit her lower lip to hold back the tears. *There is no reason to cry,* she told herself. *Nothing has happened. Everything is as it was. Nothing has changed at all.*

Nick cleared his throat. "I know this is…this must be incredibly difficult for you, Libby. To have your life in jeopardy."

"It's surreal," she said. "It's like replaying a memory."

He looked at her. "Replaying a memory?"

"Yeah. Sometimes I'll remember something and I'm outside of myself. It's like I'm watching myself do something—passively observing from a safe distance." She took a breath. "It's like that. I sometimes wonder if it's really happening at all."

Nick watched her, his forehead creased. "I hope that you at least feel a little safer with me around."

Was that hopefulness in his voice? She didn't know what to say to that. "I suppose."

Out of the corner of her eye she watched his face fall and felt a pang. Was that a harsh answer? Maybe she should have told him how desperately she needed him right now. How his presence was the only thing keeping her from becoming completely unhinged.

They watched the falls for a few more minutes, and then Libby told Nick that she was ready to go. They began the short walk back to the car, huddling under the umbrella. When they were about ten feet away Nick grabbed Libby by the elbow, stopping her midstride.

"What the—?" She did not continue with her question when she saw the grim look on his face, his lips pulled into a tight, thin line as he looked at the car.

"Stay here," he said, and handed her the umbrella.

Libby watched, slack-jawed, as Nick walked to the car. He stopped several feet short, staring at the front passenger-side tire. That was when she saw it: something white wedged underneath. Libby's stomach churned. "What is it?"

"Stay there," Nick ordered. His eyes were hard as he looked around the parking lot. There was no one there.

She'd never seen him so angry. He knelt beside the car and carefully moved the white object. As he turned it over in his hands Libby saw that he held a doll with porcelain skin and long wavy jet-black hair.

He lifted it. "Looks like someone left you a gift." The doll's wide glassy eyes stared unblinkingly.

Libby's light jacket felt oppressively hot. "What's it mean?" she managed from between her trembling lips.

She saw him grit his teeth as he examined the doll. "It's missing three fingers." He lifted the doll's shirt and then pulled it down, glancing around the parking lot again. "He wrote 'Elizabeth' on the back."

Libby stumbled backward. Her legs were no longer working. She felt an overpowering heat and steam rising from her skin.

"Libby?"

She knew Nick was at her side, and she felt his arms trying to keep her steady.

"Libby, talk to me!"

But she couldn't speak. There was the heat on her skin and the nausea rising from her gut, and all she could see were the staring eyes of the doll.

"Libby." Nick wrapped his arms around her torso to hold her upright. "Come on. I need to get you home."

"Bag it," she mumbled.

Nick stiffened. "What?"

"That doll." She took a few deep breaths, and when the tremors in her legs had subsided she took a step back. "Bag the doll. Protect it." She gritted her teeth. "There could be trace evidence. I want him to pay for this." A bracing wind passed straight through her, extinguishing the fire that had burned below her skin. She shivered.

"He'll pay for it," Nick growled. He balled his fists until his knuckles turned white. "He's going to pay for all of it."

CHAPTER SEVEN

LIBBY was curled up on the couch, wrapped in a hand-knit blue blanket that Nick recognized from her college dormitory room. Her mouth was slightly open, and every now and then she would inhale deeply and then sigh contentedly. Nick watched her with a smile. How could a person who looked so peaceful make so much noise?

His gut clenched as he thought about the stress the poor woman was under. After Libby had nearly fainted in the parking lot earlier that afternoon, his resolve to get the man threatening her was only strengthened. His pulse quickened as he imagined finally getting his hands on that creep with the twisted smile. Nick's throat tightened. He'd kill him with his bare hands.

His BlackBerry beeped, alerting him that he'd received an email. It was from Sergeant Katz, and it listed the names and ranks of the officers investigating the arson and the murder at the warehouse. Nick knew a few of the officers, but not all of them. He saved the message.

Libby's brow furrowed and she groaned. He watched her lips flutter slightly and then grow still, and then the tension in her brow relaxed. Nick felt something in him stir. He wondered if she had any idea how much he wanted her, or how much he fought the desire to take her in his arms every time a flash of worry crossed her face. He couldn't look at her without remembering the way her skin felt under his fingers. When she spoke he became transfixed on those sweet lips, watching her as if her very breath was food and he was starving.

Nick rubbed his temples. There were those old feelings again, bubbling to the surface. He wanted her—so what? She was smart as hell and she happened to be the sexiest woman he'd ever seen in his life—and also apparently oblivious to the effect she had on him. A heady combination… The truth was, he thought ruefully, that all she had to do was deliver the invitation to share her bed and he'd be powerless to resist. He had no weapons against those beautiful blue eyes. He was helpless against the soft curves of her figure, twisting like the sweetest lines of smoke each time she moved.

Libby moaned softly, and Nick felt a charge through his body. He observed his physical response with anger. *What does it matter how much I want her?* he thought. He'd gone down that path before, and it hadn't worked out. Libby was a number of things: beautiful, sweetly vulnerable under her tough exterior, clever…she had many facets. She was complicated. He liked the way she kept him guessing.

He shook his head. No, they were all wrong together. At the end of their relationship Nick had watched the fracture between them expand to a chasm. He'd thought that a marriage proposal would bridge the rift, show her how much he wanted the relationship to work, but then she'd simply buried herself in wedding preparations. He'd responded by putting in longer hours at the Bureau. Maybe that had been the wrong response, he grudgingly admitted, but between work and wedding planning they'd barely seen each other, and when they had, Libby had acted as if she didn't want him around. There was a reason they'd broken up. Besides, she'd pulled away from him. Whatever he was feeling, it wasn't mutual.

Things between them were different now. This was work, and he was being paid handsomely to guard her.

He settled back in his seat and reached for his coffee. When they'd been together he would watch Libby as she confidently worked any social situation. Nick had taken a lot of pride in gazing at that strong, confident woman and knowing that when they went home she was *his*. He found it unnerving to watch her now and to feel that same admiration and desire. Libby had the ability to talk to anyone as if they were the most important person in the room. She was magnetic. Just like her father.

Her father. Nick was learning more and more about Judge Andrews, and that knowledge was leaving a taste as bitter as the coffee in his mouth. Only a desperate man would have signed over his entire estate just to keep the police from poking around in his past. As Nick watched Libby sleep, his chest began to ache with guilt as he thought about his agreement with her father. At the time he'd planned simply to do what was necessary to protect Libby, collect his money and leave. He needed the money to pay some debt and get a head start on his new life in Washington, D.C. He was risking his life on this job, and he *deserved* that money. Nick hadn't expected to care about what Libby thought, or how the agreement might affect her. He'd expected to feel nothing but satisfaction at the thought of controlling the judge's estate. Instead, he felt rotten.

Nick's BlackBerry began to vibrate on the table beside him, jarring him from his thoughts. He grabbed the phone and walked to the hallway. "Nick Foster," he answered as soon as he was out of earshot.

"Nick, it's Molly," came a woman's voice.

Molly Ericson was the colleague he'd sent the handwriting samples to the previous night. When he'd first moved to Pittsburgh he'd been eager to get over Libby and find someone new. He'd taken Molly to dinner one night and enjoyed her company, even offered to take her out again the following night.

She'd laughed kindly at him and patted him on the arm. "Nick, all you did was talk about your ex-fiancée tonight," she'd said. "Frankly, you can't afford to hire me as your therapist."

Instead of dating, they'd become good friends.

He'd scanned and emailed a copy of a letter the Glen Falls Strangler had sent to the third victim's family, and asked Molly to compare it to the letters sent to Judge Andrews. On a whim, he'd also sent Henderson's handwritten confession.

"Molly," he said. "How are you doing?"

"Uh…better than you, from the looks of it. What's this I hear about you being at the scene of an arson and a murder yesterday?"

Nick swore under his breath. "I told Morgenstern and Leonard to keep their mouths shut."

"Leonard and I are working on a few cases. I called him yesterday afternoon and he let it slip that he was photocopying documents for you. Naturally I was curious."

He rubbed his forehead. "It's kind of a long story, and I can't go into the details right now."

"So this is a Bureau case, then?"

"Not exactly. The Stillborough P.D. is investigating those crimes. I'm just taking an interest. I'd like to keep our discussion…quiet, if you understand?"

She was silent on the other end for a moment. "You take care of yourself, okay? You're supposed to be on vacation, anyway."

"I will. Take care of myself, I mean. I promise."

He heard her sigh. "These samples you sent over are interesting. I have two letters here, one from the seventies and one from a few months ago. Both contain intriguingly similar characteristics—narrow, tense handwriting, oddly shaped letters that defy any convention I know, extreme height differentials." She paused. "I'm disadvantaged because I'm not looking at the originals, so I can't comment as to the pressure of the writing on the sheet. But I think it's fairly safe to conclude that each letter was written by a person with a schizoid personality."

"A schizoid personality? As in schizophrenic?" Nick felt his muscles tense.

"No—schizoid is different from schizophrenic. This is what

I would expect to see in a serial killer's handwriting," Molly said. "This indicates a person who is emotionally cold or even emotion*less*. Secretive. A loner."

An image of the dark-haired man with the sharp white teeth flashed in Nick's mind. "All right."

"I can also tell that the individuals who wrote these letters are highly organized and intelligent," she continued.

"Wait." Nick froze. "You said 'individuals'—with an *s?*"

"Yes. These letters were written by two different people. The handwriting is similar, but there are enough differences."

So there it was: based on handwriting analysis, the person hunting Libby was not the Glen Falls Strangler, after all, but a copycat. As the realization settled into the pit of his stomach Nick wasn't sure whether he should feel relieved. He didn't. "Two different writers," he said quietly, almost to himself. "I'm not sure that helps anything, but it answers a question. Thanks, Molly."

"Anytime. Hey, did you want to hear about the other sample, too?"

Henderson's handwritten confession. Nick had almost forgotten he'd sent it to her. "Yes," he replied. "I got distracted for a minute."

"Oh, no problem. I thought you'd be interested in knowing that it's another unique writer."

Nick's head spun. "Sorry—can you repeat that?"

"Sure thing. All of these documents were written by different people. The person who signed this confession did not write the letters."

Nick headed toward the kitchen. He had to sit down. If Molly was correct, then Henderson *hadn't* written the letters to the victims' families—which meant he had confessed to crimes he hadn't committed. Nick's thoughts were swirling around his head at light speed.

"Molly. Tell me about the person who wrote the confession."

"Well, let's see." She cleared her throat. "I'd say this was a male with a grade-school education at best, based on the formation of the letters and the language being used. I wouldn't guess he was a schizoid personality, but I wouldn't be surprised if he was involved in some criminal activity."

Nick's pulse pounded in his ears as she paused.

"If we compare the confession with the letters you sent, I would say there's a significant disparity in education and possibly social class."

"With both of the letters?"

"Yes. If you look beyond the handwriting style, and consider the vocabulary being used, both letters appear to be written by highly educated individuals. This confession looks like it could have been written by a kid in middle school."

Nick tapped his fingers against the kitchen table and leaned forward in his chair. "The person who wrote that confession is dead. So what we're looking for now is a person who would be considered a loner, right?"

"Well, not necessarily," she replied. "That's often how a schizoid personality will present itself, but sometimes people are very skilled at hiding their antisocial tendencies. You may be looking for someone who is quite charming."

Nick groaned. "So a loner or the life of the party, then? I thought you were supposed to make this easier for me."

Molly laughed. "Sorry, Nick. People are complicated."

His forehead was tense. "I'm kidding. You have no idea how helpful that was. Thank you."

"Glad to help. This stuff does get the pulse racing, doesn't it?" She sounded breathless. "You're going to miss this when you go to public corruption."

His gut clenched and he instinctively glanced around to see if Libby was listening. He hadn't told her that he was moving his job track at the Bureau from violent crime to public corruption or, more significantly, that he would be transferred to Washington in a few weeks. He wondered why he felt the need to hide it. What did he care what Libby thought about him?

"Yeah, I love violent crime," he said wryly. "I'll probably still get my share of schizoids when I investigate politicians, though."

Molly laughed. "I think you mean sociopaths, Nick. But, yeah, you probably will. We'll miss you here in Pittsburgh. Will you be living in Virginia or Maryland? Or did you score some town house in Georgetown?"

He caught a movement out of the corner of his eye and looked up. Libby was standing in the doorway, looking at him with a puzzled expression. "Molly, sorry—something came up and I have to go. I'll talk to you later," he said, watching Libby uneasily. "Thanks for your help." He disconnected the call and turned to Libby. "How was your nap?"

She fixed her blue eyes on him firmly beneath a creased brow. "Did I hear you correctly?" she asked. "Are you leaving the violent crime unit?"

The news was almost too good to be true. She'd always worried about Nick on that unit, investigating violent criminals and gangsters, and the raids that he would have to go on as a member of the SWAT team… He'd never told her where he was going, or why, or for how long, and so Libby had frequently found herself waking in the middle of the night, in tears, torn from the grip of a harrowing nightmare about Nick's whereabouts. Now he was leaving the violent crime unit? This *was* an improvement. Not that it mattered to Libby anymore.

Nick looked at his BlackBerry, turning away from her gaze. "The Bureau has a need in the public corruption unit," he said evenly. "I've offered to…fill in for a while."

Libby pressed her lips together to stop herself showing how happy she was at this news. Nick's face remained dark, and he was avoiding her eyes. She smoothed her hair back from her face. "I don't know how you did it in the first place, to be honest—working on violent crime investigation. I can barely sleep when I'm working on a murder trial, and that's what you dealt with on a daily basis."

Her words weren't having the intended effect. Nick clenched his jaw and turned in his seat. Then he changed the subject. "I sent some handwriting samples to an expert over at the Bureau. That was her on the phone just now."

Libby held her breath. "And? What did she say?"

Nick nodded to the seat across from him at the table. "You may want to sit down." She obliged, and he leaned forward. "I sent over three samples. The first was a letter written by the Glen Falls Strangler, the second was a letter sent to your father, and the third was the confession written by Will Henderson." He paused. "Libby, they were written by three different people."

Her breath snagged in her lungs. "Oh, my God." She propped her elbows on the table. Three different authors. "That means that the Glen Falls Strangler isn't after me. It's a copycat."

"It also means that Henderson wasn't the Glen Falls Strangler." Nick's voice was quiet and he watched for her reaction out of the corner of his eye. "It means he was falsely accused of those crimes."

"My God," she said, her words no louder than her breath. This was the news she'd feared, and yet she'd learned over the past few days that her father had been a man of many secrets. Could anything in his past surprise her? "My dad prosecuted the wrong person," she whispered. "The wrong man went to jail—died in jail—for those crimes while the real murderer went free." Her own words left her feeling numb. She looked at Nick. "What else did the handwriting expert say?"

"She's also a psychologist, and she said that the person who sent the letters to your father probably has a schizoid personality, which could make him antisocial and a loner. Or, conversely, he may be extremely charming."

Libby raked her fingers through her hair. "Well, okay. That

doesn't seem to help very much, though. Do you think that this is payback for a wrongful conviction?" She knitted her brows. "But why now? Henderson's been dead for years."

"Could be, Libby," Nick said. "Maybe someone else just learned about the wrongful conviction, too. Who else would know that your dad made this...mistake?"

She flinched at his words. "A mistake? Do you think he made a mistake?"

Nick didn't move and looked away, confirming her suspicions.

"No, you don't think that at all. You think my dad knew about this, don't you?"

He rubbed the bridge of his nose. "I would have no way of knowing that."

"But that's what you think." She tried to keep her voice calm, but her throat was tightening and her tone was becoming strained. "You think that Dad knew Henderson wasn't the Glen Falls Strangler. He must have said something like that to you when you met with him."

"No, he didn't say anything like that," Nick replied. His eyes softened as he looked at her, and he reached across the table to cover her hand with his. "All he said was that he had reason to believe the threats against you were credible. He was worried about you, Libby. I think he knew that the Glen Falls Strangler had never been caught and that you were in danger." He squeezed her hand. "He never said anything to me about it, but I think he knew that Henderson was the wrong person. The only question in my mind is when he figured it out."

That was her concern, too. She found it impossible to accept that her father, the very man who'd taught her right from wrong and fostered her unwavering faith in the justice system, would have knowingly prosecuted the wrong person for a crime. This wasn't any crime, either: her father had prosecuted the wrong person for a series of murders and requested multiple life sentences. Her father had helped to lock away an innocent man for the rest of his life.

She felt that same rush of heat she'd felt in the parking lot. "I think I'm going to be sick," she mumbled.

Nick rose. "Can I get you something? A glass of water?"

Waves of heat and nausea passed over her, and she took deep breaths to calm her nerves. After a minute or two the nausea receded and she was breathing easier. "I'll be all right."

Nick was behind her and his hands were on her shoulders, kneading her muscles. "You're so tense."

She sighed at the sensation of his touch. His warm hands were heavy and reassuringly strong, and his grip was firm but gentle as he worked his fingers into the knots on her upper shoulders. She sat up and leaned her head back, relaxing against his tight stomach. Her shoulders were tinged with slight achiness as her muscles softened, sending a dizzying rush of blood to her head.

She moaned softly. "That feels amazing."

The compliment only served to encourage him, and soon his fingers were tracing slow, firm circles to the base of her neck. His touches on her shoulders and her neck stirred memories of his touch on other parts of her body. Libby felt another rush of heat, except this one was centered between her thighs. Her breathing became shallow as she fell into a trance, her head tilting softly this way and that as he commanded her body. She was utterly under his control, and she wouldn't want it any other way.

He stopped, resting his hands on her shoulders and whispering, "Feel better?"

"Oh..." She sighed. "You stopped."

She felt his body stiffen, and when he spoke his voice was tense. "Do you want me to keep going?"

Her body felt alive for the first time in a long time. Her skin was hypersensitive, her muscles quivering with the electric charge he had sent surging through her with his touch. If he could do that just by working out a few knots in her shoulders, she wanted to see what he could do if he let his hands wander.

But sensibility prevailed. "No," she said, immediately regretting it.

Nick released her and stepped away, returning to his seat. Was it her imagination, or was his breathing as labored as hers?

Her cheeks were flushed as she tucked her hair behind her ears. "Thanks," she managed. "I feel better."

He swallowed. "We were talking about your dad. I think that we need to talk to someone who may have some insight. Someone involved with the trial."

"We've already talked to Jack MacGruder." The man had helped her father through the entire trial, and he didn't seem to have any doubt that Henderson was guilty. "If Jack didn't have any idea that Henderson was the wrong person, what makes you think anyone else would?"

"Maybe we need a different perspective."

She considered the question. "Who do you have in mind?"

"Henderson's defense attorney—Christopher Henzel. He's near seventy, but I looked him up and he's got a small law practice in the center of Arbor Hills."

"What's he practice?"

"Real estate."

Libby blinked. "He's no longer a public defender, huh?"

"He hasn't been for a long time. In fact it seems he opened this firm in 1981—less than a year after Henderson went to jail."

"In other words Henderson was the last criminal he represented before he decided he wanted to practice in real estate?"

"Exactly."

Libby laughed drily. "Yeah, I agree. We need to talk to Attorney Henzel."

CHAPTER EIGHT

Day Four

"Day four," she whispered to Nick. "Do you think he's going to show up?"

Nick's eyes shifted as he studied the diner patrons. "He's got to appear at some point, or the game's over."

Libby bristled at the thought that this psychological torture was simply a game to someone. She'd barely slept, awakening with a start every time she heard a creak of the floors or the tapping of a branch against her window. Even with Nick sleeping on the couch and Ben and Zack watching the house from their car Libby couldn't get to feeling safe. She was realizing that she'd always taken that feeling for granted.

"Ben and Zack are outside, right?"

"Right," Nick said. "They'll be trailing us all day. I have Sergeant Katz's direct line, and he can work with the Glen Falls P.D. to arrest this guy for murder and arson as soon as we give the word."

Libby worried her lower lip and wrapped her hands around the golden-brown ceramic diner mug. "So I'm basically a lure? He's going to approach me today and I just have to wait for it to happen?" Her fingers trembled as she rubbed her forehead. Her gut felt raw. "I don't think I can do this."

Nick leaned forward and took her hand. "You can do this, honey."

Her eyes widened, and Nick let her hand fall.

"Sorry," he mumbled. "Old habit."

Except that Libby didn't want the affectionate pet name to fall under the rubric of old habit. She missed having someone care about her enough to call her honey. She missed hearing Nick call her that.

She took a sip of the coffee. It was lukewarm and watery; she'd have to drink massive amounts to feel any jolt of caffeine. Fortunately she didn't have to rely on a drug to stay alert—adrenaline would do the trick just fine.

Libby glanced around the old diner. It hadn't changed since the first time her parents had brought her here. The blue-and-white-gingham wallpaper was pulling from the walls at the edges, but who would notice that detail amid such a distracting amount of kitsch? The ceramic animals lining the randomly placed wooden shelves had to be at least fifty years old—perhaps the only items in the diner actually older than the booth cushions, which were generously patched with silver duct tape. An entire wall was decorated with old dented license plates collected from around the country. Old advertisements for cornflakes and white bread cluttered another wall.

The Main Street Diner was simultaneously unique and exactly like every other diner Libby had ever visited or passed by. She'd always felt comfortable here. Until today.

Today they were looking for the man who'd nearly killed them in a fire two days ago. Today was the day he would make personal contact with Libby. If locking her in a room with a burning box and a disabled smoke detector was considered contact from afar, she shuddered to imagine what would constitute personal contact.

She was brought out of her thoughts by the sound of Nick chuckling. "I can't believe you're ordering pancakes." He shook his head.

"And sausage," Libby said as she skimmed her thumb across a chip on the rim of her mug. "Why are you laughing?"

"Because I looked over this menu and thought for sure you

were going to pick something like yogurt and granola with a side of seasonal berries." He made a face. "What's in season now? It's only April."

She smiled and poured milk from a small metal pitcher into her coffee. "You can't go to the Main Street Diner and order yogurt and granola. That's just wrong."

"Since when have you been concerned about appearances?"

Libby rolled her eyes. "It's not about appearances. It's about accepting a place for what it is." She reached for one of the cheap, nearly flat metal spoons. "They make the best pancakes I've ever had. No one orders the yogurt. It's probably hours away from becoming cream cheese."

Nick smiled. Libby loved the way his eyes crinkled around the edges like that—it always made her want to smile, too. She felt her chest grow warm, and she fidgeted with her napkin.

"The Libby I know has always been rigid with her diet," Nick said with a wink. "Maybe I don't know you as well as I thought I did."

Her cheeks flushed. "Maybe you don't."

She toyed with her napkin again, this time unrolling it and placing it in her lap with unusual attention to the task. *What is wrong with you?* she scolded herself. She'd been ready to tear off her clothes after that back rub last night. The memory of the way her body had responded to his touch made her feel ashamed. Was she so desperately lonely and starved for affection that she'd subject herself to Nick Foster again? Hadn't he done enough damage already?

Libby recalled the lecture her mother had given her a year before she died, when Libby was only thirteen years old. Her mother had been a high school biology teacher who'd proudly tossed her bra into a trash can as part of a public protest, and she'd warned Libby that she should never let a man prevent her from doing anything she wanted to do. Libby never had. Not her father, and not Nick. No one stood in the way of her goals, and she wasn't about to live a life of compromise. Any man lucky enough to win her heart would have to take her as she was: an ambitious woman who loved her job and aspired to be a judge, just like her father. That was how she'd always lived, and that was how she planned always to live.

But since Nick had returned she'd started to wonder what was wrong with being a woman who aspired to balance her love for her career with her love for another person. She questioned whether she was truly happy burying herself in her work if it meant she would remain alone. The thoughts made her uneasy.

A waitress brought their plates over and set them on the table, resting a check between them. "Thank you," said Nick.

"Anytime," said the waitress with a wink and a flirty smile.

Libby tightened her mouth and reached for her fork.

They ate in silence, each of them tense as they watched the diner door.

After a few minutes the waitress returned with more coffee. "Warm you up?" The question was directed at Nick. Another wink.

He gave her a polite smile and pushed his coffee cup toward her. "Please."

She began pouring and the black liquid came out too quickly, filling the cup to the brim before spilling over the table and onto his lap. Nick jumped up from the booth. "Oh, I'm so sorry!" the waitress gasped. She fumbled in her apron for a handful of paper napkins and began dabbing at Nick's pants. "Let me give you my number and you can tell me what the dry cleaning bill is."

Libby groaned. She had a feeling this wasn't the first time the waitress had had such an "accident" with an attractive man.

"Thank you, I can handle it," said Nick, stepping away from her touch. He turned to Libby with an apologetic look. "I'll be right back. We'll finish up and then go see Attorney Henzel."

She nodded. "Okay."

"Stay here."

"I will."

She watched him as he walked to the restrooms, then turned back to her plate. She didn't have much of an appetite, and she pushed the plate away and sat back in her seat. She watched the patrons at the counter for a moment, and then heard the jingle of the bell above the front door. A large family entered and walked to the right, leaving one person standing alone by the door. That was when her lungs seized.

It was him, and he was looking right at her.

Her heart flailed and she sat in the diner booth, frozen with terror, as he locked his gaze on hers and walked steadily in her direction. She wondered if he was going to draw a weapon and finish things right then and there. The thought crossed her mind, but she was paralyzed as she watched him approach. He seemed so calm. His black curly hair was once again hidden by a hat—this time a New York Yankees baseball cap. He wore a black windbreaker jacket with white trim, and his hands were hidden in his jacket pockets. His lips were raised in the slightest grin, revealing a set of pointed teeth.

He's going to kill me. The thought drifted easily through her mind without activating a coordinating flight response. Her hands turned ice-cold. She had no defense. She couldn't fight him off, and there was nowhere to run.

He was right by the table then, and he paused to look around the room. Libby's senses were dulled by the pounding in her ears. He seemed to move in slow motion as he turned to her and peeled back those lips in a sinister grin. His eyes were jet-black. Hard. Unflinching. She realized with horror that he was enjoying every minute of this.

Her tongue wasn't working when she opened her mouth to tell him to leave her alone. Even if her tongue had worked she doubted her voice would have been louder than a squeak, considering how tightly her throat had tensed around her vocal cords. He leaned closer.

"Elizabeth," he said, in a calm, even voice, "you look surprisingly well. Did you get that gift I left you?"

She tried to speak, to tell him to go to hell, but she choked on the words.

"What's the matter?" he hissed, clearly enjoying himself. "Cat got your tongue?"

"Bastard," she sputtered, shaking with fear and rage. "You bastard—"

"Now, now." He smiled menacingly. "Keep your voice down or things are going to get unpleasant. Understand?"

Libby glared at him.

"Good." He glanced around the diner to see if anyone was listening in on the conversation. "Unfortunately I don't have time to chat. Let's plan to spend some time together in a few days. How's that sound?" With that he rapped his knuckles on the table and turned on his heels, walking at a rapid pace toward the entrance.

Libby's hands were shaking violently, and as he left she slumped forward against the table, her palms over her mouth as she struggled to regain her composure. *I should follow him,* she thought to herself. *He's going to get away!* But her body felt limp, as if her bones had vanished.

Nick slid into the booth across from her. "How are you supposed to treat stains? Hot water or cold?" He glanced down at the large wet mark on his lap. "I thought I was supposed to use hot, but there was only cold water." He stopped suddenly as he saw Libby's face. "What just happened?"

Her hands were still over her face, her fingers still trembling. "He was here."

Nick's face darkened. "The suspect?" She didn't have to answer. Nick removed his wallet and threw several bills on the table. "Let's go."

Libby's knees shook as she tried to stand. "Where are we going?"

"We're going to follow him. Did you see where he went?"

"I think he went south."

They walked quickly toward Ben and Zack's car, and Nick gestured for them to roll down the window. "The suspect was just here. Libby, tell them what he was wearing."

"A black jacket. Blue jeans. A baseball hat." She gestured to her head. "Yankees."

"We think he went south," Nick said.

"We're on it," Ben said, and he started the engine and pulled out of the space, heading south down Main Street.

Nick cursed. "How did they not see him enter?"

"He followed a family inside. He blended right in with them."

Nick turned to her as he pulled out his BlackBerry. "I'm going to put a call in to the Stillborough P.D.—tell them that the suspect is around here."

She nodded and sat on a bench while Nick made the call. She crossed her fingers together to keep them from trembling and took deep breaths to steady her nerves. She was only partly successful.

"They're sending some officers from Glen Falls out," Nick said as he put his phone away.

"Do they know that he is trying to kill me?" Libby asked in a small voice.

"No, just that he's a suspect in the warehouse arson and murder."

"What?" She felt anger beginning to build. She didn't understand why Nick was going to such great lengths to hide the fact that her life was in danger. "I want them on high alert, Nick. I want them to know that someone is trying to kill me!"

"Ben and Zack know. I know. What difference would it make if a couple of cops knew? We're going to find him."

"Why the secrecy, Nick?" She choked on the question. "What are you hiding from me?"

"Nothing," he replied, but he avoided her gaze. "I'm trying to comply with your father's request."

"My father's request was absurd!" She rose from the bench to square off with him.

"Are you sure of that, Libby?" Nick spun to face her. "Your father told me he couldn't trust the police. Why should we? We don't know who's after you, or who's on his payroll." He looked away, staring down the street. "Thanks to the fire and the murder at the warehouse, the police are too involved as it is. Adding more details to the file could attract the wrong kind of attention, and I can't take that risk."

Libby considered the logic of the argument. She couldn't shake the feeling that Nick was hiding something from her, but he was right—they couldn't trust anyone.

"I want to make a report as soon as they find him. I want him to be locked away for the hell he's put me through." She watched Nick. He appeared tense, even agitated, the way he was looking up and down the road and checking his Black-Berry. "You want to try to find him," she said. "Go ahead. I'll be fine."

"I'm not leaving you." Nick turned to her. "What did he say to you?"

Libby closed her eyes, trying to hear the conversation again. "He wanted to know if I received his gift." She wrinkled her nose slightly, disgusted by the memory. "He said that he didn't have time to talk now, but that he would see me in a few days."

"Anything else?"

"No." She looked down at her feet. "Nick, I don't understand any of this. Why me? I've never met him before in my life, and I don't have any idea why he would want to hurt me. He doesn't even look familiar."

"It must have something to do with your dad," Nick said. "With Henderson being wrongfully prosecuted."

"Revenge?" Libby asked.

Nick shrugged.

"But *I* didn't wrongfully prosecute Henderson!"

"Libby." Nick walked over to stand in front of her. "You're

trying to make sense of actions that are inherently irrational. I went into law enforcement thinking that I could get inside the head of some of these criminals and understand what would lead someone to kill." He shook his head. "I'll never understand psychosis. I'll never understand what would make a person rape and kill a child."

Libby watched the slight twitch beside his left eye. "You've had too many of those cases." She paused. "Is that why you're leaving that unit?"

Nick's lips thinned. "There's so much red tape. I can't get anything done. We don't get the suspects in time, and they kill again and again." He swallowed and shook his head. "Each time a new victim appears it's another failure, Libby. I'm failing them."

Her heart ached at hearing his confession. "Investigations need to be done properly if a case is going to hold up in court. You can't help that."

"It's easy to say those things from behind a desk at the District Attorney's Office."

Her cheeks felt hot. "You think victims don't get under *my* skin? You think you're the only one who cares about saving lives?"

He looked away. "I'm under a lot of pressure to get things done the right way. If I mess up, lives are at risk."

Libby narrowed her eyes. "Are you talking about your job, or are you talking about what's happening with me?"

He turned his body away slightly and glanced at his watch, pretending not to hear her.

"Nick?"

"We should get going. Attorney Henzel is expecting us, and we don't want to keep him waiting."

She tried to ignore the words ringing in her ears as they walked to Henzel's office. *It's easy to say those things from behind a desk at the District Attorney's Office.* He was so infuriating sometimes.

* * *

Nick tugged at the locked door of Christopher Henzel's office, located on the first floor of a small office building near the center of Glen Falls.

"Sorry to keep you waiting."

They heard the voice from behind and saw an older but still sprightly man in a white polo shirt and khaki pants approaching them.

"I played a round of golf this morning and lost track of the time."

"We just got here," Nick said.

"We're grateful you agreed to meet us on a Saturday."

Henzel's frame was thin, and his brown eyes contained a warmth that Libby found reassuring. "An FBI agent left me a message about wanting to discuss William Henderson," he said. "It piqued my interest."

"I left you that message. Special Agent Nick Foster." The men shook hands. "And this is Libby Andrews."

"My father prosecuted Mr. Henderson."

Henzel seemed unsurprised. "You have your father's eyes."

He led them through a small reception area and into a modest conference room and library. Libby and Nick pulled up chairs.

"I would offer you something, but I don't know how to use our coffee maker," he said apologetically. "Would you like some milk or orange juice?"

They both shook their heads. "Thank you, Attorney Henzel," said Libby. "We're fine."

"Well, then, what brings you here? You know I haven't practiced criminal defense in almost thirty years? And I haven't looked over the Henderson files in nearly as long."

Nick said, "We've been reviewing some old files, and we have noticed some…discrepancies."

"You've been reviewing the case files?" Henzel looked interested. "For what purpose, if I may ask?"

Libby and Nick exchanged a glance. "We're writing a book," Nick replied.

Henzel replied with a short, "Hmm…" before sitting back in his chair. "Please continue. I didn't mean to interrupt."

"As Nick said, we've noticed some discrepancies in the files. A handwriting expert at the FBI compared the letters the Glen Falls Strangler sent to his victims' families with the confession Henderson wrote," Libby said. "She concluded that Henderson didn't write those letters."

"You've involved a handwriting expert at the FBI? This must be some book." Henzel's face remained still, and he pressed the tips of his fingers together. "What kinds of discrepancies did she notice?"

"The person who wrote the letters to the victims' families was highly educated and showed signs of having a schizoid personality, while the person who wrote the confession had a grade-school education at best and showed some proclivity to criminal activity," Nick said.

"We know that Henderson wrote the confession," Libby said. "What we don't know is why he would confess to crimes he didn't commit. We're here because we're wondering whether Henderson may have said something to you." Noticing Henzel's hesitation, Libby continued, "Henderson is dead, so there's no longer an attorney-client privilege to preserve."

"Of course," Henzel replied, folding his hands in front of him. "Of course." He paused to scratch his eyebrow, and he seemed lost in thought. "I must have looked at those letters and that confession dozens of times, but the truth is I never noticed a difference in the handwriting." He raised his gaze to meet Libby's. "If I had, I would've raised that question at trial."

She leaned forward and lowered her voice, speaking to Henzel kindly. "That must have been quite a trial for you. You were charged with defending someone who'd confessed to being a serial killer. That couldn't have been easy."

"I received death threats for defending him," Henzel said,

his voice calm. "I became a criminal defense attorney out of a sense of…obligation, I suppose. I had ideals. I believed in innocent until proven guilty, and I thought that by putting forth a strong defense I would protect all of society from overzealous prosecution." He looked at the table and assumed a faraway expression. "I was a fool."

The statement thrust Libby back against her seat. "Why were you—?"

"Henderson was arrested at work. He was a dishwasher at the Country Club," Henzel said. "Someone spotted what appeared to be bloody clothing in his duffel bag and reported him. The police later identified that clothing as belonging to the sixth victim. Of course Henderson told me he was innocent. He swore the clothing had been planted in his bag—said he'd never killed anyone. You know how it goes," Henzel said, turning to Libby.

"They're all innocent." She smiled. "At least I'm not the only one who hears that."

"In that way, at least, he was just like all of my other defense clients."

"But something made him different?" Nick said.

"Quite a few things, really. I realized early on that Henderson had a benefactor of some kind," Henzel continued. "I don't know who he was. I just know that Henderson was receiving lots of money from someone. His wife was, at least."

"Did this benefactor pay your legal bills?" Nick asked.

"No, I was the public defender assigned to the trial, so I was paid by the taxpayers. But you have to understand that Henderson didn't have a penny to his name. He'd never been able to hold down a steady job in his life. Suddenly his wife was buying fur coats and going out for fancy dinners." Henzel shook his head. "I remember Will telling me about the job at the Country Club. He would talk about it like it was the funniest thing in the world. He was washing dishes for people who could, as he put it, buy and sell him twice before sunset.

I always got the sense that he hated those people—the upper echelon of Glen Falls, so to speak. But he also wanted to be accepted by them. He desperately wanted their approval."

Libby rested her chin on her palm. "Do you think that's where he met this benefactor? At the Country Club?"

"Could be," Henzel said. "We never talked about it. To be honest, I didn't want to know. But at the beginning, when he was first arrested, he was desperate to get out of jail. He said that he needed to work, that his family needed him to support them. Then he changed."

"Changed? How so?" Nick asked.

"He wasn't as desperate to get out of jail. He seemed untroubled by the usual court delays." Henzel frowned. "Then one day he told me he knew who the real killer was—that he was…how did he put it?…'negotiating a price.'"

"Negotiating a price? With the Strangler?" Nick leaned forward over the table.

"Yes. I would have dismissed that comment as the delusions of an unstable person, but I'd already suspected that something strange was going on, and that his wife was receiving payments of some kind."

"Henderson was in prison this entire time, wasn't he?" Libby asked.

"Yes, he was being held without bail."

"So if he was having visitors," Libby said, her brow creasing as she thought, "then the prison would have a record of that. If the Glen Falls Strangler was coming to see him—to 'negotiate,' if you will—then he would have had to fill out paperwork like everyone else."

Henzel shook his head. "Except that there is no such record. I checked. Henderson's wife came to see him every now and again, and that was it. If he was negotiating something with the benefactor, then that benefactor had friends who didn't make him fill out the visitor paperwork."

"In other words Henderson professed his innocence and

seemed impatient about being held in jail, but then he received a lot of money from an anonymous benefactor. Later, he signed a statement confessing to have played a part in the murders." Nick sat back against his chair and stared out the window as he thought about this. "You think that he was paid to take the fall?"

"Yes," Henzel said. "I do. I think that the Strangler was a very powerful person in Glen Falls, and I think that he must have cut some kind of a deal with Henderson. If I had to guess, Henderson was promised the things he'd always wanted. Money. Respect. Notoriety. I think he reached an agreement with the Strangler whereby Henderson would sign a confession, plead guilty to lesser offenses and suffer through the trial. There had to be a murder trial. The Mayor wanted his pound of flesh. In return Henderson would be treated well in jail and his wife would be cared for." Henzel's face darkened. "But his wife wasn't cared for. Not for long, anyway. Several years after Henderson was sentenced she was found dead in their home. Strangled."

Libby felt a wave of coldness wash over her. "I thought she'd taken her own life. Was she killed by the Strangler?"

"The police never made that connection. If they had, they would have had to admit they'd locked up the wrong person. No, the medical examiner ruled her death suicide by hanging. But Henderson told me she'd been killed. He was certain of it." Henzel was quiet. "That's when Henderson started telling anyone who would listen that he was innocent, that the Strangler had paid him to take the fall. As soon as Henderson started threatening to talk, of course…"

"He was killed," Libby finished in a whisper.

Henzel nodded.

"We found newspaper accounts of a woman who claimed to have seen the Strangler walking from a victim's house covered in blood," Nick said. "Why didn't you call her to the stand? She could have introduced reasonable doubt."

"Yes, Mrs. McGovern was one of the first people I tried to contact when I received Will's case." He sighed. "Unfortunately she'd died a year or two earlier. Natural causes. I suppose that can happen when it takes six years to arrest a suspect and then another two years to bring him to trial." His tone was bitter. "I offered those newspaper articles into evidence, and I even brought in the reporter who interviewed her as a witness. In response the state introduced evidence that Mrs. McGovern had been legally blind, and the reporter couldn't remember whether she was wearing glasses or not. It was a disaster."

"But someone must have known something," Nick said. "Henderson was talking—people were being bribed to look the other way when a mysterious visitor came calling at the prison—"

"Believe me," Henzel replied, "even if someone knew something, no one was willing to *say* anything. It was a death sentence to go up against someone as powerful as the Glen Falls Strangler must have been. And for what? A happy feeling? A sense of justice?" He snorted and shook his head. "No one ever said a word." He was quiet for a moment. "No, I take that back. There was a prison guard who approached me once, telling me that Henderson had been receiving a strange visitor, that all kinds of rules were being broken to protect this visitor's identity. The guard told me that something was going on, but he wouldn't be more specific than that. He said he was going to speak with his superiors about it." Henzel closed his eyes. "He was found dead in his home a few days later. Shot in the head."

"Oh, God." Libby covered her mouth with her hands.

"The police report said all signs pointed to burglary. I knew better."

Libby shivered as silence fell across the room. Then Henzel continued.

"Henderson only confessed to having involvement with three of the murders. That was the arrangement, I suppose. I think he thought that he would have some leverage with the Strangler if he didn't confess to all of the crimes—that he could turn state's witness if the Strangler stopped making payments or something. Will Henderson wasn't the smartest client I've ever had. Someone took advantage of that."

Libby bit her thumbnail as she thought. If the Glen Falls Strangler was a powerful, well-connected person in the community, there might have been a vast conspiracy to convict Henderson. She felt sick to her stomach. What had her father done? What had her father *known* when he went to trial?

Her mouth was dry as she said, "Do you think my father knew about this?"

Henzel's eyes narrowed slightly. "I would have no way of knowing that."

"I'm only asking your opinion. I would ask my father directly, but he died two weeks ago."

"I'd heard. I'm sorry for your loss," said Henzel, but he remained unmoved.

"We need to know what Judge Andrews knew," Nick interjected.

"For your book, I suppose?"

Libby swallowed and tucked a strand of hair behind her ear. Based on his icy response, she suspected that Henzel knew something about her father—something that made him think less of him and of her. Guilt by association.

"Look," she began, "I don't know what my father did. I've learned over the past few days that you can know someone your entire life without ever actually *knowing* them." The words brought tears to her eyes again and she blinked them back. "I just want to understand what happened. That's all."

Henzel's face softened and he took a deep breath. "Your father was a complicated man, Libby. He had many sides, and he was capable of things that surprised me."

A tear rolled down her cheek and she wiped it away. Nick placed his hand on her knee. She let him.

"I didn't want to be the one to tell you this," Henzel continued, "but it seems that you already have your suspicions." He sighed. "Libby, I firmly believe that your father knew everything. I believe he knew that Henderson was being paid to do the time for someone else, and he knew that he was prosecuting the wrong man."

"God…" Libby brought her hand over her mouth. Her head reeled at hearing those words.

"Someone had to take the fall. *Someone* had to pay when the public was in a panic about a serial killer." Henzel's voice was low.

"Why Henderson?" Nick asked. "They could have framed anyone on the street, but they chose him. Was it because he needed the money? Did someone take advantage of him?"

Henzel smiled tightly. "I've wondered that myself. Unfortunately he never told me, and any answer I gave you would be pure speculation."

The nausea was back, rolling over Libby in another wave. She rested her hand on her stomach. "The Strangler was able to control Henderson with money, power and access. He was labeled a serial killer, and in many ways Henderson was another victim."

No wonder her father had told Nick that he didn't trust the police—if what Henzel said was true, they'd helped protect a serial killer and sent an innocent man to prison. Were they going to cover up whatever happened to *her,* too? She felt hot again, as if there wasn't enough air in the room.

Nick was watching her. "I think we have taken enough of your time, Attorney Henzel." He stood and extended his hand. "Thank you. This information has been invaluable."

Henzel shook his hand mutely, but his eyes were fixed on Libby with an expression of concern. "I've upset you."

"No, you haven't." Libby stood and pressed his hand warmly as she tried to force a smile. "You had nothing to do with this." She tried to take her hand from his but he was clutching it, staring at it. She was alarmed by the expression on his face: a haunted, fearful look. "Attorney Henzel?"

He looked up at her with hollow eyes. "Not a day goes by that I don't think about that trial and wonder what I could have done differently."

Nick approached them. "Like Libby said, this wasn't your doing. You didn't know what was happening."

"I could have talked to someone. I could have done something." His lips were shaking. He dropped Libby's hand. "I knew the killer had bribed the prosecutor. I was afraid that he had also gotten to the judge, or even the jurors. I didn't know who the good guys were anymore."

"You could have ended up like that prison guard. No one could blame you for keeping quiet." Libby bit her lower lip. "It would be easier if the good guys dressed in white."

A sound like a short laugh escaped from Henzel's lips, and he wrapped his arms around himself as if he was cold. "Thing is, I suspect good guys *do* dress in white." He brushed a hand over his face. "I just don't think we have many of them around."

CHAPTER NINE

"WELL, now we know why Dad didn't trust the police," Libby mumbled as they walked out of Henzel's office. "They helped orchestrate a massive cover-up to protect the Glen Falls Strangler."

"The officers who were involved are probably retired by now," Nick said. "But it's possible a few of them are still working. I imagine your father acted out of self-interest, too."

"You mean that he didn't want anyone in the police department or FBI to uncover his own misdeeds as part of an official investigation? Yeah, you're probably right."

Nick's BlackBerry began to vibrate. He frowned as he looked at the number. "Who is it?" Libby asked.

"Stillborough P.D." He held the phone to his ear. "Nick Foster."

"Nick, it's Sergeant Katz. I believe we've located the suspect's vehicle."

Nick's pulse quickened. "The white van?"

"Yes. It matches the description you provided, and we found bloody clothing in the back. We also found some materials that appear to be consistent with the homemade device that was planted in the box that caught fire. I can't say for sure yet."

"Of course," said Nick. "You're still processing the scene."

He turned his head to see Libby watching him with rapt attention. She mouthed the words, *What's going on?*

Nick covered the mouthpiece with his hand and said, "They think they've found the van."

She clapped her hands across her mouth.

"The van was parked in a residential neighborhood just on the outskirts of the downtown area," Katz said. "We're working with Glen Falls P.D. to process the scene, and a few of their men are patrolling the downtown, looking for the suspect."

"Thanks for keeping me informed, Sergeant. Let me know if you learn anything else."

"Will do."

They hung up.

Libby stepped closer to Nick and placed her hands on his stomach, clutching lightly at his shirt. The contact sent a flood of warmth through him. "They found his van?" she asked eagerly. "That means he can't be far away, right? They may find him soon?"

"I hope so, Lib." Nick placed his hands gently over her forearms, leaving mere inches between them. He could feel her breath on his face, see the hopeful glint in her blue eyes as she searched him for an answer. Nick should have been relieved to learn that the police had found the van and were closing in on this creep—so why did he feel unsettled by the news?

Libby wrapped her arms around him and pressed her ear against his chest. He tensed, unsure of what the gesture meant, or where to place his hands. After a moment he rested his palms awkwardly on her back.

"Oh, Nick," she gasped. "I hope they find him! And then we can go back to our normal lives."

He felt his stomach knot. If the police located the man pursuing Libby he would have fulfilled his promise to her father. He would be free to collect his money, move to Washington and start a new life. Move on. Without Libby. Wasn't that what he wanted?

He looked down at her as she hugged him, uninhibited in her exuberance at the thought of returning to a normal life without him. He felt tension collect in his shoulders. Gently but firmly he untangled himself from her embrace, ignoring the confused look she gave him in response. "Let's not get ahead of ourselves. He's still out there."

Libby stepped away, folding her arms across her chest. She looked up and down the street. "What are you going to do now?"

"I'm going to place a call to Ben and Zack, check on the status of their search for the suspect."

Libby nodded. "All right." She pointed to a deli behind him. "I'm going to grab something to eat. Can I get you anything?"

"Surprise me," he said as he began to dial on his Black-Berry.

He felt her staring at him. Nick shrugged to himself. *Let her be confused,* he thought. Things were different now, and he didn't have the same feelings for her that he'd used to.

He stood by the glass door of the deli as Libby walked inside, keeping an eye on her while he called Ben and Zack. They were driving around the downtown area, still looking for the suspect.

"Libby and I are grabbing lunch, and then we'll drive around, too."

"This guy's like an eel," Ben said. "He ducked down an alley and we pursued him on foot for a while, but he got away. Now we're just circling. He has to be around here somewhere—he doesn't have a car anymore, and there's no such thing as a taxi in this part of New York."

A blue bus pulled up to the curb, opened its doors and released several passengers. "He could have taken a bus," Nick said. "We'll want to alert the drivers. He's armed and dangerous."

"Good point," said Ben. "I'll start asking around, and I'll tell you if I hear anything interesting."

Nick tucked his phone back into his pocket and watched the bus as it closed its doors and drove away, leaving a plume of gray smoke behind it. He glanced up and down the sidewalk, not knowing whether he seriously expected to see the suspect or not. Then he strummed his fingertips against the top of the bench and waited for Libby.

Moments later she bolted out of the deli, pale and breathless, her pupils dilated.

"Libby," he said.

"I saw him, Nick. He's here."

He unbuttoned his holster. "Where is he?"

"I saw him through the back door, walking across the patio."

Nick felt his entire body tense. "You stay here in this deli, where there's lots of people."

"You can't go alone—"

"Stay here, Libby," he said. "Don't move."

With that, he entered the deli and darted to the back door, which opened onto a small brick courtyard—empty except for a few customers eating their lunch at the wrought-iron tables behind the deli. Nick looked around. The suspect could only have gone toward the street, and he set off in that direction, pulling his phone from his pocket.

He hit redial. "Ben, I need some help. I think we've found the suspect."

She'd been waiting for her order at the deli when she saw him pass the back door. At first glance she thought he'd been waiting for her, but then he'd continued without making eye contact. Libby had watched him leave, her breath coming in shallow bursts, her heart deafening.

Now her hands were shaking with pent-up energy as she waited in the deli for Nick to return. She chewed on her fingernails, studying the shoppers on the sidewalk. They seemed so calm, so oblivious to the manhunt continuing around them.

Then her breath halted. There he was, walking casually behind a young couple. He was still wearing the baseball cap but he'd changed his jacket—perhaps it was reversible? Libby frantically scanned the crowd, looking for Nick. She didn't see him.

The suspect was passing by the deli. Libby ducked behind a brick column, her heart thundering. She glanced out at the sidewalk again. Nick was still nowhere in sight. Libby tried to steady her breath. She could follow him, just a little way, and then call Nick or flag down a police car. Or, she reasoned, she could wait right here, as Nick had directed, and risk the suspect getting away. End it now or end it later...if ever.

She crept out from behind the column and slipped out the door.

The suspect didn't see her, Libby was sure. She was keeping a safe distance, blending in with the window shoppers. Every now and then he would stop and look behind him, and she would turn into a shop and watch him through the window. As soon as he turned around and began walking she would continue following him.

She pulled her cell phone from her pocket to call Nick. She hit the on button and received a flashing message warning that her battery was extremely low and she needed to recharge immediately. *Perfect,* she thought, *I left it on overnight again.* Libby turned the phone off and slipped it into her pocket. She would have to explain herself later. She just wanted to follow him for a few blocks and get an idea of where he might be hiding. Helping the police to capture him would be the only way to end this nightmare.

The suspect was walking quickly now, heading away from the downtown area into the wealthy residential neighborhoods. The farther they went from the deli, the more Libby began to wonder if she was making a mistake. It seemed so far to be walking, and there were fewer and fewer people around. Then again, she needed to learn more about this man. Maybe he would walk into a home or a building, and that would be the breakthrough they needed to figure out who he was and why he was following the pattern of the Glen Falls Strangler. She had no choice.

"Oh!" Libby cried out as she collided with a woman and her shopping bags. "I'm sorry."

As the woman smiled good-naturedly Libby saw the suspect turn to look at them. She turned her face away and shielded herself from view by sliding behind a large blue mailbox. If he'd recognized her, he didn't give any outward sign, but Libby's stomach turned. Should she continue to follow him? If he'd seen her, what might he do?

He continued walking. Libby felt her breath release.

He turned down West Maple Street, which sat at the very edge of the downtown and the Victorian-era houses of the residential neighborhoods. Libby turned the same corner and then stopped. He was gone.

Libby's pulse pounded in her throat as she glanced into a narrow alleyway behind a string of restaurants and small independent businesses. She wrinkled her nose at the cloying smell of baked bread and rotting garbage emanating from the brown metal Dumpsters. The alley was empty except for the garbage and the many rats that were undoubtedly living near it, and the cloudy green garbage water that drained into the vents on the road.

The suspect was gone.

Libby was acutely aware of the silence around her, of the sound of her own breath. She walked slowly toward the alley, craning her neck, staying on the sidewalk. He must have ducked into one of the restaurants, she reasoned. She would suggest to Nick that they return here later. She turned to leave.

Her breath hooked against her lungs and her heart stopped. The suspect was standing ten feet behind her. He was smiling.

"Looking for me?"

Libby's knees went weak as panic swept over her. "No," she said.

The lie seemed to amuse him, because he only smiled wider.

God, his teeth were sharp—as if he planned to rip her apart like a dog with a steak. There was that nausea again. He came closer, and Libby instinctively backed away, right into the alley.

"It must be a happy accident that we met like this, then." He smiled. "What's it called—serendipity?"

She was frozen. There had to be a way to escape. She glanced at the back doors to the restaurants.

"They're closed until dinner, if that's what you're wondering," the man said. "No one will arrive for another hour. Of course I don't need that long."

Libby started. "For what?" Her voice was barely a whisper.

The man was still smiling as he reached into his jacket and flashed the blade of a long serrated knife. "To talk, Elizabeth. Just to talk."

"You take one step closer and I'll scream," Libby snapped, surprising herself with her boldness.

The man in the black jacket paused and seemed to consider this threat. "No one's around to hear you."

"You don't know that. I'm a hell of a screamer."

He seemed amused by that, and his lips twisted in something resembling a grin. "I can cut your throat in less than ten seconds and reach the main street in another twenty." He tilted his head coyly. "From there I can walk into a coffee shop, order a cup and read the paper. All before whoever heard you scream—assuming anyone even cared—finds you here, bleeding to death, and calls the police. Do you understand me, Elizabeth?" He was inching closer. "We can have a rational discussion, or you can scream your pretty little head off and I can go have a cup of coffee."

He was beginning to look agitated, and his lips were wet with spittle as he discussed her options. Libby's body flooded with energy. She decided not to test him. "Okay," she said, trying to breathe. "Let's talk."

If she'd hoped he would calm down she'd been mistaken.

He was trembling, though she was slightly relieved to see that the knife remained tucked away in his jacket.

He pulled off his baseball cap and scratched at his dark curly hair. "Don't you understand? You are ruining *everything.*"

She fought to remain still as every inch of her body shook with fear. She thought she'd read somewhere that victims should remain calm in such situations. Easier said than done. "What am I ruining?" she said in a soft voice.

"Everything!" His fists were pulled tight, and his shriek was pinched through his tightly clenched jaw. "It's only day four, and now I have to kill you." He tilted his head and ran his fingers aggressively up and down his jawline. "It's not time."

"No," Libby answered, feeling the burn of tears as her vision became blurry. She tried to blink them back. "You don't have to kill me now. You can let me go and we can pretend this never happened."

He threw his head back and gave a quick laugh that echoed like a gunshot down the empty alley. "And then what's supposed to happen tomorrow, huh? I'm supposed to put you in danger *again.* Day five! That's how this works, Elizabeth!"

"Yes," she said, feeling the tears begin to trail down her cheeks. "We can do this again tomorrow."

He folded his arms across his chest and shook his head as he mumbled to himself. "No. No. It's all wrong. All bets are off now." He paced the alley, turning back and forth like a caged animal. Finally he spun to face her with sadness in his eyes. "Don't you see? I don't have a choice, Elizabeth. All bets are off now."

Her chin trembled and the tears were falling freely. She had her hands raised for some reason, and she began to lower them, shaking, to her sides. "All bets are *not* off," she whispered. "We can just walk away—"

Her voice stopped as she caught a movement at the top of the alley entrance. A tall, dark shadow had slipped into the alley and hidden behind a Dumpster. As he peeked around the side, his gun raised, and signaled her to keep quiet, Libby felt weak with a mixture of relief and gut-twisting fear.

Nick.

Nick struggled to quiet his own breath, which was coming in stops and spurts as his heart raced. He thought he'd seen Libby duck down this alley and he'd been right. She'd defied him and left the deli. Anger balled in his stomach.

He pressed his shoulder against the side of the Dumpster and peeked around the corner. She looked frightened half to death as she spoke with the suspect, but Nick was reluctant to act just yet. The man must have some kind of a weapon, but he needed to see it first. He strained to hear their conversation.

"Let me go," he heard Libby plead. "No one has to know about this."

"No more talking," snapped the suspect.

Libby screamed.

Nick turned around the Dumpster, weapon raised and pointing at the suspect. "FBI!"

The man spun to face Nick. He held Libby in front of him, grabbing her by her hair. A long silver blade was pressed against her throat.

"Let her go!"

The suspect pulled tighter on Libby's hair, baring her neck to the blade. Her face was white as she gazed imploringly at Nick. He couldn't stand to look at her, not to be able to help her.

"I said let her go!"

"So you can shoot me?" the man spat. "You drop your gun."

Nick felt a burning rage swirl in his chest. "If you hurt her, you're as good as dead." He seethed when the man smiled at him.

"You'll shoot me if I kill her, and you'll shoot me if I let her go. What choice do I have?"

"I just want her—got it? I'm going to lower my gun, and I

want you to take the knife away from her throat." Nick slowly lowered his gun.

To his relief, the suspect rolled the blade away from Libby's throat, watching Nick, that infuriating smile spilling across his mouth. He held her head tightly against his shoulder, and Libby was perfectly still, her gaze fixed on Nick.

"I'm going to put my gun back in its holster. I want you to put your knife away."

"Put it on the ground," the suspect snapped.

"If I put it on the ground you'll let her go?"

He seemed to consider this. "Yes."

Nick slowly bent forward to place his gun on the ground, keeping his eyes on the suspect the entire time. He stood. "There. Now let her go."

"Kick it away first."

He felt the cords in his neck tense. "You said you'd let her go."

The suspect loosened his grip just barely. "I will, but only if you kick the gun away."

He kicked the gun out of reach, feeling slightly sick to his stomach. "Let her go."

Libby fell forward then, landing on her knees. Nick ran to meet her as she crawled away, her breath coming in squeaks and pants. He helped her to her feet and placed his hands around her face to look at her before he proceeded to check her body.

"Libby," he breathed. "Are you okay? Did he hurt you?"

She leaned against him. "No," she gasped.

The suspect was watching the reunion with apparent amusement. He clenched the knife in his fist.

"Get out of here," Nick ordered.

The man snorted. "You're blocking my exit."

Nick pulled Libby to the side to allow the suspect through, shielding her from him with his body. He walked cautiously toward them, his knife still flashing in the sun. Libby pushed herself tightly against Nick, trembling.

He wrapped one arm around her shoulders, keeping her close to him. "It's okay," he whispered.

His eyes were drawn to a sudden movement as the suspect lunged for the gun. Nick pushed Libby to the side and sprung toward the man, knocking him to the ground. He kicked the gun toward Libby, who ran to retrieve it. Then Nick pressed his knee against the suspect's chest, pinning him down. Libby screamed. That was when Nick saw the blade flash—right before he felt it tear into his side. He screamed and rolled away, and the suspect sprinted down the alley.

"Oh, my God!" Libby was on her knees beside him, pressing his shirt to his side. "We have to call the police!" She reached for his BlackBerry.

"No police." Nick grabbed the phone from her. "They'll ask too many questions."

"Nick, for God's sake. You've been stabbed! I'm calling the police."

"I said no." He dialed his phone. "Ben. The suspect is heading south down Main Street." He ground his teeth together as he sat up, clutching his side. "He has a knife. He stabbed me."

He heard Ben curse. "Do you need an ambulance?"

"No. I'm taking Libby home. That's where we'll be." He hung up the phone and turned to Libby, who was wild-eyed with shock and concern. "Do you have first aid supplies? Gauze and antiseptic?"

"Of course."

"Good. I need you to drive me to your house. Quickly."

Libby lunged for the phone. "Absolutely not. I'm calling an ambulance!"

Nick pulled the phone from her reach and then winced and rose to his feet, keeping his hand pressed firmly to his side. "I don't need an ambulance."

"You've got to be kidding me. I'm going to drive you right to the hospital, then."

He stopped. "I just saved your life. The least you can do is stop arguing with me."

Libby stared at him in silence.

"Good. Now, I said no ambulance."

"Nick, I—"

"No ambulance," he growled. "Let's go."

Nick clenched his teeth and peeled the T-shirt off his chest, revealing an expanse of drying blood and a jagged gash on his left side.

Libby's knees weakened. "You really should go to the hospital," she said.

"And leave you unsupervised after that little stunt you pulled in town? Not likely." Nick removed the shirt and lowered himself onto the edge of the bathtub.

She knelt beside him on the floor and tentatively stroked his side with wet gauze. He jumped at the contact. "Try to hold still." Just the sight of the knife wound, deep and still weeping fluids, was enough to make her head reel. "You need stitches."

"I said no," Nick replied, his entire body gripped with tension. "Clean and dress the wound. Pretend your life depends on it."

Libby took a breath and continued, trying to distance herself from the task. Each of Nick's gasps was a reminder that this was her fault. Her stomach rolled.

She taped dry gauze over the ugly wound and sat back on her haunches. "Okay," she said.

Nick released a deep breath but didn't move. Libby bit her lower lip. "I shouldn't have run off," she said. "I saw the suspect and I thought I'd follow him. It was stupid." Nick remained still. "We should tell the police. They can send someone out to guard me. You don't have to... You've already done enough." Libby swallowed. "Please—say something."

His jaw was clenched shut, his eyes set firmly ahead, staring at nothing. "I realize that I'm not welcome here, Elizabeth."

Libby winced at hearing him use her full name.

"You have your plans. Career, marriage, kids, right? No room for the unexpected. No room for me."

Libby's breath caught as he turned to her, his eyes steeped in a stormy, foreign anger.

"Give me another forty-eight hours or so, and I promise I'll never bother you again."

She looked away. He had every right to hate her. He could have been killed. They both could have. "I'm sorry."

Nick grunted in response. He touched the gauze bandage on his side gingerly.

Libby's eyes began to sting. "No kids," she whispered.

Nick continued to examine his bandage. "What?"

Libby sniffed. "You said career, marriage, kids." She wiped under her nose with the back of her hand. "No kids."

"I didn't realize there'd been a change in plans." Nick rose. "Although I hear kids do make it hard to work seventy hours a week."

Libby hunched over and began to sob as her confession settled between them. She pressed her hands against her face, shaking against her own emotion.

Nick froze. "Libby, what did I say?"

She shuddered, unable to catch her breath.

He eased himself down to kneel in front of her and placed his hands on her heaving shoulders. "Libby, please don't cry. I didn't mean it."

"No," she gasped, lifting her head. "No, you're right. You're right to be angry with me." She inhaled, her breath ragged. "But I won't have children. I...can't." Her breath halted and she looked away. It was too late to take back those words, but she couldn't bear to see his reaction.

Nick placed a finger beneath her chin, tilting her face to meet his. "What are you saying?"

"I wanted to tell you." Her voice was tight with emotion. "But how do you tell your fiancé that you're infertile?" She pulled back from his embrace. "I don't think it gets more awkward than that."

Nick's dark eyes were fixed on her. "Tell me now, Libby."

She sniffed again. She'd rehearsed her story so many times, deliberating over the exact words she would use when she finally told him. Funny how in this moment she spoke without thinking.

"I went off the Pill when you went to Quantico." She gave a small shrug. "You were away, so what was the point of using birth control? And I figured we were going to get married when you came home. But nothing…happened. For months. I obviously wasn't pregnant, so I went to the doctor, who referred me to a specialist." Libby ran a finger under her eye. "Premature menopause. They said it was from the cancer treatment." Her chin trembled. "I always knew it was a possibility. The doctor said I didn't do anything wrong."

Nick swallowed and tucked a loose strand of black hair behind her ear. Libby's pulse quickened at the pain in his gaze. Every time she'd imagined this moment she'd anticipated several reactions. Nick would be angry, or disappointed, or withdrawn. But he was none of those things. He was hurt.

"Of course you didn't do anything wrong," he whispered.

Libby shook her head. "There must be a reason. I must have done something—"

"Stop it right there." Nick cupped her jaw in his hand and looked into her eyes. "I won't hear self-pity, Libby. Not from you."

He tightened his hold on her slightly and Libby became aware of his bare chest, and the way he was on his knees, his strong legs bracketing her own.

The pads of his thumbs moved in slow, lazy lines against her cheeks. Libby reached up to place her hands over his. She'd almost forgotten how well their bodies fit together, each piece of her interlocking with its counterpart of him. She'd almost forgotten how it felt to melt against him, to unload her physical and emotional weight.

"You should have told me," he whispered. "I could have…" He paused. "You just should have told me."

Libby's heart pounded as the breath from his words bounced against her cheeks. He was breathing harder now; both of them were. He held her captive, his fingers easing to the back of her neck to thread themselves together, his arms holding her still. She opened her lips to say something—anything—in response.

"Would it have changed anything?" Her voice was raw. "Nick, you left me. You left and you never called."

His forehead creased. "I didn't know, Libby."

As if that made it better, she thought. As if closing himself off and walking away was forgivable so long as he hadn't known. He really was impossible.

He was looking at her with an intensity she'd never seen. He might have died for her today. Libby's chest tightened. And if he had…?

Tell me you're sorry, she thought. *Tell me your life has been empty without me the way mine has been empty without you.* She stared into his deep brown eyes, willing him to tell her the words she needed to hear. *For God's sake, tell me you'll never leave me again.*

Instead he pressed his lips against hers, silencing her thoughts. She was only aware of the heat of his body and the pressure of his lips and the soft moan from the back of his throat as they kissed.

Then he pulled away.

"What is it?" Libby's eyes were wide.

"You're upset," he said. He was breathing heavily, his body shaking as he fought to get control of himself.

Libby blinked. Her nose was pink and her blue eyes were

bloodshot, and she was doing that thing with her hands, wringing her fingers. He'd almost forgotten how she did that.

Not like this, he thought. Not with her crying and emotional. Not with her scared, hurting and looking for anything to fill that void.

Nick took a deep breath. "We've both been through a lot." His side burned as he eased himself from the floor, leaning on the bathtub. "You need to rest."

Infertility. Nick tried without success to swallow the lump in his throat. Libby had been lonely as a child, growing up with only her father and her much older brother. Having children meant everything to her—how could she have kept something like that from him?

He'd started to walk toward the door when he heard her say, "Wait." He turned.

She was still on the floor, her arms wrapped around herself. She was looking at him as if she'd never seen him before.

"Nick," she said, her voice cracking slightly, "you saved my life today. I made a stupid mistake and I could have died." Her eyes began to pool again. "And it's not even over, because I could still die tomorrow."

"Libby," Nick whispered, "you'll live to be one hundred."

"No." She shook her head. "I have this minute, and that's all."

His face tightened. "And what do you want, then?" He searched her eyes. "What do you want if this is it?"

The sight of her in that alley, held at knifepoint, had flooded his body with blind energy. He hadn't thought about the knife, or the man holding it. He hadn't thought about his own life. At that moment all he'd thought about was Libby walking to school at twelve years old, and all the years they'd had together since then, and he'd realized that those years weren't enough. He would never have enough time with Libby.

She was still looking at him, and her mouth was still twisted in that way she had while she thought.

His heart pounded in his ears. *It's not a hard question,* he wanted to say. *Say you want me the way I've always wanted you. Say you would die happy tomorrow if I was all you had tonight.*

But what she said was, "I don't want to be alone."

Nick paused. He gave her a stiff smile. "You're not alone, Libby," he said. "I'll be on the couch."

He turned and walked out of the bathroom, leaving Libby still sitting on the floor, her mouth slightly open.

As he walked down the hall the house echoed with his footsteps and the unspoken words hanging between them. Step, step. *I wouldn't have cared about not having children.* Step, step. *You were all I ever wanted, anyway.*

Nick looked down. The bandage was already red. Libby was right. He should go to the hospital. He just didn't have time.

CHAPTER TEN

LIBBY practically jumped out of her skin when the doorbell rang. She peered out of the window and saw Ben standing with a middle-aged man holding a duffel bag. When she opened the door their jaws dropped, and Libby looked down and realized for the first time that her clothes were not only torn but smeared with blood and grime. She smoothed her hair self-consciously.

"Libby," said Ben. "This is Dr. Stevenson. He doesn't ask questions."

The doctor looked at Libby steadily. "I hear someone's been seriously injured."

She nodded. "Nick." She opened the door to let them through and gestured toward the living room. "He's in there."

The doctor pressed forward. "Nick, I'm here to stitch you up," he said. He turned back to Libby. "Is it okay if we sit in the kitchen?"

"Whatever you need."

Libby followed them wordlessly to the kitchen and stood in the doorway. The doctor pursed his lips when he saw the wound. "This is going to take some work," he said as he pulled on rubber gloves.

Nick gritted his teeth. "Do what you have to do."

Dr. Stevenson worked quickly, but Libby kept her gaze on Nick's face. He was tense, and perspiration gathered on his brow as the doctor stitched him back together. Libby's throat tightened and she excused herself from the room. She couldn't bear to see him in such terrible pain.

"You'll be all right," she heard the doctor say. "You're lucky, it could have been much worse."

"Thanks, Doctor."

"Stay out of trouble."

Ben and Dr. Stevenson left quietly and without saying goodbye. Moments later Nick joined Libby in the living room. She looked up.

"I'll go," she said, but without standing.

He looked at her from beneath his dark brows. "You don't have to go." He sat beside her on the couch, wincing slightly.

"Is it— Are you feeling better?"

"It's going to be okay, Libby. It will heal."

"Nick, I'm so sorry—"

"I know." He took her hand in his, turning it over gently and raising it to his lips to kiss her on the inside of her wrist. The touch of his lips against that sensitive skin sent sparks up Libby's spine. "I'm sorry, too." He continued to hold her hand. "You could have told me, you know. About not having kids."

"There never seemed to be a right time."

They sat in silence. "Do you think you'll adopt?"

Libby shrugged. The question was an obvious one, but it still struck a nerve. "I'm not there yet. I don't know if I could ever afford to, anyway. Not with my salary. I'm not married…" She broke off. "It seems like a complicated process."

He was quiet. "I know you wanted to be a mother. I always thought you'd make a great one."

She squeezed his hand. "Thanks." She moved closer to him and leaned her head against the back of the couch.

"You were so distant those last months we were together. I never understood why." He swallowed. "I was afraid you were going to leave me."

"And so you left first?"

Nick didn't answer except to give a slight shrug.

"Nick, what happened to us?"

He smoothed her hair back from her face. There was desire smoldering in his dark brown eyes as he ran his gaze lazily across her face. "I don't know," he admitted. "I always thought we were good together."

He ran his index finger softly from her temple down to her cheekbone, stroking across the sensitive skin near her ears before trailing down her jaw. Libby felt a shudder rush through her as he lifted her chin with that finger and brought his mouth to hers. He kissed her hungrily, tracing the crease of her lips with the tip of his tongue, coaxing her to open herself to him. As they kissed, he ran his strong, confident hands down her arms and to her waist, lifting her to sit across his lap. Libby felt his hardness press through his jeans against the fleshy part of her thigh. She raked her fingers through his golden-brown hair, delighting in the soft moan her touch elicited.

"Nick..." she whispered.

"Yes?" He pulled his mouth away just long enough to reply, then continued to taste her neck.

Libby sighed against him, turning her body to straddle his lap, to be more available to him. "Oh, God, I forgot."

He chuckled as she arched her neck back and he ran his lips lightly over her pulse points. She felt her body ignite at the attention, a sensation like the sweetest burning beginning to flood her veins. An aching need to have him, all of him, coiled itself deep within her.

"Libby," he whispered against her ear, the heat of his breath flooding her with desire. "Do you want me?"

Her answer bubbled from her throat in the form of a whimper. "Yes..." she whispered, her breath shaky.

She felt Nick tense in response, pulling her tighter against him, pressing himself against her heat. He slid his hand beneath her shirt and fanned his fingers against the softness of her stomach. She arched forward to taste his mouth as he slid one finger beneath the strap of her bra, sliding it down to touch the side of her breast. She gasped as he teased her.

"Say it," he groaned, his voice husky with arousal.

Her nipples tightened, her need for him intensified. "Please," she whispered.

He deftly unhooked her bra and took her aching breasts in his hands, running the pads of his thumbs across her nipples. Libby relaxed against his skillful touch.

"Tell me," he said, and the words jumped like a blaze of electricity down her spine.

"I want you." She sighed, settling her mouth against the salty taste of his neck. Her senses were flooded with his musk—the smell of his sweat and his desire for her. "Should we go to my room?"

He lifted her sweater over her head and eased her bra from her shoulders, dropping them both unceremoniously to the floor. "I want you here," he said, running his fingertips along her back and admiring the way her nipples responded. Then he took one breast into his mouth, teasing her with his teeth.

She couldn't argue with that.

Libby reached down his back to slide his T-shirt gently up and over his head, interrupting the attention he was paying to her breasts. He hastily removed the shirt and returned to tasting her, and the feel of his tongue on her delicate flesh caused her knees to weaken with need. She tightened her hold on his muscular shoulders, delighting in their feel as they tensed and released beneath her fingertips. She was in a trance, lost except for the sensation of Nick's hot mouth against her skin, his warm hands holding her to him, and the quivering of his muscles as he strained to contain his need for her.

She tenderly ran her fingers down his sides, avoiding the newly stitched wound, feeling a swell of love and gratitude for him. Nick knew everything about her, and he still found her desirable. Despite all of the pain in their shared past, all of the ups and downs, he was prepared to give his life for her.

She thought of all the time they'd spent apart, and how they'd been brought back together now, when someone was threatening her life. Tonight was barely certain, and what could tomorrow bring?

She pulled away, feeling a lump rising in her throat.

Nick sensed her hesitation and paused to look at her with confusion. "What's wrong?" he whispered.

She shook her head and smiled at him. "Nothing's wrong," she replied. "This is perfect."

He smiled and moved his hands lower to unfasten her jeans. Libby stood to help him, then grinned as his eyes widened at the sight of her lacy black panties. He pulled her back onto his lap and traced his fingers across the juncture of her thighs, then teased off her panties, sliding them slowly down her legs before tossing them aside. Libby settled back against the couch as Nick removed his remaining clothes, slipping out of his jeans and boxers with admirable speed.

He returned to the couch to position himself above her, bringing her ankles to rest on his shoulders. Libby reached for his hardness, smiling as he closed his eyes and stiffened at her touch. "What about protection?" she asked.

He looked at her through half-open eyes. "But you said you can't—"

"I can't," she whispered. "But we should be careful, you know. If there's been anyone else…" There was a knot in her stomach as she verbalized that fear. She'd been living like a nun since their breakup, but she could hardly expect that Nick would have done the same.

He smoothed his hand across her forehead, looking into her eyes. "There's been no one else, Libby," he whispered. "No one."

Relief passed over her. "Me neither," she whispered. "I mean—"

"I know what you mean." He smiled, and then she felt him press himself against her heat.

He groaned softly into her ear.

He took her gently but with urgency, thrusting in and out with long, deep strokes. He watched her face as she lifted her hips to meet his, matching his pace with her own. He held her waist, assisting her. Libby felt the tension mounting as their dance became faster, and she closed her eyes against the sensation of her body rising into the air. Finally she began to tense and shudder with sweet release, and Nick collapsed against her moments later, his body misted with light sweat.

"Oh, Libby," he whispered, kissing her once again.

Libby angled her body so Nick could lie beside her. He pulled a blanket over them and they entangled their limbs, his muscular legs pressing against her soft thighs. She sighed into his neck, feeling a blissful contentment. Then they fell asleep.

The room was dark when Nick awoke. Libby was breathing steadily, her face calm in the moonlight that splintered through the curtains. He paused, relishing the feel of her skin against his, the soft shape of her curves underneath the blanket. He kissed her lightly on the nose, smiling at the sigh she gave in response. Then he carefully disentangled himself from her and dressed.

Just past midnight. *Day five.* The realization brought him crashing back to reality. He wandered into the bathroom to splash water on his face. Day five and he'd never predicted he would be here right now, feeling the way he did for Libby. Yet he found whatever he *was* feeling difficult to define. Making love to her again, savoring the feel and taste of her body, had inexplicably felt the same way it always had and yet completely new. He felt like he'd just discovered something wondrous—as if he'd stumbled across a beautiful sight known only to him.

There hadn't been anyone else. Even now, hours later, Nick's heart galloped at her confession. How many nights had he lain awake in bed, alone, wondering where Libby was and who she was with? His insides had churned on such nights, twisting at the thought of her with another man. To think that all that time she'd been alone, too... The thought of her saving herself for him was almost too much to entertain.

He stepped into the kitchen. He was hungry, and the stitches in his side were aching. He took some aspirin with water and searched Libby's cupboards, deciding that pancakes sounded good.

Nick didn't fully understand the implications of what had just happened between them. He'd established his own boundary, deciding that he would not make love to Libby. Then he'd helplessly given in to his need for her. He smiled to himself as he realized that he'd always been powerless to resist Libby. He was drawn to her by some kind of gravitational force, some need he couldn't define or control. Or escape. He stopped smiling. The realization terrified him.

He heard a sound behind him and turned to see Libby stumbling into the kitchen as she pulled on her sweater. "What are you making?" She yawned.

"Pancakes." He felt his face soften at the sight of her. Who knew that Libby rumpled and yawning could be so damn sexy?

She grinned playfully. "At midnight? I think it's a little early for breakfast. Even for you." She steered herself into his chest, carefully wrapping her arms around him and resting her ear against his heart.

Nick's body responded to her, and he lifted her face to kiss her on the lips. Those beautiful, billowy lips, he thought as he pressed his mouth against hers. What would he give to taste that mouth every morning?

He pulled away to ask, "Do you want some?"

Her eyebrow arched. "Some what? If pancakes, then, yes. But if you had something else in mind..." She ran her hand tantalizingly across the zipper on his jeans. "Yes to that, too."

He groaned and kissed her forehead. "Libby, if you do what you just did to me again, I'll have to quit my job and follow you for the rest of my life."

"Well, we wouldn't want that, now." She nipped him lightly on the lower lip and then drifted away to the refrigerator. "Orange juice?"

"Sure, why not?"

Nick finished preparing the pancakes while Libby set the table. She squealed as he placed her plate before her. "You made a Libby pancake!" She smiled, pointing to the *L* Nick had cooked into the largest pancake on her plate.

"You know me and my fancy culinary skills." He beamed.

How much had he missed these moments, when he and Libby could just be themselves? He kicked himself for not asking her why she'd become so withdrawn—to think she'd been harboring her infertility from him, afraid that he would judge her for it. He reached across the table to hold her hand, delighted when she entwined her fingers with his to deepen the contact between them.

"Nick," she began, "you know I've told you a lot of things tonight?"

"Yes," he said, tightening his hold on her. Her confession had been so intimate—possibly more intimate than the moment they'd finally given in to their passion.

Libby turned her face to his. "I'm wondering why you've decided to leave the violent crime unit. I thought it was what you'd always wanted. At least when you were with the Glen Falls Police Department you seemed to feel so frustrated that you couldn't work on larger cases." She stroked his fingers with her thumb. "You've always wanted to be a hero."

A hero? Nick supposed that was true. Then he'd actually joined the Bureau and learned that maybe he wasn't cut out for the job, after all.

"When I first transferred to Pittsburgh I had a child abduction and murder case." His chest tightened as he thought of it. "I was there at the scene, Libby. I saw her body, thrown away like trash in a field. Knowing that another human being was capable of that…I felt like a part of me died."

Libby swallowed. Her eyes were soft and compassionate as she listened to him. "That's an awfully large burden to carry on your own."

He looked at her. "We've both been shouldering burdens alone."

She nodded, seeming to know exactly to what he was referring.

"I couldn't stop thinking about that little girl," Nick continued. "Her name was Greta Littlefield. She was ten years old. He took her as she was walking home from a friend's house. Just...plucked her right from the sidewalk."

Libby sighed and shook her head. "I'm so sorry."

"I met her parents. They gave me her school picture." His brow tightened at the memory of their faces, torn with grief. "They asked me to remember her. I kept that picture on my desk. I felt like it was my duty to find whoever did that and stop him before any more children were hurt."

She gazed down at their hands, and then began to trace his fingers with her thumb. "That's a lot of lot of responsibility for one person to take on."

Nick clenched his jaw. "There were so many things going on, Libby. We'd just broken up, I was in a new office in a new city..." He shook his head. "I did everything I could to find him. I looked at that picture of Greta when I felt too tired to continue and was able to keep going." He paused, dropping his voice. "But nothing I did was enough. He struck another child. Then another."

Libby's looked down. "Nick, you did everything you could—"

"But it wasn't enough." He looked her in the eyes. "That's the thing. I did my best and it wasn't enough. I failed her." He leaned back in his seat, pushing his plate to the side. The memories still sat like lead in his stomach. "That's when I asked to be put on other cases. I just couldn't face Greta's picture anymore, knowing how short I'd fallen."

Libby leaned forward to touch his arm. Her face was open, her expression sympathetic but not condescending. "Did they catch him?"

Nick nodded. "Yeah. Another agent did after I asked to be removed from the case."

She was silent.

"I know what you're thinking," Nick continued. "You're thinking that I ran away. From Greta. From you. From everything painful in my life."

She winced, and Nick realized that he'd just referred to Libby as a source of pain. To his relief, she simply said, "I wasn't thinking that. I was thinking that I'd want to leave, too."

"Maybe I did run away," Nick admitted, almost to himself. "Maybe that's what I'm doing now by transferring to public corruption. It's just that I think that if I was *meant* to do this kind of work, to investigate violent crimes, it shouldn't…get to me in that way."

"Oh, I wish that was the case," Libby sighed. "The cases I work on haunt me, too. All of those victims, each of them going about their normal routine when suddenly everything changes. Like *that*." She snapped her fingers. "Maybe I don't remember every detail of every file, but those stories become a part of me, too. I don't know how to deal with it. I just keep going." She rubbed her forehead. "And, you know, I wonder why Dad didn't feel the same way. I can't stop thinking about him knowing that Will Henderson was innocent and prosecuting him anyway."

Nick felt a pain as he looked at Libby's downcast expression. Her father had been her hero. She'd wanted to follow his path, to be just like him, and in the past few days she'd learned that he hadn't been who she'd always believed him to be.

"I'm so angry, Nick," she said, her voice rising with emotion. "I loved him, and I trusted him, and now I find out that I had no idea who he was. And I feel guilty because I still love him, even in spite of all of these bad things he did."

"Of course you love him, Libby. He was your father. Emotions run on a spectrum, and we rarely feel simple love or hate." He smiled sheepishly. "Sorry. I'm friends with a psychologist."

She placed her hands in her lap. "I know. Emotions are complicated."

She looked at him and Nick felt like she was sizing him up, wondering whether she should say something more.

He shifted away, suspecting that she wanted to discuss feelings. He realized he was unprepared to have a discussion about what they'd just done, or where they stood. The fact remained that he was scheduled to move to Washington, D.C., in a matter of days, and asking Libby to join him would be like asking the earth to reverse its course around the sun.

He cleared his throat. "Your father was a complicated man, Libby. The threats on your life suggest that he made some enemies, and yet the revenge angle doesn't make sense to me. Your father did everything the Strangler wanted him to."

Libby sighed. "I know. Maybe someone from Henderson's family learned what really happened and is seeking revenge?"

"But why not seek revenge against your father? Why you?"

"Are you asking me to apply logic to psychosis?" Libby twisted her napkin between her fingers. "I suppose that to a person with a schizoid personality one life is as meaningful as another, and they're all worthless. Besides, Dad died knowing that someone was after me because of something he did," she said quietly. "I'd say that's pretty harsh."

She withdrew again, visibly retreating into her own thoughts.

Nick imagined the Strangler approaching Libby's father, offering him money and power in exchange for an innocent man's life. He wondered how a man could trade his integrity for something as empty as money. Then his thoughts drifted to his own bargain with Judge Andrews, and the moment he'd demanded his estate in return for protecting the woman he'd once loved. The woman he still loved. *You've always been a man after my own heart.* Nick's stomach heaved as he remembered the judge's words—in his desire for revenge, had he proven him correct?

He was about to take Libby's entire inheritance—and for what reason? So that Nick could afford a nicer house and pay off his car? So that he could get some juvenile satisfaction from exacting revenge against a man who'd insulted him? A man who was no longer alive? Libby's salary was meager, and her law school debt was astronomical. An inheritance could give her financial security, help her to pay for things she couldn't otherwise afford. He grew cold. What if that money was Libby's only chance to finance an adoption?

He turned in his seat, unable to get comfortable. If he went to the police now and explained everything he'd violate the judge's terms and Libby might never know that he'd almost taken her entire inheritance. That could be a way out for him—except that he still wasn't sure he could trust the police, and if he didn't have that reward money he'd be saddled with tens of thousands of dollars in expenses for guarding Libby. Hiring two dedicated private investigators for a month wasn't cheap. He cursed himself for being so brash and thoughtless. Why hadn't he simply demanded to have his expenses covered?

He cleared his throat. "Your Libby pancake is going to get cold."

She gave him a small, wistful smile. "Maybe I'll save it for the real morning. I'd like to go to bed." She paused. "And I'd like you to come with me."

He tried to force down the anxiety rising from his stomach. She was looking at him so sweetly, with a suggestive smile. "I'm pretty tired, Lib."

The smile wavered. "Me, too," she said quickly. "I just thought I would feel safer. But if you don't want to—"

"No, it's fine." He touched her hand. "It's fine. Let's go to bed."

CHAPTER ELEVEN

Day Five

DAY five.

It loomed like a threat, and Libby's skin prickled every time she glimpsed a movement out of the corner of her eye as she walked with Nick down Main Street.

"I need you to be vigilant," he said. "Hypervigilant, even."

"Done and done," she replied, darting her glance right to left. The morning rain had kept the crowds away, but there were a few shoppers scattered down the sidewalk.

"The suspect has been watching our every move," he continued. "He's planted the signs like clockwork. Now we need you to lure him out of hiding again."

"You're using me as human bait," she muttered, rubbing her arms to smooth down the goose bumps. She'd never imagined the suspect would still be at large on day five. Her stomach burned at the possibility that they would not catch him in time.

He wrapped his arm around her shoulders and gave her a kiss on the forehead. "I'll be right with you, sweetheart."

Now the hair on her arms rose for a different reason entirely, and she eased her head against Nick's shoulder. "Will the police be around? Or Ben and Zack?"

She felt Nick tense slightly and remove his arm from her shoulders. "Ben and Zack will be watching, of course. They're on their way."

"But not the police?"

Nick shook his head.

Libby clutched his jacket lightly, leading him to the side of the road. "No," she said. "Enough with the 'no police' rule. I want them called."

Nick's eyes were dark, and he avoided her gaze. "I promised your father I wouldn't," he said. "Besides, we don't know if we can trust them."

She searched his face. "What if, in the end, my father was only concerned with protecting his own reputation? With ensuring that no one found out what he did to Will Henderson? What if we're avoiding the police for no other reason?"

"Libby, we just don't—"

"Someone is trying to kill me. He's already killed someone else and stabbed you. He was prepared to kill me yesterday, and today he's going to set a trap. We know he's going to place me in a life-or-death situation." Her voice gave out as she heard her own words. "We're not building a case against him, and you won't involve the police out of some weird sense of obligation to my father. Nick, you couldn't stand my father!"

Nick turned to her. "Libby, there are things I can't…tell you."

She blanched. "Things? What things can't you tell me?"

"Not now, okay? Not yet."

"No." She clasped his jacket in her hands as he tried to turn away from her. "No more secrets, Nick."

He touched her hands and she relaxed her grip on him. Her fingers felt like ice against his warm palms. "Do you trust me?"

Her gaze darted back and forth between his eyes. "Yes, of course."

"Then believe me when I say that you're safe with me."

Nick's bargain with Judge Andrews was corroding his insides. He hated the thought of keeping that information from Libby. But how would she react if she knew the truth? Last night as he'd lain awake in her bed he'd decided that he would only collect enough money to cover his expenses—he would hand everything else over to Libby. It was the right thing to do. He'd explain it—somehow convince her that he hadn't intended the demand to be a cheap shot at her dying father.

He felt sick. Libby adhered to a rigid moral code. In her mind there was right and wrong, justice and injustice, and he was pretty sure his actions would fall under "despicable." Who was he kidding? Once she found out what he'd done she'd never speak to him again.

"If you don't call the police," she said, "there's no case being built against him for the hell he's put me through. There's no evidence, and there's no way that he can be prosecuted for this. I think we need to trust them. I don't see what choice we have."

"He'll be prosecuted for arson and murder," Nick said. "He'll go to jail for the rest of his life—if he even makes it through the day alive."

Libby's face was troubled. "I trust you with my life," she said, and the words cut through his very being, "but I won't blindly follow you." She pulled out her cell phone and began to dial. "I'm calling the police. I'm telling them everything."

Nick pressed his hand against his eyes. Then he heard her drop the phone and looked up. He froze.

The suspect was staring at him, his eyes glinting with an almost palpable delight. *This is a game to him,* thought Nick.

He had something in his jacket pocket, pressed against Libby's back. "It's a gun," he hissed into her ear. He glared at Nick. "You move and I'll kill her right here on this sidewalk—got it?"

Nick nodded and held his hands up, palms out. "No trouble," he said.

"There better not be."

He turned back to Libby. The barrel of the gun was angled upward and forced against the bottom of her rib cage. She winced in pain as he pulled her closer to him, pressing the gun still farther into her back.

"Let's go for a walk, darling." He shot another glare in Nick's direction. "And I'll take your BlackBerry, too."

Nick reached slowly into his pocket and handed over his phone. He stood frozen in place as the suspect picked up Libby's cell phone and placed it in his own pocket. "Now, turn around and slowly count to one hundred—out loud," he ordered.

Nick complied.

When he reached one hundred, he turned around. They were gone.

He pushed her through a wooden gate into a narrow alleyway. The nozzle of the gun was now shoved painfully against her spine, and Libby had difficulty walking straight. "You can relax the gun," she snapped. "You've made your point."

She heard him laughing—a low, dry laugh. "Have I? And what do you think my point is?"

"You're some sick bastard who has a twisted fascination with a serial killer. You copy him because you lack the imagination to do anything original."

She saw sparks when he cuffed the side of her head with her cell phone. "Show some respect," he growled against her ear as she stumbled forward, "or next time I'll use the hand holding the Glock. Now, keep walking."

Libby's vision blurred as she righted herself. He was walking her down an empty alley blocked from view by windowless brick buildings. *Keep him talking,* she told herself. Talking was the one thing she could do to get information and try to regain some control of the situation. Besides, this creep had proven that he followed the Glen Falls Strangler M.O. to the letter, which meant that she had time left.

"You know you can't kill me," she said. "It's only day five. The Strangler wouldn't have used a gun, anyway."

"I told you yesterday that all bets were off," he snarled. "I don't care about all of those things anymore."

He pushed the gun into her back again and Libby winced. Her head was throbbing where he'd hit her. "So you intend to kill me now?"

"Maybe. Maybe not."

"I think I have a right to know." *Careful, Libby—don't push him too hard.*

"Stop. To the left."

Libby looked to her left and saw a white door with peeling paint and a shattered lock. "What do you want me to do?"

He pushed the gun into her side. "Get in there."

She froze. She'd worked in law enforcement long enough to know that victims who stepped into a car under the threat of violence rarely survived. She suspected that walking through a door with a man with a gun would be equally deadly.

Her thin frame vibrated with the thrust of her heart. How ironic that now, as she was under the threat of death, she felt so alive. There were birds building a nest under the awning that hovered above the white door and she could hear them shuffling. She could feel the afternoon sun as it crept from behind a cloud. She could smell coffee and cinnamon rolls being prepared in a bakery nearby. Was this how it ended?

No. She wasn't going to die. Not today.

He pressed the gun harder, this time hitting a nerve and sending a spark of pain through her body. "I said get in there."

She stood firmly in place. "No."

She felt the gun waver just slightly and realized she'd thrown him off guard with her disobedience. Then he jabbed the nozzle roughly against her, this time twisting her upper arm until the back of her head was resting against his shoulder.

"What did you just say to me?"

Libby gritted her teeth. "I said screw you, and I'm not opening that door."

He flung her to the ground. Libby cried out in pain as the

asphalt tore at her elbows and knees. When she turned her head to look back at him he had the Glock pistol pointed at her.

"Open that door."

She looked around, considering her options. She was surely as good as dead if she did as he asked; the door looked like part of an abandoned building.

He glowered at her and said, as if reading her mind, "You don't have many choices, Elizabeth."

She couldn't very well continue to lie in the alley, so she began to rise to her feet.

"That a girl," he said, his shoulders relaxing just slightly as she cooperated.

Then her phone rang. He looked down.

Libby lunged forward, landing her right shoulder squarely against his sternum. He gasped and released his hold on the gun, dropping it just out of reach. She felt mad with rage as she dug her nails into his face, drawing blood. Thrusting the palm of her hand against his nose, she heard a sickening crunch as the cartilage broke. He screamed, clutching at his face, while Libby rolled away to reach the gun that still lay only inches from his fingers. She'd started to wrap her fingers around the cool metal grip when the gun flew out of her grasp.

He had reached it first.

Libby took off running, hearing him cursing behind her as her feet pounded the pavement. A bullet ricocheted, zipping past her ear. A blood-curdling scream escaped her throat, and she heard her own breath coming in shrill spurts. There *had* to be a way out of here.

Another shot rang out, this one puncturing a metal trashcan as she ran by. He was shrieking in pain as he pursued her, but gaining ground. Libby approached a gate that seemed to lead out of the alley and crashed her shoulder up against it. She could hear him coming, and a bullet shattered the top of the board on the gate—too close to her head.

"Help me!"

With clumsy fingers she fumbled at the latch on the gate. The latch was locked, or jammed—she couldn't tell which. But it didn't matter because the result was the same. She was trapped, and her killer was quickly closing in.

Nick approached the first person he saw and flashed his credentials. "Special Agent Foster. I need to borrow your cell phone."

The woman looked puzzled but she opened her purse and handed over a pink phone studded with multicolored rhinestones. "Bring it back," she said.

A dark car pulled up to the curb and the passenger window was rolled down. Zack and Ben peered at him. "Nick, where's—?"

"He has Libby," he said.

The men jumped out of the car, their hands placed on the guns in their hip holsters.

"Where'd they go?" Ben said.

"They can't have gone far. We'll need to circle this block. He has a gun."

Zack nodded. "I'm heading north." He took off running.

"I'll head south, then." Ben looked at Nick. "We should alert the P.D."

Nick swore under his breath. Now that he knew the extent to which the police had protected the Strangler he still wasn't certain he could trust them. But did he have a choice? He wondered if his reluctance to involve the police had anything to do with the payment he stood to gain if he complied with Judge Andrews' conditions. Nick felt cold. Had he just traded Libby's life for money?

He called the police.

"This is Special Agent Nick Foster. A woman was just abducted at gunpoint on Main Street. I'm in pursuit but I need backup." He gave his location and hung up.

Ben removed his gun from its holster and gripped Nick's arm. "We'll find her," he said, before he took off.

Nick dialed Libby's number, praying the suspect hadn't already smashed her phone to pieces. He listened for ringing, but couldn't hear anything above the noise of the street. He dialed it again, this time pacing back to where the suspect had been standing when he'd approached Libby. There was a fence blocking the entrance to an alley. He heard a gunshot.

Nick's body went rigid. He pushed on the gate but it wouldn't budge, so he rammed his shoulders against the boards, splintering them until he had created a hole large enough to pass through.

More gunshots. A woman was screaming.

He took off sprinting down the alley. Fear twisted his gut as he saw Libby's cell phone lying on the ground, ringing next to a puddle of blood.

More gunshots, and this time they came in rapid succession.

He fled down the alley, his lungs burning and his body heavy with dread. If he lost Libby now—he couldn't bear to complete the thought.

As he neared the end of the alley he saw another wooden gate. His gaze rested on a figure on the ground—a body, twisted and bleeding.

"No!"

His weapon was drawn as he hurtled down the alley toward the gate. A person hovered over the body, standing in a shadow, holding a gun. Nick stopped in his tracks and raised his weapon.

"FBI! Drop your weapon!"

He heard the metal hit the ground. "Nick!"

His body shuddered with relief as she stepped into the sunlight. *Libby.* He ran to her, sweeping her into his arms, kissing the soft black waves of hair that fell across her cheeks. "Oh, God, Libby. Honey, are you all right?"

She nodded, but her teeth rattled as she tried to answer him. "I killed him," she said, and pointed to the body.

Nick dropped to his knees. The man's nose was broken and bloody, and his jacket was riddled with bullet holes. He turned to Libby, his eyes wide. "How did you—?"

"I managed to get away when my cell phone rang. He got distracted. Then I broke his nose, like you taught me one time, and I tried to run away but he kept shooting at me. And then I reached this gate and I saw that." She pointed to a black bottle of wasp spray on the ground. "They must have it because of the trash cans. The can says that it sprays up to thirty feet, so I tried it and got him in the eyes. He dropped his gun."

Nick's jaw was slack. "And then you shot him?"

She shook her head. "No. I was going to hold him there, but then he lunged at me again and I shot him." She looked at the body with contempt. "I kind of enjoyed it, too."

Nick's eyebrows shot up. "Well, we'll strike that last comment from the record."

There was a crash behind them as the gate burst open. Ben stepped through, his gun raised.

"It's all over," said Nick, standing.

Ben exhaled and lowered his gun. His eyes widened when he saw the dead body. "Damn, Nick. You did a number on him."

"Actually, Libby killed him."

Ben's jaw dropped and he looked at her with visible admiration. "Well, I'll be…"

Zack climbed through the gate then, breathless. He gave a low whistle when he saw the scene and placed his gun back in its holster. "Looks like you boys have it covered."

"Girl," Ben corrected him, and laughed as he saw the shock on Zack's face.

"She's something else, all right," Nick said, surprised by the tension in his voice. He swallowed. The sound of police sirens approaching pierced the sudden quiet.

Libby wrapped her arms around herself. "Nick, does this mean it's over? Am I safe now?"

He brushed his lips against her cheek. "Yes, sweetheart, you're safe now."

CHAPTER TWELVE

Day Six

LIBBY placed a pitcher filled with icy green liquid on the patio table and distributed salt-rimmed glasses.

"I should be the one making the margaritas. You should relax." Nick smiled, running his hand up the back of her leg.

"Nonsense," she replied, handing him a bag filled with little paper umbrellas. "You can be in charge of decorating our drinks. Besides," she said as she leaned over his chair to plant a kiss on his cheek, "you know I don't do well with relaxing. Oh—and none for me, thanks. I can't handle my tequila."

He slipped his hands around her waist, pulling her onto his lap. "You have to have a paper umbrella on a toothpick—we're celebrating."

"Stick it in my wine glass, then." She sighed as he kissed her softly, savoring the warmth of his mouth, then giggled as she felt his fingers tugging at the bottom of her shirt. "Not now! They're going to be here any minute!"

"Come on, just a little—"

"No." She laughed, standing and fixing her shirt.

Nick sat back in his chair and groaned. "We're like an old married couple already."

Libby arched an eyebrow. "If old married couples do what we did last night, then I'm fine with that." Her cheeks grew pleasantly hot as she thought about their lovemaking, and she was pleased to see Nick's lips twist in a devilish smile. "I'll take a raincheck, though," she said as she returned to the house.

Nick was probably right about relaxing, she thought as she prepared a bowl of tortilla chips and salsa for her guests. Libby was bruised and scraped from yesterday afternoon's narrow escape, and her body felt achy as she came down from the adrenaline rush. The police had seemed satisfied with her statement, and Libby wasn't concerned about the inevitable investigation. Killing him had been a matter of self-defense.

Him. He had a name now, didn't he? Reggie Henderson— Will Henderson's nephew. All the pieces had fallen into place once they'd learned that bit of information. Reggie Henderson was taking revenge for his uncle's wrongful imprisonment and murder, and what better target for revenge than the prosecutor's daughter? Libby's stomach churned acid as she thought about how close he'd come to succeeding. *You messed with the wrong girl, Reggie.*

She'd told the police that Reggie had been stalking her in the same way his uncle had stalked his victims. She hadn't been able to bring herself to tell them what she knew about her father: that he'd knowingly prosecuted an innocent man to protect the reputation of the real Strangler—a powerful, wealthy, still-unknown person—and that he'd probably received some kind of financial benefit from the Strangler in return for his cooperation. That he'd sold his soul to the devil.

Libby reached for jars of cumin and red pepper and began to mix seasoning for the grilled fajitas. She wondered what her father's deal had been with the Strangler. What had he negotiated—money? Political support when he ran for judge? She washed her hands, examining the scrapes on her wrists. The physical pain was nothing compared to the emotional ache that came with learning that the father she'd idolized had sold his ideals. She needed some distraction from her own thoughts tonight.

She watched through the window as Nick rose to greet

Ben and Zack, who'd each brought a bottle of wine. Libby felt warm at the sight of Nick. This week had been filled with unexpected surprises, and she supposed that one day she would look back and think that her father had ultimately reunited her with Nick. She didn't know where they stood, or where they were going, and she knew that he would be returning to Pittsburgh soon. But maybe, she thought, the distance would only be temporary.

She felt a pang of guilt as she thought about David. He'd come home last night, and he wanted to see her. Libby intended to call him to invite him to have coffee, and to explain in person what had happened while he was in Zurich. David was a good, kind person, but they just weren't right for each other.

But she and Nick? They deserved another chance.

Nick dried the last plate and returned it to the cupboard before folding the dish towel in careless thirds and flinging it over the side of the sink. "A delicious dinner, Libby," he said, nuzzling her neck.

She twisted away from him, giggling. "I want to take a bath. I think I've earned that much."

He stood back up, suddenly tense. "Yes, you certainly have."

He tried to suppress a nagging feeling as she walked away. It had started yesterday afternoon as Libby gave her statement to the Glen Falls Police. Nick had watched her with a mixture of admiration and astonishment: that beautiful, elegant woman had somehow managed to overpower an armed man. If it had happened in a movie he wouldn't have believed it, but when he considered the way Libby was when she set her mind to something how surprised could he really be?

And yet that feeling swirled in his gut. Inadequacy. Failure. Judge Andrews had hired Nick to protect his daughter, and she had saved herself.

He shook his head, trying to scatter the thoughts. He was being selfish. Libby was alive, and that was all that mattered.

Except that being with Libby this past week had made Nick realize how much he needed her in his life, how much he'd always wanted her. Libby's heroic efforts yesterday were just another example of her persistent independence and self-sufficiency. She didn't need him the way he needed her. She could protect herself. She didn't need anyone. His stomach tensed.

He heard the bathwater running as Libby sang to herself, and he felt a sudden sadness pass over him. Nick knew it was only a matter of time before they had a conversation about their future—and what kind of future could they have? Now that Libby was safe he needed to return to Pittsburgh so he could pack his belongings and head to Washington, D.C. Libby wouldn't react well to the news. His mouth tightened. What was his choice, other than to quit his job completely? He loved his career as much as Libby loved hers. Was he supposed to give up everything he'd worked for so that he could support Libby in her dreams? So that he could be the man behind the successful woman? No. That wasn't an option.

Libby still didn't know about Nick's bargain with her father, either. He'd called Everett yesterday evening to tell him the news.

"Everett," he'd said as he heard the attorney answer. "It's Nick Foster."

"Hello, Nick," came the cold response. "Is Libby all right?"

"She's fine. Actually, she's better than fine. The man who was stalking her is dead. Killed yesterday afternoon."

"I see. I think I know why you're calling me…"

"Everett, I need my expenses covered. That's all. I want everything else to remain with the estate. Give it over to Libby."

He'd been silent. "It's more complicated than that, Nick."

"It shouldn't be," Nick had replied. "Do what you need to do."

Giving Libby the money was the right thing, Nick told himself, but it wouldn't solve anything. Libby would still find out what he'd done to her father, and she'd never forgive him for it.

He was fooling himself to believe they had a chance together. Nick gritted his teeth. No sense in long goodbyes. It was time to leave.

He collected his clothing, folding it up quickly and shoving it to the bottom of his duffel bag. He added his toothbrush and travel toothpaste, his soap and shampoo. It would be dark soon, but he could still make it to Pittsburgh before midnight.

Nick zipped his duffel bag and stepped back. Was that everything?

He heard Libby turn off the bathwater. His gut knotted. He would leave a note. It would be easier that way.

The doorbell rang just as Libby was undressing to climb into the bathtub. "Nick?" she called. "Can you get that?"

She waited for a response. The doorbell rang again. She sighed and dressed, then ran down the stairs to the front door.

"Oh, Everett." She smiled. "This is a nice surprise."

"Libby," he said with a reserved smile, "are you alone?"

She blinked. "Uh...no, actually. Nick is here." She turned and saw him walking toward her. "Nick, you remember Everett?"

"Yes," he said, offering his hand stiffly.

"I'm glad you're both here," said Everett. "I would like to come inside for a few minutes, if I may?"

"Oh, of course," Libby said, and stepped aside. "Let's go into the living room. I see Nick has already cleaned up."

Nick and Libby sat on the couch and Everett seated himself on a chair facing them. He was carrying a worn brown leather briefcase that he opened, retrieving a file. "Libby, you recall that when we met a few days ago I told you that certain conditions had to be met before I could disclose the terms of your father's trust." He closed the briefcase with a snap. "I am happy to say that those conditions have been met."

"Oh, good," Libby sat up straighter. "This should answer some questions, then." She saw Nick shifting in his seat.

"Your father knew your life was in danger before he died. Knowing that, he turned to the one person he trusted to keep you safe—Nick Foster." Everett hit him with a stony gaze.

Libby reached over to squeeze Nick's hand, surprised when he returned the gesture limply.

"Your father asked that I read the following letter to you—preferably with Mr. Foster in the room." Everett cleared his throat and proceeded. "'My dearest Elizabeth—if this letter finds you, it means you have survived a horrific threat against your life by a madman out for revenge against me. Rest assured, my dear child, that you have done nothing wrong, and that the fault lies entirely with me.'"

Libby's lip began to tremble. Hearing her father's message made her heart hurt.

Everett continued. "'Elizabeth, I leave this world with a number of regrets, the least of which is that I am unable to leave you anything of financial value after my death.'"

Libby looked at Nick in confusion. He shifted again in his seat.

"'When I learned of the threats on your life,'" Everett read, "'I turned to a man whom I believed cared enough about you to guard you with his life. He was the only man I trusted to protect you. That man was Nick Foster.'"

Nick leaned forward, seemingly agitated.

"'I asked him to protect you. It was my dying wish. Regretfully, he informed me that he could only comply with my desires if I promised to pay him the value of my entire estate.'"

"Oh, that's bull!" Nick stood, red-faced.

"Nick!" Libby gasped.

"You can't listen to this, Libby. Your father—" He bit his finger, trying to keep from saying anything else.

Libby felt stunned, as if someone had slapped her. She turned to Everett. "What is this? I don't understand."

"Perhaps you should hear the rest of the letter," Everett replied calmly.

"I won't listen to this!" Nick shouted.

"Nick, please." Libby felt her stomach churning. "Continue, Everett—I want to hear this."

Everett cleared his throat again and continued to read the letter. "'Libby, I have never considered Nick to be especially worthy of your love and affection. He is hot-headed, arrogant, and, as this situation demonstrates, morally bankrupt. Since he has demanded every penny from my estate in exchange for saving your life, I can only leave you with the following words of advice: do not throw the pearls of your youth at this swine.'" Everett folded the letter. "It is signed, 'Affectionately yours forever, Dad.'"

Libby turned to Nick, who was almost purple with rage. "Nick, is this true?"

"Of course not!" he said, turning to Everett. "Tell her the truth, that I was only going to deduct my expenses and leave her everything."

Everett looked at Libby and sighed. "It's true, Libby. All of it. Nick is owed the entire estate—but he did ask that I give it back to you after deducting his expenses."

Libby felt light-headed. Nick had demanded money from her dying father to protect her. Worse, he had demanded every last penny in her father's estate.

She gripped the side of the couch, steadying herself. "Everett," she said, "Nick and I need to talk."

Everett nodded and left the house without another word.

"Libby, I—"

"How dare you?" she said softly, her voice strained. "To demand my father's estate in return for protecting me? Nick, what were you *thinking?*"

"Libby." He laughed drily. "You never knew your father the way the rest of the world did. He was a *monster*. This week we learned that he accepted a bribe to send an innocent man to jail for the rest of his life! Are you going to believe anything he says?"

A weight began to build in her chest. "And you think you're better than he was?" Her voice cracked. "My father was dying. Desperate. And you told him that you wanted everything he owned. You took revenge on him when he came to you for help." She glared at him. "I know my father was far from perfect, and I know that he was hard on you. To be honest, I loved you more because you never returned his insults. I believed you were better than that." Her chin trembled. "I thought you were here because you still cared about me. I was wrong."

Nick was perfectly still. "Libby—"

She noticed the packed duffel bag by the doorway for the first time. Her heart skipped a beat and she turned to him, her mouth open. "Your bag is packed."

He looked at his feet. "I need to get back to Pittsburgh. I'm moving in a few days." He lifted his head to meet her eyes. "I'm being transferred to Washington, D.C."

Libby hunched forward. Her mouth opened but no sound came out. She closed her eyes and shook her head. *"Washington?"* A cry lodged in her throat. "When were you planning to tell me this?"

"The FBI requires all agents to spend a few years at a major office. These plans were in place long before I came here."

"Then why would you—?" She stopped herself. She'd been about to ask him why he'd allowed her to believe that there was something permanent between them. But he had never made her any promises. He'd never told her he would stay, as much as she wanted him to. "And you were just going to leave? Just like that? While I was in the *bath?*"

Nick was silent, watching her.

"I don't even know you," she whispered. "I must be a terrible judge of character."

His eyes flashed. "I'm not leaving anything—"

"That's how you deal with difficult problems, Nick," she

said, her voice eerily calm in spite of the storm of emotions swirling in her chest. "You leave them. I'm nothing but a problem to you."

"Libby, you know that's not true—"

"It's not?" She glared at him. "I thought things between us were different. I thought that *you* were different."

He squared his jaw. "I have as much right to a career as you do."

"But don't you see? It's not that at all. Nick, I've never told anyone that I can't have children. I told *you* because I am tired of the secrets between us. I trusted you. But you don't feel the same way. All of these secrets—and when were you planning to tell me?" She rose. "We've made a terrible mistake."

"I'm sorry you feel that way."

The hard tone of his voice wrapped an icy fist around her heart. How had she been so foolish? How had she allowed herself to actually believe their relationship could work? They couldn't change who they were.

She leveled a steady glare at him. "You have five minutes. After that I never want to see you again."

Libby set the timer on her watch. Five minutes.

Nick was gone in two.

Her head was throbbing. Every time she closed her eyes Libby's mind replayed the scenes from the last week. The doll lodged under the car tire. The sound of gunshots reverberating in an empty alley. The feel of Nick's bare skin on hers. The sight of him in the moonlight as they made love in her bed. The sounds of their last words.

The clock read nearly eleven, and she'd been crying for hours. She reasoned that she'd eventually pass out from exhaustion. In the meantime she could at least have some tea.

Her cell phone vibrated to indicate she'd just received a text message. *Nick.* Libby lunged forward but frowned when she saw the message was from David. He wanted to come over.

She sighed and dialed his number. So much for sparing his feelings, she thought, but they needed to have this conversation now.

"Hello?"

"David, it's Libby."

"Hey, you!"

She'd almost forgotten how chipper he could be.

"Did you get my message?" he asked.

"Yeah. Look, it's not a good time. I've kind of… It's a long story."

"I have time," he said. "And I was just on my way over to see you."

"Now?" She glanced at the clock. "It's late."

"I know, but I was in the neighborhood and I wanted to see you. I have some chocolates from Switzerland."

She smiled feebly. "Ah, you've figured out my weakness already."

"So I can come over? I'm about five minutes away."

She thought about it. What difference did it make? Maybe hearing about David's trip would be a pleasant distraction.

"Sure, why not. I was just about to make some tea."

"See you in a few."

Libby rushed to her room to change into something more presentable: jeans and a simple T-shirt. She splashed cold water on her face, but her eyes were still swollen from crying. It would have to do, she decided.

There was a knock at the front door. David held out a small blue gift bag.

"Oh, you shouldn't have." She smiled politely. She opened the bag and removed a box of chocolates. "These look amazing."

David smiled and Libby looked away. They were barely dating. So why did she suddenly feel so guilty?

She stepped back to allow him inside. "How's your father doing?" she asked.

David's father, former Mayor Jeb Sinclair, had been diagnosed with dementia several years ago, and had been in a nursing home for some time.

"He's not doing too well, to be honest. The doctors want to move him to a locked unit. He needs more care than he's currently receiving."

"I'm sorry," Libby said as she poured two cups of tea. She'd known Jeb Sinclair practically her entire life, and she'd always remember him as he'd been in her youth: a smiling, towering figure of a man. "You know, I was looking through my dad's old files and I found some of your father's campaign flyers. I can show them to you later."

David smiled. "Isn't it funny how our fathers were friends and we found each other years later?"

Something about his tone made her skin prickle. Libby brushed the feeling aside. "Funny."

He looked around the room. "Should we sit?"

She led him to the living room, trying not to look at the couch where she and Nick had made love only two nights earlier.

She cleared her throat. "So, tell me about your trip to Zurich."

David tilted his head slightly. "Are you okay? You look like something's wrong."

She took a breath and got ready to assure him that she was fine, but instead she slumped forward and said, "Oh, God. You have no idea what's been going on this past week."

She told him how her father had hired her ex-fiancé to protect her, and how he'd appeared out of nowhere to tell her that someone was stalking her.

"This stalker—Reggie Henderson—David, he knew all these things about me. Where I work, what I eat for lunch, the roads I take." She shuddered. "I was terrified."

He leaned forward, his forehead creased with concern. "Tell me what happened."

"He was copying the Glen Falls Strangler, so he planted signs. There were supposed to be six. The first one was a picture of me walking into court—he was 'firing a warning shot,' so to speak. Then he locked us in a room in a warehouse and tried to kill us by planting a device that started a fire. He even hollowed out the smoke detector and left a note for me there."

David frowned. "Do you think he was trying to kill you on that day? Or was it all part of some game?"

Libby flinched. "I don't know. I guess maybe he was going to save us at the last minute. Why?"

He shrugged. "Just a question. Continue."

"On day three he left a gift—a porcelain doll with black hair and blue eyes. He planted it under Nick's car tire."

"Nick?"

"My ex-fiancé. The guy my dad hired."

"Oh. That must have been terrifying."

She nodded breathlessly. "I almost fainted I was so scared. The next day he approached me right in the Main Street Diner and told me he'd be seeing me in a few days. I later saw him in a deli. Nick took off after him, but he must have lost sight of him because I saw Henderson later. I followed him."

David frowned. "That was foolish."

She hesitated. "Yes, I know. He almost killed me there. He had this long knife—" She indicated the length with her hands. "Nick saved me." She looked at David. "He's FBI—SWAT team." She saw his lips twist and realized that she was being inconsiderate, talking about another man that way. "Anyway, yesterday was day five."

"And what was the sign?"

"Laying a trap. It was a life-or-death situation. He abducted me at gunpoint right from the sidewalk. God, David, it was awful."

He sat stiffly. "But…you escaped?"

"Yes, thank God. I broke his nose and ran away. He was shooting at me. I was cornered. Then I sprayed him in the eyes with wasp spray left out near some trash cans. I grabbed his gun when he dropped it, and when he lunged at me I shot him."

She sat up straighter. She couldn't help but feel some pride as she remembered the incident.

"But you said there were meant to be six signs, didn't you? What was sign six supposed to be?"

"Oh." Libby shrugged. "I don't know. Henderson is dead, so I guess it doesn't matter. As far as I know the police never figured that out."

David nodded and sat back thoughtfully. "Interesting."

She snorted. "Interesting? How about terrifying? Or how about *Gee, Libby, I'm glad to hear your stalker didn't kill you yesterday.* Is 'interesting' the best you can do?"

He stared at her, and Libby froze. There was something odd about his glare.

"Is that what you want me to say, Elizabeth? That I'm glad you made it out alive?"

She swallowed. His response made her uncomfortable. "I think I've upset you. I shouldn't have talked about Nick like that. Don't read anything into it—we're completely over."

"Oh?" David arched a brow.

"Yes," she said slowly, glancing at the clock. "You know, I'm tired, David. Maybe we can have coffee or something tomorrow."

He smiled. "It's almost midnight, Libby. If we wait twenty minutes or so it will *be* tomorrow." He took a sip of his tea and then placed the mug on the coffee table. "Day seven."

Her heart skipped. "That's not even funny," she said, but the look on his face told her that he hadn't meant it as a joke. She stood. "I think you should leave. Now."

"Now?" He laughed, and the sound raked her spine. "You didn't even tell me the best part of the story!"

Libby's lips grew cold. "What are you talking about?"

"You forgot to tell me the part where you learned that your father, the Right and Honorable Michael Andrews, agreed to prosecute Will Henderson in exchange for the *real* killer's political and financial support when he ran for judge a few years later."

He had a sick smile as he spoke to her, and his eyes had grown wide. He was taking an obvious delight in her unease. Her mouth went dry. "How did you know about that?"

"I do my research, too, Elizabeth," he sneered as he rose from the couch.

Libby's muscles quivered—she knew she had to run, and yet she felt paralyzed.

"Can you imagine? Judge Andrews knowingly prosecuted the wrong person for political gain. He knew who the serial killer was and he allowed him to go free. Of course he made him promise not to kill again, but even still…" He shook his head and clucked his tongue. "You must have been *so* disappointed."

"Get—get out," she stammered.

"Get out?" He laughed. "Don't you want to know what the sixth sign is?"

"No," Libby's mouth went dry. A chill flushed her body. "You—"

"Me, Libby. Reggie Henderson planted the signs for *me*. You killed my accomplice. Well, that shouldn't stop us from proceeding. And you've guessed what sign six is by now, haven't you?" David reached into his pocket and retrieved a long hunting knife. He smiled. "A false sense of security."

CHAPTER THIRTEEN

AFTER driving aimlessly for an hour, Nick stopped at the Main Street Diner for a cup of coffee. It tasted stale, like it had been sitting there all night.

Nick sat back in a booth and stared out the window. Growing up, he hadn't been able to wait for the day when he packed up and left this town for someplace more exciting. He'd seized that opportunity as soon as the FBI offered it, and he admitted now that he hadn't thought about how Libby might have felt. He'd reasoned at the time that if they were meant to be together the pieces would fall into place. He'd thought he loved her, but now he realized that it had been a selfish love.

But the past few days had felt different.

He'd felt the same passion for Libby that he always had, that same sexual spark that had always burned between them. It burned even hotter now, and try as he might he couldn't forget the taste of her, or the way their bodies fit together so perfectly. But, even more than that, he'd been astonished by her strength. In the midst of being stalked she'd learned that her father was a criminal, and yet she'd handled herself with grace. He shook his head. Libby was amazing.

Anxiety settled in the pit of his stomach. Libby was amazing—and where did he fit in? She was right—everything she'd said to him tonight was right. He was selfish. He was ugly in his need for revenge. He ran away from problems because starting over was easier than seeing something difficult through. He'd failed Libby. He'd started the week thinking that he could be her hero, that he could save her from the monster pursuing her. But Libby didn't need a hero with a gun. She needed a man who wouldn't let her down, who wouldn't leave when the going got tough.

The coffee was bitter in his stomach. Who was he?

He was just another man who had failed her.

He heaved a sigh and rubbed his forehead, wondering if he should continue to Pittsburgh or whether he should return to her house and beg for forgiveness. *She already gave you a second chance,* he thought bitterly. Asking for a third seemed like too much.

He stared at the coffee ring stains and scratches on the Formica table and tapped his index finger against it. She'd told him that she never wanted to see him again. He should respect her wishes for once. And yet he couldn't bring himself to leave town.

The bell above the door rang and a man came in to sit at the counter. Nick looked around at the nearly deserted diner. He was tired of drinking coffee by himself. Being alone meant he called all the shots. He was tired of calling all the shots.

His mind floated back to the case. He was still troubled by something that he couldn't define. How was it possible that Reggie Henderson had known so much about Libby's whereabouts? He'd always been right behind them, no matter where they went, except Nick had never seen anyone trailing them. Was it possible that Reggie Henderson had known where he and Libby were going in advance? His pulse began to quicken. That would only be possible if he'd been spying on them somehow.

Nick left a few dollars on the table and walked quickly to his car. He popped the engine hood and opened it wide, examining it by the light of a streetlamp. He didn't see anything out of place. He closed it and opened his door, checking under the seats and the floormats, not knowing exactly what he was looking for. He checked the trunk, but it was empty. Nick paused and wondered whether he should check under the vehicle's carriage.

He called Sergeant Katz. "Somehow I knew you'd be working," Nick said when the man answered.

"I'll be working late for a while. We're still processing all of the material we took from the Stillborough warehouse," he said. "We haven't even started with the van yet."

"I'm actually calling about the van," said Nick. "I need to know if you saw some kind of listening device in it."

"You think Henderson planted something so he could spy on Ms. Andrews?"

"That's exactly what I think."

"I can take a look if you give me a few minutes. Can I call you back?"

"Sure."

Nick got in the car and sat in the driver's seat. He thought about the way Henderson had planted that doll underneath his front tire—a little "gift" for Libby. He'd watched carefully to make sure they hadn't been followed to the falls. There *had* to be something in his car that had allowed Henderson to track them.

He ran his fingers under the steering wheel and then searched the glove compartment, coming up empty. He began knocking on the panels on his dashboard, listening for any signs that a device had been planted and feeling for loose parts. He took the small flashlight he carried on his keychain and shone it into the vents. Nothing.

Nick sat back, feeling frustration tighten in his chest. He looked up at the streetlamp, watching it flicker. That was when he saw it.

A little piece of rubber, just slightly out of place on the seam where the driver's-side door closed. Nick's pulse quickened as he tugged at the rubber and shone the flashlight on the metal beneath. Taped to the metal was a thin black wire with a small plastic microphone.

Nick's phone vibrated. "Nick Foster."

"It's Katz. I'm in the van."

"Good. What I need you to do is look for any kind of a listening device."

Nick heard the creak of the van doors opening. "I don't see anything. The back is empty."

"Check for false panels," he said. "I'm looking at a wire in my car that I believe is a bug, so there must have been a way for him to monitor me."

"Wait a sec." Nick heard some shuffling. "I think I see—yep, there's a false floor in this van."

His heart was pounding now as he heard the sound of metal parts smacking together. "What are you looking at?"

"It's some kind of radio device. It looks pretty expensive."

"Let me know when you've turned it on."

He waited for a minute, listening to Katz flipping switches on the device. The sergeant sighed. "I need to find a power source. Let me call you back again."

They hung up and Nick strummed his fingers on the steering wheel, deep in thought. So Henderson had bugged his car and probably Libby's house in order to get enough information to plant the signs. Rage began to stir in Nick's chest at the thought of that creep listening in on his conversations with Libby.

More than his conversations…

His phone vibrated again. "What do you have for me, Katz?"

"Hello? Is this Nick?"

Nick pulled the phone away to stare at the number. It was Christopher Henzel—Will Henderson's defense attorney. "Attorney Henzel? This is Nick."

"I just turned on the news and saw that Libby shot someone in self-defense. Someone by the name of Reggie Henderson. You want to finally tell me the truth about that 'book' you two are writing?"

Nick rubbed at his forehead. "He was stalking her," he said. "Following the pattern of the Glen Falls Strangler and planting signs. We didn't want to alarm you."

Henzel was quiet. "Is she okay now?"

"Yes. He's dead and it's over."

There was a long pause on the other end.

"Hello?"

"I'm still here."

Nick heard him take a breath.

"There's something I neglected to tell you."

His heart skipped. "What's that?"

"Henderson—Will Henderson—he wasn't as innocent as he claimed to be. He said some things…he knew some details that he would only have known if he'd been involved in the crimes in some way."

"I don't understand…"

"The Strangler hired Henderson to plant the signs for him. His fingerprints were all over some of the photographs mailed to the victims. I remember Andrews making a big to-do about that at trial."

Nick's pulse quickened. "Damn it, Henzel, why didn't you tell us this sooner?"

"Henderson was my client. I've never discussed my suspicions with anyone." He paused. "For God's sake, you should have been honest with me. I had no reason to believe Libby was in danger."

Nick gripped the wheel. In a true reenactment of the Glen Falls killings Henderson would plant the signs and the real killer would enter the scene on day seven.

He picked up his BlackBerry. It was nearly midnight.

"Henzel, I have to go. I have to check on Libby." He put the key in the ignition. "And Henzel—thanks."

Almost as soon as Nick hung up the phone vibrated again. "Nick Foster."

"It's Katz. Look, I got this device to work and I'm picking up something weird."

He felt perspiration bead on his brow. "Weird?"

"It's muffled, but it sounds like a man and a woman talking. I can't make out much."

Nick's spine went rigid. *Libby was with the killer.*

"It's Libby," Nick said as the car engine roared. "She's at her house and she's in danger. See if you have a recording option on the device. I'm on my way to her house and I'll need backup."

David bound Libby's wrists and ankles with duct tape as she sat on a kitchen chair. Her hands grew cold as the tape disrupted her circulation.

"The sixth sign is a tricky one," he explained merrily. "It took me a while to figure that one out, myself."

Libby's mouth opened and closed, her voice frozen.

"Oh, come now, you can talk to me," said David. "We have so much in common. You see, your father was a corrupt bastard and *my* father was the psychotic bastard who corrupted him." He grinned. "Destiny!"

Her knees weakened. "Your father?"

She remembered sitting with Nick, Ben and Zack in her living room, reviewing her father's notes from when he'd interviewed the woman who'd claimed to see a tall, ruddy-faced man covered in blood walking from one of the victim's homes. Jeb Sinclair was easily six-foot-four, and his complexion had always been spotted by rosacea. The witness wouldn't have recognized him in 1972 because he hadn't run for mayor until 1976. She kicked herself for not drawing the connection when she found those campaign flyers mixed in with the case documents.

"That's right. Jeb Sinclair. The longest-serving Mayor of

Glen Falls. A simply charming man, by all accounts." He stepped back to study her. "But he was also the Glen Falls Strangler. And a vicious child abuser."

Libby winced reflexively. "I'm sorry."

"Your apology means nothing to me," he said flatly. "Your father could have saved me from years of torture if he'd been man enough to do the right thing."

She tried to wet her lips, but her mouth was bone-dry. "*You* could still do the right thing, David," she said softly. "You're more of a man than either of our fathers were. If you left right now no one would have to know about any of this."

"I'm not stupid, Libby. The second I left here you'd be on the phone to the police."

She watched him circling like a shark. The hunting knife lay on the kitchen table. "H-how did you find out about your father?" Her lips felt rubbery.

"He told me. I was fifteen. He'd beaten me up again—broken a few bones. I threatened to call the police. He told me that he could do whatever he wanted and no one would care. That he was responsible for eight murders and he'd pulled some strings so that someone else agreed to take the fall." He laughed drily. "He actually bragged about it."

As David paced the kitchen Libby began to twist her hands, trying to loosen the duct tape. Her senses felt heightened again, the way they had when Reggie Henderson told her to walk through that white door in the alley. She could hear the rush of blood in her veins, the blinking of her eyes, see the flickering of the lightbulb she'd been meaning to change for weeks now. Yesterday she'd pushed aside her regrets. Today she thought of Nick.

What wouldn't she give to take back those final words when she'd told him that she never wanted to see him again? This past week she thought she'd gained some perspective on what mattered in life, and then she'd gone and lost it again. A rush of sadness washed over her. Nick had made a terrible mistake when he'd made demands of her father. But he'd tried to right the wrong. She swallowed. She loved him and she always had—why couldn't she just *tell* him that? And why wasn't love reason enough for them to set aside their hurt feelings and try to work out their problems? To try to figure out a way to make their relationship work?

Then she remembered that duffel bag. He'd been about to sneak out on her. He was probably halfway to Pittsburgh by now.

Libby sat up. She had to stay sharp. There would be a way to escape. She just had to take a deep breath and figure it out. She watched David pace like a caged lion and her gaze drifted to the glinting blade. A cold terror collapsed across her as she realized how alone she was.

Nick didn't even remember the roads he'd driven as he pulled onto Libby's street. All he could think was that she was in serious danger. He couldn't entertain the thought that he might already be too late.

He cut the headlights and parked the car three houses away. The road was silent except for the faint chirping of crickets, and dark except for the stars and the bright light of an almost-full moon. The police backup he'd requested hadn't arrived yet. He wasn't about to wait.

Nick made his way stealthily across the grass until he reached Libby's house. The shades were all drawn but light filtered through. He tried to peer through a gap in the living room curtains, but didn't see any movement. Crouching low, he darted around the house to the kitchen and felt a burst of adrenaline when he saw that Libby had neglected to draw the curtains in the back of the house.

He crept silently across the back patio toward the window, straining to hear voices. His heart thrust against his rib cage when he heard only silence. Then he saw her, sitting in a chair, her wrists and ankles bound, her head sagging forward on her chest.

He was too late.

Nick struggled to breathe, his breath coming in sporadic bursts as he pressed his hand against the side of the house to steady himself. He was too late and beautiful Libby—*his* Libby—was gone. His body went numb.

He was a fool, and his own selfishness had just cost him the only woman he could ever love. He'd only wanted one more minute with her—just one minute to tell her that he loved her, that he would give up everything he owned for her. Then he would have been out of her life forever, just as she wanted.

He saw a figure in the kitchen move through a shadow. Nick ducked and drew his weapon. If he couldn't risk his life to save Libby's, he'd risk it to send her murderer to hell.

Libby glanced at the clock on the wall. It was well past midnight and David was still pacing the kitchen, peering out of the windows. "You're nervous," she observed. "David, you know this is wrong."

"Shut up."

"Why would you kill me, anyway? For revenge? My father is dead—you can't hurt him anymore. And I never hurt you. I kind of liked you."

He snorted. "That's why you hopped into bed with your ex-fiancé as soon as I left town? Because you liked me so much?"

Libby's face grew warm. "You bugged my house?"

"A long time ago," he mumbled, peeking out the side of the window.

He'd bugged her house—was it possible that there were tapes somewhere? Could he be recording this moment? She needed to keep him talking, because that would help the police to build a case.

She took a breath. "How did you bug my house?"

"Reggie worked for a security company," David said nonchalantly. "He put wires all over the place. You wouldn't guess it from looking at him, but Reggie was a technology guru. He actually figured out a way for me to listen to you over the internet." He turned to her. "Is it a correct use of the word 'ironic' to say that it was ironic that your father paid him to install your security system?" He shrugged. "That's rhetorical."

"You still haven't answered my question," she said. "Why me?"

"You're wearing my patience thin with these questions," he growled.

Libby continued, resolute. "Is it to hurt my father or to impress yours? A little of both?"

"A little of both? How's that?" he snapped.

"You must have hired Reggie Henderson to do your dirty work while you were out of the country. That was clever," she mused. "Of course allowing Reggie to take the fall for your crime doesn't work anymore, seeing as he's dead. You didn't count on that, and that's why you're going to get caught."

David paused. "Reggie was a disappointment in the end. Oh, he performed adequately for a while, don't get me wrong, but when you told me that he stabbed what's-his-face in the alley and was going to kill you on day five?" He clicked his tongue. "For shame. We had our arrangement. He knew the rules. Anyway…" He sighed. "Let's just say I'm glad that you took care of that one for me."

"You're glad? But that leaves you without someone to blame for—" She stopped.

"For your death?" He grinned. "I thought so at first, but then I heard the most wonderful argument between you and what's-his-face tonight. It was like an omen that this was meant to be."

Libby's heart skipped. "You're going to frame *Nick?*"

"Yes," he said. "Or at least use him to cast reasonable doubt on my own case." He snorted. "Isn't it strange the way Nick never contacted the police when he knew your life was in danger? I think a jury will agree."

"But the cell phone records. You texted me—"

"And I'll be the one to discover your body, my dear. I'm going to claim I arrived to find you." David smoothed her hair. "Don't you trouble your pretty head. You just leave the planning to me."

The intensity of his gaze made Libby's stomach roil.

"No, on second thought be scared. I like it when you're scared."

Libby heard a rustle outside the window. She turned her head toward the sound and then turned it back, afraid that David would see her response.

He stopped. "Did you hear that?"

"No," she lied.

He walked to the window. "Something went past the window."

Her pulse picked up speed. Was it possible that someone had contacted the police? The thought that someone might have realized she was in danger was almost too much to hope for, but she needed a reason to keep going. "It's probably an animal. There are a lot of raccoons around here."

He spun to face her. "It's day seven. There's no reason to wait any longer."

Panic flooded her, squeezing the air from her lungs. "You don't have to do this, David."

"You don't understand, Libby," he said, leaning forward until his stale breath bounced off her face. "I'm a really bad guy. I *want* to do this."

The house was surrounded by police officers, all waiting for the lights to go out.

Nick led a team of three officers to the basement door. "Don't bother picking the lock," he said, and retrieved the key from its hiding place under a planter in the garden.

How many times had he told Libby that she was inviting trouble by keeping a key outside? Now he was glad she'd never listened.

The door flew open quietly and the officers stepped into the basement, flashlights poised above their drawn weapons. Nick ran to the gray circuit breaker panel and looked back at the other officers, giving them a nod. When they nodded in response he flipped a switch, cutting electricity to the house.

"Go!" Nick shouted, and the police stormed up the basement stairs. Seconds later there was a crash as more officers broke through the front and side doors.

Nick felt a white-hot rage pumping through his veins. His muscles pulsed with pure energy as he pounded up the steps. He could think of nothing else but getting his hands on the man who'd killed Libby. He'd make him pay.

"In here!" one of the officers called, and his heart caught in his throat. Two officers were in the living room, kneeling beside a bespectacled man, pressing him to the ground. "He tried to run," explained the officer.

Nick towered over the killer. "You killed Libby!" he shouted.

The man was stunned. "Elizabeth," he said softly, his eyes glassy.

Nick advanced on him but was restrained by the other officers.

Then he heard her. "Nick!"

Libby.

He sprinted to the kitchen and shone his flashlight on the chair in the center of the room. She saw him and burst into tears. "I thought I'd never see you again!"

"Libby."

He darted to her side and cut away the duct tape on her wrists and ankles with a pocket knife. She moaned, and in the dim light he saw her rubbing her wrists. As he came to face her she started to stand, but then fell back in her chair.

"My feet are numb," she explained through her tears.

"Oh, honey." He took her into his arms, kissing her mouth, her cheeks, her lips. "Oh, Libby, I thought I'd lost you."

"Nick." She wrapped her arms around his shoulders and sobbed into his neck. "I was so scared I'd never see you again." She threaded her fingers through his hair. "I thought you'd left me."

"I couldn't leave, Libby." His throat tightened. "I won't ever leave you. Never again."

The lights came on and he stepped back to look at the most beautiful face he'd ever seen. She had her hands against his cheeks, and she was smiling as the tears fell.

"Nick," she began, "I shouldn't have kicked you out like that."

"Yes, you should have. I messed up. Royally. I'll do anything to make it up to you."

"Then promise me something."

"Anything."

"No more secrets between us."

He smiled. "No more secrets. I promise." He leaned in and kissed her, dwelling on the softness of her lips. His legs were shaking and he fell to his knees. "We've wasted too much time. All of those months apart... I never realized until now how much I need you in my life."

She stroked his face softly. "I need you, too, Nick. I like to imagine I'm fine by myself, and I guess I've gotten by." Her lower lip trembled. "But life is so much better with you."

His heart grew warm. "I'm not going to Washington. I have to relocate to a large office, but I'll request a transfer somewhere closer. New York City, or maybe Boston." He looked into her eyes. "Nothing else matters. You're all I've ever wanted. I love you."

Libby's chin trembled and thick tears streamed down her face. "I love you, too, Nick. I've always loved you." She held his jaw in her hands, stroking her thumbs against the stubble of his cheeks. "We'll figure something out."

He slipped his fingers through her jet-black hair. "Maybe after I finish my paperwork and you've given your statement I could take you somewhere nice for pancakes." He grinned. "Or yogurt and granola—whichever you prefer."

His heart ached when he saw her lips part in a broad smile. "There's nothing I'd love more."

CHAPTER FOURTEEN

"THAT'S everything," Libby said.

Nick closed the door to the moving van. "Beautiful day for a road trip."

Libby didn't respond. She was looking back at her empty house, smiling sadly.

Nick wrapped an arm around her shoulder. "I'm going to miss this house, too."

"I was so proud when I bought it. I planted all of those flowers in front, and I chose all of the room colors." She rested her head against him.

"Are you sure you're okay with this? I don't want to force you into anything—"

She nodded. "Yes. I love this house, and I have lots of happy memories of my time here. Then some not-so-happy ones…"

Six weeks had passed since Nick had rescued her, and although logically she knew that she was no longer in danger, she hadn't slept well in the house since. Every creak made her heart pound and disrupted her sleep for the night. Moving to Virginia would be a welcome change.

She wrapped her arms around Nick's waist. "I hope a nice couple buys it. This house is meant to be filled with love."

Nick brushed his lips against her forehead. "Your new home has a lot of white walls that need painting, and a big green lawn that needs a garden."

Libby sighed. "Fresh starts are nice."

"Come on," Nick said. "We have one more stop before we leave."

Nick helped Libby climb into the large van, holding her hand so she could step up. A few months ago she might have resisted such aid and informed him that she wasn't helpless. Now she recognized the gesture for what it was to Nick: a desire to protect her, to be her hero every day, and not just under extraordinary circumstances. She'd always prided herself on being independent, but Nick's sweet little gestures made her heart melt.

As they twisted through the roads of Glen Falls, Nick pointed out landmarks. "Here's our middle school. I saw you walking to school one morning, right over there." He slowed the car to point. "Love at first sight, Libby."

Warmth spread over her cheeks. "You never told me about that. And here I thought you fell in love with me because of my vast eighth-grade geography knowledge."

"It's true—you could rattle off the continents like a pro. And I remember you pointing out that North America was distorted on our world map to appear much larger than it is."

"Cold War propaganda," she mumbled.

Nick chuckled and turned the corner. "Mostly I remember getting a C in that class because I couldn't focus on anything but you."

The warmth on her cheeks began to spread down her neck.

"There's the grocery store," Nick continued. "I bought you a sandwich there on our first date, and we walked to the library afterward to study algebra."

"That wasn't a date!" Libby laughed. "I'm pretty sure you were just following me around."

"Guilty. But we ate a meal together. Sort of. I'd consider that a first date."

Libby looked at her favorite grocery store for the last time, bade farewell to her favorite roads and the Victorian homes she'd always admired, and gave a little wave to the Main Street

Diner. "Even though someone nearly attacked me in there, I still kind of love that place," she said.

"Hey, I was the one assaulted by the waitress." Nick shook his head. "She ruined a perfectly good pair of pants."

She smiled and sat back in her seat, looking out the van window. "Oh, the District Attorney's Office," she said. "I said goodbye to everyone yesterday. I admit I cried buckets."

Nick reached over and took her hand.

"I took that job expecting to be there forever, or at least until I became a judge. It was hard to let go of that dream."

"I can understand that."

"But that was when I wanted to be like Dad," she said quietly. "I've realized that I'll never be like him. It's time for me to be Libby."

Nick was quiet. "Your dad... Well..."

"He made some mistakes," she said, finishing the thought for him. "Terrible mistakes. Not the least of which was that spiteful letter disclosing your arrangement with him." She swallowed, her chest tightening as she thought of that moment when Everett had come to her house to read the letter. "Dad always wanted to have the last word."

Her head still felt foggy when she thought of her father trading his integrity for his ambition, and of all the havoc he'd wreaked as a result. He'd taught Libby to look out for victims, to seek justice for the powerless, and yet he'd failed to protect Will Henderson—a poor, uneducated man—from the powerful Jeb Sinclair. Worse, he'd used his position and his knowledge to advocate the imprisonment of a man who was not guilty of the charges against him, knowing that his prosecution would allow a killer to go free.

She struggled to reconcile this image of her father with memories of him handing her presents on Christmas morning, or giving her affectionate hugs when he came home from work. The contrast left her disoriented.

"I'll always love my dad," she said, her voice trembling. "I will struggle with who he was, but for all of his shortcomings I believe he tried to be a good father."

Nick took a deep breath. "You know your dad and I didn't always see eye-to-eye, but I have to give him credit for raising a hell of a daughter." He kissed her hand. "You amaze me, Lib."

She squeezed his hand. True to his word, Nick had returned every penny of the award to Everett, who had then reimbursed him for his expenses. Libby and her brother James had inherited the rest of their father's estate. Libby had already begun using her share of the inheritance to establish a nonprofit organization to pair indigent persons who might have been wrongfully convicted with attorneys to appeal their cases. She'd located a small office out of which to run it in Washington, D.C. Nick would be working only a few blocks away.

"I can't help Henderson, but I can help others like him. The wrongfully accused and the powerless. I need to do this, Nick. I need to find forgiveness."

He swallowed. "You found a lot of forgiveness already. For me."

"And for myself," she added. "I've done a lot of thinking over the past few weeks about my infertility. I felt guilty about it for a long time. Guilty and ashamed—like it was something I had to hide. I blamed my diagnosis for making me feel inferior." She looked at him. "Then I realized that you still loved me, and that all of those bad feelings were my responsibility."

"*Still* loved you?" Nick's voice tightened. "Libby, I doubt there's anything that could make me *stop* loving you, honey."

"I feel like I've taken the first step toward healing, at least. Forgiving myself for being imperfect. I don't know about adoption yet." She paused. "I think I'd like to be a mom one day."

"You think about it, and you let me know what you decide."

She sat back and looked at him. "You don't care about having a family?"

"Don't get me wrong—kids would be great." He shrugged. "But honestly? I have my family right here."

Libby felt a swell of emotion, and for the first time in a long time she didn't know how to respond, except to grip his hand tighter.

Nick pulled into a parking lot at the base of the trail to Overlook Point. He turned off the engine and faced Libby. "The day we hiked up this trail and looked down at Glen Falls was one of my favorite memories with you. I'd like to hike it one more time before we move away for good."

She looked outside at the warm, cloudless morning. Getting some exercise before the long drive to Virginia was a great idea.

"I'd love to." She beamed.

They locked the van and set out on the trail, which started out as a gentle slope but then grew steep about fifteen minutes in. Libby welcomed the vigorous hike. Her heart was pounding in a steady beat and the air was cool and sweet-smelling below the canopy of trees. The man beside her was smiling with that adorable dimple, and wearing khaki shorts to show off his muscular calves. Better still, he was holding her hand. Tightly. Life was good.

They came to a clearing and hiked the remainder of the path to Overlook Point, from where they could see the entire town of Glen Falls and hundreds of miles in the distance. From that vantage point the world could be divided into colored squares and rooftops, lazy rivers and highways. From above, the world below made sense.

Libby sucked in her breath. "It's so gorgeous. I wish I could put this all in a bottle and take it with us."

Standing in companionable silence, they watched as the morning sun burned off the haze in the valley below. Libby closed her eyes to listen to the stillness around her, feeling the warmth of the sun's rays on her skin and the earth under her feet. She inhaled. She was alive. She was still *alive*. The realization made her want to throw her arms around someone—so she did.

Nick laughed and hugged her back. "Hey, what's that about?"

She wanted to tell him that it was about the way he'd brought her back from death, that he'd saved her in more ways than she could explain. She had her life, and she had Nick, and he made her life worth living.

"I'm not very good at talking about my feelings," she said. "So I'll just say I love you."

She looked at the valley and pointed to a spot where a white tent was being erected. "Oh, look! Do you think someone's getting married today?"

"Could be."

She sighed. "This would be a beautiful place to get married. I know we were supposed to be married in the chapel, but I would love to be married here."

"Libby, you know I'd marry you anywhere, but, yes, this does seem like the perfect place." Nick smiled. "So let's get married."

She grinned and her eyes widened. "Really? I'll start planning as soon as we—"

"No." His voice deepened. "Let's get married today."

"I don't understand—"

Nick knelt on one knee and opened a black velvet case. Inside was a glistening solitaire diamond.

Her jaw dropped. "Nick, what is—?"

"Marry me, Libby. Here. Now. Today."

Her cheeks grew warm as he took her left hand into his trembling fingers. "Oh, my…"

"I ordered everything you chose when you planned our wedding. The flowers, the caterer, even the officiate. I snuck your wedding dress out of the van after you packed it. Your cousin Caroline is down there already, and she's going to help you get dressed."

"Nick, I—"

"Our friends and family will be here," he continued. "Your

friends from the District Attorney's Office, your brother James and your nephews."

Libby's eyes brimmed with tears. She looked down at herself and began to laugh. "I'm all sweaty! My hair is a mess—"

"Caroline's going to drive you to a hotel. I've reserved a suite, and you can get dressed there and do whatever you need to do." His eyes were intense as he gazed at her.

"Why, Nick Foster," she whispered, "you threw me a surprise wedding."

"Or an elaborate engagement party, if you're not ready. I even ordered the chocolate wedding cake you've always talked about."

She laughed, sputtering tears. "You actually *listened* to me?"

"I've hung on your every word since we were twelve years old. I love you, Elizabeth Andrews, and it's a beautiful day for a wedding." He swallowed. "Marry me. Please."

Libby lost herself for a moment in his beautiful, dark brown eyes. "Yes." The word spilled from her mouth. "I want to marry you today."

He beamed and slipped the solitaire on her ring finger. He then stood and took her into his arms, kissing her soundly on the lips. Libby's heart swelled as she stepped away to look at Nick—the man she'd always loved and always would.

"You are full of surprises, Nick."

"Hold on, Libby. You can't believe what I have in store for you today."

She was breathless as she grabbed him for another kiss. They stood in an embrace, watching the wedding preparations below.

Finally Nick kissed her on the forehead and said, "I think we should go get ready for our big day."

Libby nuzzled against his neck. "I'm feeling pretty perfect

right now," she said. "Do you think we can just stay here for a few more minutes?"

"Anything you want, Libby," he said, pulling her closer against his side. "Forever. Anything you want."

* * * * *

Come home to the magic of
Nora Roberts

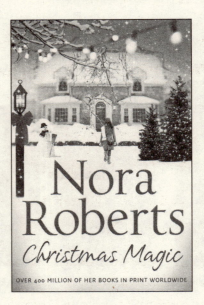

NORA ROBERTS

Christmas Magic

OVER 400 MILLION OF HER BOOKS IN PRINT WORLDWIDE

Identical twin boys Zeke and Zach wished for
only one gift from Santa this year: a new mum!
But convincing their love-wary dad that their
music teacher, Miss Davis, is his destiny and
part of Santa's plan isn't as easy as
they'd hoped…

Have Your Say

You've just finished your book. So what did you think?

We'd love to hear your thoughts on our 'Have your say' online panel
www.millsandboon.co.uk/haveyoursay

- 🌹 Easy to use
- 🌹 Short questionnaire
- 🌹 Chance to win Mills & Boon® goodies

Visit us Online

Tell us what you thought of this book now at
www.millsandboon.co.uk/haveyoursay

YOUR_SAY